THE KEEPER OF EDELYNDIA

Benjamin J. Denen

THE KEEPER OF
EDELYNDIA

TATE PUBLISHING
AND ENTERPRISES, LLC

The Keeper of Edelyndia
Copyright © 2014 by Benjamin J. Denen. All rights reserved.

No part of this publication may be reproduced, stored in a retrieval system or transmitted in any way by any means, electronic, mechanical, photocopy, recording or otherwise without the prior permission of the author except as provided by USA copyright law.

This novel is a work of fiction. Names, descriptions, entities, and incidents included in the story are products of the author's imagination. Any resemblance to actual persons, events, and entities is entirely coincidental.

The opinions expressed by the author are not necessarily those of Tate Publishing, LLC.

Published by Tate Publishing & Enterprises, LLC
127 E. Trade Center Terrace | Mustang, Oklahoma 73064 USA
1.888.361.9473 | www.tatepublishing.com

Tate Publishing is committed to excellence in the publishing industry. The company reflects the philosophy established by the founders, based on Psalm 68:11, *"The Lord gave the word and great was the company of those who published it."*

Book design copyright © 2014 by Tate Publishing, LLC. All rights reserved.
Cover design by Jim Villaflores
Interior design by Jomar Ouano

Published in the United States of America
ISBN: 978-1-63185-318-0
1. Fiction / Fantasy / General
2. Fiction / Action & Adventure
14.05.26

Dedication

First, I would like to thank Jesus Christ without Whom I can do nothing. I would like to thank all of the wonderful people who have helped make this novel possible. To my mom and dad, I thank you for instilling in me a love for the written word and for encouraging me so often to pursue my creative dreams. To all the people at Tate Publishing, thank you so much for investing an incredible amount of time and effort into my manuscript. There are not very many people in the publishing world who would invest so heavily in a first-time author. A special thanks to everyone who participated in my focus groups by helping me shape the final version of this including Alec, Anna, Bryan, Debbie, Gary, Heidi, Jim, Kris, Tyler, and Neal. To my restless ball of creative energy, Carter, I literally could not have prayed for a more perfect son. You are the embodiment of all the imagination and creativity jumbling around in my head. It is such a blessing and privilege to call you my son.

Lastly and most importantly, I would like to thank Tessa, my beautiful and wonderful wife. I shudder to think where I would be without you in my life. Without your incredible support, patience, and dedication I would not be able to accomplish a fraction of what I can do with you at my side.

PROLOGUE

This night will change everything. He could feel it in the air. Something was off. Branches and thorn bushes tore at his flesh as he made his way quickly through the dense forest. The weighty feeling that this night would see heartache, sadness, and terror was inescapable. This night would see bloodshed.

The air was too cold. The forest was too quiet. Despite the fact that the moon was at its fullest, the light seemed to die before it hit the earth. It was a night of shadows.

He shook his head, trying to clear his system of this overwhelming sense of foreboding. *Focus*, he told himself. *Superstition is for children.* In truth, he was far too old for something as silly as being afraid of shadows. Yet…

Normally the forest was alive with sounds. But not this night; the silence was oppressive. Unnatural silence has a way of unnerving even the bravest of men. Never had he ventured so deep into the forest only to find himself completely alone. There was no evidence of deer, bear, or elk. Not even a squirrel could be found.

Breathe. Connect. Focus. The mantra repeated over and over in his mind. Slowly, he began to find his center, the place where concentration and determination meet calm.

Then he heard it. Later, when he would have time to reflect, it would strike him how one sound had the power to change the course of history. Even the greatest and most significant revolutions start with a small, seemingly insignificant push. Only, for the people of Havenshae Valley, this push was far from insignificant.

As soon as he heard the sound, every fiber of his being froze. He was instantly transformed into a state of complete awareness. Because it had been so silent, he first thought he must have imagined the sound. It had started to feel like sound itself had ceased to exist.

Then he heard it again—the scream. Only this time, he didn't just hear it. He felt it. It tore through his chest, threatening to stop his heart. He knew this scream. *It came from her.*

At this point in his journey, he was not terribly far from the village, just over a four-hour journey on a clear day. Somehow, he traversed the distance back to the village in less than a quarter of that. He couldn't be sure of the exact time his flight took, but he knew that he made it in exactly twenty-seven screams.

His heart nearly exploded with each scream, each driving him faster than the last. Agony and terror filled his core and began to overwhelm him. *She is in pain. She needs me.*

Though his instincts told him to be prepared for the worst, what he saw when he arrived at the edge of the village was far more terrible than he could have ever imagined. The village center was strewn with corpses. Dismembered hands and heads littered the ground. It was complete and utter carnage. His eyes were immediately drawn to where they stood. *Keepers.* His darkest fears were confirmed.

They were huddled together surrounding someone whom he couldn't see. The screaming had stopped. One of the Keepers moved to the side to retrieve a fallen weapon, giving him a view of the horror that would haunt his dreams for years to come. A female body, broken and bloody from incessant beating, lay on the ground, a man still above her clearly having defiled and humiliated her in the worst possible way. Her clothes were torn apart, and what he could see of her face was nearly unrecognizable. She was no longer making sounds, but he could sense in his soul that she was still alive. Then, with an almost imperceptible motion, her head turned slightly and her remaining eye found his. It pleaded with him to run. Though he knew it might be her last request, it was one that he could not, would not honor.

Breathe. Connect. Focus. The mantra kicked in without warning. Only this time, instead of finding center, he found something else—something dark, something wild. Suddenly, everything around him slowed to a near stop. All of his senses kicked into a sort of hyperactive state. He could smell the blood of every corpse. He could feel every blade of grass beneath his boots. He could hear the beat of the violator's heart. Then, it happened.

All he had was his staff. Gripping it with his right hand, he pushed the hidden notch just above the center grip, ejecting the blade that was concealed within. No longer was it a simple staff; what he now held in his hands was a deadly weapon with one purpose—*justice.*

Only once before had he used his weapon in this way, but never with the deadly intent that now drove him. *Tonight will be a night of firsts.* There were ten battle-hardened Keepers and only one of him. They were outnumbered.

He tore them apart with a savage, methodical intensity. His staff, hands, feet, and teeth were his weapons. In this newly discovered state of complete and total rage, he found himself moving faster than he thought humanly possible. Maybe it wasn't human at all. At the time, he didn't feel like he was moving fast. Quite the opposite. It seemed as though he was fighting while completely submerged in water. He willed his arms to move faster, killing with such a fury that later the remains could hardly be identified as human.

It was over before most of the Keepers even knew he was there. He threw the violator off her body so hard that when he struck a nearby wall, most of his bones snapped on impact. As the rage slowly ebbed, he once again became aware of his surroundings. The anger quickly turned to sorrow as he knelt by her side, cradling her ruined body in his arms. She had drawn her last breath. Never again would they laugh together, sing together, enjoy the Valley together. She was gone. Her last moments on earth were spent in complete and utter agony.

He slowly rose to his feet. The village had become a home of the dead. Many of its residents had shown him genuine kindness. Now they were gone, all of them. In one night, his world had been obliterated. Behind him, he heard the violator stir. He turned to see the wretched man trying to drag himself away with broken arms, feeling the agony of every movement that he made. Before that night, he would have felt mercy, but never again. The time for mercy had ended.

He lifted his staff in his right hand, and with righteous anger and vengeance coursing through his veins, he threw it with inhuman strength. It struck the violator in the back of his skull, passed though, and buried itself a full two feet into the ground.

Thus ended Orron's life as he had known it. Even then, he knew that the end had begun. Sorrow overtook him, and he collapsed. Despair mixed with the exertion of his superhuman flight and fight dragged him into unconsciousness. He would never forget his last thought before darkness enveloped him. It was the thought that would determine the fate of Havenshae Valley and beyond. *The Age of Reckoning has come.*

Part 1

Chapter One

One Year Earlier...
"*Orron, you know it has to be this way!*" *said a disembodied voice, emanating from the darkness.*
"*Does it? There must be another way!*"
"*I know it's hard, but—*"

⌒⌒

A scream tore through him, and his eyes fluttered open as he gasped for breath. The world spun crazily around him. Everything was a blur. He closed his eyes again as tightly as he could, trying to will away the dizziness.

Another cry. This time it was less of a scream and more of a plea for help. Forcing himself to open his eyes, his vision slowly began to focus. He gingerly looked around. He was lying in a large, wet clearing, surrounded by trees, his body covered in a long black cloak. The air smelled like lightning. In his right hand was a long staff.

I have to get up, he told himself urgently. Sitting up brought on another wave of dizziness, causing him to lean over and wretch. The throbbing in his head mixed with his spinning surroundings made everything foggy.

I can do this. He rolled over onto his hands and knees. His limbs shook violently, the icy cold air freezing his lungs with each breath. The snow on the ground numbed his hands.

Another cry, distinctly female. This one fainter than the last. Something about her voice motivated him. *I have to help her.*

He reached behind his head and felt cold blood dripping down from a quickly forming lump. Completely devoid of hair, his skin was smooth and icy to the touch. He pulled the hood of his cloak over his head and used his staff to pull himself upright. As the ground seemingly swayed beneath him, he gripped his staff so hard that his knuckles turned white. Slowly, the swaying stopped, and he once again opened his eyes.

Unsure of what to do next, he simply waited, hoping for another cry, something, anything that would help him find this girl. *Who is she? Why do I care so much?* His mind was flooded with questions.

Who am I?
Where am I?
Why am I here?
What do I do now?

The voice in his dream called him Orron. *Is that my name?* he wondered. As to where he was, the answer was apparently some kind of forest in the dead of winter. He had no idea why he was there or what his next course of action was, but when the female voice once again cried out, his questions no longer mattered. The only thing he cared about was finding this girl.

Reacting on instinct, he dove into the forest, running as fast as his unsteady legs would carry him. Branches clawed at his face as he made futile attempts to knock them away with his staff. Gnarled tree roots grabbed his feet, causing him to stumble and fall repeatedly. With grim determination, he picked himself up and continued running.

Pausing every so often to pick up the sound of her voice, he ran for what seemed like hours. Sometimes he heard a cry, other times he heard a whimper. Hearing her pain compelled him to run faster.

He slid to a stop as he reached the edge of a deep ravine. The night was so dark that he could barely see the bottom. Somehow, he could *sense* that she was down there. *Where is she?*

The moon finally broke through the clouds, illuminating the ravine. He began to make out the shape of a girl among the rocks, but he could not tell if she was alive. As quickly as he dared, he made his way to the bottom.

Razor sharp rocks ripped his palms as he slid to a stop next to the girl. She was young, no older than nine or ten. Laying his staff beside her, he gently touched her face, and she stirred. *She's alive!* Her eyes opened and looked at him with confusion.

"You're bald," she said with a quizzical look on her face. Fresh tears shimmered in her green eyes in the moonlight.

"Where are you hurt?" he asked, ignoring her remark.

"What happened to your hair?"

She's lying at the bottom of a deep ravine in the middle of razor-sharp rocks, and all she can think about is my lack of hair! He couldn't help but smile despite the precariousness of the situation.

"That doesn't matter right now," he replied. Any sense of frivolity left the moment he noticed the boulder resting on her left leg.

The ravine was roughly fifty feet from end to end and no more than ten feet at its widest point where the little girl now lay. Looking up, he guessed that it was at least twelve feet to the top, maybe more. Rocks ranging from the size of pebbles to larger than a warhorse were piled on the ground. They appeared to be freshly disturbed, as if there had been a rockslide. He figured that was how the little girl found herself trapped beneath the boulder that looked to be among the largest around him. *Maybe two warhorses is more accurate.*

He examined the boulder that was pinning her leg. Upon further inspection, he could see that the weight of the boulder was distributed on the rocks surrounding her, keeping it from completely crushing her leg, but a sharp corner of the rock was penetrating her skin just below the knee. He could see blood pooling on the rocks beneath her leg. She had already lost a lot. If he didn't do something soon, he could lose her.

"What is your name?" he asked, trying to keep her talking as he assessed the situation.

"Ly'ra," she said. "W–What's your name?" Her voice was growing weaker.

He hesitated, unsure of how to answer. Remembering what the voice in his dream called him, he replied, "My name is Orron. Ly'ra, I need you to stay awake. Can you do that for me?" His voice rose as she struggled to remain conscious.

"I'm...so...cold," she said weakly.

Orron took off his cloak and laid it across her upper body. He turned to face the boulder and tried to move it with all the strength he could muster. *Not even an inch*, he thought in frustration. Ly'ra moaned. *Come on, Orron. Do something! If you don't, this girl will die.* The thought of this innocent girl dying filled him with rage, and he struck the boulder with his fist so hard that blood started to flow from his damaged knuckles.

From somewhere deep within the recesses of his mind, three words began to repeat themselves. *Breathe. Connect. Focus.* At first, he resisted them, but then he let the words wash over him. Slowly, his heart rate slowed until he found his center and, with it, a new source of strength. Without opening his eyes, he bent down and placed both hands under the boulder, ignoring the sharp edges that dug into his fingers. Power flowed through his muscles as he lifted with all of his might. A primal scream erupted from deep within him as the boulder began to move.

First one inch, then another. Inches became a foot, then two.

She screamed as the boulder lifted off her leg. With one last surge of strength, Orron heaved and the boulder came crashing down with a thunderous crash several feet away. He collapsed.

Ly'ra was sobbing uncontrollably as blood poured from her left leg. Gritting his teeth, Orron pulled himself to her. *I can rest later.* Examining her wound, his stomach turned at the sight of the gaping hole. Her leg was broken and the bones were exposed. The boulder had been keeping the blood flow to a trickle. Now that the pressure was gone, it seemed as though a flood had been unleashed from her wounded leg.

Quickly, he tore off part of his shirt and wrapped it tightly around her thigh, forming a tourniquet. He knew she might lose the leg, but right now, he was more concerned with the blood loss. He held her in his arms trying to will away the pain.

After collecting his breath for a moment, he looked down at her, "Ly'ra, I am going to get you some help, but first you need to tell me where to find it. Can you do that?"

She struggled to catch her breath between sobs.

"Th–there's a trail…" Her eyes fluttered and Orron shook her gently trying to keep her awake.

"Where, Ly'ra?" Desperation crept into his voice. "Where is the trail?"

She was quiet for a long moment. Orron began to fear the worst. Finally, she spoke. Her voice was barely a whisper. "At the top. By the…the old, sad tree. It takes…it takes me home. I want to go home."

She began to cry again. Orron's heart broke at the agony in her face. "Thank you, Ly'ra. You are being so brave. I'll take you home now, I promise. Just stay with me."

Wrapping her in his cloak, he gathered her small frame in his left arm and grabbed his staff with his right. He struggled to the top of the cliff. Once he reached the top, he scanned the forest until he found an old tree with limbs sagging low to the ground. It leaned heavily to one side, giving the impression of an old man bent low with age. He could see the trail that she had told him about.

Her crying had stopped. Orron looked down at her face and saw that her breath was ragged and short. Worried, he tried again to shake her gently, but she would not wake up. Pushing back his fear, he repeated the words that kept playing in his mind. *Breathe. Connect. Focus.* Finding his inner strength, he set off down the trail as fast as he could.

The exertions of the night were taking their toll on his body. He struggled to remain upright as every overhanging branch continued to find his exposed face and neck. Blood began to pour into his eyes from the numerous cuts and scrapes. His arms and legs burned. The air seemed to lack the amount of oxygen that he needed. With steely determination, he pressed on. *I have to save this girl!*

The trees began to thin as the trail lead up a small hill, and he burst out of the forest into a snow-covered field that stretched as far as his eyes could see. His head throbbed. His body ached. To his left, he could make out the faint light of a distant house. Then he noticed the voices. There were people calling out for Ly'ra, searching the field and edge of the forest with torches.

He sank to his knees as exhaustion threatened to overtake him. Mustering all the strength he had left, he pulled back his hood and cried out, "Here! I have her here!"

One of the torchbearers was kneeling by the trees not far to Orron's right. He looked over at him, leapt to his feet and started running toward them. Stumbling a couple of times in the thick snow, the man finally reached Orron and Ly'ra.

He was huge. The light from the torch in his right hand made his red hair and beard appear as if they were on fire. When he saw the blood covering Orron and Ly'ra, he let out a terrifying war cry and raised the club he had in his left hand.

In his exhaustion-induced stupor, Orron was unable to react. He knew what was about to happen, and for some reason he smiled. As the club arched through the air, he found himself welcoming the blow that was coming. The club struck his head with shocking force, and he returned to the same state of unconsciousness with which his night began.

Chapter Two

"*Orron, you know it has to be this way!*" *said a disembodied voice emanating from the darkness.*

"*Does it?*" *challenged Orron.* "*There must be another way! The Maker—*"

A noise at the door brought Orron out of his dream. His attempt to open his eyes was met with tremendous pain shooting through his head. The brilliant light flooding the room from a nearby window was more than he could handle. It was as if daggers were stabbing through his eyes into his brain. He closed them tightly, trying to shut out the pain, and struggled to prop himself up.

"There, there. Don't you bother with trying to move." The melodious voice was definitely female. "You've had enough excitement to last you two lifetimes. Rest that head of yours, and don't mind me."

Orron raised his hand to his head, feeling the soft bandages that encased it. The events of the night before—or, well, whenever it was—flooded back.

"Where…how long have I been out?" His throat burned, and his voice was weak.

"It's been two days since they brought you here. It's a wonder you're still alive. When Mattox gets the foolish notion in his head to hit something with that club of his, it rarely gets back up if you catch my meaning," she said with amusement. Her voice was soothing and kind. It, more than anything, calmed his pain.

He opened his eyes as wide as he dared and was greeted by a kind smile from a woman sitting on a chair next to him. Instantly he knew her to be the mother of Ly'ra. Though he only saw Ly'ra in the dark, the resemblance was remarkable. They shared the same bright green eyes. She was plainly clothed in a long, brown dress made of wool, gathered in the middle by a single white cord. Her hair was gathered in a pile on the top of her head.

"Now, if it is all right with you, I need to remove these bandages before the infection gets you."

Slowly, she removed the bandages from his head, mindful of the dried blood. Her hands were steady with practice and skill.

When she finally pulled it off, she caught her breath in surprise. "Well, I never…"

"What is it?"

"Your head! It's nearly whole again!"

"Well, I guess whole is better than the alternative." He made the effort to sit up. The pain subsided as his eyes adjusted to the light.

"True enough," she replied with a wondering smile. "You are a mystery, aren't you?"

"Ma'am?" he said, unsure of what she meant.

"First, Ly'ra tells us the most remarkable tale of her heroic rescue. I can scarcely believe her! Then—."

"Ly'ra, is she all right?" He had nearly forgotten about the small girl he had gone to great trouble to save.

"Oh, she is a terror, what with the broken leg and all. She is darn near reveling in her chance to be the center of attention. I have half a mind to scold you for bringing her back!" Her eyes twinkled with mirth.

Overcome with relief, he finally laid back. He could not seem to understand why the safety of this girl was so overwhelmingly important to him. She was little more than a stranger. *There is something about her…*

Suddenly serious, the woman looked at him with a hint of tears glistening in her eyes. "I owe you more than you can know, young man. This family has seen too much sadness, I…" She looked to the side and wiped her eyes.

With a slight shake of her head, her lighthearted demeanor returned. "Then my fool husband tries to kill you! He's a brute of a man, mind you," she said with a wink, as if to confide in him a secret. "And here I was, doting on you night and day, worried that we would have a death on our hands, and you go and wake up right as rain!"

He blushed. "I'm sorry for the trouble, Ma'am."

"Oh, it was no bother at all." She dismissed his apology with a wave of her hand. "And you can stop calling me 'Ma'am.' Any hero who rescues my fair Ly'ra deserves to call me by name. I am Me'ra."

I am no hero. He didn't know what he was, but he sure didn't feel like a hero. "I was just in the right place at the right time. My name is Orron."

"Well, Orron, I will never stop thanking the Maker for putting you there when my Ly'ra needed you most," she said with genuine appreciation. "Where do you hail from, Orron?" Her eyes were probing his. She was fishing for something.

"I…um…honestly, I don't know," he replied. He sensed her confusion at his answer but was not sure how to respond.

"No matter, the important thing is that you were here when Ly'ra needed you."

Apparently, that was enough of an answer for now. She stood up and made to leave the room. "You will find that there are fresh clothes on the table next to you. I'm afraid that all but your cloak were ruined, with the blood and all. You're a bit taller than Mattox, which is saying something, but they will do fine."

He looked at her with confusion over the name. "Mattox is the brute who tried to bash your skull in," she said with another wink. "Ah, but the brute is the man of my heart. Don't worry, he warms up over time."

As she turned to leave, Orron struggled to sit up causing the blanket to slide down. Me'ra froze as her eyes locked on his chest. He followed her gaze and noticed that it was covered with strange black markings. Looking back at Me'ra he saw that her hand was now covering mouth. *Is that terror in her eyes?*

She once again shook her head and the smile returned to her face, though it appeared to Orron to be a bit forced.

Clearing her throat, she said, "When you are ready, Ly'ra would like to see you." She glanced one more time at the markings then left the room and closed the door behind her.

Orron gingerly touched his head. He could feel that the scabs had nearly healed. The bump on the back of his head was gone entirely. Two days had passed and his head and face were still as smooth as silk. Not a sign of hair growth existed.

Slowly, he swung his legs out from under the wool blankets and cautiously stood up. He was pleased to find his legs steady. In truth, other than the now subsiding ache in his head, he felt great, though still a bit tired.

Stretching out his cramped muscles, he noticed the table that Me'ra had mentioned. He walked over and picked up the clothing. There was a pair of soft, dark brown pants and a warm-looking shirt of a light tan color. Both were made of wool. Me'ra was right; the pants and sleeves were a little short but they fit well enough. Though he was apparently taller than Mattox, he was quite a bit slimmer. The shirt hung loosely on him and the pants had to be cinched tight with a belt.

He put on his own boots, which he found next to the bed. Looking around, he saw his staff leaning in the corner. For reasons he could not yet understand, knowing it was close at hand made him feel more at ease.

The room was small but clean. There was a bed in one corner and a table next to it with a small chair tucked underneath. On the opposite wall stood a tall mirror. Orron made his way over to the mirror and took himself in for the first time.

He was tall, maybe six and a half feet. As he had noticed, he was completely bald save for thin, dark eyebrows. He guessed his age to be eighteen or nineteen. His appearance was young, but his deep, bright blue eyes were not.

Remembering that Ly'ra wished to see him, he opened the door and walked into a larger room that apparently served as their primary living space. To the right there was a large fireplace with an ample rug made from the hide of a bear lying on the floor in front of it. Four wooden chairs with soft-looking cushions formed a semi-circle around the fire. To the left of the fireplace was a hand-operated spinning wheel and wooden loom. Across from the door he had just exited was a closed door. It was a simple home filled with warmth. A delicious scent filled the room from the meal Me'ra was preparing over the fire.

She turned as he walked into the room. "Hmm," she said with disapproval. "My first order of business will be to make you some clothes that fit."

"You don't need to bother with that, Ma'am—I mean Me'ra. These are more than fine."

"Oh, it's no bother. Making clothes is what I do. She motioned to the window. Looking out, Orron could see a weathered barn with a fence extending out over the snow-covered field. "Wool is certainly not scarce around this house. Mattox is a shepherd, the only one in Lillyndale to be exact," she said proudly. Then remembering that Orron was unsure of his surroundings, she added, "Lillyndale is the small village just a ways across the meadow."

Lillyndale. As he looked out the window across the meadow, Orron realized that there was something familiar about that name, just as there was something familiar about Ly'ra. He had so many questions and so few answers.

"Would you like a bowl of soup?" Me'ra asked, breaking his daydream. "It's got just a touch of venison and spice in it. Although it's a bit bland for my liking, it's better than nothing."

"That would be wonderful," he said. Having not eaten in—well, he had no idea how long—he was famished. Taking a seat next to Me'ra, he had to force himself to down the soup slowly. It was delicious.

"Careful there, young man." She let out a small, lyrical laugh. "There's no sense in having you choke on it. There's plenty more where that came from." In total, she filled his bowl four times. She handed him a cup of cold water when he finished.

Feeling full and refreshed, he sat back and closed his eyes. The warmth of the fire and the food in his stomach made him sleepy. He dozed off and awoke with a start to find himself alone in the room.

Me'ra entered the room from the door to his left, and when she noticed that he was awake, said, "Good, I'm glad to see you getting some more rest. If you're feeling up to it, Ly'ra would like to see you."

Orron stood and followed Me'ra into another room, and he saw Ly'ra for the first time in daylight. Her hair was the same deep auburn as her mother's hair. Freckles abounded on her face, which lit up as he entered.

"You really are bald!" she exclaimed as he sat in the chair next to her. "I had wondered if I had imagined that. The only people I've ever seen who are bald are either really old or Keepers, but you're not old. And you're *definitely* not a Keeper," she said with a roll of her eyes, as if that were the most obvious statement anyone could have made.

Unsure of what a Keeper was, Orron looked to Me'ra. Darkness clouded her face. "Keepers are the enforcers of the Council—soldiers, brutal men with brutal hearts." There was a bite to her words, perhaps even the hint of a threat. It was clear that she had no love lost for these Keepers.

"Orron is not a Keeper, Mother," Ly'ra repeated.

"No," Me'ra agreed. "No Keeper would ever rescue anyone, let alone a dirty little daughter of a shepherd!" She walked over to wipe off Ly'ra's face. "Honestly, child, I swear that you wear more of your food than you eat!"

"Mother," pleaded Ly'ra with embarrassment.

"You were very brave," he said, rescuing her from Me'ra's doting.

"Was I?" asked Ly'ra.

"Yes, you barely made a noise the entire time. You were even able to tell me how to find your father."

This pleased Ly'ra very much. "It hurt so badly."

"I can imagine. How are you feeling now?"

Her face brightened. "Better. Mother says that my leg is going to heal up real good."

Orron smiled. "I'm sure you will be running around before you know it."

"Oh, bless the Maker, I hope not," interjected Me'ra. "Nothing but trouble you are, child."

"I am *not* a child! I am nine and a half," she said defiantly.

The door opened and Orron turned in his chair to see Mattox entering the room. His face darkened as he saw Orron sitting next to Ly'ra. "What is *he* doing in here?"

"I wanted to see him!" Ly'ra said protectively.

"Quiet, young lady!" he bellowed. Mattox pointed his finger at Orron in disgust and anger. "You, get out of my daughter's room. It's bad enough to have a Keeper under my roof, but you *will* stay away from my daughter."

"Mattox!" Me'ra said with reproach.

"He is *not* a Keeper!" cried Ly'ra.

Orron started to stand and raised his hands defensively. "I am sorry, sir, I can go."

"No, you will not," declared Me'ra with authority. "It is bad enough that you nearly killed the boy, Mattox. I will not have you treating our daughter's rescuer with such poor manners." She stood with her hands on her hips, and the look in her eyes warned Mattox not to push her any further.

Clearly over-matched, Mattox looked at Ly'ra and Me'ra then glowered at Orron. "If you even try—"

"Mattox," Me'ra said softly but with steely force.

He looked at Me'ra and relented. Dropping his eyes, he turned to leave. "Fine, I will be tending the sheep." He stormed out and slammed the front door so hard that Orron could feel the floor shake.

"You will have to forgive him," Me'ra said apologetically. "He is a good man, but these days it's hard to trust anyone."

"It's all right," replied Orron. "He is just trying to protect his daughter."

"I don't need him to protect me all the time, I'm—"

"Yes, dear," chided Me'ra. "You're nine and a half, which is still young enough to get your leg broken in a rock slide." She turned to Orron. "Thank you again for your kindness and understanding. I will leave you two alone." She kissed Ly'ra on the forehead before she exited the room. "I'll be just outside if you need anything, sweetheart."

Orron noticed that she left the door open this time.

"I hate it when he gets so mean," said Ly'ra as Orron returned to his seat.

"He just cares about you and wants to keep you safe. I would do the same if you were my daughter."

"Do you have any?" she asked.

"Any what?"

"Daughters?"

He had to think about that for a moment. Though he knew little more than his name, he felt pretty confident that he had no children. "No."

"Where do you come from?"

"I'm not really sure."

"How can you not know? Everyone knows where they come from." She appeared perplexed.

Suddenly uncomfortable with the direction this conversation was headed, Orron changed the subject. "How did you get trapped under that rock?"

"I was out collecting winter berries like I always do, and I was walking down my favorite path when I came to the ravine. That's where the best berries are," she explained. She shuddered as she recalled the next part of the story. "I saw a nice patch of bushes at the bottom, so I climbed down to gather them. That's when the ground shook. Rocks started falling all around me." She started to tear up.

"The ground shook?"

"It was so scary. It seemed like the world was falling apart. The big rock fell on my leg and I couldn't move. It hurt so badly."

"How long were you alone?"

"I left the house just after lunch, so it must have been hours and hours. It felt like forever."

"It must have been horrible."

"It was. I felt so alone…like I was going to die." Her face brightened. "Then you came and saved me!" she said beaming from ear to ear. She grabbed his hand.

He smiled and squeezed her hand. "I am just glad that I happened to be in the right place at the right time."

"How did you know where I was? It was so dark outside."

"I heard you crying for help"

"Me? You heard me?" Her face was full of confusion. "I could barely make a sound. My leg hurt so badly I could barely breathe!"

"You must have been louder than you thought," he replied, unsure of himself.

"I don't think so."

It struck Orron that he heard her calling for help from very far away. He had run through the forest for a long time before he found her in the ravine. No one who had lost that much blood could have called out and been heard over such a great distance, not even on the clearest of nights. *So many questions…*

"Well, the important thing is that I *did* find you," he said, trying once again to change the subject.

"That reminds me," she said. Orron could sense another difficult question coming. "How in the world did you move that rock? It was huge!"

"It wasn't that big," Orron said, knowing that was a lie. The boulder was massive. "It just looked bigger in the dark."

"Maybe…" she replied, clearly unconvinced. They sat in silence for a few moments, lost in their memories of that night. Ly'ra yawned, breaking the silence.

"Well, young lady, I'm just glad that you are all right," Orron said as he stood up. "You need your rest."

Ly'ra was reluctant to let go of his hand. "Orron?"

"Yes, Ly'ra?"

"Thank you for coming when I needed you…for saving me."

"I would do it a thousand times over," he said as he patted her on the head. He meant it. Something about this little girl tugged at his heart. He wanted nothing more than to protect her, to keep her from pain and suffering. It was as if he had always known her, and he cared for her as he would a little sister.

He returned to his room and laid down on the bed. Every time he tried to answer one of the many questions swimming through his head, he was greeted with even more questions. With a frustrated sigh, he gave up and closed his eyes. Restless sleep soon overtook him.

Several hours later, he was awakened by the sound of arguing. Sitting up, he was disoriented by the change in light. Night had fallen and long shadows were cast by the light of the moon streaming through the window. The loud voices in the room outside his door grew more hushed as Me'ra and Mattox continued to argue. Curiosity got the better of Orron, so he crept quietly over to the door to listen.

"You have no way of knowing that he isn't a Keeper! Have you seen him?" Mattox said, trying to keep his voice down. "You saw the symbol on his chest! It's the mark of the *Keepers*!" Even through the closed door, Orron could feel Mattox's hatred when he said that word.

"Aye, I have, but I have also seen his eyes. *Those* speak only the truth. They are not the eyes of a Keeper."

"Ah," Mattox replied with frustration. "Woman, you and your fascination with eyes! I don't trust him. I don't care what his eyes are telling you."

"Mattox, you don't trust anyone—"

"And you know as well as I do why that is." There was tinge of sadness in his voice.

A long pause followed. Finally, Me'ra spoke up. "You don't have to trust him, but you should at least be thanking the Maker that he was there for Ly'ra." Her voice broke as she continued. "Without him there, I–I can't bear to imagine…"

"Aye, Me'ra, thankful I am," Mattox replied gently with a conciliatory tone. "It doesn't mean I trust the boy. It wouldn't be the first time the Maker used evil for good."

"And it wouldn't be the first time we tried to see evil in the Maker's good."

"Aye." Another long pause followed. Then, with softness in his voice, Mattox whispered, "I do love that girl, and I do love you."

"I know, dear. You're not too awful yourself."

Mattox gave a half laugh then asked, "So what do you suggest we do with the boy?"

"Well, I think we should *both* start by showing him the kindness the Maker expects us to show."

"I guess that means you don't want me clobbering him again?"

"Precisely, you old brute."

"Who are you calling old? You're not exactly young yourself, woman!"

Through the door, Orron heard Me'ra smack Mattox on the arm. They both laughed quietly and headed into another room.

Orron moved away from the door and stood in front of the mirror. He pulled his shirt off. The markings on his chest formed some kind of symbol. His skin was very white and seemed to glow in the moonlight that streamed in through the window. The markings were three lines as black as the darkest of nights and were about an inch wide. One line started at his right shoulder, curved inward across his right breast, and curved back out to his right hip. A mirror image of that line curved in from his left shoulder to his left hip. A third line cut through the center of the other two and stretched from the center of his breastbone to his naval.

He traced the lines with his hand. The blackened skin was slightly harder and raised. He shuddered as he remembered the look on Me'ra's face when she saw the symbol. *Why was she afraid?*

Just like his head, his skin was smooth and devoid of hair. His shoulders, arms, and chest were thick with muscle. There was no trace of fat. He flexed his hands and they felt powerfully strong. His thoughts returned to the look in Me'ra's eyes. *What am I?*

As Orron returned to bed, his eye caught the staff resting in the corner. He retrieved it and sat on the bed to look it over.

It was no ordinary walking staff. Though it appeared to be made of a wood-like substance, it had a feel to it that seemed harder and smoother than any natural wood. There were numerous small, strange symbols engraved throughout the shaft.

One end was slightly thicker than the other was. It appeared by the balance that the thicker end was the top. At the smaller end was a slender hole that appeared to go deep into the center. The hole was actually more of a slit, with the center slightly wider than the pointed ends that reached nearly to the edge of the staff. Standing straight, its height came up to just above his breastbone.

He sat back down and laid the staff across his lap. As he examined the symbols more closely, one in particular caught his eye. It was located in the center of the staff, the same symbol that was on his chest.

He brushed his thumb over it and realized that the oval was nearly identical to the size of his thumb. Out of curiosity, he pressed down. He let out a gasp as a blade ejected from the hole at the top.

Orron's heart pounded as he realized the true nature of his staff. *This is definitely not a walking stick.* He leaned over and lightly touched the dark blade with the thumb of his left hand. Though he barely brushed it, the blade sliced his thumb drawing blood with its razor-sharp edge. The blade stood about a foot in length, was nearly as wide as the staff, and tapered to a sharp point. It was thicker in the center. He could not determine whether it was metal or stone. Its surface was so dark, it appeared to absorb the light around it. There was not a single notch or flaw to be found.

He pressed the symbol again and the blade silently retracted with lightning speed. The weapon felt so natural in his hands. When he held it, there was tremendous familiarity with every notch and symbol.

What am I? he asked himself for what seemed like the thousandth time. Perhaps it was his fatigue, but he felt as if the staff emitted an almost imperceptible energy. It felt alien, ancient. Dread crept over him as he remembered the strength he had shown while rescuing Ly'ra. That memory combined with the familiarity of this spear in his hands spoke a truth that he was afraid to accept. *I am a weapon.*

Chapter Three

"Politicians!" Draedon muttered to himself as he splashed icy cold water on his face. It had the satisfyingly jarring effect of washing away the last remnants of early morning fatigue. "Einar, how long have we served together?"

"Too long, sir," he replied, handing Draedon a towel.

He wiped his face. "Right you are, my good man!" He motioned emphatically with his towel hand. "And how many times has the Council sent out an Elder to meddle in our business?"

"Too often, sir."

"Right again!" He handed the towel back to Einar. "I had hoped that when they shipped us off to the far reaches of the Avolyndas Territory we would be free of them." Draedon sighed in resignation. "I guess that would be asking too much. Thank you for listening to my many rants, Einar. You are a good friend."

"Of course, sir. If that will be all, I will take my leave and meet you at the South Gate at noon."

"Thank you, Einar. You may go." Einar bowed slightly as he left the room. Draedon turned back to the mirror and leaned on the edge of the washbasin. *Thirty-two years of service and I am still treated like this.*

Draedon looked at the aging man in the mirror. His hair and beard were both kept short and neat with streaks of gray. Both were minor rebellions. The Keepers had a strict dress code including a shaved head and face. *Thirty-two years. I would say that has earned me the right to protect my head and face against the cold of winter,* he told himself, though he knew the real reason was to infuriate the blasted Council.

He had debated shaving today. Elder Zittas had sent word that he would be accompanying the annual new recruits. Each year, the Council rotated Keepers out of the outlying territories so that every Keeper was given the privilege of serving in the Holy City. *Privilege? More like a curse!* He shook his head, glad that he had decided to keep his hair. Secretly he hoped that his little act of rebellion would waste precious minutes of the Council's time as they debated what to do with him. He knew that his status and respect protected him from punishment over such a small infraction, but the pleasure he derived from their annoyance was well worth their disdain for him.

Like many Keepers who served as long as Draedon, he had grown quite weary of the Council. Though they claimed to be the righteous leaders of the One True Church of the Maker, he saw them for what they really were: power hungry men who cared far more about political manipulation than saints and souls.

There were five Elders who formed the governing Council of Edelyndia—one representative for each of the four territories and one for the Holy City. Zittas represented the Avolyndas Territory in the northeast. Rynov, the oldest and longest tenured member of the Council represented the wealthy Great Plains Territory in the southeast. The mysterious Seidar represented the Great Desert Territory in the southwest. Draedon had only encountered Seidar on one occasion, and the very memory of that moment sent a shiver down his spine. Filo, the newest member of the Council, represented the northwestern corner, the North

Woods Territory. Iorane represented the Holy City, a massive city that occupied much of the center of Edelyndia.

Draedon had enlisted in the Keepers two years before the end of the Great War. Through war and peace, he had served the Council faithfully, sacrificing greatly to ensure peace for the citizens of Edelyndia. Starting out as an enlisted soldier, he had risen through the ranks to the position that he now held— Legion Commander. There were five legions in all stationed in the four territories and the Holy City. Though his post in the Avolyndas Territory located in the Great Avolyndas Mountains was considered by many to be the "backwoods" of Edelyndia, he enjoyed where he served. He found the mountains to be quite serene and peaceful. His territory was one of the safest and annually reported the fewest run-ins with Heretics, the remnants of the losing side of the Great War. The legion at his command was well-trained, and he felt it was the most efficient and effective legion in all of Edelyndia. Still, that was not enough to keep the Council off his back.

Though visiting the territory he represented was well within the normal practice for most Elders, Draedon knew the true reason that Zittas chose to return to the Avolyndas Territory, and it filled him with anger. *The cursed Inspections…*

He straightened up and adjusted the long, black cloak that all officers wore. Unlike some Legion Commanders, Draedon chose not to further embellish his uniform to show off his rank. In his experience, a commander revealed himself through his actions, not his uniform.

Satisfied with his appearance, he turned and left his bedroom and headed down the stairs to the dining hall. It was the largest room in the house. Decorative tapestries and valuable paintings adorned the walls, depicting elaborate portrayals of battles from Edelyndian history and legends. Numerous candles in golden sconces lit the room. Hanging from the ceiling was an impressive chandelier made of crystal. It, too, held numerous candles, but it was not lit.

When he arrived, he was surprised to see his daughter laying out food on the table. "Kor'lee, you know that we have servants for that."

"Yes, Father, I do." She gave him a quick hug. "That doesn't mean a daughter can't fix breakfast for her father, does it?"

"No, of course not. Sit, sit! Let's see what wonders you've cooked up this time." The breakfast was exquisite. Eggs cooked to perfection with bacon, bread, and honey. The bacon was a special treat since it was so rare in this part of Edelyndia, to which Draedon inquired.

"Einar brought a pig to me yesterday," Kor'lee explained. "Honestly, Father, I don't know where he finds these things."

"He is quite resourceful."

"When he gave it to me, I knew immediately that we had to have bacon for breakfast! I hoped you would like it."

"Of course I like it! You are old enough to know by now, my dear Kor'lee, that bacon is the true path to a man's heart. What have I done to deserve you?"

Kor'lee got up and walked around the table to kiss her father on the cheek. Wrapping her arms around his neck from behind she said, "Father, you know that you could never deserve me."

He patted her arm. "True, true."

Eighteen years…my, how fast they have gone. He shook his head sadly. *If only her mother could have lived to see her grow. She is beautiful and looks more and more like her every day.*

Kor'lee was tall for a woman, only a few inches shorter than Draedon. She possessed the same long, midnight-black hair that her mother had as well as her noble, high cheekbones.

Her personality, however, she had inherited from her father, something that sometimes led to brief, but heated exchanges between the two of them. They were both incredibly stubborn.

But she is good…a lot better than I'll ever be. That, she inherited from her mother.

It pained Draedon as a father to see her grow into such a beautiful woman in this dirty Keeper Citadel. Seeing the lustful stares of the Keepers who thought he didn't notice almost drove him to insanity. The only thing he had known to do was to pass on the one skill set that he possessed. He taught her how to fight.

After catching one Keeper attempting to make a pass at her when she was only ten, Draedon took it upon himself to teach Kor'lee how to wield a sword and bow. He knew that it was not the way a young woman should grow up, but it was the only way he knew how to raise her. *If only her mother were here…*

Shaking himself from his reverie, he rose from the table and left his quarters to face the day.

The morning passed quickly as the hours were filled with last minute inspections of the soon-departing Keepers. He said his final good-byes to the officers who had served him well.

The Keeper Citadel of the Avolyndas Territory was located within the massive walls of Farovale. Before the Great War, it had been one of the grandest cities in all of Edelyndia. Sadly, like much of the country, Farovale had still not completely recovered from the devastation brought on by the war even thirty years later. The Citadel boasted a legion of five thousand Keepers. Combined with the support staff needed for a legion its size, most of the city's fifteen thousand citizens were in some way affiliated with the Keepers.

Just before noon, Draedon met Einar at the South Gate. They could see the force of one thousand Keepers entering the mouth of the Valley in perfect formation. Toward the rear rode two men on splendid warhorses. Draedon knew that one of the riders was Elder Zittas and the other he assumed to be his new captain.

His previous captain had served him for the better part of ten years and abruptly decided to take his retirement. Their good-byes were as emotional as one would expect from battle-hardened soldiers. *Too many of the good ones are retiring or dying*, Draedon lamented. He was not particularly fond of the new breed of Keepers coming out of the Holy City. *Too enthusiastic for bloodshed if you ask me.*

As the formation drew near, he turned to his servant and asked, "What do you think, Einar? Should we let them in?"

"It would be advisable, sir."

Draedon gave the order, and the drawbridge lowered over the moat that was fed by the Havenshae River from which the Valley derived its name. They proceeded up the small hill that separated the outer from the inner wall of the fortress and into the South Courtyard where the departing Keepers were waiting.

Elder Zittas and the new captain dismounted and climbed the narrow stairway to the top of the wall. "Here we go," Draedon muttered under his breath as they approached him. "Greetings Elder Zittas. I trust that your journey was uneventful."

"It was dreadful." He ignored Draedon's hand offered out in greeting. "Let's get this over with. The sooner I can get out of this wretched place the better."

Zittas was a proud, pretentious man. Draedon tried his best to hide his contempt for his superior. Zittas wore clothes made of the finest linens. The cloak he wore alone cost more than most peasants earned in a year. His skin was milky white and as smooth as one would expect from someone who had never really worked a day in his life. The Elders were not required to shave their heads. His hair was long, roughly the color of dung. Gray was beginning to speckle his carefully styled hair and his long, flowing beard. Draedon figured he was at least fifty years old, probably older. He was tall and slightly overweight. Overall, he carried himself like a man who thought himself better than anyone who crossed his path.

Draedon forced himself to turn, lest his contempt become unable to hide. He turned to the captain. "And you must be my new captain. I am Commander Draedon, and you are?"

"Captain Valtor, sir. It is an honor serving under someone as experienced as yourself."

Valtor spoke with silky flattery that reminded Draedon of a snake. He looked to be in his mid-twenties. Medium height and build, he was clean-shaven. Though his somewhat beady eyes widened a little at the sight of Draedon's hair and beard, he said nothing.

Looking back to Zittas, Draedon motioned toward the courtyard. "At your leisure, Your Grace."

With an annoyed sigh, Zittas turned to the courtyard and launched into a passionless liturgy. He droned on about the glory of the Church and the honor of serving the Maker by serving the Council. Draedon had to make a concerted effort to hide his boredom. Mercifully, Zittas's oration finally ended. With the ceremony concluded, the new Keepers made their way to their new quarters as the departing Keepers gathered outside their walls to wait for Elder Zittas to lead them to the Holy City.

Draedon motioned to Zittas and Valtor. "If you will follow me, we have refreshments prepared in my quarters." Einar followed as they made their way through the city to the officers' quarters, which was not far from the southern wall.

They entered his front door and settled into a sitting area to the left of the entrance. A fire was burning in the ornate fireplace in the center of the far wall, where three chairs faced the fireplace. Four glasses filled with wine and a bowl containing grapes were sitting on a table in front of the chairs.

Zittas sat down in the center chair and Valtor took one on the left. Draedon sat opposite of him, and Einar stood quietly behind him. Once they were settled in, Elder Zittas spoke first. "What is the current state of your Keepers?"

"With today's replacements, we are standing at five thousand Keepers. They are divided into five brigades—one archer brigade and four general infantry—."

"There are no cavalry?" asked Valtor incredulously.

Draedon looked over at Valtor, not appreciating the breach of etiquette. A captain never interrupts his Commander. *You and I will have issues, I see.*

"You will see, *Captain*," he said succinctly to remind Valtor who was in charge, "that in the terrain of the northern territories, cavalry is quite useless. The only horses here are for carrying equipment, not Keepers." This apparently came as quite a shock.

Draedon continued, "As I was saying, we have five brigades headed by our brigade chiefs, all of whom are quite experienced. Each brigade contains ten companies led by their company marshals." He sighed. "Unfortunately, many of the Keepers being replaced today were our better, more experienced marshals, which leaves us a little green for my liking. As it stands, we have 57 officers and 4,943 enlisted men."

"I trust you will be ready for the summer Inspections?" Zittas asked.

"Yes, Elder Zittas. We will be ready as always."

"So you say, but how long has it been since you have made a selection?"

"I have not made a selection since I was promoted to Legion Commander, but you know this already." Draedon knew that this was coming and had braced himself for the inevitable confrontation.

"Commander Draedon," Zittas said with disapproval thick in his voice, "you know that it is your responsibility as Legion Commander to provide the Church with worthy selections."

Fighting back the urge to speak what was truly on his mind, Draedon replied, "Your Grace, when a worthy selection presents itself, I will be more than happy to provide her to the Church."

"You *do* know that you are far behind the other Commanders. You are making me look bad to the rest of the Council." The whininess of Zittas's voice grated on Draedon.

"I will do my best to find one this year," Draedon assured, though he had no intention of doing so.

"Very well. Do better, Commander." Motioning to Valtor, he continued, "Captain Valtor comes with the highest praise of the Council. I trust you will use him well."

"I look forward to having you serve under me," Draedon said to Valtor.

"And I am looking forward to eradicating the Heretics from these hills under your command, sir," Valtor said with that same annoying, snake-like voice.

Zittas stood, signaling that the meeting was over. As they stood up, Draedon shook Valtor's hand. "I'm afraid you may find this territory a bit boring. There is not much action against the Heretics to speak of around here."

"We will see about that."

Something in the way that he said it made the hair stand up on the back of Draedon's neck. *We will see about you, Captain.* After they had left, Draedon pulled Einar aside. "Do me a favor. Find out all you can about our new captain."

"That may require me to spend some time in the Holy City."

"Take as long as you need."

Chapter Four

Orron woke up early hoping to be able to sneak out without waking anyone. He had spent much of the previous day in seclusion, claiming that he was still not feeling well. In truth, he was completely recovered, and even that disturbed him. From the way Me'ra had described it, he should still be feeling the effects of the blow he had received. His head raced with so many unanswered questions. *What is the symbol on my chest? Why do I have such a lethal weapon that feels so at home in my hands?* These questions and so many more pounded at him relentlessly. He hoped that by returning to the clearing where he first awoke a few nights ago, some answers might begin to emerge.

As quietly as he could manage, he slipped out his door. The house was completely silent. His stomach growled, and he momentarily considered taking some food for his journey, but stealing anything from this family that had shown him such kindness—even just a bite of bread—didn't feel right. *I can just hunt for food in the forest.* He made his way through the room and carefully opened the front door, slipping outside.

The frigid, early morning air took his breath. With his staff in his right hand, he buried his left hand deep inside his cloak.

Winter appeared to be at its fullest, and the chill in the air stole the warmth from his bones.

Snow was falling lightly as he made his way across the field toward the path down which he had traveled just a few nights ago. Since his initial journey took him to the ravine where he had found Ly'ra, it made sense to try to backtrack his way to the first clearing.

As he walked, he realized that this was his first full view of the rolling, snow-covered hills in daylight. A towering mountain rose up majestically to the north. The world was silent as it lay covered under the soft winter blanket.

He found the trail quickly and made his way through the forest. Traveling at a much slower speed, he enjoyed not having branches tear at his skin. His leather boots and warm cloak were able to keep much of the cold out, but his face was soon burning from the icy wind. He hunched his shoulders and trudged through the forest. The thick tree growth kept the snow cover lighter than in the field, making the journey somewhat easier. Preoccupied with his thoughts, Orron failed to notice that he was not alone when he arrived at edge of the ravine.

"I was wondering when you might be coming by here," a gruff voice said, startling Orron. He looked down and saw Mattox sitting on a rock at the bottom of the ravine. He had scraped away the snow where Ly'ra had lain and was looking at the dried blood that had not yet faded.

"I–I'm sorry to disturb you," Orron said. "I'll leave you–"

"I don't know what I would have done without her," Mattox said, seemingly lost in thought, his face full of sadness. Orron thought he could see evidence of crying. Running his hand through his hair, Mattox looked up at Orron for the first time. "I don't know who you are or why you were in these here woods, but I–I owe you a debt I can never repay."

"You don't owe me, Mattox," Orron said quietly, leaning on his staff. "I'm sure you would have done the same for another."

"I–I don't know anymore," he said bitterly. "Everything has been–well, it's been hard." He touched the rock where Ly'ra had lain in so much agony. "When Ly'ra didn't come back that day, I was so…"

His voice trailed off as fresh tears spilled over, rolling down his cheeks. Embarrassed, he wiped them away quickly. He cleared this throat and continued. "I was ready to kill you, you know. I even tried, but it seems that shiny head of yours is too thick."

Barely, thought Orron. The memory of the blow from Mattox's club still made him wince.

"It's just that…I've come to this place every day since you brought her back to me. It has made me realize how close I came to losing her." He absently brushed traces of snow from the rock. Orron could see him imagining what she had endured. Mattox solemnly looked up at Orron and stared him in the eyes. "I mean it, Orron, I thank you from the bottom of my heart for saving my daughter." There was genuine humility in his words.

Orron bowed his head slightly in acknowledgment. Mattox clapped his hands on his knees and stood up. His eyes examined the ravine and landed on the huge boulder. He motioned to it with his hand. "Ly'ra said that you threw a giant boulder off her leg. Is this the one?"

"Yes, it is."

Mattox's eyes grew wide with astonishment. "How in the holy name of the Maker did you move that?" he asked as he stroked his beard. "That must weigh more than ten horses!"

Orron spoke the simple truth. "I don't know."

"You are a mystery, lad." He climbed his way out of the ravine, needing Orron's outstretched hand to exit the top.

"I see you are planning to steal away quickly and quietly," Mattox said. It wasn't an accusation, just an observation. "Where are you headed?"

Orron motioned deeper into the woods. "That way. I have questions that need answers."

"Don't we all, lad, don't we all."

Orron turned to leave, but Mattox caught him on the arm. "Listen, Orron. Ly'ra is fond of you. So is Me'ra." Mattox looked down and shuffled his feet. "You have no food and apparently no real place to go. Well, I could use some help around the farm come spring. These are dark times, and one can't have too many people around protecting the ones he loves."

Orron could tell that this was difficult for Mattox to say. When he was slow to respond Mattox added, "I can't pay you much, but we have a warm bed and mostly good food for you. Well, if you can stomach Me'ra's cooking, that is."

That brought a smile to Orron's face. He had fully planned on setting off on his own, but Mattox's offer intrigued him. There was something about this family that felt right, like this is where he was meant to be. He glanced in the direction where he knew deep down he had come from several nights ago. He was torn. "I don't want to be a burden to anyone," he said in weak protest.

Mattox smiled broadly and clapped Orron on the back. "You won't be a burden at all. Why, it is about time we had another man around the house," he said with a wink. "It might even the odds a bit."

Though his unanswered questions burned within him, Orron pushed them aside. His soul told him to accept Mattox's offer. "If you are sure, I would be honored to accept."

"Then it's settled! So tell me, Orron, what do you know about sheep?"

"Um…nothing," he replied.

"No matter. That will give us something to talk about during these dreadful winter months."

Before they made their way back toward the house, Orron looked one last time in the direction of his clearing. He had no idea what his future held, but somehow he knew that clearing held the key to his past.

Chapter Five

Winter in Farovale was a miserable time for the healers. Sickness abounded and for many, the only cure was the sunshine and warmth that was many months away. It was a particularly frustrating time for Kor'lee. Though she had considerable skill with medicine, the healers often treated her as if she was little more than a servant. In their eyes, she had two things going against her. She was young, and she was a woman. Not even having the Legion Commander as her father could buy her any respect, though that was fine with her. She never wanted to live off the reputation of her father anyway.

At the moment, the healers stationed in this ward located in the northeastern part of the Citadel were away tending to other matters. Before leaving, the chief healer, a wretched, fat little man named Erez, charged Kor'lee with the disgusting task of cleaning vomit off the floor with tattered old rags.

She stopped scrubbing and surveyed the ward. It was a cramped, one-room, rectangular building. The floors were made of dried, warped pine, stained with the fluids of countless Keepers over the years. The walls were made of plaster that had probably been white at one time. Now they were a disgusting shade of gray streaked with yellow that she sincerely hoped was just from age, but she couldn't be sure. Most of the room was packed with cots that were little more than sanded wooden frames. The beds were hardly a comfortable place to recover from illness or a wound, but they were all that she had to work with.

There were no windows. She had heard that none of the healers' wards in Edelyndia had windows. It had something to do with an ancient superstition that certain deadly diseases could be transmitted by simply looking at the sick and dying while passing by. Obviously, that was an absurd belief, but every ward that she had ever seen contained no windows.

She hated this room; it felt like a prison. *I should just give Erez what he wants and quit.* Though she wanted nothing more than to leave this job, her pride would not allow her to give in. Though she was often mistreated, there were times when helping the sick and wounded brought her a semblance of joy. The desire to help others was in her blood. Her father often told her that her mother could ease the greatest of pain with just a smile. Kor'lee had followed in her footsteps and served as a healer. *Well, I'm more of a servant than a healer...maybe even a slave.*

With a sigh, she returned to her scrubbing. She knew that she was among the better archers in Farovale, and she knew more about the craft of medicine than most of the men who lorded their positions over her, but the leadership of the Church forbade a woman from holding any rank above servant. She certainly would never have been allowed to fight alongside men. There were even certain villages in the realm that went as far as to require women to keep their heads covered and remain silent. Fortunately, she knew her father would never allow such silliness. *Thank the Maker for small favors.*

She finished scrubbing the floor and went over to the washbasin. As she was scrubbing her hands of the filth, the front door opened. In walked a man whom she had never seen before.

He wore the cloak of an officer. Without bothering to look in her direction, he said, "Excuse me, servant girl, where can I find Erez?"

Servant girl? She did not appreciate that one bit. "I am not sure where Erez is at the moment, but I can have my father, *Commander Draedon*, send for him." Emphasizing her father's name had the desired effect. His head whipped around, and he looked closely at her.

"You must be Kor'lee." His face contorted into what she assumed must be his attempt at a dashing smile. *I'm sure the ladies must be lining up for you where you came from,* she thought with disgust.

"I am," she replied stiffly. "And whom might you be?"

"I am Captain Valtor. I just arrived from the Holy City." If that fact was supposed to impress her, it failed. When she didn't respond, he continued. "I heard the Commander had a beautiful daughter, but the reports did not do you justice." He moved over and leaned on the counter next to her, a little too close for her liking.

Kor'lee moved away to a nearby table and busied herself with refolding a stack of bandages that clearly did not need folding. "Do you want me to give a message to Erez for you?"

Undeterred by her lack of interest, Valtor followed her. "Actually, I was hoping for a tour of the medicinal wards in Farovale."

She could tell that he expected her to offer her services, but cleaning up the dried bile sounded more appealing. "I'll be sure to tell him when he comes back." Her lack of interest seemed to perplex Valtor. It appeared that disinterest from a woman was new territory for him.

"Perhaps *you* would be able to give me the tour?" he said, pushing on.

This guy can't catch a hint. "Unfortunately, I have *far* too much work to do. Perhaps another day." She did not intend ever to see that day.

Something about Valtor repulsed her. Perhaps it was the way he looked at her. Though she didn't consider herself to be all that beautiful, she had grown into her womanly figure and, living in a Keeper Citadel, she had grown accustomed to lonely men eyeing her like a piece of meat. But it was more than the way he looked at her. His voice reminded her of something, but she couldn't quite place it.

"I am Captain of the Keepers," he said proudly. "Surely *I* can give you new orders."

A snake! That's what it is, she realized. *The way he says the letter "s." He sounds like a snake!* With a thinly veiled attempt to hide her mockery, she replied, "But, alas, I don't receive orders from the Keepers. I am but a lowly woman."

"And a beautiful one at that," he said, eyeing her lustily. His hand found the small of her back. She abruptly stopped folding the rags and looked him squarely in the eye.

"Will that be all, Captain?" she said sharply, abandoning any pretense.

His hand started to slide lower as he said, "It doesn't have to be."

That's it! With lightning fast reflexes and surprising strength, she grabbed his hand and swung his arm around sending his face crashing into the table. With a groan, he croaked, "Unhand me, wench!"

Instead, she applied more pressure. His wrist neared its breaking point. She leaned over and whispered in his ear. "Try to touch me like that one more time, and I will make sure it is the last thing that you touch."

The front door opened and Erez walked in. Kor'lee quickly let go of Valtor's hand and he fell to his knees. "Erez, there you are. The Captain was just looking for you. You will be happy to know that he has offered to clean the floor for the next week as a way to…" she started to stall, searching for a reason. "As…

um…a way to give back to the fine healers who work so hard for the Keepers."

Valtor stood to his feet holding his injured wrist. Finding his voice, he spoke through clenched teeth. "I never—"

"He never expected that you would agree to it," she quickly interrupted. Her eyes fixed on Valtor's own eyes. The threat in her eyes was unmistakable. "If you agree to let him clean the floor, I told him that I would keep the details of our conversation a secret from my father, lest he be given other…responsibilities."

Valtor didn't miss this hint. For a moment, his face turned an ugly shade of red. He quickly regained his composure and turned to the chief healer, who was oblivious to what was really going on. "I would love to clean your floors," he said slowly.

Erez consented and Kor'lee excused herself, leaving the ward as quickly as her legs would carry her. Once outside, she took off running. Tears streamed from her eyes, blurring her vision as she ran.

She headed for the North Gate. When she arrived, she turned to the left and dashed down the alley that ran along the wall. When she passed the seventh building, she stopped. After making sure no one was looking, she pulled on the torch holder in front of her. One of the slate stones that formed the pathway along the wall slid back, revealing stairs hidden underneath. Einar revealed this secret passage to her not long after they arrived in Farovale years ago.

Quickly she descended the stairs and pulled another lever. The hidden mechanism that controlled the trapdoor pushed the stone back into place, and she was alone in the tunnel. Light streamed through tiny slits carved in the ceiling.

Still upset, she made her way swiftly through the winding tunnel. Finally, as she rounded the last curve, she reached what appeared to be a dead end. Hanging on a hook was warm clothing she kept there to protect her from the forest's harsh winter.

Though she was underground, it was still quite cold. She changed out of her dress and donned the dark green and brown pants, shirt, and cloak as quickly as her chilled hands would allow. Dressed more appropriately for the outdoors, she pulled on the hook and part of the ceiling above her slid back, making an exit. Instead of stairs, notches in the wall served as a ladder. She climbed out and onto the forest floor. A large pine tree stood next to her, shielding the secret opening. After pressing what appeared to be a large knot, the door closed.

She collapsed, completely alone in her forest sanctuary. Though her toughness, strength, and the training her father had given her allowed her to best Valtor, she was still quite shaken. The tears flowed out of anger and hatred. She hated Valtor for assaulting her. She hated herself for not breaking his arm. Moreover, she hated the Church for creating a world where she didn't matter.

Pulling herself up, she began to walk through the forest as she often did when days like this occurred. Before coming to Farovale, her father had been stationed in the North Woods for as long as she could remember. She always felt more at home in the freedom of the forest than she ever did in the confines of the Citadel. The smell of pine trees soothed her wounded spirit.

After about an hour, she came to a large clearing where she often went to think. This was her secret place. To her knowledge, no one else knew of it; however, something was different this time.

Though snow was still falling, the ground was completely bare. It looked as if something had burned away the remnants of grass. The trees were charred. She couldn't be sure, but the air almost smelled faintly of lightning. The clearing seemed to pulse lightly with unseen energy. *What happened here?*

She approached one of the blackened trees, running her hands along its trunk. It was hardened, as if turned to stone. Seeing her favorite place in all of Havenshae Valley transformed in this way filled her with tremendous sadness. *Must everything change?*

A lump formed in her throat as she remembered the moment the unceasing changes in her life began, the night her mother died twelve years ago. Since coming to Havenshae Valley, this small clearing had been the one thing in her life that seemed pure, innocent, and constant. This was the one place where she felt safe, significant. Now even that was taken from her.

Hugging herself tightly, trying to fight back the tears, she made her way back to the entrance of her tunnel. *Someday,* she tried to convince herself. *Someday they will no longer treat me like a nobody. Someday I will matter.*

Chapter Six

Orron brushed the sweat from his forehead. *It's on me now. I can do this.* Staring the creature in the eyes, he willed it to do what it needed to do. He futilely tried to dry his hands on his pants in an attempt to wipe away his nervousness, acutely aware of the eyes burning into his back.

The creature bellowed in pain. *Clearly, this is not going well. Should I do something?* He looked at Mattox, hoping for some kind of guidance.

"You're on your own with this one, lad," he said with a grin.

Great. Thanks for the help. Turning back to the ewe lying in front of him, he rubbed his head in frustration. *Of course, the first birth on my own has to have problems.* He had assisted Mattox during the lambing process of several ewes over the last few days. All had gone quite smoothly. His luck seemed to run out just in time for Mattox to insist on switching roles. The process had lasted over an hour, and it had grown apparent that something was wrong.

"You can do it, Orron," Ly'ra said encouragingly.

Rolling up his sleeves, Orron wiped his brow one more time. He reached his right hand slowly inside the ewe. *Breech.* The now familiar words that he used to find his center played in his mind, and his breathing slowed.

He found the rear fetlocks and cupping them in his palm, gently pulled. Once the hind legs were facing rear, he grasped the hooves and slowly pulled them forward.

"That's it, boy. Just like I told you!" Mattox said.

Slowly, the lamb emerged from its mother. After making sure it was breathing, Orron laid it down. Nature's instincts took over as the ewe found her offspring and began to lick it clean. Orron sighed with relief and sat back against the barn wall.

"I knew you could do it!" Ly'ra said joyfully.

Mattox patted him on the shoulder. "Well done, lad, well done. Me'ra has supper on. Why don't you wash up and join us inside." As he stood up, he turned to Ly'ra, "You too, young lady. I don't want your grubby hands touching my food!"

Ly'ra rolled her eyes and stood to her feet with the help of a wooden crutch that Mattox had fashioned for her. She brushed the hay and dirt from her simple dark brown dress. Orron stood to join her. They walked over to a tub of water by the large barn door that Mattox had just walked through. Orron and Ly'ra washed their hands thoroughly in the cold, murky water.

When they were finished, Ly'ra hugged him tightly, catching him off guard. He looked down to see a familiar smile. "What was that for?"

"Oh, no reason. I just love having you here."

"I love it, too," he said genuinely as he stroked her hair. These last three months, he had grown very close to Ly'ra. In many ways, she felt like family. "Come on, we better get inside before your mother scolds us both!"

Winter had been soothing for Orron. The daily routine of helping around the farm eased the burden of all the unspoken questions about his past. Mornings were spent feeding the sheep and cleaning the barn with Mattox. In the afternoons, when he wasn't needed to help mend the fences, he enjoyed helping Me'ra and Ly'ra operate the spinning wheel and loom. The work was steady and peaceful.

Some nights they were joined by Aton and Rhi'rra. Aton was a farmer who grew corn on a neighboring field. Rhi'rra was Me'ra's older sister, and the two were spitting images of each other. *Oh, the stories that Mattox and Aton could tell!*

When he was in a particularly merry mood, Ly'ra could talk Mattox into getting out his graivar, a stringed instrument native to the people of the Avolyndas Mountains. Despite his gruff exterior, Mattox possessed a hearty singing voice, though nothing could compare to the heavenly sound of Me'ra's singing.

As winter's icy grip on the Valley thawed, lambing season had begun on the farm. The air grew warmer, melting the blanket of snow that covered the hills. Soon they would be taking the sheep out to the pastures.

Orron was careful to walk slowly as they made their way toward the house. Ly'ra was recovering remarkably well, but she still walked with a noticeable limp. They joined Mattox and Me'ra at the table. In honor of Orron's first delivery, Me'ra had fixed a delicious smelling roast lamb. He found it somewhat ironic that they celebrated the birth of a lamb with the death of another.

Famished, Orron tore into his dinner after Mattox thanked the Maker for the food.

"Goodness," Me'ra said, "It must have been some lambing!"

"Aye," said Mattox between bites. "It was quite the ordeal. The poor girl couldn't do it herself."

"How'd you do?" Me'ra asked Orron.

"Fine, I guess."

"He was wonderful," Ly'ra said, beaming with pride.

Mattox chuckled. "Oh, he was all right. I got a little nervous, though, with the way his hands were shaking and all."

"They were not!" Orron protested. Then, he conceded. "I guess I was a *little* nervous."

"A *little?* Lad, you were sweating like you were running laps around the Great Desert!"

Me'ra tried to conceal her smile. "Oh, be nice to the boy. Why, you vomited the first time you had a breech."

"I never—"

"You vomited?" Ly'ra's mouth fell open in disbelief. Her father was something of a hero to her, and Orron could tell that she was not used to hearing of his weaknesses.

"Well, maybe a little, but the situations were nothing alike."

Me'ra raised an eyebrow. "Really? How so?"

"Well, for starters, it wasn't a wee little ewe like the one today. She was huge!" He had a tendency to exaggerate details. Spreading his arms wide he said, "She was at least this long and the lamb…it was huge, too!"

Me'ra rolled her eyes as he continued.

"The birth lasted for over twelve hours, and I was deathly ill with the mountain fever."

"I'm sure you were," she said wryly.

Desperate to change the subject, Mattox looked to Orron. "Well, now that the weather has cleared up a bit, I was thinking about heading into the woods tomorrow for a hunt. It's been a while since I nabbed an Avolyndian elk. Want to tag along?"

He hadn't returned to the woods since the night in the clearing. Part of him was afraid of what they might hold for him. He pushed the last bite of lamb around on his plate. "I don't have a weapon to hunt with."

"You can use my old bow," he replied. "Well, if you're strong enough to handle it, that is."

Knowing that he had no real reason to say no, he tried to hide his unease. "Sure, that sounds good."

"Can I come too?" Ly'ra asked.

"Sorry, deary. You're leg isn't quite healed enough for that. Perhaps in the fall," Mattox said as he patted her arm.

She sighed and crossed her arms in frustration. The long recovery had gone far too slow for her liking, something she complained about often. She was unaccustomed to being so cooped up.

After dinner, Mattox, Me'ra, and Ly'ra gathered around the fire, but Orron excused himself to his room. With the door shut, he sat down on his bed and stared out the window toward the woods. *There's something out there, something connecting me to my past.*

That night, he had the reoccurring dream that had plagued him off and on since that first night in the woods. The conversation was always the same–a faceless voice telling him he knew what he needed to do, and Orron was arguing against it. Sometimes the voice came from a bright light, other times everything was completely dark. Every time he had this dream, he woke up drenched in sweat, his heart racing.

After a restless night, he woke early and dressed for the hunt, donning his warm, black cloak. He paused as he was about to open the door. Turning around, he retrieved his staff that had remained concealed under his bed for months. Though he didn't know why, he had a strange feeling that he was going to need it.

When he entered the main room, he noticed that Mattox had an old sword strapped to his waist. "What's that for?" he whispered, not wanting to wake Me'ra and Ly'ra.

"You can never be too careful these days," Mattox replied somewhat ominously. Then he nodded toward Orron's staff. "And that?"

He shrugged his shoulders. "The same reason I guess."

Orron and Mattox grabbed what supplies they would need for the next few days and left the house. Mattox grabbed his extra bow and quiver from the barn and they made their way across the field toward the forest. There was a chill in the early morning air.

As they entered the forest, Mattox broke the silence. "Now, I'm not sure what you are used to hunting, but we are not after small game or even deer." He puffed his chest out and stroked his beard. "Avolyndian elk! These woods are full of the giant beasts. As big as horses they are, and fast. Smarter than a fox. Now those are a prize worth winning!"

"Have you ever killed one?"

"Aye, of course I have! I was only a little older than Ly'ra when I killed my first."

Though Mattox had a propensity for exaggeration, Orron could tell he was speaking the truth. Their first day in the forest yielded little results, but Mattox proved to be a more than capable tracker. They were able to pick up the trail of several deer, but no signs of the elk.

The spring growth was beginning in earnest, and the forest was thick with undergrowth. Greenery was far more plentiful now, giving it a far less intimidating feel than he remembered. His fears began to melt away as enjoyed his time in the forest with Mattox. There was something invigorating about being on a hunt. Orron felt more alive than he had in months. They spoke little, focused solely on their quest for the elusive creatures.

As the day wore on it became apparent that the elk were not in the area. Mattox stopped to rest. "Well, we should at least try to nab some rabbits, or we will go hungry."

The area around them was littered with small tracks. Orron bent down and touched one. "Yellow rabbits, heading that way," he said as he pointed at a small thicket.

Mattox raised an eyebrow. "And how did you know that? Those rabbits are only found here in this forest."

"I just do," he said. Mattox looked at him curiously but let it go.

"Well, boy, watch and learn. Not too many men can claim to have killed a yellow rabbit. They are slippery little buggers. I, myself, have killed my share," he said proudly.

They both nocked arrows and slowly followed the trail. They were approaching a small creek when Orron saw a blur of yellow.

Acting on instinct, he fired his first arrow. Everything seemed to slow down as he saw something yellow streak through his peripheral vision. He spun, loaded a second arrow and crouched, firing the arrow all in one smooth motion with the bow held parallel to the ground so that the shot could fly under an overhanging branch. The arrow passed through a very narrow gap between two trees and struck the rabbit a good fifty yards away.

Orron turned to Mattox and saw him standing with his mouth open. The arrow was still nocked in his bow.

"How...?" was all that he could get out.

Orron ignored him and went to retrieve the rabbits. *How did I do that?* he wondered. His skill with the bow had shocked him more than it had Mattox. As he gathered the rabbits, he realized that the arrows had pierced them both in the center of their left eyes. They were both perfect shots.

They decided to make camp. Finding a relatively flat patch of ground where the undergrowth was sparser, Mattox made a fire to cook the rabbits. Because it was still early in the spring, night fell quickly. Before long, the fire was casting long shadows on the trees that ringed their camp. The night brought with it a slight chill, not so cold as to make it uncomfortable, but cold enough to make the fire inviting.

Mattox declared the food was ready and handed Orron one of the rabbits. As they ate, Mattox kept staring at Orron and finally said, "I can't figure you out. I have never known another man that could do what you did today. Where did you learn to shoot like that?"

"I don't know. I just...there's just a lot about me that I don't know or understand," he said. He tossed his last bite of the rabbit into the fire with frustration. "Today, it felt like I had been hunting all my life. If you would have asked me yesterday how to shoot a bow I couldn't have told you, but once it was in my hands, I..." his voice trailed off. With a frustrated sigh he blurted out, "What I did with that boulder, the fact that I can use a bow? You can't deny that I carry the mark of a Keeper. I–I just..." He didn't want to say it. "I'm afraid I'm some kind of...weapon...a killer," he said bitterly.

Orron pulled his knees up to his chin and hugged them tightly to his chest. Mattox was lost in thought. They were both silent for a while. Finally, Orron spoke quietly, "Don't you ever wonder?"

"Wonder what?"

"Who or what I was before I came here."

"Aye, but then I remember that none of that matters."

That was not the answer Orron was expecting. "What do you mean?"

"I know you're frustrated, but who you are is not found in your past," Mattox said. "It is found in your future, in the decisions you make every day." He gazed intently into the fire. "Orron, I'm going to tell you something that I have never told anyone, not even Me'ra." He looked up, searching the sky for how to proceed. "I am not a great man. I'm not even a good one. After..." He caught his breath. "After what happened all those years ago, I turned my back on the Maker. I blamed Him, hated Him for what the Keepers had done."

Orron wondered what could have happened to make this seemingly devout man hate the Maker, but he kept his questions to himself.

"When Ly'ra went missing, it felt like what happened before was happening all over again." Mattox's eyes glistened in the firelight. "I yelled, screamed, and cursed the Maker. *How could You do this again!*" His hands shook as he remembered that night. "Then, when my anger accomplished nothing, I fell to my knees. I did the only thing left that I knew I hadn't done. I asked Him for help." He looked at Orron with a heaviness in his eyes.

"Orron, I asked, and you walked out of the forest holding my Ly'ra." His eyes gave way and tears streamed down his cheeks, disappearing in his beard. "My damnable pride blinded me with hatred for the Keepers, and I struck you down." He was silent for a moment. "Do you see what I'm getting at?"

Unsure, Orron shook his head.

"What I'm trying to say is...well, I asked the Maker for help, and He sent you. I don't know who you are, but I do know this," he wiped his eyes and leaned over, placing one of his massive hands on Orron's shoulder. "It doesn't matter what you were before, I believe. I *know* that you are someone He saw fit to use. That is all that will ever matter to me."

The weight of Mattox's words resonated with Orron's soul. After sitting in silence a while longer, Mattox rolled over and went to sleep. Orron lay awake, staring at the stars and the eternal darkness that held them.

Who am I to be used by the Maker? According to Mattox the *why* didn't matter, only the fact that he *was*. He trusted and respected Mattox profoundly and wanted desperately to believe him. With a sigh, he rolled over, closed his eyes, and forced himself to give in to his overwhelming exhaustion.

Orron awoke the next morning to find Mattox putting out the fire.

"We better get a move on. Today we get our elk, maybe two. I can feel it in my bones."

Orron just grunted in acknowledgment. It had been a restless night. The dream had come back more vivid than ever before.

If Mattox noticed Orron's unease, he chose not to acknowledge it. They packed up what little supplies they had and were ready to return to the hunt in less than ten minutes.

"I woke up early and got to thinking," Mattox said as he picked up his bow. "Maybe we should split up today and cover more ground. The Avolyndian elk is a clever beast. The two of us are not small men, and we are likely to just scare her off before we catch sight of her."

Orron shrugged his shoulders. "I'll head south."

"Aye, I'll head east. Let's meet back here at dusk." He clapped Orron on the back. "I need to warn you. I may be a bit late, what with the massive elk I'll be dragging behind me."

Finally, Orron smiled. Mattox had a way of breaking the tension. They said good-bye and headed their separate ways.

Like the day before, once he was on the hunt, his tension melted away. The first two hours of the hunt were uneventful. Then he saw it—his first Avolyndian Elk. Orron had just finished climbing to the top of a steep ridge, and from his vantage point, he saw a giant beast grazing on the underbrush in the ravine below. He knew instantly this was the elk that Mattox had described. Though its antlers had just started their spring growth, it was clearly male. Even from this distance, he could see that the animal was strong, lean, and powerful.

The mighty animal's head rose as soon as Orron spotted him. They stared each other straight in the eye, daring the other to move. Orron was unsure if he could shoot him through the overhanging branches. As though he understood Orron's intentions, the great elk snorted and leapt away.

Having taken so long to find his first elk, Orron was not about to let this one get away. With his staff in his right hand and bow in the other, he half ran half slid down the steep bank and charged after the fleeing giant.

Orron was fast. He was abnormally fast, but this elk was just as fast and the pursuit carried the two deeper and deeper into the forest. Up hills, over streams, and through thorn bushes they ran. The hunted could not shake the hunter, nor could the hunter gain any ground. They were evenly matched.

The chase went on for at least an hour, maybe more. Just as Orron was beginning to feel like he would not be able to go on, he began gaining ground. *He is slowing down!*

The animal burst through two trees, and only seconds behind, Orron followed into a large clearing. He skidded to a halt. The elk was nowhere to be found. Panting heavily, trying to catch his breath, he leaned over grabbing his shaking legs. *Where could it have gone?*

He straightened up and looked around, noticing there was something strange about this clearing. Everything in the center was completely dead. What little grass could be seen was brown as if scorched by the sun. The trees that surrounded the clearing were blackened as if they had burned suddenly and at great temperatures. Then, it hit him. *This is my clearing.*

A deep sense of foreboding turned his stomach. The hair on the back of his neck stood up as he looked around cautiously. His heart beat loudly in his ears. After a moment, he realized that this clearing was completely devoid of sound. Even though his concentration had been on the chase, he had still noticed the natural sounds of the forest until he entered the clearing. Now no birds, insects, or squirrels could be heard. Not even a breath of wind stirred.

His heart was beating so hard he was worried that it might explode. *Breathe. Connect. Focus.* The words had no effect this time. The panic in his heart raged on with abandon.

An overwhelming energy began to emanate from all around him. The staff in his right hand started to glow. The silence was transformed as the energy began to hum. It started as a low rumble and built to a deafening roar.

Orron dropped his bow and staff. Clutching his ears and closing his eyes tightly, he fell to his knees in agony. He thought he could hear a distant voice screaming only to realize that the scream was his own.

Pulsing, crashing, cacophonous noise echoed around him. He wanted to cry for help, but he didn't know who would hear him. The relentless pounding threatened to tear him apart from the inside out. Fear clawed at his heart. *I am going to die.* With final desperation, he cried out with all his might, "*Maker, help me!*"

Instantly, the noise stopped. The clearing returned to its previous state of eerie silence. Orron remained frozen in place. After mustering the courage, he cautiously opened his eyes. The sun had made its way across the sky and shadows were beginning to fill the clearing. *It's been hours!*

He got to his feet and picked up his bow. Looking down at his staff, he was unsure if he should take it with him. Tentatively, he bent down and placed his hand around the grip. It felt normal.

What happened? It was almost as if he had just been awakened from a dream, a nightmare. The slight ringing in his ears told him otherwise. Shaken, he didn't know what to do next.

Clang! He whipped his head around in the direction from which he had entered the clearing. *That sounded like a sword.* He strained to hear where it could have come from. For several moments, he listened. Just as he was beginning to believe he had imagined the noise, he heard faint shouting and another clash of swords.

A thought filled his mind that was so farfetched he dismissed it immediately. *There's no way...*

He heard the clash again. The thought returned. This time it carried with it an image. It was an image that he recognized and filled him with dread. He knew exactly whose sword that was. *Mattox!*

He took off running as fast as he could manage in his weakened state in the general direction he thought the sounds had come from. After hearing no other sounds, he skidded to a halt and realized that he had never before seen these particular trees. *I'm lost.*

Breathe. Connect. Focus. The words came back, and unlike his experience in the clearing, they took him back to a place of peaceful calm. He leaned back and sat cross-legged. Tranquility flowed through him as his shoulders relaxed. He let the sounds of the forest envelop him.

Thump, thump. Thump, thump. Thump, thump. He tensed. *What was that?* Momentarily his concentration was broken, and the panic tried to claw its way back in. The words repeated in his mind, and he once again relaxed.

Thump, thump. Thump, thump. Thump, thump. The sound returned. *Could it be?* This time he recognized the sound, but could hardly believe it. *How…?* He opened his eyes. The "how" didn't matter. *Helping Mattox is all that matters right now.* The sound was coming from somewhere to his right.

He stood up and took off running. This time the sound stayed with him, guiding his every step as the sound of Mattox's heartbeat grew stronger.

Chapter Seven

After an arduous journey through the thick forest, Orron finally arrived at the source of the sound. He crouched down next to a large tree and surveyed the scene in front of him.

A group of five men stood conferring together with their backs to Orron. Two others lay on the ground, dead or unconscious he could not tell. The sky was growing darker by the minute, limiting visibility. He could make out Mattox lying on the ground at the edge of the circle of trees. The fact that he could still hear the beat of his heart told him that he was still alive.

Looking up, Orron noticed that the tree in front of him was one that he could easily climb and there were branches that extended over where the men were standing. He climbed stealthily up and onto one of the stronger branches. Careful not to alert the men, he made his way along the branch until he was directly over them.

They were dressed in dark green and brown cloaks that blended in well with the forest. He listened intently to their conversation.

"Then what should we do with him?" one of the smaller men asked.

"I say we slit his throat and dump him in the river."

That earned him a slap upside the head.

"We are not murderers."

"Then why'd we grab 'em?" he countered, rubbing his head.

"I told you already. He's Lillyndale's only shepherd. If he stops providing the Keepers with wool, they will suffer. That's a win in my book."

"I'm with you on this one, Raulin. Just tell us what to do," said a particularly large man.

"Well, we can't leave him here, and we are *not* Keepers. We don't kill at random," the one called Raulin replied. "The way I see it, we have no choice but to bring him with us." He motioned to the two on each side of him, and they walked over to where Mattox lay.

Orron knew he had to act fast. This was as good a place as any to stage a rescue. The trees were spread out enough for him to swing his staff. Though they had attacked Mattox, he was unwilling to use his bow. He did not want to turn into a killer. He drew in a breath and let it out slowly, calming his beating heart.

Grabbing the branch with his left hand, he transferred the bow and staff to his right. He swung around so he was hanging from the branch, directly above the two men who had stayed behind. With one last calming breath, he let go.

He landed on one of the men, dropping him to the ground with a thud. Swinging his staff around, he caught the other one sharply under his chin. The man's head snapped back and he was unconscious before he hit the ground.

Orron glanced down at the one on whom he had landed. He was breathing, but not moving. *Two down, three to go.*

Raulin and the two other men let go of Mattox and spun around drawing their swords. Orron gripped the staff in his right hand and slowly twirled it around him, tracing intricate patterns as he passed it from one hand to the other. His heart beat slowly, and he felt deadly calm. The hood of his black cloak concealed his face in shadows giving him a ghostly appearance in the fading light.

"Well, what do we have here?" Raulin said calmly. He was clearly no stranger to conflict. "That's a cute little stick you have there." Turning to the smaller man on the left he said, "Would you please show our visitor what swords do with sticks?"

He nodded his head and approached Orron carefully. Orron stopped spinning his staff and gripped it in the center with both hands. He held it vertically close to his body with his weight resting on his back foot and remained perfectly still.

The swordsman stopped a few feet away. The sword, though somewhat short, appeared to be battle worn, and its handler held it confidently. Orron's complete lack of movement appeared to unnerve him. He licked his lips nervously not sure what to do next. With a cry, he attacked, swinging the sword at Orron's head.

At the last possible second, Orron spun away and twirling his staff over his head, he brought it down hard on the swordsman's back. His next blow was to his temple and the man fell to the ground in a heap.

Orron turned back toward Raulin who was picking at his nails as if he was bored. "Impressive." he said. He turned to the hulking man on his right. "Bruschian, would you mind?"

"It would be my pleasure," he replied with a wide smile. He hefted his weapon, a huge hand-and-a-half sword. It, too, was notched from heavy use. He was easily seven feet tall, and he must have weighed close to three hundred pounds. Orron was a large man, but Bruschian towered over him as he approached. He was thick with muscle and bones so large he appeared to have been bred for battle.

No matter, the bigger they are... Orron resumed his previous fighting position.

Bruschian struck first. Orron had assumed that a man his size must be slow and was caught off guard by his surprising speed. He deflected the crushing blow with his staff, but the power spun him around allowing the bigger man to land a punch to the back of his head that sent Orron sprawling.

Bruschian let out a very ugly laugh. In the fall, Orron's hood had fallen back. Bruschian's laugh caught in his throat when he saw Orron's bald head. "Keeper," he said with deadly hatred.

"No," Orron said somewhat surprised at the reaction. "But I seem to be getting that a lot these days."

Bruschian started walking menacingly toward him with his sword in his right hand, raised slightly.

"Now, if I were you, I would work on your posture," Orron chided. "Your technique is atrocious."

Bruschian tilted his head in confusion. *Not the smartest are you?* With blinding speed, Orron swung his staff upward, catching his sword-hand on the knuckles, breaking bone with the force of his blow. Bruschian bellowed in pain.

Before he could react, Orron pushed himself up and swung around, kicking the massive man in the front of the left knee so hard that he could hear the kneecap snap. Twirling the staff around, he prepared to deal him a final blow, but Bruschian fell to the ground, writhing in agony.

With the big man disabled, he turned to Raulin who was holding the now-conscious Mattox in front of him with a dagger to his throat. Mattox looked furious, but was completely helpless. Exasperated Raulin said, "This has gone far enough. I don't know who you are, but I have no quarrel with you."

"You *do* know that you are holding a dagger to my friend's throat, don't you? That sounds like something worthy of a quarrel to me," Orron replied calmly.

Raulin shifted his weight and gave him a sheepish smile. "Good point. I guess you have me there. What now? I can't let him go; you will kill me. Although I am not bad with a blade, I am no match for anyone that can defeat Bruschian so easily—"

"And I cannot attack you while you hold my friend's life in your hands," Orron finished his thought for him. Then, with a glint in his eye, he swung the staff around to his right hand and pressed the hidden button extending the blade."

"Well that's a neat trick!" Raulin exclaimed. "I'm impressed. But I'm afraid your little toy changes nothing."

"Doesn't it?"

Mattox's eyes widened as he sensed what Orron was about to do. "Don't do it, boy," he warned.

Raulin glanced at the spear and back at Orron's face cautiously. "Listen, this is obviously just a misunderstanding."

"Then help me understand."

"You can't; you're not from around here."

"Why do you say that?" Orron was genuinely curious.

"Well, for starters, you would not have been surprised that Bruschian thought you were a Keeper. Anyone who's from around here knows that the only people wearing hooded cloaks and bald heads are Keepers."

Orron shrugged his shoulders.

"Second," Raulin continued, "you don't seem to be aware of the fact that you are standing in my forest."

"Your forest?"

"Yes," Raulin said proudly. "This is my forest. I am its king."

"And that gives you the right to attack innocent men?"

Raulin's eyes grew dark. "No one that stands by and does nothing while the Church does what it wants is innocent."

What is he talking about? Orron's mind raced quickly. He didn't like where this was going. He was afraid that if he did not do something quick, this could have a very unpleasant ending. He breathed in slowly as he made up his mind.

It happened so fast that Raulin didn't even have time to blink. With little more than a flick of his wrist, Orron sent the spear flying toward them. It barely missed Mattox's throat as it buried itself into Raulin's shoulder sending him crashing to the ground.

Orron exhaled and looked down at his hands. They were shaking. He walked over to where Raulin lay and pulled the spear out of his shoulder, causing him to cry out in pain.

"Go ahead, Keeper. Finish what you started." Raulin looked at him with grim determination. Orron couldn't help but be impressed with his bravery.

Holding the tip of the spear dangerously close to Raulin's throat Orron said, "I already told you, I am neither a Keeper nor a killer." He buried the spear in the dirt next to Raulin's head. To his credit, he never even flinched. "My friend and I will be going. Try to follow us, and I will be less inclined to show mercy."

Grabbing his spear, Orron wiped the blade on the ground and converted it back into a staff. After untying Mattox, he helped him up. Together, they left Raulin and his band behind.

When they were safely away from the bandits, Orron stopped, bent over, and vomited. Sinking down next to a tree, he wiped the bile from his chin. He noticed that his hands were still shaking violently. The stress of his day's experiences had caught up with him. Mattox came over and sat down next to him. His hand was holding his head where blood flowed from a nasty looking gash.

"Are you alright?" Orron asked.

"Aye. You?"

"I'm just a little shaken up."

"Aye."

They both sat in silence. The quiet felt good to Orron. He was disturbed to realize that he had enjoyed himself while he was fighting those men. Every move, every blow felt natural, like he was meant to fight. It only made him feel more miserable.

After a few minutes passed, Mattox spoke up. "Orron... thank you."

"You would have done the same for me."

"I don't mean about rescuing my sorry rear. I mean for not breaking my knee cap when I hit you with my club!"

Orron laughed despite himself. Mattox got up and pulled him to his feet. "Let's go home."

Chapter Eight

It's going to be a hot summer, Draedon thought as he swatted at a bothersome fly. Under the heavy black cloak required of his rank, he wore the simple breastplate, greaves, and bracers made of hardened leather that all the infantry wore. *Oh, to be a common archer.* They had the good fortune of wearing only a thin gambeson. No soldier in the Keepers wore a helm so that "the peasants can see their hairless heads and tremble in fear," or some such nonsense Elder Zittas had once said.

Draedon stood at attention as the peasants of Covenglade poured into the cramped square at the center of the small village. Covenglade was nestled in the foothills of the mountains, just outside of Havenshae Valley. Draedon, along with a company of one hundred Keepers, had traveled to the village to perform the first Inspection of the summer. They now formed an imposing perimeter around the village square.

Old buildings, worn from the harsh, northern winters, formed a ring around a large, dirt courtyard. One of the buildings was Cleric Torker's manor. Clerics were low-level leaders in the Church. From their ranks, some were selected to govern the various villages of the realm. Some were good people, but many were ambitious, power-hungry men who desired nothing more than advancement. Cleric Torker was not one those.

Directly across the square from the Cleric's manor stood an old, weathered church made of sagging wood and cracked stone. It stood apart from most of the churches that Draedon had come across in his many travels. Most stood in stark contrast to this humble structure. In times of bad, it didn't matter how many starved to death, most churches would always be filled with enough ornamentation to feed a village for months, if not years. It seemed to Draedon that this ramshackle house of worship was a perfect fit for the unassuming cleric who served as the caretaker of it and the villagers who worshiped there.

The One True Church of the Maker, Draedon thought to himself with disgust. *It's the One True Church all right, but it has nothing to do with the Maker, at least not anymore.* Of course, Draedon would never say these things aloud, at least not in front of most people.

His new captain had insisted on accompanying Draedon, eager to experience his first Inspection. *Valtor, cursed snake of a man.* After Kor'lee had told Draedon of their encounter in the northern ward, he had wanted vengeance. He felt it was his duty as a father; however, as a Legion Commander, he could do nothing. He had no legal right according to the Church to punish a Keeper based solely on the word of a woman, not even his own daughter. The worst he could have done was issue a stern reprimand that would have had little-to-no effect on Valtor. Instead, he was forced to spend a great deal of time alongside the man. *Something I find about as pleasant as standing under this summer sun in this blasted black cloak...*

After the last of the villagers arrived, he turned to his captain and gave him a curt nod. Valtor stepped forward and began to read the official decree of the Council.

"Citizens of Covenglade. Your Council of Elders, the Holy Seer and Voice of the Almighty Maker has decreed that today shall be the chosen day of the eleventh annual Inspection. This is the will of the Maker. Thus, any girl who is eleven years of age on this day must step forward and present herself. The Legion Commander, as appointed by the Holy Council, shall inspect her to see if she is both pure and fit for service unto the Maker. Any girl who has the blessed fortune of being chosen will have the honor of serving the Council in the Holy City from this day forth." Valtor finished with a flourish.

He is enjoying this far too much, Draedon thought, sickened by the smile on Valtor's face. As a father of a beautiful daughter, the thought of turning her over to the whims of the Council infuriated Draedon. Though he did not know what happened to the chosen girls once they arrived in the Holy City, he had heard terrible rumors of slavery and abuse. For this reason, in the six years since being promoted to Legion Commander, he had not chosen a single girl much to the consternation of the Council.

Six young, terrified girls stepped to the center. He could hear the choked sobs coming from their mothers as the other villagers tried to comfort them. *Let's get this over with.*

He stepped to the center of the gathering and walked around, examining the girls from all sides. He knew that Valtor was watching him closely. *I better give him a show.*

He turned to Cleric Torker. "Is this *all?*" Draedon said with all the annoyance he could muster.

"Yes, my lord," the gentle old man replied nervously.

He turned back to the girls and placed his hands on his hips. Most of the girls were unkempt and poorly nourished. Winter had been harsh and sickness abounded. One girl stood out.

"You there," he said to a beautiful little girl shaking with terror, "what is your name?"

"Fle'ra," she said, her eyes never leaving her feet.

"Look at me and stand at attention when I address you, you filthy whelp!" Though it pained him to verbally abuse the young girl, he knew that it was the only way to protect her.

Tears streamed from her eyes as she lifted her head and stepped forward. Draedon had to force himself to keep from comforting her. *I didn't sign up for this.*

Thirty years ago joining the Keepers had been about adventure, nobility, and earning the respect of his village. *Now...now I'm nothing more than a monster to this helpless child.* He sighed, his frustration not an act. Looking over at Valtor, he could see a slight smile forming. *He thinks I'm trapped.*

It hadn't taken long for Draedon to realize the true reason why Valtor had been assigned to him. The Council felt he needed a watchdog. Now he knew he was being tested.

"Open your mouth so I can see your wretched teeth."

She complied. *Well, that won't work.* He saw that they were perfectly intact and remarkably even. This was going to be tough. He knew that according to the requirements of the Council this girl should be selected.

"Bend over and touch your toes," he ordered, trying to stall.

She once again complied. He then made her perform a number of pointless exercises trying to find some flaw, something that would allow him to return her to her mother.

Tension filled the air as it became apparent that she was a worthy selection. *Where is it?*

He was preparing to simply dismiss her for no good reason and accept the consequences that would surely follow when he noticed the smallest of flaws. As she turned her head during one of his exercises, he caught a glimpse of a tiny scar behind her left ear.

He grabbed her head so hard she cried out in pain. Twisting her head, he made a show of examining the scar. He had to hide his relief.

"This," he said to the cleric, "is the best you can offer the council? She is too flawed to serve the Church as even the lowest of slaves!" He pushed her roughly back to the other girls. She stumbled and fell to the ground.

"Scars, poor teeth, bones showing! All of these girls are unworthy," he declared. Out of the corner of his eye, he saw the cleric sigh with relief. "Yet again, Covenglade shall spend the year bearing the shame of failing to provide even one halfway-decent selection for the Council!"

Turning sharply to Valtor he ordered, "Captain, gather the men. This Inspection is over."

Valtor opened his mouth to protest. "But, sir–"

"Captain, was my order unclear?"

"No, sir. But that girl is a perfect–"

"Captain Valtor, I do not recall asking your opinion!" Draedon's eyes flashed with anger. "I'm not sure what they are teaching these days in the Keeper Academy, but when you are in *my* Territory, the only response you will give when issued an order by a superior officer is 'Yes, sir.' Is that clear?"

Valtor returned his stare, and for a moment, Draedon thought he might actually defy him in front of the other Keepers. *That would be unwise, young man.* Part of him wanted Valtor to rebel.

Then with crisp military precision Valtor said, "Yes, sir. My apologies, sir."

"Very well. Carry on." Draedon dismissed him with a wave of his hand, very much enjoying the look of embarrassment on Valtor's face as he was humiliated in front of the other Keepers.

Valtor turned, issued the order and followed the Keepers as they paraded out of the village. Draedon stayed behind and turned to the cleric.

"Cleric Torker, I will have a word with you before I leave." Valtor shot him a quizzical look. Draedon then said loudly enough for Valtor to hear, "I do not take your failure to provide a suitable selection lightly!"

"Yes, my lord."

Draedon pulled the cleric aside. After the captain left the village square, he said softly, "Torker, I must ask your forgiveness. I meant no harm to that poor girl."

"I know, Commander. You gave a wonderful gift, even if she doesn't see that yet."

Draedon looked down at his feet. "How are things going? The children look a little on the weak side."

"It's been a long winter," he said with sadness in his eyes. "We lost a few to the fever."

"What do you need?"

"Medicine, a quality healer, more food."

Medicine and food were hard to come by in the years after the Great War. The devastation wrought by the long years of fighting still left their mark on the farming communities. Toward the end of the War, locked in an evenly matched struggle, the Council followed the leading of Elder Seidar who unleashed a terrible plague that affected both land and people. *It may have won the War, but at what cost?*

"I will send Kor'lee when we can spare her. As for food and medicine..." Draedon raised his hands in exasperation.

"Thank you, Commander," he said with a kind smile. "I know you do what you can. It would be a pleasure to see Kor'lee again. It has been quite a while since I have seen her."

Draedon had known Torker for many years. They first met when Draedon was a Captain in the North Woods Territory. He had been there for his family during the dark days of his wife's passing. Kor'lee, in particular, had really found comfort in his presence. When Draedon was promoted and assigned to Farovale, Torker transferred to Covenglade shortly after.

He was a slight man, bent with age, who had served the Church for many years, more years than Draedon had been alive. He was bald on top with a flash of snow-white hair that ringed his scalp. His eyes were gentle and full of the kind of wisdom that comes from walking the earth for over seventy years.

"I'm sure she will be happy to get out of the Citadel," Draedon said. Before he walked away to rejoin the rest of the Keepers, he said, "Oh, and Cleric..."

"Yes, sir?"

"You cut it a little too close this year. I don't care what it takes, just make sure we have no obvious selections next year."

Chapter Nine

"Wake up, sleepy head!" Ly'ra said as she jumped on Orron's bed, startling him out of his slumber.

"What? What is it?"

"Don't tell me you forgot!"

"Forgot what?" he said with a playful twinkle in his eye.

"Orron!" she said with a pout on her face.

Orron laughed. "Oh, of course I didn't forget. Happy birthday, Ly'ra!" He sat up and gave her a big hug. "How old are you now, seven?"

"Hey, I'm ten!" She hit him with mock anger.

He released her and looked intently at a spot on the floor and pointed. "Hey, isn't that…"

"What?" she asked.

With her head turned, he grabbed the pillow behind him and smacked her in the head. "That's for jumping on my bed to wake me up!"

She laughed and jumped off his bed before he could land another blow. "You know you love me," she said as she gave him a curtsy.

"Yes, but I think I liked you better when you couldn't walk!"

"Ly'ra," called Me'ra through the open door. "Leave the boy alone and get in here. You have chores to finish."

"But, Mom–" Ly'ra whined.

"No buts! It may be your birthday, but the chores won't start doing themselves!"

Ly'ra rolled her eyes. Orron threw the pillow at her, but she caught it and sent it flying back. He could have blocked it easily, but instead let it hit him in the face and fell back, feigning unconsciousness.

She laughed and skipped out of the room. Orron stayed in bed for a few more moments, not quite ready to be fully awake. Ever since the hunt, things had been different. Though questions still plagued him, he felt more at ease. Many nights after the others would go to sleep he would sit cross-legged and let the three words wash over him. He had found an inner peace that held the uncertainty at bay.

He finally dragged himself out of bed, changed into clean clothing, and joined the family at the breakfast table.

"So what are we going to do first?" Ly'ra said with excitement.

"Whatever you like, dear," Mattox said. He looked distracted.

"Can we have a party tonight?"

"A party sounds nice," mumbled Me'ra.

What is wrong? Orron wondered. Ly'ra had been telling him for weeks that birthdays were full of joyful celebration in Havenshae Valley. *Ly'ra's the only one who looks joyful.*

Ly'ra seemed oblivious to the dour moods of her parents. She just kept chattering on about the party. After breakfast, they cleaned the table and Mattox disappeared out the door, saying he had to take the sheep to pasture.

The day was spent preparing food for the party. It was going to be a small gathering with just the four of them, Aton and Rhi'rra. Aton's farmhand, Zafilo, dropped by in the afternoon to tell Me'ra that he and his father Daedar, the village miller, would be coming as well.

Orron couldn't wait for the party to begin. He had spent weeks working on Ly'ra's present. With a knife that Mattox had given him, he spent countless hours carving a life-size imitation of a yellow rabbit. Me'ra had shown him how to crush certain flowers so that he could paint the carving. It wasn't perfect, but he knew she would love it.

Ly'ra bounced around the house all day. Her enthusiasm seemed to break through the gloom that hung over Me'ra. By the start of the party, she was finally smiling.

Evening fell and Aton and Rhi'rra arrived first. Rhi'rra gave Orron a hug. From the first time he met them, he was struck by the genuine warmth and kindness they showed him. Mattox had told him early on that he should not go into the village because of how people would react to the way he looked. They didn't seem to notice.

When Daedar and Zafilo arrived, their reaction was quite different. Orron answered the door, and Zafilo jumped back in surprise.

"Who are you?" he asked. Zafilo was tall, very skinny, and had a head full of red hair that seemed a little too large for his body. Daedar just eyed him silently. Mattox was returning at that moment from the fields and quickly interjected.

"Daedar, Zafilo it's good to see you. This is Orron." Orron offered his hand and Daedar shook it reluctantly. He couldn't take his eyes off Orron's bald head.

Sensing their discomfort, Mattox added, "He's my cousin's boy from Farovale. He caught a nasty case of the fever over the winter and lost his hair. The healers sent him up here to get well." He put his arm around Orron and said with a wink to Daedar, "The mountain air seems to be doing him some good. He's eating us out of house and home."

Daedar seemed to buy his explanation, but Zafilo still kept his distance. Orron didn't take it personally. Mattox had warned him that the people of Lillyndale had endured a lot of abuse at the hands of the Keepers that he apparently so closely resembled.

With everyone having arrived, they made their way outside where Mattox had setup a table. When everyone was seated, the party began. As was the custom of Lillyndale, the birthday festivities started with everyone at the table saying the one thing that they appreciated most about Ly'ra.

Suddenly nervous, Orron listened while the others spoke. *What should I say?* The others mentioned things like her smile, her laugh, and so on. Finally, it came time for Orron to speak. He stood up and his mouth was dry.

He looked at Ly'ra who was beaming at him. Looking in her eyes, he knew what he wanted to say. "Ly'ra, you are what is right with this world. Thank you for being light in this darkness." As he sat down, he noticed Me'ra discretely wiping away a tear that she didn't want anyone to see.

After dinner, they gathered around a bonfire; they sang and danced merrily. Orron noticed that Mattox and Me'ra did their best to appear happy, but their smiles never quite reached their eyes. He could sense that something was deeply bothering them both.

Daedar slowly began to warm to Orron. They ended up being seated next to each other for dinner, and Daedar kept him entertained with stories of Mattox when he was young. He was in his fifties, at least fifteen years older than Mattox, and had many amusing stories to tell. Something about Zafilo, on the other hand, struck Orron as odd. There was something in the way that he talked and watched everyone at the party. It bothered Orron, but he couldn't understand why.

As the night began to wear down, Ly'ra begged and begged her father to get out his graivar and sing one of her favorite ballads. He tried to resist, but eventually she got her way. He went inside and brought out the instrument.

All were silent as they waited for Mattox to begin. After a long pause, he started to play a song that seemed incredibly out of place at a birthday celebration. The melody was hauntingly beautiful, but the words were what unsettled Orron.

In the Avolyndas Mountains
There lived a girl so pure
Her laughter filled the valleys
With a peace so secure

The birds sang out a chorus
Every time she wandered by
Theirs songs filled up the valleys
Her joy lit up the sky

One day the sky
Turned dark and gray
The birds could not be found
What now filled up the valley
Was a sad and mournful sound

Her tears streamed down
And soaked the ground
Her laugh forever lost
Now sadness fills the valley
Like a long harsh winter's frost

In the Avolyndas Mountains
There is nothing left that's pure
No laughter fills the valleys
There is nothing that's secure

For when the will of men runs wild
Purity is no more
And tears flow through the valley
With darkness forevermore

His last note rang out mournfully in the dark summer evening. No one dared to make a sound. Orron looked over at Me'ra and saw that her eyes were damp with tears.

Mattox walked over to Ly'ra and held her face in his hands. It was as if he wanted to say something but couldn't get it out. He kissed her on the top of the head instead and went back inside the house. Me'ra got up and gave Ly'ra a long hug, and as if on cue, everyone got up to leave.

Orron sat by the fire bewildered by Mattox's song. *Why are he and Me'ra so sad?* Something was deeply wrong, and it frustrated him that he could not begin to understand what it was.

Before Ly'ra went inside he said, "Wait here. I have something for you." He ran inside, grabbed the carving and returned with it hidden behind his back.

"Close your eyes," he said. With her eyes closed, he put the carving in her hands. "You can open them now."

Her eyes flew open and lit up the second they took in the beautiful object before her. "Oh, Orron! I love it!" She traced her fingers over the surface, admiring the workmanship. Then she wrapped her arms around his waist.

"Orron," she said as she held him tight. "Is it all right if I adopt you as my big brother?"

Orron smiled. "Of course, Ly'ra. I'd like that."

She let go and looked up at him. "Good night, big brother."

"Happy birthday, little sister."

The next morning, the family seemed to be more itself. Orron desperately wanted to ask what last night had been all about, but he kept his questions to himself.

When they finished eating, Ly'ra asked, "Can I go into the woods and gather berries today?" She had been asking this question for weeks.

"I don't see why not. If it's all right with your mother," Mattox said.

"I don't think she should go alone."

Mattox looked over at Orron. "Would you go with her?"

"Of course! It sounds fun." Ly'ra beamed at his response.

"Then go, have fun. But Orron," he said, suddenly very serious, "keep this girl safe."

"I will," he replied, and he meant it.

The day passed quickly as they wandered the forest. Orron made sure they didn't stray in too deeply. Ly'ra was a chatterbox as always. Being cooped up for all those months had been hard on her, and now that she was out in the woods, she couldn't contain her excitement.

As they walked, she went on and on about the different kinds of berries, which ones were edible and which ones were not. She pointed out the various types of undergrowth. Orron was impressed with her knowledge of the forest and told her so.

"Father used to take me into the forest all the time. He knows a lot," she explained.

It seemed a little strange that a shepherd would know so much about the forest, but he let it go. As the day moved on, they soon found themselves at the ravine where Orron had first met Ly'ra. They stopped, and Orron watched Ly'ra's face.

"Maybe we should go," he said.

"No, this used to be my favorite place in the whole world. I like it here."

"Even after that night?"

"Well, I don't really like to think about it too much." She paused. "Yes, I still like it here."

They sat down, dangling their feet over the edge of the ravine. Both were silent for a moment, lost in thought. Ly'ra was absently twirling a flower in her fingers.

"I used to have a sister," she said abruptly.

A sister? Why didn't Me'ra or Mattox ever say anything?

"She was taken during the Inspection when I was two."

The Inspection? He had heard it referenced once when Aton was over. When he said it, he looked embarrassed as if he had said something very wrong. He hesitated, and then asked, "What is the Inspection?"

"Every year, during the Mid-Summer Festival, everyone in Lillyndale and the surrounding farms has to gather in the village square." She looked down. "They are really scary. All the girls who are eleven have to gather in the middle while a big, scary Keeper decides whether or not to take them."

"Take them where?"

"I don't know. The Holy City, I think."

"Can't the parents stop them?"

"If they do, the soldiers kill everyone." She looked around as if to make sure no one could hear her. "They say that's what happened to Garondale."

"Garondale?"

"Zafilo once told me that there was another village in Havenshae Valley. It was somewhere in the forest, I think. Anyway, apparently, they tried to stop the Keepers, and they were all killed. The Keepers then burned the village." She shuddered at the thought.

"So your sister was taken?" he asked.

"Yes. My father never talks about it, but one time I found some old clothes in the barn that belonged to a little girl. When I asked my mother about it, she told me about her."

They fell silent again. "What was her name?" Orron asked softly.

"A'ra. All my mother said was that she was very pretty and loved to laugh."

Then it hit Orron why Me'ra and Mattox had been so sad.

As if she guessed what he was thinking, Ly'ra said, "I have to be in the Inspection next year." She looked into his eyes and added softly, "Orron, it really scares me."

His heart broke as he saw the fear in her eyes. He felt anger well up within him. *No one is going to take this beautiful little girl.* "I won't let them take you, Ly'ra."

"Promise?" she said. Her eyes now filled with hope. He knew that if he promised, she would believe him and trust in him completely.

With conviction, he replied. "I promise."

Later that night as they were eating dinner, Me'ra looked over to Mattox and signaled with her eyes. Mattox wiped his mouth, cleared his throat, and turned to Orron. "I've been thinking, Orron. The Mid-Summer Festival is next month, and well, we have a lot of wool and clothing to sell. Normally, this is something we do as a family."

Things grew awkward around the table as Mattox looked to Me'ra for reassurance. She nodded.

"Well," he continued, "I know that I've been saying that you need to avoid the village, but Me'ra–" he grunted as Me'ra kicked him under the table.

"You men, always struggling to speak your feelings," Me'ra chided.

Mattox glared at her and continued, "What I was meaning to say is we *all* look at you as part of the family now and, well, we'd—*I'd*—like it if you would accompany us to the festival."

Orron looked around the table and saw Ly'ra and Me'ra smiling at him.

"I would be honored," he replied.

He knew from the way that Me'ra and Mattox made eye contact that this was more than an invitation to a festival. This was an informal adoption into the family.

Family. First Ly'ra, now Mattox and Me'ra were affirming him as part of the family. *This feels right.* It felt so good to feel like he was truly home.

Chapter Ten

Five weeks of freedom. Kor'lee sighed. Her visit with Cleric Torker in Covenglade had been exactly what she needed after her encounter with Valtor. Today was her last day. Her heart sank as she thought about what awaited her back in Farovale.

She gathered the few possessions that she had brought with her, a few changes of clothes, her bow and quiver, and what little medical supplies that were available to her. Her father had nearly brought her to tears of joy when he returned from the Covenglade Inspection with the news that her skills were needed at the specific request of Cleric Torker. Deep down, she knew that her father was just giving her the chance to escape her misery in the Keeper Citadel, and she loved him even more for it.

As she looked around, she realized it wasn't just the escape from the city that had made her so happy. Spending time in the presence of someone as kind and gentle as Cleric Torker had worked wonders on her wounded spirit. Torker was different from the other clerics she encountered on a daily basis. He actually cared about her, and not just because she was the Commander's daughter. Try as she might, she could not understand how someone who had seen so much hardship in his life could be filled with so much joy.

The place she had been staying was a simple, one-room dwelling with a soft bed and a table and chair in the corner. It was located above a small space that served as Covenglade's healing ward. In reality, it was just a dingy room with rotting floorboards. It contained only one bed for patients and a cracked washbasin that could only hold water for one minute at most. Convenglade was a poor village, but then again, every village in the Avolyndas Territory was poor in some way or another. She turned as she heard a knock on her door.

When she opened it, she found Torker standing with a large, delicious smelling loaf of bread in his hands.

"I thought that you might want some food for your journey."

"Thank you, Cleric Torker," she said as she accepted the gift. She knew that a freshly baked loaf was a bit of a luxury, but to refuse it would have been insulting. She took it, wrapped it in a clean cloth, and added it to her traveling knapsack.

"I trust your stay was pleasant?"

"It couldn't have been better!" She looked down at the knapsack in her hands and found herself hating it for what it represented. *A trip back to prison.* "But, I guess I have to go back now."

Torker moved quietly behind her. "What is it, child?"

She glanced at the ceiling. It was beginning to sag from years of water damage. Covenglade did not have a carpenter. He had died a few winters ago. Time had not been kind to this village.

"It—it's nothing."

Torker put his hand on her shoulder, and she turned to look at him. It was almost as if his eyes could see past excuses and right to the heart of the matter.

"Kor'lee, I may be an old man, but I can see when someone is carrying a burden on her heart."

"I just— I don't know." She sat down on the bed, frustration evident in her body language. "I feel like...like I don't matter."

"But, Kor'lee, you matter greatly."

"To whom?"

"Why, to your father, to me, to the Maker—"

"The Maker? If I matter so much to Him, why did He let my mother die? Why did He leave me alone in a world where I'm not worth anything just because I'm a woman?"

Torker just stared at her patiently with sadness in his eyes. She looked down, suddenly embarrassed.

"I'm sorry, Torker. I didn't mean that." She placed her hands in her lap. "I just don't know where I belong anymore. I hate it in Farovale. The men treat me horribly. One of them, a new captain, makes me feel so dirty with the way he looks at me. I feel like I'm little more than just a piece of meat to those people." Her voice grew quiet. "I feel like no matter what I do, I am destined to always be a slave."

"Are you a slave?"

It was a simple question, one without any accusation or pretense, but Kor'lee didn't know how to respond. "Sometimes I feel that way."

"But not always?"

"Well, no, I guess I realize that I have some freedom to make choices."

"Such as?"

She had to think about that. A slight smile crossed her face.

"I chose to nearly break the captain's wrist when he made a pass at me."

Torker returned the smile. "See, no one can take away all of your freedom. You always have a choice."

"But I don't have the freedom to make the decisions that I really want to make."

He looked at her carefully. Normally, when someone stared at her for that long it made her feel uncomfortable. Torker's gaze did not have that effect. It made her feel good, like there was actually someone who was willing to listen to her.

"And what decisions would you like to make?"

She looked at the door as if she were staring at the world that lay outside of it.

"I want to matter. I want to be able to make a difference in this world."

Torker took her face in his hands. They were rough from years of hard labor, scarred and calloused.

"Kor'lee, when I look at you I see a woman of great strength and courage. I believe with all my heart that you will make a difference in this world, greater than you can possibly know. Have faith, child. The Maker has great plans for you. Just wait, and you will see."

Her heart swelled as his words washed over her. *If there were anyone who would be able to hear the plans of the Maker, it would be Torker.* She gave him a quick hug and they stood up.

"I guess I'd better be going," she said.

"Yes, you want to make sure to be safely in the city walls before nightfall. There are rumors of bandits roaming throughout these hills." There was a twinkle in his eye when he mentioned the bandits. It was as if he knew something, but he did not elaborate.

She said her good-byes to the villagers and found a battalion chief named Orcai waiting for her on the road just outside the village. Her father did not want her traveling alone, so he sent one of his most trusted officers for protection. Though Kor'lee did not know Orcai very well, she did not mind him. He treated her very respectfully.

"Are you ready, Ma'am?" he asked when she approached.

She took one long look back at Covenglade and sighed. "Yes. Let's go."

The journey was uneventful, and soon after returning, she was back to her old routine. She spent her first few weeks working in one of the southern healer wards. It was light work, mostly bandaging blisters and minor training accidents.

Finally, when she had a day to herself, she was able get away to spend some time alone in the woods. She returned to her secret clearing and was dismayed to find that it was still charred. It no longer felt inviting and peaceful.

She sat with her back against one of the blackened trees and gazed out over the cheerless clearing. Torker's words occupied her thoughts. *The Maker has great plans for me. What does that mean?*

With a sigh, she looked at the heavens. The sun shone brightly in a cloudless sky. "If You have plans for me, would You mind showing me some time? Anything...anything at all would be just fine with me."

Not surprisingly, she heard no reply. Actually, she heard nothing at all. The clearing had an eerie silence that felt unnatural.

She stood to her feet and made her way back to her secret tunnel and into the Keeper Citadel. *Maybe someday I'll be free of this place,* she thought wistfully. She knew, however, that was little more than a dream. Independence was not a quality that the Church favored in a woman.

As she walked aimlessly through the streets, she passed a couple of Keepers who were busy taking inventory of their equipment.

"Why do I always have to go on these stupid Inspections?" the younger of the two complained a bit too loudly. *He's lucky my father isn't around,* Kor'lee thought.

"Well at least it's in Lillyndale," the older Keeper replied.

"What's so good about that?"

"Haven't you been to one of their Inspections before?"

Kor'lee stopped just around the corner of a building so that she could eavesdrop.

"No, this is my first summer here."

"Ah, then you don't know what you've been missing! The Lillyndale Inspection falls during their annual Mid-Summer Festival."

"So?"

The older Keeper smacked himself in forehead and shook his head. "You new recruits have no culture in you. The Mid-Summer Festival used to be quite renowned. Well, before the Great War anyway."

"I never heard of it."

"My point exactly, you uncultured brute!"

"What was so special about it?"

"Oh, let me see. Where do I begin?" he said as he stroked his chin thoughtfully. "The artisans from all over the mountain range used to come and hawk their wares in the fields, and at night there was the merriest dancing in all of Edelyndia. And don't get me started on the food."

Now that seemed to interest the younger man. "Is it still like that?"

"Sadly, no," he said with a shake of his head. "After the War, most of the hill-folk stopped coming down out of the mountains. Now they mostly keep to themselves. Secretive buggers they are."

"What about the dancing?"

"Oh, they still do the dancing. I was there a couple of years ago. It's still a nice little festival. Nothing like what it was back in the day, mind you, but definitely worth seeing."

Kor'lee tried to look busy as they came around the corner and paid her no attention as they passed. She rushed back to the officer's district. This festival sounded like just the diversion she needed from this city. *Maybe I can convince father to let me come along this time!* She knew there was little chance he would agree. He didn't like having her around the Keepers when he could help it. *I can always try,* she thought hopefully.

When she arrived at their quarters, she discovered that her father was away. She paced the floor nervously for the next hour waiting for him to return. Finally, just in time for dinner, Draedon came through the front door.

"Father, I missed you!" she said as she hugged him before he had time to remove his cloak.

"Well, what did I do to deserve this?"

"Oh, nothing," she replied sweetly. "I just couldn't wait to see you!"

He gazed at her suspiciously. "What do you want, Kor'lee?"

"Want?" she said a little too innocently.

He held her at arm's length and smiled, "I've been wrapped around your little finger for too long to be fooled by this little act."

"Fine, you got me." She breathed in expectantly. *Here it goes.* "I want to come with you to the Lillyndale Inspection."

His face hardened. "Absolutely not." He dropped his hands and moved into the sitting area at the front of the house.

Not willing to give up so easily, she followed him and protested. "Why not? I won't be in the way. Besides you always like to travel with a healer."

"You're not a healer," he reminded her as he took off his cloak.

"I *should* be. I'm better than most of the buffoons who boss me around every day," she said bitterly. She crossed her arms and summoned her best pouty face. "You have dragged me all over Edelyndia, and now I'm stuck in this awful city. I can't stay cooped up here forever."

Draedon walked over to his daughter and placed his hands on her shoulders. "I can see how miserable you are here, and it breaks my heart, but I don't have a choice about where the Council sends me."

"But you *do* have a choice about letting me come with you to Lillyndale." She pulled away from him.

"Kor'lee, the Inspections are no place for—"

"For what, a *woman?*" she said angrily. "I'm not as weak as everyone thinks I am!"

He raised his hands in surrender. "I know, I know. I meant that the Inspections are no place for my daughter." He looked down and Kor'lee could tell that something was bothering him. "I...I just don't want you to see it."

"But—"

"That's my final answer, Kor'lee."

The look in her father's eyes signaled that the matter was no longer up for discussion. She stormed out of the room and made a point of slamming her bedroom door. Deep down, she knew that her father just wanted what was best for her, but she was still angry with him.

Then a thought crossed her mind bringing a smile to her face. *I shouldn't.* But why not? She was old enough to take care of herself. *But what if I get caught?* She looked at her bow and quiver hanging next to her door. *What's an adventure without a little danger?*

The next morning, her father gathered the company at the north gate, and they headed out of the Citadel and into the forest. From her vantage point atop the building across from her secret passageway, she could see that Captain Valtor marched next to her father. *Maybe it* was *a good idea that I didn't travel with them,* she thought to herself.

She waited until they disappeared into the forest and climbed down the side of the building. After making sure no one was in the alley with her, she pulled the torch holder and quickly made her way into her tunnel.

After closing the trapdoor behind her, she ran down the tunnel as fast she could to catch up to her father's company. Though she didn't want to be seen by them, she still knew that it was unwise to travel the forest road to Lillyndale alone. Rumors of attacks by the Forest Bandits constantly circulated the healing wards. She knew if she traveled close enough to the Keepers, she should be safe. The Forest Bandits would never risk openly attacking a company of Keepers.

She was nearly out of breath when she reached the end of the tunnel. Panting hard, she donned her forest garb and decided to wear the dark green cloak to help conceal her identity if she were seen by a Keeper. She had brought her bow and a quiver full of arrows. *Just in case...*

She decided to travel in the woods just west of the road, as the Havenshae River often ran on the eastern side, leaving her little in the way of concealment. Though the secret tunnel had taken her on a somewhat lengthy detour, she was able to catch up with the company in just over an hour. Walking in a defensive formation, they were not moving terribly quickly.

The fact that they were intently gazing the forest for any sign of bandits made it hard for her to remain hidden. She often had to stray a little deeper into the forest than she would have liked, making her journey taxing. As the day dragged on, she silently cursed herself for forgetting to bring a water skin. She was so focused on figuring out how to sneak her bow and quiver out of the house without her father noticing that she had simply forgotten to bring provisions like food or water.

It grew dark more quickly in the forest than in Farovale due to the thick tree cover. The Keepers stopped to make camp for the night, spreading themselves out along the road. Some chose to make camp in the surrounding trees, forcing Kor'lee to backtrack behind where they had stopped.

Once she felt like she was far enough away to avoid detection safely, she made her way to the river. The long journey had made her as thirsty as she had ever been in her life. The water moved swiftly, but she decided to wade a short way in and crouch down to drink. As long as she stayed close to shore, she felt she wouldn't have to worry about the current causing her to fall, which was a fear since she wasn't a very strong swimmer. The water was icy cold and felt very good on her skin. Though she was dressed lightly under the cloak, the mid-summer sun still bore down through the trees on her all day.

As she drank, she had the distinct feeling that she was being watched. She assumed it was a Keeper and kept her head down. As long as whoever it was didn't see her face, he would assume she was just one of the forest dwellers that were scattered throughout Havenshae Valley.

She tensed as she heard a stick crack underneath a boot. *That came from the opposite shore.* She readied herself, suddenly thankful that she had thought to bring her bow with her into the river. *Bandits?*

With her head down, she pretended to be oblivious to the person creeping toward her. She could see him fairly well in her peripheral vision. When the person was in range, she suddenly whipped her bow around and nocked an arrow, startling the stranger. He was dressed in dark brown and green clothing. His hair was long, a dark shade of brown. It was parted in the middle, and instead of a beard, he wore his facial hair in a well-trimmed goatee.

He raised his hands as if in surrender. "Well, hello there. My apologies for disturbing you."

She glanced down at the sword strapped to his hip. *Definitely a bandit.* The only weapons that non-Keepers were legally allowed to carry in Edelyndia were bows for hunting.

Her heart beat furiously, but she managed to respond calmly, "Apology accepted. Now, if you please, slowly remove that sword and throw it in the river."

"I'm afraid I can't do that, m'lady."

She wasn't sure what annoyed her more, his refusal or the way he called her a lady. "And why is that?"

"It belonged to someone very dear to me. I promised him that I would care for it after he—." He paused. "Well, after he could no longer care for it."

Something in his voice told Kor'lee that he was either a very good liar or he was telling the truth. "Fine, take it off slowly and throw it in the forest behind you."

"That I can do." He did as she asked, and with his hands still in the air said, "So, what now?"

"How do I know that you don't have any more weapons on you?"

"Well, I could take off my clothes if that would make you feel better." He started to lift his shirt.

"No!" she said with her face blushing.

The stranger smiled as he lowered his shirt. "I guess my word will have to do."

Kor'lee thought for a moment. *I can't trust him. He's obviously a bandit.* An idea came to her. "Swear on the person who owned your sword before you."

His smile vanished as he just stared at her. He apparently hadn't expected that.

"It's that or I shoot you where you stand, Forest Bandit," she said, though she doubted she could actually shoot him. Somehow, her hands were not trembling, but her heart was racing.

"Fine," he said, the merriment gone from his voice. "If I do this, will you lower your bow?"

She nodded.

"I swear on my father that I am unarmed."

His father. Now she was the one caught by surprise. Without thinking she asked, "What happened to him?"

"Begging your pardon, miss, but I am not usually one to bare my soul to a stranger aiming an arrow at my chest."

She had already forgotten their agreement. Lowering the bow, she watched him warily. "Sorry."

"Apology accepted," he replied and his smile returned. "Now that you know that I am unarmed, may I beg the indulgence of your name?"

"You first."

With a flourish, he bowed and said, "My name is Raulin, and I am king of this here forest."

She laughed aloud. "King? This forest has no king."

"Oh, doesn't it? Then why is it that the company of Keepers up ahead is keeping such close watch as they lie down to sleep?"

She had no answer for that. "So you don't deny that you are a forest bandit?"

"Oh, some call us forest bandits." He ran his hand through his hair. "I prefer freedom fighters."

"Freedom fighters? From what, may I ask, are you trying to free yourself?"

He looked at her as if that was a stupid question. "Why, the Church, of course, and that cursed Council of theirs."

Kor'lee had never heard someone speak so openly against the Church or the Council before. Though she certainly was not overly fond of them herself, it made her a little uncomfortable.

"You still haven't told me your name," he reminded her.

Should I tell him? Her name was rather common, so she figured that it was safe enough. She didn't want to know what he would do if he realized that he was standing in the presence of the Legion Commander's daughter.

"Kor'lee," she said.

"Well, Kor'lee, I am pleased to make your acquaintance."

"Likewise," she said, keeping their little dance going. Neither spoke for a moment, taking the opportunity to size up each other. He was tall, and though she didn't want to admit it, quite handsome. He looked to be a few years older than her, maybe twenty-three or twenty-four. For an outlaw living in the forest, he was surprisingly clean and well-mannered. He appeared to be quite muscular, and he had a strong chin. What struck her the most was that she didn't feel like a piece of meat in his eyes as she did with many of the Keepers.

Finally, Raulin broke the silence, "Well, Kor'lee, correct me if I am wrong, but you do not live in the forest do you?"

"And how would you know that?"

"For starters, anyone who lives in the forest knows that if you stand still too long in these waters you will find that your legs make a very good meal for the Havenshae leeches."

She looked down and pulled up her pant legs. To her horror, she saw that her calves and shins were covered in slimy, brown leeches. With a gasp, she threw her bow on the riverbank and quickly reached down to remove the vile creatures. The sudden movement caused her to lose her balance, and she toppled head first into the swiftly moving current.

She struggled to right herself as the current carried her over a small waterfall. Her head went under water, and she began to panic. She couldn't tell which way was up. Her lungs screamed for air, but instead she swallowed a mouthful of river water.

Another waterfall poured more water into her nose and mouth. She thrashed her arms and legs, desperately trying to find something to hold onto. Her chest felt like it was going to explode. Black dots began to cloud her vision.

The river sent her over yet another short waterfall, and her head struck rocks. Before she lost consciousness, she vaguely felt someone or something grabbing her around the waist, and then everything went black.

Chapter Eleven

Warmth. A bright light. Am I dead? Slowly, she tried to open her eyes, but the pain in her head forced her to close them again. She reached her hand up and felt a large lump on her forehead. *The river.* Memories of her ordeal in the river washed over her. *The leeches!* Involuntarily, she sat up quickly to reach for her legs and the nausea swept over her.

"Whoa, there," a voice said, "not so fast. You need to lie down." *Raulin.* "Don't worry, the leeches are gone."

"How…what?" she said, her brain had difficulty processing full sentences. *My head is pounding!*

"Take it easy, Kor'lee. You hit your head pretty hard."

"How did I…? Did you save me?"

"Well, yes, I guess I did."

"Why?

"What do you mean, *why?*"

"Why would you risk your life for me?"

"Hey, you may just see me as a lowly forest bandit, but I'm not heartless." She sensed genuine hurt in his voice.

"I'm sorry. Thank you."

"You would have done the same."

"You saw how well I swim."

"Point taken. Are you feeling well enough to eat?"

"I don't know," she said as she propped herself up. The throbbing in her head had lessened some, and she slowly opened her eyes. Raulin was sitting a few feet away, cooking what looked like a rabbit over a fire. The sight of the fire concerned her as she remembered that there were Keepers on the forest road.

As if he read her mind he said, "Don't worry. They won't be able to see the fire. We are far enough away."

"Far enough away? Where did you take me?"

"It wasn't me. It was the river."

"It carried me that far?"

"Actually, it was pretty impressive how long you were able to hold out."

"I don't feel very impressive." She gingerly rubbed the lump on her forehead.

"You should feel lucky. Not too many people who get caught in that current live to tell about it." He finished cooking the rabbit, pulled a dagger out of his boot, cut off a piece, and handed it to her.

"Hey, you swore that you weren't armed!" she said.

"Well, I am a Forest Bandit," he said with a wink.

She took the meat and tore into it. It had been a long day without any food.

Raulin kept looking at her as they ate. It wasn't the same kind of look that she was used to. It didn't make her feel dirty, but for some reason it made her blush. He was the first to speak after they finished eating.

"We already established that you don't live in these woods. That means you are from either Farovale or Lillyndale. My money is on Farovale."

"Good guess."

"Where are you headed?"

"Lillyndale, for the Mid-Summer Festival."

"Alone?"

"Is there something wrong with that?" she asked defensively.

"Not at all. It's just not very safe, what with all the Forest Bandits running around," he said with a grin. "And we know how they are."

She smiled back. "They *are* pretty brutish."

"I prefer dashing," he said, putting on his most debonair smile and puffing out his chest.

Kor'lee let out a small laugh. "I'm sure you do."

"In all seriousness, I don't think it is the wisest idea for you to be traveling alone."

"I can handle myself," she said.

"I'm sure you can, but these are dark times, Kor'lee. Not everyone you meet in the forest is, well, like me," he said in a serious tone. "Some would have let you drown or worse."

"Do you care about my welfare now?" she challenged.

"Listen, Kor'lee. I've already braved the Havenshae River and removed leeches from your legs. What do I have to do to earn your trust?"

"I'm sorry, Raulin. I *am* being rude," she said apologetically. "I guess I'm just not good at trusting strangers."

"Then let's change the 'strangers' part," he said holding out his hand. "Friends?"

She looked at him for a second. *He did go to great lengths to rescue me.* She took his hand. "Friends."

Pleased, he stood up and retrieved his sword from behind a tree. "Good, then you won't be mad if I still have my sword. I couldn't leave it behind."

"I guess that's all right," she responded. It no longer worried her for him to be armed. If he wanted her dead, he could have just let her drown. Then she remembered her bow.

"My bow! I left it by the river," she said, tensing up. Her father had given it to her for her birthday when she turned sixteen. It had been her mother's, and it had always been very special to her.

"I saw where you threw it. I'm sure it will be fine," he said reassuringly. "We can retrieve it in the morning."

"We?"

"I am going with you."

"To Lillyndale?"

"It's been a while since I've been to the Mid-Summer Festival. It sounds like fun."

"Don't you have any 'kingly' duties to attend to?"

"My realm can govern itself for a few days," he said with mock seriousness.

Her hand went to her head as a fresh wave of pain swept over her.

"You really should lie down and rest," he said with a worried look on his face.

Why does he care so much? Brushing the question aside, she laid down, using her cloak as a pillow. Raulin laid down on the other side of the fire, mindful to keep a respectful distance from her.

It had been a long day and her eyes were heavy. Before sleep overtook her she said, "Raulin?"

"Yes, Kor'lee?"

"Thank you for saving my life."

"Any time, m'lady." This time it didn't bother her at all.

Kor'lee awoke with the first light the next morning feeling much better and refreshed. Looking over to where Raulin had slept, she saw that he was gone. She felt a twinge of sadness. *Oh well.* She sat up and wiped the sleep from her eyes. As she gathered her things and prepared to leave she heard footsteps behind her.

"Leaving without me?" Raulin asked.

"I thought—"

"You thought I'd left? After all we've been through." He shook his head with mock disapproval. "I was just passing a message on to some…friends," he said mysteriously.

"What did you say?" She was suddenly worried. Though she felt like she could trust Raulin, she wasn't about to trust the other bandits.

"Don't worry, it wasn't about you. I just told one of my men that I was going to be gone for a few days. That's all."

"You have 'men'?"

"I told you. I'm the king of the forest," he said proudly. *Who are you, Raulin?* she wondered.

They broke camp and began heading north. A little while after reaching the road, they found the place where Kor'lee had fallen in the river. Her bow was right where she left it. With it retrieved, they followed the road the rest of the way through the valley.

They talked as they hiked through the forest. Raulin told her stories of his life growing up in the foothills outside the valley. His family was clearly very dear to him, but he conspicuously avoided any details about what happened to them. She kept her questions to herself, not wanting to invite any questions about her own past. On that subject, she was completely silent. Whenever Raulin asked her questions about her childhood, she quickly changed the subject. He seemed to notice her reluctance but respected her privacy.

Making good time, they reached the edge of the forest by late morning. She pulled her hood over her face. Raulin looked at her questioningly.

"There are certain Keepers whom I don't want to recognize me," she said carefully. He just nodded his head and accepted that. "Aren't you worried that you might be recognized?" she asked him.

"Who would know me? I may be a king, but I'm a pretty secretive one."

Before leaving the forest, Raulin hid his sword. They came to a large wooden bridge that spanned the Havenshae River. Crossing over it, they entered the village of Lillyndale.

The view was breathtaking. Lillyndale was nestled around one corner of a large lake. Water cascaded down the side of a majestic mountain that formed a picture so gorgeous that she almost wondered if it was a painting.

The festival was far better than the way the old Keeper in Farovale had described it. There were various artisans strewn about the field and throughout the village selling all sorts of treasures. Clothing, food, candy, jewelry, and many more items were being sold all around her. She could hear music coming from somewhere in the village square.

The only dark spot in the all the gaiety was the group of Keepers, who were gathered in the field just outside of the village. Kor'lee knew her father was most likely among them, so she hurried into the village. Raulin stuck close by, and soon they were swept up in the festivities. There was so much to see!

Lillyndale was a quaint village. It had fared much better than Covenglade. The homes were well kept. Healthy looking children ran through the streets, and the people seemed genuinely happy.

Kor'lee's attention was broken by the sound of a commotion off to her left. Turning, she saw a young girl near tears as another mean-looking girl her age was talking to her condescendingly.

"I bet you're taken next year," the mean one declared.

"Don't say that, Aly'siah!"

"Why? You know I'm right. Better you than me."

"Why do you have to be so mean?"

"Oh, grow up. All I'm saying is they liked your sister. It makes sense that they'll like you too."

That was apparently too much for the other girl to handle. She burst into tears and started to run away. Coming around a corner with a cup in his hands was someone Kor'lee very much wished to avoid—*Valtor*. The scene unfolded so quickly that she was helpless to stop it.

The crying girl was so distraught that she wasn't watching where she was running. She crashed hard into Valtor, causing him to spill his drink all over his cloak. He threw the cup to the ground in anger.

"Wretched little girl," he said with unfettered rage in his eyes. The girl cried out in pain as he viciously grabbed her by the hair. He pulled a nasty looking dagger from his belt and held it to her cheek.

"I'm going to teach you some manners," he said with an evil glint in his eye. He flexed his arm as he prepared to cut into her flesh.

Kor'lee reached for her bow, but she knew she would not be fast enough. Then, seemingly out of nowhere, a cloaked man exploded into the square. With inhuman speed, he grabbed Valtor's dagger hand, spun him around and struck him in the chest so hard that he flew back several feet, crashing off a building and tumbling to the ground. His dagger went flying to the ground several feet away.

"Keep your hands off her!" the man said with fire burning in his eyes. His hood had flown back in the tussle exposing his bald head. He appeared to be about Kor'lee's age.

To her left, Kor'lee heard Raulin suck in his breath in surprise and mutter to himself, "You again!"

"*Heretic!*" Valtor managed to say through clenched teeth as he tried to find his breath. "I will have you arrested!"

"*You* are going to arrest *me*?" the man replied. "One as mighty as you, who apparently needs to pick a fight with a ten-year-old girl, presumes to make accusations against me?" His eyes flashed as if daring Valtor to attack. He did not.

Seeing that Valtor was too cowardly to act, the man bent down and gently helped the girl up.

"Are you alright, Ly'ra?" he asked.

"I–I think so," she said through her tears.

Then, not at all surprised by his cowardice, Kor'lee saw Valtor draw another dagger from his boot and move toward the unsuspecting young hero. Catching him off guard, he slipped the dagger around his neck from behind and whispered something into his ear.

Kor'lee panicked as she realized what was about to happen. At the last possible moment she threw back her hood and cried out, "Valtor, stop!"

He scanned the crowd trying to determine where the voice had come from. His eyes settled on Kor'lee, and it took a moment before he recognized her.

"Kor'lee?" he said with surprise. "What are you doing here?"

"The better question is what do you think *you* are doing?"

"You presume to lecture me?" he said angrily. "I am–"

"Yes, I know," she said interrupting him. "*You* are the Captain of the Keepers. And you know that *my* father is the Legion Commander." She could feel Raulin's eyes boring into her. "Shall I call him over so you can explain why you chose to strike a harmless child or why you want to kill an unarmed man?" Her words were like daggers.

Valtor glared at her menacingly, then let go of the man. He returned the dagger to his boot and straightened up, smoothing out his cloak. "It's always a pleasure, Kor'lee," he mumbled as he walked away.

She let out her breath in relief and turned to Raulin who was staring at her.

"Well aren't you just full of surprises," he said, and she knew she was going to have some explaining to do. Before she could start, the young hero approached her.

"I owe you my thanks, ma'am," he said.

"It was nothing," she replied.

"Saving someone's life is never nothing," he replied. Something in his eyes caught Kor'lee's attention. She saw something pure, something noble.

"My name is Orron, and this rascal is Ly'ra," he said, looking down at the little girl who was now beaming proudly.

"It's a pleasure to meet you both. My name is Kor'lee–"

"And I'm Raulin," he interjected. They stared at each other for a long moment. The tension in the air was thick. *They know each other,* Kor'lee realized. Finally, Orron offered his hand and Raulin shook it a little harder than Kor'lee thought he needed to.

"Well," Orron said after an awkward pause, "Ly'ra and I better be getting back to her parents." With a nod, he turned and walked away. *Something is very different about him,* Kor'lee thought.

"So, about your father," Raulin interjected, breaking her concentration. She turned and saw Raulin looking expectantly at her.

"About that," she said apologetically. "I didn't want to tell you. I didn't know what you'd think."

"Legion Commander?"

"Yes."

"And you're fine with that?"

"What do you mean?"

"You don't have any idea, do you?"

Suddenly defensive, she said, "Any idea about what?"

Anger clouded his face. "Have you seen what your father and his men do?"

"They protect the peace," she said. She didn't like where this was going.

"Protect the peace?" He had to struggle to keep his voice down. "Open your eyes, Kor'lee. The only thing they protect is the evil will of the Council!" He turned and stormed away toward the village center. Kor'lee chased after him.

"Raulin, wait!"

He stopped and turned. She could see the pain in his face.

"My father is not a bad man!"

"Your father..." he grabbed her and pulled her behind a building so that no one could overhear them. "You want to know why *I* don't have a father?" He looked deep into her eyes, and she could feel the pain and sorrow coming from his. "Keepers like your father came into my home when I was the same age as that little girl. They kicked in our door in the middle of the night and dragged us all out into the center of our village." His eyes flashed with anger.

"Someone had accused my father of being a Heretic. It was all a lie, but they wouldn't listen. They made my father watch as they killed my two older brothers one by one. Then they took their time with my mother."

Kor'lee felt as if she was going to vomit.

"I can still hear my father's screams in my ears as they slit my mother's throat. Then they stabbed me here." Raulin lifted his shirt revealing a large scar just below his heart. "I'm only alive because the idiot didn't know how to use a sword."

He turned and punched the wall in anger. "Then…then they really enjoyed themselves as they tortured my father. I was barely conscious as I lay there bleeding, but I could hear the whole thing. They tried to get information out of him. It took a long time for him to die."

"Raulin, I–" her voice faltered, as tears fell from her eyes. She didn't know what to say. *My father would never do this.* She knew it with all her heart, but she knew that right now it didn't matter. She did the only thing she knew to do; she embraced Raulin tightly.

"I've never told anyone that story," he said with a hint of embarrassment in his voice.

"Thank you," she said, though it rang hollow in her ears.

"You needed to know."

"I…I know you won't believe this, but my father *is* a good man."

He looked at her for a moment. Before he could respond, they were interrupted by shouting. The Keepers were rounding up the villagers. Raulin clenched his jaw and said, "The Inspection."

Dread filled Kor'lee's stomach. "We should leave."

"No, you need to see this," Raulin said firmly. Kor'lee nodded.

The two of them climbed to the top of the house behind which they had been standing. Shimmying carefully to the edge of the roof, they were able to see the village square, safe from detection.

The Keepers were nearly finished rounding up the villagers. Once everyone was settled, Kor'lee's father motioned for Valtor to begin the proceedings. He stepped forward and read a lengthy proclamation. Then, three terrified little girls stepped forward.

Kor'lee's heart jumped into her throat as she watched the scene unfold. Her father began examining each of the girls. He was rough and mean, saying the cruelest things that she had ever heard him say. *Who is this man?* she wondered as tears streamed down her face once more. Raulin just lay next to her, silently watching with a grim look on his face.

The scene seemed to play out forever. Though Kor'lee had heard rumors of the Inspections, she had never actually witnessed one. It horrified her to see her father inspecting these little girls as if they were little more than cattle. The power that he wielded over them was perverse, maybe even evil.

To her great relief, her father finally dismissed all three with a wave of his hand. He turned and stared at Valtor for a minute and said something that they couldn't hear from their perch. Valtor appeared livid, but he turned and barked an order. The Keepers marched out of the village with her father in the rear.

When they were gone, Raulin and Kor'lee climbed down from the roof and sat in the shade of the building, saying nothing for a long time.

Finally, Raulin spoke up softly. "Kor'lee, there is a lot going on in this world that you are not aware of."

"I–" her voice gave out as she buried her face in her hands and began to sob. The weight of what she had just seen came crashing down on her. Raulin put his arm around her, holding her close as she laid her head on his shoulder.

"I'm sorry you had to learn this way," he said gently.

After a while, Kor'lee stopped crying and wiped away her tears. The sun was beginning to fall in the sky as night was quickly approaching. They sat in silence for several more moments.

"So, about that food…" Raulin said lightly, breaking the tension.

Kor'lee laughed and wiped her nose. "That sounds good," she replied.

Raulin stood up and helped her to her feet. With a gleam in his eyes he said, "We came here to have some fun, and as King of the Forest, I decree that fun is what we shall have." He offered her his arm. "M'lady?"

She took it, and as they headed off to enjoy what was left of the Mid-Summer Festival, she couldn't shake the feeling that somehow her life had just changed. But for good or ill, she did not yet know.

Chapter Twelve

After the run-in with the Keeper, Orron had stayed very close to Ly'ra throughout the Inspection. The man that Kor'lee had identified as Valtor shot them menacing looks, but kept his distance. After the Inspections were over, the Keepers left quickly. There were no more run-ins between him and Valtor.

Since this had been his first experience with the Keepers, it had caught Orron off guard how similar his appearance was to Valtor's own appearance. He wore a very similar cloak that Orron had left back at the farm and was nearly identical in build and height. His head was shaved clean, though unlike Orron, Valtor had evidence of stubble growing. Their similarities disturbed him. *The way he looked at Ly'ra with that hideous blade to her face...* Orron shuddered at the thought. *I am nothing like that man.*

As much as Valtor's appearance had bothered him, the Inspection was far worse. It had pained him greatly to watch that cruel Commander poke and prod those girls as if they were animals. He couldn't bear the thought of Ly'ra enduring that next year. *Not if I can help it*, he thought grimly.

How could anyone grow so perverse, so evil? He shook his head, trying to erase the memory from his mind. Then he stopped. *I don't want to erase it.* Today he had seen the evil that would try to take Ly'ra next year. He wanted to remember it, to burn the image of the snarl on Valtor's face into his memory. *I have to protect her.*

After the Inspection was over, Orron had tried to distract Ly'ra by taking her to the field where the other children were playing games. It was to no avail as she refused to leave his side. He knew that Valtor had terrified her to her core, which made him burn with anger even more.

When they had returned to where the family was selling their wool and clothing, Mattox had noticed the look in Ly'ra's eyes, but the rush of customers kept him occupied.

Finally, Mattox came over bent down to Ly'ra. Gently, he cupped her face. "There's my girl. Why don't you run along and join your mother? I've heard rumor of a vendor selling a rare candy so delicious you'll never want to eat anything else ever again!"

That seemed to lift Ly'ra's spirits some. Candy was a rare treat for the people of Havenshae Valley. She ran over and joined her waiting mother, and they set off in search of this wondrous treat.

Mattox straightened up and looked at Orron expectantly. Sticking to the facts, Orron filled him in on what happened. Mattox's face turned to stone as he clenched his fists tightly. Orron was worried that he might do something rash, then he remembered that the Keepers were long gone by now and relaxed.

"That wretch was lucky I was not there to see it," Mattox finally said. "As it were, I thank the Maker that at least *you* were there and had the good presence of mind to let him live."

"If it wasn't for the Commander's daughter I might not be here to tell you about it."

"Aye, I'll thank the Maker for her as well." Then he added, "In *spite* of her father."

Orron folded his arms and looked toward the darkening sky, deeply troubled by what Ly'ra faced next year. "Mattox," he said slowly. "Next year is..." his voice trailed off, not wanting to finish the thought.

"Aye, it is. Not a day goes by that I don't think about that vile Inspection." Pain and anger filled his voice.

"What are we going to do?"

"Well, it's funny you should ask," he said with a mysterious look on his face. He grabbed Orron by the shoulder and pulled him toward the edge of the village. "There's some people I'd like you to meet."

Without knocking Mattox entered the front door of the mill and motioned for Orron to follow him.

"They are expecting us," he explained, leading Orron down into the cellar.

In the center of the darkly lit room was a large round table at which sat four men, three of whom Orron already knew. Aton, Daedar, and Zafilo were there and next to them sat a very large, imposing-looking man. His hair and beard were black as night, and his arms were massive. The clothes he wore bore the stains of a man who spends many long hours with his hand at the forge. At the sight of Orron, he stood up, ready for a fight.

"Easy, Morven," Aton said. "He is *with* us." Unsure, Morven stood his ground.

Mattox clasped Orron by the shoulder and said, "This boy here is family. Anything I can hear, he can hear."

Morven shot Mattox a dark glare, but relented and sat down. "I don't like you bringing in new faces at this stage," he said darkly.

Orron looked around. The floor was made of hard-packed dirt and the walls were stone, smoothed by age. It smelled musty, and the room was filled with tension.

As they sat down around the table, Daedar spoke up. "Gentlemen, you know why we are here. If anyone is uncomfortable with where these talks will take us, I suggest you leave now."

They all sat in silence. An ominous weight filled the room.

Daedar continued. "All right then. Who would like to start?"

Aton cleared his throat and spoke up. "Well, as you all know, I—we—lost our little girl to the Inspection a year after Mattox and Me'ra lost theirs." He nodded to Mattox who sat silent with a hard look on his face.

"She was the last to be selected from Lillyndale. It's been seven years since then, and well, we don't know if or when there will be another."

"It's only a matter of time." Mattox said.

"We don't know that!" Morven said emphatically. "I've heard reports that this new Commander hasn't made a selection anywhere in the six years he's been here!"

"And how long do you think the Council will let that go on?" Daedar countered.

"Did you see the new captain?" Zafilo said. It seemed to Orron that there was something off about the way he said it. It almost felt like he was trying to stir something up.

"Aye," Mattox said turning to Orron, "Why don't you tell them what happened with Ly'ra?"

Orron filled them in on the events of the afternoon. As he described his fight with Valtor, he noticed Morven growing angrier.

"That was a foolish thing you did, boy!" Morven said hotly, interrupting the end of Orron's story.

"What was I supposed to do?" Orron shot back.

"Attacking a captain of the Keepers, why—"

"Enough!" Mattox said as he slammed his hand down on the table. "Are you telling me you wouldn't have done the same for Aly'siah?"

Morven shifted uncomfortably in his seat.

In a softer voice Mattox continued. "Morven, your Aly'siah is the same age as my Ly'ra. You know as well as I that she is up for the Inspection next year." Morven remained silent.

Aton spoke next. "What do you propose that we should do, Mattox?"

He looked down at his hands. "I have thought long and hard about this. Part of me wants to fight, to take revenge on the Keepers for what they've done. I feel it is my right to make them pay."

Orron looked around the room. No one made eye contact with Mattox. Everyone knew that they could be executed just for listening to someone say what Mattox had just said.

Mattox shook his head. "As much as I want to do that, I know it to be foolish. We would lose, and many would suffer." His eyes scanned the men at the table. "I propose…well…I think that we should take our families and head into the mountains."

Everyone just stared at Mattox. Apparently, this was not what they were expecting.

"Are you crazy?" Morven finally said. "You know what happened to Garondale when they resisted—"

"Like I said, I'm not proposing that we fight."

"That may be true, but the law says that the entire village is punished when even one family keeps their daughter from the Inspection," Aton added.

"I don't see a better way," Mattox replied. He threw his hands up in exasperation. "All I know is that I will *not* risk losing another daughter to the damnable Inspection!"

"Then you will sentence us all to death!" Morven said nearly shouting.

"Gentlemen," Daedar interjected, trying to calm the situation, "let's take a breath here. I don't believe that Mattox wishes any of us harm." He leaned back from the table and placed his hands carefully on the arms of his chair. "I am the oldest one here by a good number of years. I was fortunate enough to have raised my children without this cursed Inspection. The fever took my first boy and that was hard, but I can't imagine having to submit my child to the Council's will." He paused, and then continued with conviction in his voice. "I know that what Mattox proposes carries tremendous risk for the entire village, but if we don't stand up for what is right and defend our children at all costs, the Council wins, and evil will have its day."

The room descended into uncomfortable silence. Finally, Aton spoke up. "I know the pain the Inspection can bring all too well, but I'm not sure that I am ready to do what you ask, Mattox."

Orron remained silent through most of the proceedings. He could feel the pain and fear that filled the room. Though he didn't know all of the details, he could sense that what Mattox was proposing carried tremendous risk and possibly death for many innocent people.

After the silence hung in the air for several minutes, Daedar sat forward and leaned on the table. "Well, gentlemen, we knew what we were meeting to discuss was going to be dark and fraught with peril. Mattox has given us a lot to consider. Let's take the next several weeks to think on it and meet one last time at the Harvest Festival to reach a decision."

They all gave their assent and the meeting broke. Morven gave Mattox one last glare as he stormed out of the cellar. After shaking hands with the other men, Mattox and Orron made their way out.

"Morven doesn't seem to care for you all that much," Orron said once they were outside.

"Aye, you picked up on that?" he said with a chuckle.

"It was pretty obvious from the moment we arrived."

"We have a bit of history." Mattox stopped and stretched out a cramp in his back.

Orron waited patiently for Mattox to continue.

"We both grew up here in Lillyndale. My father was a shepherd and his a blacksmith. We both took up our fathers' trade, and he always considered himself superior to me." Mattox continued walking toward the village.

"When we were young men, about your age, Me'ra and her sister moved into Lillyndale after their parents passed. We both fell madly in love with Me'ra. She was the most beautiful thing I had ever seen," he said fondly. "Well, we both made our overtures and Me'ra rejected Morven and chose me instead. He's hated me ever since."

"But you said he had a daughter. Didn't he marry?"

"Aye, he did, but he still loves Me'ra, I think. Rumors were always making their way around about how poorly he treated his wife. She passed a few years back," he said sadly. "She was a gentle woman, very close to Me'ra. She deserved better."

They stopped in the field just outside the village. Orron could see Ly'ra and Me'ra sitting on a hill not far away, pointing out the shapes in the stars in the clear, night sky.

"So you really think heading for the mountains is a good option?" Orron asked.

"I don't think any of our options are good," he replied with frustration. "The only option I will *not* accept is doing nothing."

Orron looked at Mattox and felt the determination in his words. He didn't have any answers, but he trusted Mattox completely. Whatever path he chose, Orron would follow.

"I am with you, Mattox," he said solemnly. "We can't let them take Ly'ra."

"Aye," he said as he placed his meaty hand on Orron's shoulder. "I don't know what lies ahead, but I do know that I am thankful to have you as part of this family."

Mattox looked over and gazed lovingly at his wife and daughter. "I don't know how you do it, but you seem to have a knack for being exactly where this family needs you to be when trouble comes. I have a feeling that in the months to come, Ly'ra will need that watchful eye of yours."

Chapter Thirteen

It annoyed Draedon that the Keepers had to stop for the night on their way back to Farovale from the Lillyndale Inspection. Normally, this journey should only take twelve or thirteen hours, but the recent rise in the activity of the Forest Bandits forced them to move much slower along the narrow road. *Better safe than sorry.*

As much as he longed for this journey to end, he was quite relieved that the Inspection season was now finally over. Starting with the Covenglade Inspection, he had been on a nearly non-stop journey throughout the Avolyndas Territory. Every stop was brutal for him. It was exhausting trying to find excuses for why he didn't find "suitable" selections.

Valtor was a constant nuisance. He seemed to learn from the Covenglade experience not to openly defy Draedon, but in his own slippery way found ways to undermine and question his every move.

Things were building to a point where a confrontation was inevitable. He was determined to use the winter months to figure out a way to deal with him. *Maybe I can get him reassigned,* he hoped.

His concentration was broken by Valtor plopping himself down next to him as he ate his dinner in front of the fire. Draedon did not attempt to hide the fact that he didn't appreciate the uninvited interruption.

After a moment Valtor said, "Commander Draedon, may I have permission to speak freely?"

"Go ahead, Captain."

"Sir, forgive me, I do not mean to question your judgment, but how is it that you could not find a single qualified selection this season?"

"You say you don't mean to question me, but there are you are doing just that."

"My apologies, sir." Draedon could tell that he certainly did not mean it. Valtor just stared at him, demanding an answer.

He knew that he was going to have to have this conversation sooner or later. *No time like the present.* No longer hungry, he threw the remainder of his dinner into the fire. "Captain, as you know, I do not have to explain myself to you."

"Yes sir, but–"

"Look…" he said cutting him off. "I am not ashamed of who I am as a man, soldier, or Legion Commander." He looked Valtor in the eye. "I am not afraid to explain my actions, either." He shifted his weight on the stump that he was sitting on. *Well, I might as well get this over with.* "Captain, do you think me a fool?"

Caught off guard, Valtor said, "I…no, of course not!"

"I know exactly what is going on here. I know why you were selected as my new captain."

"Sir?" he said trying to look like he didn't know what Draedon was talking about. *Keep trying; I'm not buying it…*

"Don't bother with pretense, Captain. I have served the Council for most of my life, and I have learned a few things along the way." He picked up a stick and began drawing shapes in the dirt in front of him.

"Back when they instituted the Inspection over ten years ago, I was the only captain to speak out against it. Were it not for my record and the respect of my Legion Commander, I'm sure the Council would have done away with me back then." He paused, remembering the days before his promotion. *Things were so much easier back then.*

With a sigh he continued. "I was as shocked as the Council when the other Legion Commanders selected me as the replacement for this territory's Commander when he was killed six years ago. Now, we are stuck with each other."

Valtor remained quiet. Draedon could tell that this was not new information for him.

"Captain, I know that you are here to watch me. I'm guessing you hope to either catch me doing something worthy of punishment or to simply drive me to early retirement." To his credit, Valtor didn't respond.

"There's something that you really need to understand," Draedon continued. "I'm not retiring, and I am one of the—if not *the*—best Commander the Keepers have."

The tension between them was palpable. Draedon held Valtor in a penetrating gaze. "I'm more experienced than you, I'm more respected than you, and I'm smarter than you."

Valtor bristled but said nothing.

"And as long as I am Legion Commander, I will not tolerate you trying to undermine me." He leaned forward and pointed the stick at Valtor. "I don't care whose recommendations you can boast of, you are just another subordinate Keeper to me, and I am not afraid to put you in your place."

Valtor was clearly not accustomed to being talked to in this way. His hands clenched, and the veins on the side of his neck bulged.

Draedon was not finished. "So, in regards to your question, Captain, I will not answer you. I'm not afraid to; I just don't see the need. We will not see eye-to-eye. On that, I'm sure we can both agree. Are we clear?"

Through clenched teeth Valtor responded, "Crystal clear."

"Crystal clear, *what*, Captain?"

"Crystal clear, *sir!*" Draedon was really enjoying himself now. With a patronizing wave of his hand he said, "Very well, you may go."

Valtor stood to his feet and looked as though he was going to say something. Instead, he turned sharply and walked away. *Well, that went well*, Draedon chuckled to himself, though he knew it wasn't over.

They arrived in Farovale around midday the next day, and Draedon was kept busy with the updates of his brigade chiefs. It was after dark when he finally arrived at his quarters. The house was dark when he walked in.

He was not terribly surprised to find that Kor'lee was not home. *She's probably still furious with me.* They hadn't spoken since she angrily stormed out of the room after he forbade her from coming with him to Lillyndale.

He sighed. It hurt him to know that there was tension between him and his daughter. Even though she had wanted to come so badly, he knew that there was no way that he could have let her. He very much did not want her ever to see him perform an Inspection. *I can't protect her forever, but that won't stop me from trying.*

As each hour passed without a sign of Kor'lee, he began to grow worried. He was just about to head out in search of her when the door opened, and she walked inside.

"Kor'lee–" his words were cut off by her stare. Her eyes were full of anger and hurt. "Kor'lee, you can't still be mad at me."

Instead of answering, she walked away, slamming her bedroom door behind her.

The next several days passed with little change in their interactions. He saw her every morning at breakfast and again for dinner, but he could rarely get more than monosyllabic answers to his questions. When she did give him more of a response, it was to argue vehemently about some such nonsense or another. He couldn't figure out what was going on with her, but this wasn't the first time he struggled to understand the growing young woman with whom he shared a house. He often wished her mother were still alive to help her understand the world. *Life as a Keeper's daughter without a mother is hardly a life at all.*

Finally, after enduring over two weeks of this, Draedon decided something had to be done. After completing his morning rounds, he stopped by the western healing ward where he knew she was assigned for the week.

When he walked in, he saw that she was binding the foot of a Keeper. It struck him how skillfully and confidently she worked. The Keeper was giving her a hard time, obviously trying to flirt with her, but she kept her mind to the task in front of her. When she finished, she stood up and saw Draedon standing in the doorway.

Before she could speak, he stepped forward and raised his hands in surrender, "Kor'lee, I'm not here to argue. I just want go for a walk. That's all. Just father and daughter." His eyes pleaded with her to accept.

With a reluctant shrug, she took off her apron and followed Draedon out the door and into the streets. They walked for a while in silence. Finally, it was Kor'lee who spoke first.

"Father, why do the Inspections exist?"

He wasn't expecting this. "Kor'lee, I don't–"

"If you want me to walk with you, answer the question," she said as she stopped with her arms crossed.

He sighed, unsure of how to proceed. The last thing on earth he wanted to do was talk about the Inspections with his daughter, but at least she *was* interested in talking. He pulled her by the arm into an alley so that they could have some privacy.

"Kor'lee, there are things about this world that you don't understand."

"Don't coddle me, just answer the question!" she said coldly. Looking at the young woman standing in front of him, Draedon was struck by her strength. *You are so much like your mother.*

"The Council claims that it is to give pure and perfect young girls the opportunity to serve the Maker in the Holy City."

"But…" she prodded.

"But, in truth, I believe it is about control."

She looked at him questioningly so he explained further.

"After the Great War, the Heretics continued to fight. Though they took mostly to the hills of the north, they were still quite adept at disrupting the trade routes and crop production throughout Edelyndia. About ten years ago the Heretics succeeded in launching a series of campaigns in which they destroyed a good percentage of the food production in the Great Plains Territory." He paused, grimacing at the memory of the bloody battles.

"While the Keepers were focusing their attention on stopping them in the Plains, a collection of villagers in the North Woods Territory staged an uprising and succeeded in taking control of the Keeper Citadel there. Though the Keepers were able to restore order before too much damage was done, the Council began to fear another war would break out." He looked down, struggling to find the words to continue. "The Inspections are their way of ensuring that this won't happen."

"I don't understand. Won't they just inspire another rebellion?"

"Well, there's more. Only girls age eleven are subject to the Inspection; however, any village that has even one person who participates in a rebellion automatically has all of their eligible girls taken as servants of the Council." It angered him just speaking about it. "This gives the citizens of Edelyndia two choices. Either they can submit to the will of the Council and *hope* that their daughters aren't chosen, or they can rebel and *guarantee* that they are chosen."

"So it's about brutality and force."

"Yes, I'm afraid so."

"Why is it only the girls who are in the Inspection?"

"That I don't know. The Council is very secretive about what they do with them."

"What happens to the young boys if there is a rebellion?"

Draedon didn't want to respond, but knew he had no choice. "They are all put to death."

The look of horror on Kor'lee's face tore him apart inside. *This is what I wanted to protect you from.*

"And you…you're alright with this?"

He pounded his thigh in frustration. "No, Kor'lee, of course I'm not all right with this!"

She just stared at him.

"I tried to stop it. I fought it when they instituted it. They even threatened me!" He paused and looked down as his voice lowered. "It was when they threatened you that I finally gave in."

He could tell she didn't know what to think. "Kor'lee, you should know that since I have been Legion Commander, I have not selected a single girl for the Council."

She slid to the ground and hugged her knees to her chest. "I just don't understand how you can stay in the Keepers," she said softly.

"You probably can't understand this right now, but I really do believe that I am doing a good thing here."

She looked at him in confusion. "By participating in this barbarism?"

"No," he said gently, "by keeping these girls safe."

He sat down next to her and put his arm around her. She didn't resist. "I know this is all so hard for you to hear, but every time I stand in front of those little girls at the Inspections, I see you in all of their faces." His voice wavered as he continued, "I know that if I leave the Keepers, I will just be replaced with someone who will have no problem making the selections like the Council demands of them."

They remained silent for a moment.

"Kor'lee, you have to trust me. I'm doing...well, I'm doing what I can to make this world right."

She looked up at him. "I–I just...this is all so horrible."

"I know, dear, but someday things will be different," he said as he kissed her on the top of the head.

Someday, he thought with a bitter taste in his mouth. *It's always someday*. He longed for the day when *someday* was actually a reality.

Chapter Fourteen

In the days and weeks that followed the Mid-Summer Festival, a deep sense of foreboding grew inside Orron. Try as he might, he could not seem to shake the overwhelming feeling that a dark storm cloud was approaching. This storm would not be one of rain and thunder but of pain and sorrow.

His mood worsened with each passing day. It finally reached the point to where even Ly'ra could not bring a smile to his face. Mattox, too, seemed to suffer from the same malady.

One day, just a few weeks before the Harvest Festival, Me'ra finally had enough. Orron and Mattox were staring off into the distance as they ate their breakfast in silence. It was as though they were gazing at the evils that may befall them in some unknown future. She slapped her hand on the table to get their attention. Orron nearly choked on the piece of bread he was eating.

"That's about all I can take." She glared at the two of them. "I will not have another day of you two moping around this house."

Mattox started to protest. "Hey, I'm not–"

"Oh, don't go trying to deny it. Haven't they been dreadful, Ly'ra?"

She nodded her head solemnly.

"Well," Me'ra continued, "there you have it. I've never seen a more pitiful pair in all my years."

Orron remained silent, trying to look at anything in the room but Me'ra. He knew better than to argue with her. Unfortunately, Mattox wasn't so smart. With food in his mouth, he motioned to her with his fork.

"Now listen here, woman–"

The icy look on Me'ra's face silenced him. When she spoke again, her voice was calm but forceful.

"I know what is on your minds, but while the Maker still sees fit to put air in our lungs, we might as well enjoy it." She waited to let her words sink in. "Here's what we are going to do. Mattox, today you are going to take your daughter into the woods and spend the day helping her pick her favorite berries."

Ly'ra squealed with delight, and Mattox smiled in spite of himself.

Me'ra turned to Orron who was still desperately trying to avoid making eye contact. "And you are going to help me in the garden." Pausing for emphasis, she added, "And *you* are going to enjoy yourself!"

She said it as a command, but there was kindness in her words. Orron looked up and saw her smiling at him. Ly'ra giggled, and Orron couldn't help but notice that the mood at the table was suddenly considerably lighter.

After the table was cleared, Mattox and Ly'ra set off for the woods. Orron could hear Ly'ra singing as they walked. Before long, Mattox joined in. Orron smiled to himself. *Maybe things aren't actually all that bad.*

He changed into work clothes and headed outside, finding Me'ra in the field behind the house. Me'ra kept a rather sizable garden where she grew turnips, onions, and potatoes. She motioned for him to join her.

It was potato season, and they spent the day together digging through the mounds of dirt. Though it had been a harsh summer, their yield was surprisingly plentiful. The work felt good, and spending the day with Me'ra had a positive effect on his soul. They laughed, talked, and laughed some more. Orron felt himself truly relaxing for the first time in weeks. As the sun began to dip toward the horizon, they bagged up their harvest.

"We should be able to make out nicely at the Harvest Festival," Me'ra said proudly.

The Harvest Festival. Orron shuddered as he thought of the decision that he and Mattox faced. Me'ra could sense his sudden change in mood.

"What is it, Orron?"

He was going to say it was the meeting he and Mattox were to attend, but he knew that wasn't it. There was something deeper, something he had never shared with Me'ra.

Ever since the Inspection, the dreams had returned in more vivid detail. Instead of a formless voice, he could now see a man dressed in brilliant white. The conversation extended as well. Every night, his dreams featured the same argument. The man in white was insisting that someone needed to die. The name was always obscured, but whoever it was apparently meant a great deal to Orron. He would wake up every morning drenched in sweat. Sometimes he even woke up crying.

Orron knew that these were no ordinary dreams. He could remember every feeling, every thought. The Orron in his dream was incredibly strong, wild, terrifying even. He was a warrior. Even though the man in white appeared to be his superior, the Orron in his dream did not intend to listen to the authoritative being's orders and let this nameless person die.

"Orron?" Me'ra's voice brought him out of his reverie. Looking down, he saw that his hands were shaking. When he looked up, he saw the worry on Me'ra's face.

"Orron, you know that you can talk to me."

He didn't know where to begin. Haltingly at first, he began to tell her of the dreams. He told her about his experience in the clearing the night Mattox was attacked. Though it was difficult at first, it felt very good to share what he had been keeping inside for so long.

When he finished, he just stared at his hands. "Me'ra, I'm afraid."

"What are you afraid of, son?" She asked, grabbing his hand.

"I...I'm afraid of me...of who I really am." His voice faltered. He pulled his hand back and lifted his shirt revealing the symbol on his chest. "You know as well as I do what this symbol is. Who am I if not a Keeper?"

"I know that Ly'ra told you about..." Her breath caught in her throat. "I know she told you about A'ra. She would have been about your age, you know."

She wiped a tear from her eye. "I'm going to tell you something that we have never told Ly'ra." She had to gather her breath before she could continue.

"A little over two years after...after the Keepers took her, A'ra returned to us. Only it wasn't our A'ra anymore."

Orron could almost feel how difficult it was for Me'ra to talk about this memory.

"She was different somehow. Her eyes were empty, as if they had taken her very soul." By now, tears were streaming from her eyes.

"She was all skin and bones. Before the Inspection, she had been all full of life, so happy. Her laughter used to fill the Valley."

Like the girl in the song Mattox sung on Ly'ra's birthday, Orron realized.

"The A'ra that returned to us was a shadow of her former self. It was late at night, and Mattox heard a commotion outside. He opened the front door, and there she was, sitting on the porch staring out toward the mountains. She never spoke a word to us. She looked so... Well, we felt it best to have Ly'ra stay with Aton and Rhi'rra while she recovered. But she never recovered. She passed just a few days later."

The pain on Me'ra's face was so vivid it brought tears to Orron's eyes.

"At first, I hated the Maker for letting me see her like that. Then I realized why He did it. He wanted me to know what I needed to protect Ly'ra from."

She wiped her eyes and looked at Orron with an intensity that seemed to burn with purpose.

"Orron, I think He brought you here to us. You have become like a son to Mattox and me. Ly'ra all but worships you. I believe in my heart that you are here for a reason." Me'ra cupped his face in her hands. "I know you are afraid of who you might be and what power you possess, but Orron, you were there in the ravine when Ly'ra needed you. You were there in the forest when Mattox was attacked. And you were there for Ly'ra when the Keeper held that blade to her face. Whoever you are, whatever you can do, whatever your past holds, it is all because the Maker has a plan—for you and for us."

"But how can I know what that plan is?"

"You will know when you need to know. Of that I am certain."

Chapter Fifteen

It was all Valtor could do to keep quiet during the weekly briefing. He was gathered with Commander Draedon and the five brigade chiefs around a large oval table in the Legion command room. Ancient weaponry hung from the walls and murals depicting great battles filled in the gaps. Valtor noticed none of this. As he listened to the various chiefs drone on about the activities of the Forest Bandits throughout the Valley, his mind was elsewhere.

I finally have you, he thought smugly to himself, trying not to show his contempt for his Commander sitting across from him. He knew what he had was tenuous at best. *Still, there is hope.*

He had been reluctant when Elder Zittas had first told him that he was to be reassigned to the Avolyndas Territory under Commander Draedon. He was well aware of the rumors circulating the Holy City, that Draedon was turning a blind eye to the Heretics, or even worse, aiding them. His reluctance turned to excitement as Elder Zittas confided in him his true mission. He was to find a way to bring Draedon down. It was an honor to be chosen for so great a task.

Since arriving at Farovale, the suspicions of the Council proved well founded. Although he had been unable to find any evidence of his direct involvement with the Heretics, his performance at the summer Inspections had been suspicious to say the least.

Draedon had turned into quite the problem for the Council, but he had the loyalty and respect of the veteran Keepers. The people of Havenshae Valley actually seemed to tolerate him instead of showing the open contempt that the Commanders of the other territories routinely received. In his six years, there had not been a single uprising. *Something that may soon change.*

The last chief finished his report, and Draedon turned to Valtor. "Is there anything you would like to add?"

He cleared his throat, suddenly a little nervous. *So much rides on this tenuous plan.* "Uh…yes, sir. There is one other thing."

"Go on, Captain," he said, clearly annoyed. Draedon had long since stopped trying to hide his disdain for Valtor.

"My contacts in the Valley have told me rumor of a rebellion forming in Lillyndale."

Draedon eyed him suspiciously. "Your contacts?"

"Yes, sir. I was approached at the Lillyndale Inspection by someone who I believe to be credible."

"And this contact of yours, he tells you that a rebellion is forming?"

"Yes, sir."

"In Lillyndale?"

"Yes, sir. That is what I said, sir."

Draedon burst out laughing, and he was soon joined by a couple of the brigade chiefs. Valtor had to fight back his anger.

"I request permission to look into it further."

"You do that, Captain," Draedon replied between laughs.

"May I ask what is so funny, sir?" Valtor gripped the edges of his chair tightly trying to suppress his rage. *Someday I will be the one who laughs.*

Draedon finally calmed himself. "Lillyndale is one of the last places a rebellion would ever take place. They are a sleepy farming community."

"Still, I believe this source to be reliable."

"Very well, Captain, you may look into it." His eyes narrowed as he pointed at Valtor. "But you are *not* to act without my express approval, understood?"

Valtor was furious about being treated like no more than a dog on a leash. "Yes, sir. Of course, sir."

"Very well, if there is nothing else, this meeting is adjourned."

The meeting broke, and Valtor left as soon as he could. *How dare he? I am the Captain of the Keepers, not some mere whelp to be ordered around.* His anger burned hotly.

He made his way as quickly as he could through the cramped streets of the Citadel. Stopping at the northern stables, he saddled his coal-black stallion and exited the Northern Gate. *No cavalry in the Northern Territories,* he thought disgustedly to himself. *Just another sign of Draedon's incompetence.*

Valtor had grown up on a horse farm in the Great Plains Territory. He had learned to ride before he had learned to walk. In his opinion, an army without a cavalry was no army at all.

Four hours after he left Farovale, he stopped at a bend in the river that roughly marked the halfway point between Farovale and Lillyndale. As his horse drank from the river, Valtor settled in to wait for his contact.

Valtor was beginning to think he was not going to show when he heard a rustling in the trees behind him. Drawing his sword, he spun around as a man walked out of the trees.

"You're late," he said as he sheathed his sword.

Motioning to the horse the man said, "Not everyone can afford a fine beast like that to ride around on."

"What news do you have for me?"

"I want your word first."

Valtor glared at the man menacingly. "You presume to make demands of *me*?"

The man folded his arms defiantly. "If we don't have an agreement, then—"

"Fine, you have my word."

Satisfied, the man continued. "The conspirators are planning to meet again at the Harvest Festival."

"And? What is their plan?"

"There is talk of them heading into the hills."

"Have they decided on when this will happen?"

"No. That will all be decided at the meeting."

Valtor stroked his chin thoughtfully. *This is exactly what I needed.*

The man shifted uncomfortably on his feet. "What will happen to them?"

"That is none of your concern."

"But I—"

"I *said* that is none of your concern! That is, unless you are uncomfortable with our agreement. I could always—"

"No," the man said quickly. "It's…I'm fine."

"I hope so." Valtor leaned toward the man threateningly. "If you say a word or give them any indication that I know…" His voice trailed off as the unspoken threat hung in the air.

"You can count on me," the man said. Valtor could hear a morsel of regret in his tone, but knew that this man did not dare to go back on his word.

"Good. Send word when a decision is reached."

"I will." He turned and disappeared into the trees.

Chapter Sixteen

He is up to something. I can feel it. Draedon paced back and forth in the sitting area at the front of his quarters. Something in Valtor's eyes had bothered him since the meeting with the brigade chiefs. At first, it had seemed silly that Valtor had wanted to investigate Lillyndale, but the more he thought about it, the more he realized that as much as he was annoying, Valtor was that much more cunning.

He finally sat down in front of the fireplace that dominated the room. It was very large, made of exotic stones imported from the Great Desert Territory. The shiny, wooden mantle was adorned with gold etching. The previous Commander had been very fond of fancy things. The entire house was filled with elaborate decoration and furniture. He looked around the room in disdain. *This is a place for a politician not a soldier.*

Kor'lee was gone as had become her custom. Since that day in the alley, things had improved between them, but she still kept mostly to herself when she wasn't working. *I wonder what she could possibly find to do in this city.* He knew that she was not at all fond of where he was stationed.

There was a knock at the door, and in walked Einar. Draedon sprung to his feet and embraced his old friend and servant.

"Einar! It has been a long time since you departed for the Holy City. I was beginning to worry that ill had befallen you!"

"My apologies, sir."

"Come, sit...sit!" he said motioning to the chairs in front of the fireplace. "So, tell me, what did you find?" Draedon had been anxiously awaiting Einar's return, hoping he had found out something that he could use against Valtor.

"I'm afraid there wasn't much to learn about his past, at least officially. I had to travel all over Edelyndia to find anything."

"Oh?"

"His parents were horse farmers in the Great Plains Territory."

"Were?"

"Yes, sir. They were both killed when he was thirteen."

"Thirteen...he's twenty-five right now." Draedon realized what that meant.

"Yes, sir. His parents were killed in the Heretic uprising twelve years ago."

"That does tell us something."

Einar looked at him inquisitively.

"That would explain his hatred for the Heretics," Draedon explained.

Einar nodded and continued, "There's more."

"Go on."

"After the death of his parents, Valtor joined up with a group of vigilantes loyal to the Council."

"Vigilantes?"

"Yes, sir. They apparently played a key, though secretive, role in crushing the rebellion while the Keepers had to focus on retaking the Citadel in the North Woods Territory. They conducted raids and executions that were...shall we say morally gray. It broke the back of the rebels, so to speak."

This was news to Draedon. He was involved in the siege in the North Woods and was unaware that vigilantes played such a large role in the other territories.

"What kind of raids did they perform?"

"Well," he said with distaste, "it took a fair amount of digging to find this information. Apparently, they were quite brutal. They would show up in the middle of the night and drag suspected Heretics out of their homes. There were rumors of torture, murder, and even rape...all done in an effort to extract information about the Heretics."

Draedon suddenly felt uneasy. "How did he end up in the Keepers?"

"After the rebellion was crushed, several of these vigilantes were commissioned as officers by the Council as some sort of reward for their loyalty it would seem. Valtor was one of the ones chosen."

"That would have made him very young."

"Indeed, very young."

"How is it that I never heard of him?" Draedon wondered aloud.

"It appears that, even after joining the Keepers, his actions were kept rather secretive. He was assigned a small number of Keepers whom he led on clandestine missions at the will of the Council. There are rumors that he continued his interrogation techniques throughout the remote regions of Edelyndia. Dreadful stories, I must say, but they are only rumors. Finding anything official about his past was nearly impossible. It would seem that someone powerful has been protecting him and going to great lengths to protect his secrets."

Draedon was silent as he considered this. It bothered him greatly to think that someone under his command had this sort of history. What bothered him more was the memory of Elder Zittas telling him that he came highly recommended by the council. *Recommended for what?*

Looking over at Einar, he noticed that his eyes were heavy with exhaustion. His clothes were ragged, as if he had spent considerable time on the road and hadn't slept in days. "Thank you for your hard work, my good man. Please get some food in your belly and some rest. That's an order."

"Yes, sir. Thank you, sir." He slowly got up and ambled his way to the kitchen.

Draedon remained in his chair, staring into the fire. He sat that way for a long while as troubling thoughts filled his mind. *What is Valtor up to? Before Einar had returned, the Lillyndale, business was troublesome, but now—*

His thoughts were interrupted by the door opening behind him. He turned to see Kor'lee entering the room. She looked surprised to see him still awake. *Is that guilt on her face?*

"Hello, Father," she said a little too loudly.

"Isn't the hour a little late for you to just now be coming home?"

"I'm sorry, Father, I was just…" She seemed to be searching for an excuse. He noticed the bow and quiver in her hands.

"And what was that for?"

She looked at the bow. "I was…um…shooting at the practice fields."

It made sense. She did this quite often, but he had the distinct feeling that she was hiding something. He rubbed his forehead tiredly. *Things are finally getting better. I don't want another fight right now.*

"Very well. Don't stay out so late from now on. You know how these Keepers can be."

Relief flooded her face. She said goodnight and made her way quickly to her room.

Valtor, the Council, now his daughter all seemed to have him in the dark. He knew that he had to start finding some answers. *I have a bad feeling that I might not like what I find.*

Chapter Seventeen

The day of the Harvest Festival finally arrived. Orron helped Me'ra and Mattox load up their cart with the produce from their garden, and they headed into the village. Much to her dismay, Ly'ra stayed behind with Rhi'rra at their farm this time. Though Mattox was sure that there wouldn't be any Keepers in Lillyndale, he felt it unwise to take the risk. Orron agreed.

When they arrived in Lillyndale, Orron noticed that the Harvest Festival was not nearly on par with the Mid-Summer Festival. There were far fewer vendors and the villagers were not in quite as much of a celebratory mood. It seemed that a cloud hung over the villagers.

Fewer vendors meant more customers for Orron, Mattox, and Me'ra, and they were busy selling their produce the entire afternoon. When evening fell, they packed up what little they had left, and Me'ra gave Mattox a knowing look.

"I will wait in the field outside of the village."

"Aye. We will find you when we're through."

She looked at both of them. "May the Maker watch over you both in what you must do." She looked as though she wanted to say more but instead gave Mattox an encouraging smile and walked away. Mattox beckoned Orron to follow, and they headed to Daedar's mill. This time, they were the first to arrive.

Daedar greeted them at the door and led them down the stairs into the cellar. They were soon joined by Aton, Zafilo, and Morven. Four other faces that Orron did not recognize came as well. Once everyone had arrived, Daedar began the meeting.

"Well, gentlemen, we know why we are here. There's no use dragging this out." He looked around the table with a solemn look on his face. "My hope is that you all have spent time seeking the will of the Maker in this matter."

All but Morven nodded in response. Orron noticed that he never stopped looking at a knot in the table in front of him.

"Well, then," Daedar continued, "let's come to a decision." Turning to Mattox he said, "Since this was your proposal, you should go first."

Mattox cleared his throat and stroked his beard. "Aye. You all know where I stand, and I will make this quick. Having watched one daughter be taken in the Inspection I cannot—I *will not*—endure it again. I vote that we leave the Valley soon, before winter settles in."

Silence followed. Finally, Aton spoke up. "I talked it over at great length with Rhi'rra. We do not like this course of action, but…well, we both see that there is no other way." He looked at Mattox. "We are with you, Mattox."

Orron saw Morven curse under his breath.

One by one, everyone at the table sided with Mattox, leaving Daedar and Morven.

A long period of silence followed. Daedar kept looking toward Morven as if to give him the opportunity to go next. He remained silent. Finally, Daedar said, "I am getting old—too old to be traipsing through the mountains—but I agree with all of you." He looked at Morven then Mattox. "You must protect the children. They are our hope, our future. I will not go, but I will support and help you."

Suddenly, Morven struck the table so hard Orron thought he had to have cracked it. "You fool! Don't you know what you are saying?"

"Calm yourself, Morven," Daedar said softly but firmly.

Morven ignored him and continued. "If you leave, what happens to the rest of us? The rest of the children?"

Mattox looked him in the eyes. "Morven, I have a responsibility to Ly'ra as her father to protect her no matter what the cost."

"Even if that cost be my Aly'siah?" Morven challenged.

"You can and should come with us, Morven," Aton offered.

"Why? So the Keepers can catch us and slaughter us in the mountains?" Morven was half standing now. His face was red, and spit flew from his mouth as his voice rose. "Even if we come with, you will doom us all!"

Morven pointed his finger at Mattox and his eyes burned with anger. "You! You have *no* right to force this on us!"

"I am sorry you feel that way Morven, but my family is going one way or another." Despite his calm exterior, the resolve was clearly evident in Mattox's voice.

"I won't let you!" Morven was now shouting, completely out of control. "I will stop you. I—"

"You can *try*," Orron said slowly. The authority in his voice silenced Morven. He sat down in resignation.

After a moment of silence, Daedar spoke up. "Morven, I know how hard this must be for you, but you must choose. You must decide if you are going to stay or go."

Morven looked at his right hand that was bleeding from hitting the table. In a defeated voice he said, "You leave me no choice. I—we—will go with you."

Daedar let out a breath in relief and patted Morven on the arm. "Then that settles it. I, for one, agree with Mattox. You need to leave before winter makes the mountains unsafe for travel."

They spent several more minutes working out the details of their plan. After a small amount of disagreement, they finally agreed that at the next full moon in three weeks they would meet at Aton's farm and leave together for the mountains.

Once the meeting was over, Mattox and Orron left the mill and somberly made their way to Me'ra. The look on their faces answered her unspoken question.

"When?" she asked.

"Three weeks," Mattox replied. She nodded her head.

"Then we will be ready."

Later that night after they had returned home, Me'ra and Ly'ra retired for the evening, leaving Mattox and Orron in front of the fireplace to talk about what lay before them.

"The journey will be difficult," Mattox said.

"Have you ever been up in the mountains?"

"Aye. When I was a small lad, my father took my mother and me up there during the Great War. All I remember was the cold—bitter, bitter cold."

"Is there food to be found up there?"

"Aye, but the hunting is hard. The animals up there are cunning and hard to find. We are going to need to bring as much with us as we can."

"We can hunt before we go."

"That's what I was thinking too."

They fell silent, lost in thought of what lay ahead.

"Mattox?" Orron finally said.

"Yes, lad."

"Are you worried about Morven?"

Mattox was slow to answer. "He does concern me," he finally admitted.

"What should we do?"

"Nothing. Morven's a good man and just wants his daughter to be safe."

"So we should trust him?"

"I don't see how we have a choice."

Chapter Eighteen

It's all coming together! Valtor could barely contain his excitement as he made his way to where Elder Zittas was staying. He had just arrived from the Holy City, and Valtor was anxious to tell him how the plan was proceeding. Elder Zittas's chambers were located in the Cathedral.

The Holy Cathedral of the One True Church of the Maker was located in the heart of Farovale. It was the tallest and most heavily fortified structure within the city walls. Built long before the city was turned into a Keeper Citadel, it was one of the oldest buildings in all of Edelyndia. Soaring majestically above the city rose its three spires of equal height. Numerous halls filled with countless rooms filled the enormous building. Not only was the Holy Cathedral a place of worship, but in the event of a siege it could also hold thousands of soldiers and peasants. It was truly breathtaking to behold.

When Valtor arrived, he was stopped at the door by a cleric who demanded he remove his boots.

"This is holy ground, the home of the Almighty Maker," the cleric said with disdain.

Valtor wanted to say something but bit his tongue. After his boots were removed, he hurried into the majestic Cathedral and through the cavernous foyer. Even though he had been in there many times, the elaborate craftsmanship still amazed him. Gold, silver, rare gems, and diamonds sparkled everywhere. Even the floor contained ribbons of gold.

The chambers of the Elders were located on one of the upper floors. Valtor made his way up the winding staircases and finally arrived at his destination. He knocked on the door leading to Elder Zittas's chambers. As he waited, he heard a thump on the other side of the door, then another. *Someone is attacking the Elder!*

He drew his sword and burst through the door in time to see a half-naked young girl no older than twelve scurry through another door leading out of the room. Sitting shirtless on his bed, Elder Zittas looked up at him angrily.

"How dare you burst in here like this!"

Valtor's face flushed with embarrassment. "I–I am so sorry, Your Grace. I thought—"

"I don't care what you thought, Captain. Exit this room at once! I will fetch you when I am ready!"

Quickly, Valtor left the room and closed the door behind him. His hands were shaking slightly as he sheathed his sword. He straightened and re-straightened his cloak as if trying to wipe away his embarrassment.

After a moment, the door opened, and Zittas motioned for him to come in. Now fully clothed in his ornate robes he sat down in a lavish chair covered in gems and the finest silk that Valtor had ever seen. He held out his hand indicating that Valtor was to sit next to him.

"Your Grace, I have word that our plan in Lillyndale is on track and ready for our next phase."

"Good. Very good work, Captain," Zittas said with satisfaction. "So where do we stand?"

"Several of the villagers are planning to flee into the mountains in order to avoid the Inspection."

"There are eligible girls going?"

"Yes, Your Grace. There are two leaving with their families."

"Good," Zittas said with satisfaction. "They will work perfectly. This is just the kind of opportunity we have been waiting for."

"I thought so, too, Your Grace."

Zittas folded his hands together and sat back in his chair. "So is everything in place then?"

"It is, Your Grace."

"This business with the Commander's daughter…are you certain?"

"Absolutely. I have witnessed it with my own eyes."

"What a fortunate turn of events. The Maker is smiling on us."

Zittas turned and pulled on a cord that was hanging from the ceiling. A few moments later, there was a knock on the door, and shortly after, a cleric entered the room.

"Cleric, send for Commander Draedon. Tell him I must speak with him at once."

Once he left, Zittas turned back to Valtor. "How long will it take you to start phase one of the plan?"

"If preparations begin tonight, we should be able to be in Lillyndale by late tomorrow night. I took the liberty of having warhorses brought in from the Great Plains Territory last week."

"Oh?" Zittas said with a raised eyebrow. "How did you manage that without arousing suspicion?"

"Commander Draedon knows very little about horses. I arranged to have my contacts make sure they were dirty and saddled like large packhorses, and I told the Commander that we needed more for some excavation work on the southern wall. I am confident that he accepted it without question."

"Very good."

Valtor shifted in his seat. "Your Grace, if I may be so bold, I have a small request."

He raised his eyebrow. "Yes, Captain?"

"If we want to ensure the plan will succeed, it will require us to—how shall I say this—bend the law?"

"Go on."

"We need this to look like…well, it must look like Draedon was behind this. It has to look official."

"What you're saying is that this must be different than before. Less…quiet," Zittas said knowingly.

"Yes, Your Grace. Exactly."

"Very well, do what you must. The Church is behind you."

They discussed the details of the plan. Valtor knew that it would require cunning, precision, and brute force. Zittas prepared the documents that he needed while they waited for Draedon.

"You sent for me, Elder Zittas?" Draedon said once he arrived. He did not seem pleased to see Valtor.

"Yes, Commander. Captain Valtor has told me some very disturbing news about a group of villagers from Lillyndale who are aiding and abetting the Heretics known as the Forest Bandits."

Draedon looked at Valtor and studied him for a moment. "And you have evidence of this, Captain?"

"I do. Here." He pulled a letter from his cloak. "This is a letter from one of the conspirators promising aid to the bandits. It names the rest of the rebels."

Draedon accepted the letter and read it carefully. "And how did this happen to come into your possession?"

"My source was the courier. Instead of delivering it to the bandits, he brought it to me." Sensing that Draedon was struggling to accept his word, Valtor glanced over at Zittas.

"Commander, I have seen the evidence and concur with Captain Valtor that action must be taken."

"Very well, I will take a company, arrest these men, and interrogate them myself," Draedon said.

"No, Commander, I would rather Valtor handle this."

Draedon looked confused. "Why? I am the Legion Co–"

"My apologies, Commander. I did not mean to insult you. It's just that the Captain has already led this investigation to this point, and I feel it wise to have him finish what he has started."

"Plus, I would like to be able to ensure the safety of my contact," Valtor added.

Draedon was silent for a moment. "Very well," he said. "Whatever you think is best, Elder Zittas." He turned to leave, but Zittas was not finished.

"Commander, one more thing."

Draedon turned around.

"I need your signature authorizing this arrest. It is a new policy from the Council."

This didn't seem to sit well with Draedon, but he complied. Before he left, he turned to Valtor and said, "The villager who you said was leading this rebellion…what did you say his name was?"

"His name is Mattox."

Chapter Nineteen

Orron rubbed his hands by the fire, trying to bring the feeling back. *Winter came early this year.* He looked over at Mattox and saw that he appeared chilled to the bone as well.

"Maybe we'll have better luck tomorrow," Orron offered. They had been out on the hunt for two days now with no luck whatsoever. It was as if the animals knew that they were coming and had hidden themselves away.

"Aye, I hope so. There's no use freezing ourselves in this miserable weather for nothing."

Mattox had been in a rather foul mood since they had left. Me'ra and Ly'ra were back at the sheep farm preparing things for the long journey into the hills. No one really knew what to expect, but the sudden transition to winter had cast a pall over everyone's preparations. Mattox and Orron had left to try to gather some meat for the journey. Orron had suggested that they just slaughter and eat the sheep, but Mattox could not bring himself to do it.

"We can just leave them for the people in the village," he had said.

Now, just days away from their agreed upon departure and no luck on the hunt, Orron was beginning to wonder if it was the right choice. Their hunt had taken them deep into the forest, and Orron had a bad feeling they would see little change in their fortune.

"This cursed weather is unnatural," Mattox said gruffly, breaking the silence. "Snow this early? That I'm used to, but this cold…"

Orron pulled his cloak tightly around him. He could sense it too. There was something almost sinister in the wind. Even the warmth of the fire seemed to have no effect against it. He tossed and turned as he tried to quiet his unease.

Just as he was beginning finally to drift off to sleep, he saw movement in the trees not far from where he lay. *It's probably just shadows from the fire*, he told himself. Then he saw it again. Mattox sat up apparently having witnessed it as well.

They both peered into the darkness. Whatever it was, it sounded as if it was moving closer. Mattox grabbed his bow and nocked an arrow. Orron reached instead for his staff.

"Bless the Maker…" Mattox muttered under his breath as the flickering light of the fire illuminated the massive form of an Avolyndian elk. He seemed to be staring right at Orron.

Mattox slowly began to raise his bow. *Something feels wrong*, Orron thought. He put his hand on Mattox's shoulder and said, "Wait!"

Mattox hesitated, looking at Orron expectantly, his eyes demanding an explanation. The elk moved a short ways away and stopped, seemingly waiting for Orron to follow. Something moved in Orron's spirit, and he knew what he had to do.

He rose to his feet slowly and looked at Mattox. "I…I have to go."

Mattox just stared at him with his mouth open.

"You just have to trust me, Mattox," he said firmly. "There's something I have to do. I will meet up with you at the farm later."

He left Mattox behind and walked toward the elk. As he neared, the elk began walking away. Orron followed, allowing the elk to keep a little bit of distance. He felt a flutter in his stomach as his nerves were on edge. He knew where the elk was leading him and was uneasy about what awaited him there.

The journey lasted about an hour when suddenly the elk stopped and looked back at him. The noble beast then passed between two familiar trees and headed into the large clearing that Orron knew was on the other side. He paused, steeled himself, and followed it into the clearing. Not surprisingly, he was alone.

With his staff gripped tightly in his right hand, he moved to the center of the clearing and waited. His body was tense, every muscle standing at full alert. The air was silent, and the night was dark. Still, he waited.

Slowly it began. The energy started as a hum, building slowly until the earth shook with a roar louder than the loudest thunder. Orron's staff hummed with energy, sending it coursing through his body. This time he felt very different. Instead of panicking, he let the energy flow through him.

Time seemed to stand still as Orron shut his eyes and lost himself in the swirling energy. The three words flowed through his spirit, filling his heart with peace and strength. He held his staff vertically in front of his body with both hands. His head was bowed and his body relaxed. The sound built to a deafening crescendo, but still his courage did not waver. This time was different—silence. The sound stopped abruptly. Orron remained where he stood with his eyes closed at complete and utter peace with the world. Then he heard a voice so deep and full of wisdom that it could not have come from a being of this world. It was a familiar voice, the voice in his dreams.

"Greetings, Orron, True Keeper of The Maker's Plan. It is time for you to awaken."

Orron slowly opened his eyes and saw standing in front of him a majestic looking man, if that is what he was. He stood very tall in a billowing black cloak. Like Orron, he had no hair on his head, and in his right hand, he held the same staff as the one Orron held. He radiated with tremendous strength and power.

Orron did the only thing that seemed right at the moment. He fell to his knees and bowed his head.

"Rise, Guardian. I am not to be worshiped or revered. I am as you are, a True Keeper. Nothing more, nothing less."

Orron slowly rose to his feet, though he felt unworthy to look this being in the eyes.

"My name is Arlas, and you know me well. There is much that you have forgotten, Guardian."

I know this being? Orron tried to shake the confusion from his mind to no avail. "Who…who am I?"

"You are as I told you, a True Keeper of the Maker's Plan."

His darkest fears were confirmed. With dread in his voice he said, "I don't understand. The Keepers are horrible—"

"The Keepers of which you speak are nothing more than a perversion—man's way of trying to imitate the Maker's plan instead of submitting to it."

"I don't understand."

Arlas sighed and sat down on the ground cross-legged and motioned for Orron to join him. Orron sat down in front of him in similar fashion. "There is much you do not understand, Guardian. That is why I have come. It is time for you to awaken. There is much you have to accomplish."

"What can I possibly accomplish? There is so much that I don't know," Orron blurted out with frustration.

"Peace, Orron," Arlas replied. His voice sounded harsh, but a slight smile tugged at the corner of his mouth. "You are always so full of questions."

He was right. Orron's head swirled with questions, but he forced himself to be patient.

"Long before the age of man, the Maker created a race of wise and powerful beings. They served Him well until a great rebellion. Those who rebelled desired the power of the Maker. They were cast out of His Kingdom and into a vast universe."

Arlas paused as if remembering this time of strife. "With peace restored, the Maker saw fit to create a new race of beings, one that has the freedom to choose whether or not to love and follow Him. These beings were called humans and were scattered throughout the inhabitable worlds of the universe. Since that time, a great war has waged between those ancient beings who remained loyal to the Maker and those who were cast out. Those who remained loyal became known as the Keepers, for their task was to protect the Maker's plan from being disrupted by the evil of those who are always seeking to kill and destroy all that the Maker has created. These usurpers are known only as the Fallen, those ancient beings who were cast out of the Maker's kingdom."

Arlas looked at Orron. "Orron, this is who you are, why you exist. You are a Keeper, as am I."

"How is that I don't remember any of this?"

"It has to do with how you found yourself alone in the forest exactly one year ago tonight."

Has it been one year already?

"The Keepers are divided into two classes. There are those who are called the Assessors. At times when the Fallen have succeeded in drawing the hearts of man far from the Heart of the Maker, the Assessors are sent to bring about the Age of Reckoning, a time when the Maker's judgment is poured out on those who are wicked, and the Fallen are defeated at the hand of the righteous. The Maker chooses to use the Assessors in different ways. At times, they take human form and wage war in the physical world. Other times, the Maker instructs the Assessors to empower certain humans to bring about the Age of Reckoning through supernatural means."

He laughed lightly to himself. "I have once witnessed a man slay a thousand soldiers by himself with only the jawbone of a donkey."

"So the Assessors fight for the Maker?"

"Sometimes, yes. Other times they inspire, empower, or simply watch the actions of the righteous as they battle against the Fallen. They are fierce warriors, but they are as cunning and wise as they are strong."

Arlas grew serious and looked at Orron with a piercing gaze. "There is another class of Keeper known as the Guardians. They are tasked with defending and protecting those humans who have remained loyal to the Maker. As with the Assessors, the Guardians carry out the Will of the Maker in a variety of ways. Sometimes they take human form, other times they use other humans. I am a Guardian, as are you, Orron."

"How are the Guardians different from the Assessors?"

Arlas sighed. "Your memory has faded more than I had feared. The Guardians watch over a single human or, in some circumstances, a small group of humans. They are tasked with protecting them at all costs, meaning that the focus of the Guardian is always to defend. Assessors, on the other hand, are tasked with taking the battle to the Fallen. They focus on the offensive, not the defensive."

Orron had difficulty comprehending what he was hearing. *The Keepers that Arlas are describing sound so powerful, so much more than I could ever possibly be.*

"But I...how could I be what you say? I don't feel... Well, I am neither powerful nor wise."

"Just because you have forgotten and lost your way does not change who you are, Orron."

Orron couldn't bring himself to believe fully what Arlas was saying about him. "You still haven't explained how I woke a year ago with no memory of who I am."

"Haven't I?" Arlas said with an inquisitive look on his face. "Very well, I will try to be more specific. As you may have guessed, your task was to serve as Guardian over the one they call Ly'ra. From the time that she was born, you kept watch over her. Edelyndia is a land where the Maker usually chooses to have the Keepers empower humans rather than directly intervene. As evil ambition and pride perverted the Church, darkness began to reign over this land. The Maker's Plan was being undone through the work of the Fallen. Thus, the Maker tasked the Assessors with bringing about the Age of Reckoning. The Assessors decided to use the one named Mattox to bring this about."

Mattox? How…why would he do this?

Sensing his confusion Arlas explained. "The Assessors knew that Mattox would need a push. With Ly'ra and Me'ra to protect, they knew that Mattox would not do something as reckless as lead a great rebellion." He paused as if he knew that what he was about to tell Orron would be difficult to hear. "They decided that Ly'ra would need to die in order to provide that push."

"Ly'ra? Why would she—" The memory of his reoccurring dream silenced Orron. *Is that what this has all been about?*

Arlas waited until Orron's attention returned to him before he continued. "Ly'ra was supposed to die in that rock slide one year ago. The Assessors knew that if she died, Mattox would descend into hatred and despair. At the summer Inspection, there would have been an incident in which Mattox would have intervened, killing several Keepers, sparking a rebellion that would have swept Edelyndia like an uncontrollable wildfire."

The dream kept replaying in Orron's head. "So my dream… that argument between you and me really happened?"

A pained expression fell over Arlas's face. "Yes, Orron. I serve the Maker as leader of the Guardians. It fell to me to explain to you why Ly'ra was to die. You refused to accept what you were hearing. At the time, I thought that you would come around, but you didn't."

Orron closed his eyes tightly as the memories of that night began to wash over him suddenly.

That night after our argument, I was so angry that I couldn't think straight. I couldn't believe that the Maker would allow someone so pure and innocent as Ly'ra be used in such a way. I remember running down a great hallway shining with powerful light and entering a small room—my room—and donning my cloak and grabbing my staff. I ran back down that hall and stopped in front of a great door carved in symbols, the same symbols as the ones on my staff. I went through the doors and…

"I came to Edelyndia without your permission," Orron said, finishing his thought aloud.

Arlas nodded.

"Is that why my memories have been erased?"

"Yes. Choosing to come to the physical world in human form requires the permission of the head of a Keeper's class. In your case, you were required to get my permission and blessing. You did not."

He studied Orron as if trying to figure out the answer to a great mystery. "I still do not understand how you were able to pass through the Chamber and into this world without my blessing. It has never been done."

Orron didn't have an answer. Though his memories were starting to return, there was still much that he didn't know. It was like one veil had been lifted and several more were left behind it.

Arlas continued. "However, you managed to accomplish it; you came to this world. That energy that you have now twice encountered in this clearing is the process by which the Keeper enters human form."

"So, the last time I was in this clearing you were trying to come here?"

"Yes. You were apparently not ready. When you cried out for the Maker's help I was called back."

Orron sat in silence, stunned by what he had learned. *A Guardian of Ly'ra?* That explained the almost supernatural pull he felt toward her.

"So, I have…power?

"Yes. Though your human form provides many limitations, you are not fully human." He leaned toward Orron as his voice became quiet with the weight of what he was about to tell Orron. "Do not ever make the mistake of thinking that your power comes from you. Powerful you may be, but the source of that power comes from the Maker. It is never your own doing."

Recognition filled Orron. "The three words…"

"Yes, very good, Orron. I see that you have not forgotten everything. 'Breathe. Connect. Focus.' This is known as the Mantra of the Wise. This is how a true Keeper channels his power. When in human form, a Keeper is no more powerful than any other human is. It is only when he submits himself entirely to the Will of the Maker and connects to His Spirit that he is able to do great things."

Orron fell silent as this new information only created more questions.

Sensing his confusion, Arlas said, "Speak, Orron. Now is the time for answers."

Where do I begin? "The elk, was that a Keeper?"

"Yes. A Keeper can take many forms. I sent him to guide you back to the place of your beginning."

"What is my staff? I remember bringing it with me from—well, come to think of it, where did I come from?"

"You came from the Kingdom of the Maker. You will return to this place when the time is right. As for your staff, it is the weapon of the true Keeper. It possesses great power when wielded correctly. It cannot break, and the blade will never dull."

Remembering how quickly his body healed he asked, "Can I die?"

"Your body is human. A mortal wound will terminate your human existence, and you will be summoned back to the Maker to give an account for your actions. As you have already experienced, though, your body can and will heal much faster from any other wound than a normal human's would."

Orron had many more questions, but one gnawed at him as it had since he first awoke in the forest a year ago. "What am I to do next?"

Arlas stroked his chin thoughtfully. "In truth, Guardian, I do not entirely know. When you intervened and prevented the Assessors from carrying out their task, you changed the course of the Maker's plan. The Age of Reckoning must still happen, but how it will proceed is undecided. When I tried to come those months ago when I was sent to retrieve you, you cried out to the Maker. He heard you and called me back. He has seen fit to allow you to decide the fate of Edelyndia."

"I don't understand. How can I?"

Arlas regarded him carefully. Silence fell between them as he studied Orron. When he spoke, he did so with great pensiveness. "Orron, I cannot answer that for you. What the Maker is choosing to do—allowing you to be both Guardian and Assessor—it has never been done before in the history of the Keepers. You have been given a great power and even greater responsibility." He shook his head. "I confess that I do not understand why He has chosen to do this, but the only thing that matters is that He has."

Orron stood to his feet and walked a small distance away. His thoughts overwhelmed him. *How can I possibly decide the fate of so many? I barely understand who I am let alone the power of which Arlas speaks.*

Arlas stood to his feet, walked over to Orron, and placed a hand on each shoulder. "Orron, though I do not know the fullness of the Maker's plan I do know this, you are a Keeper. I have watched you for many eons, and I know that your heart is pure. What lies in front of you is a difficult road to travel. The best advice that I can give you is to trust your heart and the Heart of the Maker."

"Can you not stay and assist me?"

"No, Orron. This task is for you only. However, you are never alone. The Maker shall be your greatest ally and source of power."

He turned and walked toward the edge of the clearing. When he reached the outer trees, he looked to Orron and said, "My time has come. I must leave you now."

He walked into the forest and abruptly the deafening sound of the energy accompanied by a blinding light overwhelmed Orron's senses, and he covered his eyes. As suddenly as it began, the noise and light disappeared, leaving Orron alone in the darkness.

Breathe. Connect. Focus. The words brought calm to Orron's spirit. He felt power course through his body. Though he had no idea what he was going to do, he now knew that he was not alone. That knowledge brought him tremendous comfort.

After a while, Orron opened his eyes. The first thing he noticed was a strange burning sensation on his chest. He pulled open his cloak and lifted his shirt. The symbol on his chest was glowing ever so slightly. He touched it with his right hand. Suddenly, he jerked it back. *Did it just shock me?*

He didn't know what to make of it. Something had changed him, transforming his body. It wasn't just the mark on his chest. He felt different somehow.

With renewed determination, he started traveling quickly back toward Ly'ra. He still had many questions, but there was one thing that he knew beyond a shadow of a doubt. *I must keep Ly'ra safe.*

Chapter Twenty

The ground shook as one hundred Keepers mounted on fine warhorses flew down the frozen dirt road. As they broke from the forest, Valtor gave the signal and one third of the riders peeled off, heading toward the hills to the east. Valtor and the remaining riders rode across the bridge into the village of Lillyndale. The thunderous sound of the warhorses was a foreign sound to the villagers, and they were awakened from their slumber. At Valtor's command the Keepers dismounted and began kicking in doors and dragging out the residents.

Valtor waited in the village square as the residents were herded like cattle in front of him. He smiled to himself, enjoying the look of terror on many of their faces. The villagers were rounded up relatively quickly.

He admired the swiftness and precision of the Keepers at his command. He had handpicked them from the ranks of the general infantry. Many had trained with Valtor in the Holy City and served under him during his clandestine raids. *It feels good to be back at it again.*

One of the Keepers, a company marshal who had been with Valtor since the days of the uprising, approached him. He was the only officer that Valtor had selected for this mission. There was no one that Valtor trusted more to go into battle with. Tysion was taller than he was and outweighed him by at least fifty pounds, all muscle. He had few equals with the sword.

"The villagers are all here, Captain."

"Very good, Marshal Tysion."

"What are your orders, sir?"

"Have the men set up a perimeter. Anyone trying to leave shall be put to death."

"Yes, sir,"

As Tysion left to organize the other Keepers, Cleric Osbere, the governor of Lillyndale, made his way over to Valtor. He was clearly unhappy at having his sleep disrupted. Valtor looked at him with disgust. *Sniveling little whelp of a man.*

Something about Osbere rubbed Valtor the wrong way. He was a short, obese man that talked with a high-pitched voice that grated on his nerves, and he was always sneezing. He never stopped complaining about the weather of the Valley and made sure everyone knew just how beneath him he thought this posting was. Apparently, he had aspirations for one day being selected to the Council.

"What is the meaning of this, Valtor?" Osbere waved his arms as he walked, and the picture very much reminded Valtor of a squawking goose.

"That is *Captain* Valtor to you, Cleric, and I am here on official business. I come with direct orders from Commander Draedon and the Council."

"At this hour? Why haven't I—"

"You are overstepping your bounds if you presume to question me." Valtor made sure to include his most menacing snarl.

Sufficiently chastised, Osbere's face reddened, "My apologies, Captain. I just would have appreciated being informed about—"

"Consider yourself informed, Cleric."

"Begging your pardon, sir, but what is the nature of this… visit?"

Valtor glowered at him. He didn't appreciate having to explain himself to this sniveling little man. "We have orders to arrest the Heretics that are planning a rebellion in *your* village."

"But, sir, I can assure you, there are no Heretics—"

"Is that so?" he said menacingly. "Then would you care to explain this?" He handed the cleric the fabricated letter.

Osbere's face hardened as he read it. "My apologies, Captain Valtor. You will have my full cooperation."

"I would expect nothing less, Cleric Osbere." His words were a threat.

Orron quickened his pace as he felt a stirring deep within his spirit. *Something is wrong.* He had been running for over an hour now, and though he was very tired, something drove him on. Since leaving the clearing, he had been overwhelmed by a deepening sense of dread. *I have to get back to Ly'ra.*

He had already journeyed a great distance in a relatively short amount of time, aided by the supernatural power he now knew was available to him. The Mantra of the Wise kept playing over and over in his head. The unnatural cold and silence tried to distract him. Whenever they managed to draw his attention away from the Mantra he felt his strength wane. Fighting to gain control of his thoughts, he began to say the words aloud breathlessly.

"Breathe. Connect. Focus. Breathe. Connect. Focus." On and on he spoke until talking itself became a distraction. He then hardened his mind and drove himself onward in silence.

A new sound entered his mind causing him to slide to a stop. *Thump, thump. Thump, thump. Thump, thump.* It was the sound of a heart beating faster and faster. He instantly knew the source. *Ly'ra is scared.*

The last of the peasants from the countryside stumbled into the square as Valtor eyed them with contempt. *Heretics,* he thought with disgust. He knew that by technical definition, many were "innocent," but in his eyes, none was innocent. *Either you fight for the Church or you are against it.*

A cacophony of sounds filled the square. Angry voices demanded to know what was going on. Mothers tried to shush their crying children.

"*SILENCE!*" Valtor's voice roared above the din of the crowd. An eerie quiet filled the square. He paused for a moment before continuing, basking in the feeling of power and control. When he spoke, his face curled into an evil sneer. His voice was filled with malice.

"Has the Church not been gracious to you, unthankful miscreants? Have you not enjoyed the favor of the Council?"

No one dared to respond.

He continued. "And how do you repay them? By consorting with Heretics and fueling their unholy rebellion!" He saw the shock on many of their faces.

He turned to Osbere. "Cleric, if you would be so kind, please read the charges." The cleric just stared at him. Though Valtor knew the cleric held no love for these people, he clearly wanted no part of this.

Valtor's eyes narrowed. "If that is too difficult of a task for you, perhaps you would rather share in their fate?"

The cleric's eyes widened and he cleared his throat. With a shaky voice, he read the letter in his hands aloud.

"Citizens of Lillyndale, it has been brought to the attention of the Council that there are those among you who have turned your back on the Will of the Maker. Darkness has filled your hearts, and evil has become your mistress. As the Beacon of Light in this dark world, the Church must take a stand for righteousness. The crimes against the One True Church of the Maker include heresy, debauchery, and providing aid to the Heretics known to you as the Forest Bandits." He paused. Beads of sweat formed on his brow despite the chill in the air.

Valtor leaned toward him with his hand on the hilt of his sword. "Continue, Cleric."

Wiping away the sweat he continued, "The punishment for these crimes is death. Anyone who wishes to absolve themselves of the crimes mentioned herein must raise their voice and identify the Heretics among you. In doing so, you will receive the grace and mercy of the Council, the voice of the One True Maker. Furthermore—"

Valtor held up his hand, silencing the cleric. "Is there anyone who wishes to absolve themselves?" His eyes scanned the crowd. A large man with dark hair and massive forearms glowered at him.

"I do. I wish to make an accusation."

Valtor raised an eyebrow. "And your name is?" He turned his body to face the accuser.

"My name is Zafilo, sir."

Orron's foot caught on a tree root and he crashed down the side of a small ravine, hitting his head on a tree stump at the bottom. Dazed, he lay still for a moment trying to catch his breath. He forced himself to his feet and tried to continue. Pain shot through his ankle, and he once again fell to the ground. He let out a frustrated cry.

Pulling off his left boot, he examined his ankle closely. It had already started to swell but it didn't look to be broken. Cursing his clumsiness, he pulled himself up with his staff. Much slower now, he continued, wincing with every step.

He couldn't shake the feeling that there was something trying to keep him from Ly'ra. Every tree branch seemed to target his exposed skin. His feet seemed to find every twisted root.

Focus, he told himself. Try as he might, he couldn't shake the overwhelming sense of foreboding. It was as if doom was just around every tree. The shadows seemed to dance with unknown evils.

The silence was what unnerved him the most. At one point, it was so quiet that he tapped his staff against a tree just to make sure that he had not gone deaf. No evidence of living creatures could be seen.

His hearted pounded furiously as he pressed on as quickly as his injured ankle would allow. He gripped his staff tightly. With dread in his heart, he knew that one thing was certain. This night would see bloodshed.

Valtor could hear gasps as a tall, skinny young man stepped forward. *It didn't take much to bribe you. Make a promise of money, power, and fame, and inbreeds like you drool all over yourselves. Coward*, he thought disgustedly. Though he was very appreciative of the opportunity Zafilo had presented him with, he was still bothered by the greed that had led him to sell out his own friends and neighbors.

He motioned for Zafilo to kneel before him. "And who are these Heretics?"

Zafilo hesitated. Valtor began to worry that he might have changed his mind. Then the young man cleared his throat and spoke, "I personally witnessed Mattox convince eight others to join his rebellion."

"Zafilo, no!" a woman cried from the crowd. Valtor turned to see an old man put his hand on her shoulder to silence her as he stepped forward.

The old man spoke gently. "Zafilo, what are you doing?"

Zafilo stood and turned to the man. "Don't worry, Father. I have this all worked out."

"Son, you don't know what you are doing."

"I know exactly what I am doing! I'm making a life for myself!"

"But at what cost?"

Zafilo appeared to waver. "I...I know—"

"Son," the old man said as he approached him with his hands held out. "Stop this while you still have a chance."

Things were unraveling fast, and Valtor knew he had to do something. *He has already named Mattox. That is enough.*

The old man placed his hands on Zafilo's face. "I know I haven't always been the best father, but—" He stopped as his eyes grew wide. Looking down he saw Valtor's blade exiting the front of his body. Crying out in pain, he fell to the ground.

Horror filled Zafilo's eyes as he said to Valtor, "This wasn't part of—" Valtor's sword severed his head before he could finish his thought. Behind him a young girl screamed.

Orron froze. The scream tore through his being, and his senses became instantly and completely aware of everything around him. He waited for another, but he was only greeted by more enveloping silence.

Did I imagine it? He waited. His heart beat loudly in his ears.

Another scream tore through the silence. Without hesitation, he broke into a run, ignoring the excruciating pain in his ankle. *Ly'ra!*

Chaos descended on the village as the Keepers moved in to restore order. They dragged five of the men named in the letter to the center of the square and bound their hands behind their backs. *Zafilo's testimony would have been nice, but no matter. We have the letter.*

It took several minutes to get things under control, but the superior force of the Keepers successfully managed the situation. Tysion approached Valtor.

"Captain, all but three of the Heretics are in front of you. One named Daedar you have already killed." He motioned to the old man lying on the ground. "Two others are unaccounted for. The two missing are the leader, Mattox, and his cousin's son, Orron. They are apparently out on a pre-winter hunt."

Valtor swore to himself. He had hoped to capture Mattox with this raid. *No matter. The plan will still work.*

He looked at the cleric and noticed that he had vomited on himself. *Disgusting little man.* He motioned for him to continue reading the letter.

Reluctantly Osbere spoke up weakly. "Furthermore, as punishment for the crimes of your fellow villagers any girl that would be eligible for the Inspection next summer must immediately present herself to the Captain of the Keepers."

⌒⌒

Two more screams ripped through Orron. The second was filled with so much fear that it caused him to stumble. His ankle wanted to give out, but he ground his teeth and drove himself onward, pushing himself to go faster. *I'm coming, Ly'ra!*

⌒⌒

This time, the Keepers had to use physical force to restrain the villagers as they dragged two young girls into the square. From where he stood, it appeared to Valtor that at least two men were killed in the struggle with several more wounded. He smiled to himself. *Even without Mattox this is going perfectly.*

Valtor looked at the cleric. "Only two this year?"

"I'm afraid so, sir."

"Very well, they will do."

He looked at the two girls standing in front of him. Both were sobbing uncontrollably. Looking closer, he realized that he knew the one on the left. *She's the one from the Mid-Summer Festival,* he thought with a smile. *Looks like you will finally get what you deserve.* He grabbed both girls harshly by the hair and spun them around so the village could see their terror.

"Because of your insolence you all deserve to suffer at the hands of the Council's arm of justice. Instead, the Council has empowered me to select these wretched little things to serve the Council in the Holy City as penance for your crimes."

The burly, dark haired man that had been identified as Morven bellowed with rage. He leapt to his feet from where he knelt among the accused rebels. With incredible strength, he broke the ropes binding his hands and lunged for Valtor. Tysion struck him down before he could reach his target.

Emboldened by the heroic efforts of Morven, the villagers began to attack the Keepers. Chaos returned as the village square was transformed into a battleground.

The screams were now assaulting Orron nearly continuously. He no longer felt the pain in his ankle as he drove himself faster than he had ever thought possible.

Trees whipped by in a blur as he ran. He felt as if he were flying. Minutes felt like hours as he knew in his heart that time was his enemy. *I have to reach her!*

Valtor wiped the blood off his sword on the body of a fallen villager. The fighting had lasted mere minutes. It was a massacre. The village was strewn with the dismembered body parts of the fallen villagers. *My men have performed well.*

Sheathing his sword, he looked around for the girls who had been selected. When the fighting had erupted, they had escaped his grasp. He spotted them huddled against the side of a nearby building, holding each other and sobbing with sheer terror.

As Valtor was making his way toward them, Tysion approached him dragging a bloodied woman behind him by the hair. Deep claw marks streaked with blood adorned his face. He threw her down at Valtor's feed. "Cleric Osbere identified this woman as the wife of Mattox."

Valtor looked down at her. She was beaten badly. Many of her teeth had shattered from the blows of her attacker. Her left eye was completely ruined and her red hair was streaked with blood. "What happened?"

Tysion gingerly rubbed the wounds on his face. "She attacked me when the fighting broke out. I think she was trying to get to one of the girls. My guess is one of them is hers." He motioned to the two girls with his head.

Valtor looked at the girls and immediately recognized the red hair and smiled menacingly. *So you're Mattox's daughter.*

The redheaded girl saw her mother and ran to her screaming. Before she could get there, Valtor struck the girl in the side of the head with the butt of his sword so hard that she flew three feet and hit the ground. Her body lay still.

The screaming stopped abruptly. Orron did not slow down. He knew the screaming was coming from the village.

Even at his supernatural pace, he was still at least thirty minutes away. Grinding his teeth together, he pushed himself harder.

After making sure the girls were secured to the backs of two Keepers' warhorses, Valtor mounted his own. He looked over to Tysion who was mounted next to him.

"Select ten of our best Keepers to stay here and await this Mattox. Tell them to capture or kill him. It makes no difference to me."

Tysion pointed toward the crumpled body of Me'ra. She was still breathing but barely. "What should they do with her?"

An evil smile crossed Valtor's lips. "Have them do with her as they please."

Tysion returned the smile and left to carry out his orders.

Turning to Cleric Osbere, he noticed that the smell of vomit on him was now joined by the smell of urine. With disgust evident on his face, Valtor said, "Cleric Osbere, I am assigning four Keepers to accompany you back to your manor as protection until Elder Zittas sends for you."

Osbere stared blankly at him.

"Do you understand me, Cleric?"

He made no response. Motioning to a nearby Keeper, he told him what he had just told the cleric. Nearly catatonic, Osbere had to be led away by hand.

Tysion returned, and at Valtor's signal, the rest of the Keepers thundered across the bridge and down the road to Farovale.

Orron burst through the trees and into the field just over three hundred yards from the bridge that led to Lillyndale. His body ached from the journey, but he refused to acknowledge it. Quickly but cautiously he made his way to the bridge.

It had been quite some time since he had last felt Ly'ra scream. He could no longer hear her heartbeat. When he arrived at the bridge, he crouched by the side and looked toward the village. He prepared himself for the worst, but what he saw was far more terrible than anything he could have imagined.

Legs, hands, heads, fingers, and other various body parts were strewn about the field outside the village square. He could only imagine the horror that awaited him inside the square itself. From his vantage point, he could not see into the square, but he could hear the sounds coming from it. Men were cheering someone on with evil and lust in their voices.

As quickly as he dared, he stole to the edge of the village, side stepping the body parts remains. He tried not to look closely at what lie on the ground as bile rose into his throat.

Reaching the edge of the village, he peered around the corner of a building and saw a group of Keepers gathered in a circle among the carnage. One of the Keepers moved to grab a fallen sword giving Orron a view of the horrors within the circle. There, with a vile man on top of her, lay Me'ra.

He could hardly recognize her. Her face was beaten so badly that she barely looked human, and her clothes were torn apart, revealing various bruises, wounds, and burn marks. One of the Keepers standing next to her body was holding a torch that, from the marks on her body, Orron could tell had been used in her torture.

Rage Orron had never known filled his soul. He once again said the three words and instead of finding his usual sense of power and calm, he found something else. His being was filled with a wild and burning anger. This was not the anger of an uncontrolled human. It was the righteous anger of a True Keeper of the Maker's Plan. This was the vengeance of an Assessor.

With her one working eye, Me'ra locked onto Orron as a single tear rolled down her cheek. The look on her face pleaded with Orron to leave, to save himself. Though he was outnumbered ten-to-one, the power flowing through him made him stronger than a thousand trained soldiers.

Ejecting the blade from his staff, Orron rose to his feet. Only once before had he used his staff as a spear in combat. Then, he had only intended to wound. Now, he would leave no enemy alive.

With blinding speed, he closed the distance between him and the Keepers. When he reached the nearest one, he crushed his skull with the butt of his spear. Before the fallen Keeper's body hit the ground, two more joined him, stabbed through the heart with his spear.

He grabbed the Keeper off Me'ra and threw him so hard his bones shattered as he struck the stone wall of a house across the way. A few of the quicker Keepers leapt at Orron.

One grabbed him around the neck from behind. Another's attempt to stab him in the stomach with his sword was deflected by Orron's staff. While he was engaged with the swordsman, another Keeper latched onto his arms, pinning them to his side.

With one Keeper on his back cutting off his airflow and another wrapped around waist, Orron jumped forward with inhuman strength, crashing into the swordsman. He used the only weapon he had available to him and attacked with his teeth. The swordsman fell to the ground, bleeding profusely from the mortal wound to his throat.

Orron swung his body around with savage ferocity sending his attackers flying to the ground. Now free, he closed the distance between them and stabbed them both through the face.

This all happened so fast that the remaining three Keepers had yet to see their attacker. They died before they found him.

It was over in a matter of seconds. Orron dropped to his knees beside Me'ra. He cradled her head in his arms. Tears flowed as the woman who had been like a mother to him lay dying in his arms, her body violated and ruined.

Her breath was ragged and both her eyes were now swollen shut. She made a faint sound. Orron brought his ear to her lips.

"Orron…Ly'ra…they took her…" With the last strength left in her body, she gripped his arm.

"Save her, Orron…" blood flowed from her mouth as she choked.

"Don't let them do to her…what they did…to A'ra."

"I won't, Me'ra," Orron said with tears flowing from his eyes. "I will save her. I swear to you, I will not stop until Ly'ra is safe again…no matter the cost."

She coughed violently causing her to spew blood. Orron helplessly watched death overtake the woman who had shown him so much love and acceptance.

With her voice in the faintest of whispers, she said, "Orron…tell Mattox…and…Ly'ra…tell them that I love them so very much."

Orron felt her hand tighten ever so slightly on his as she focused what little energy she had left on her final words. He had to lean closely to hear her speak.

"Orron…don't let…Mattox…give in to…his hatred. Save him, Orron…save them both…"

And Me'ra's last breath escaped.

Orron screamed savagely. The pain was overwhelming. Never again would he hear her voice. Never again would she comfort him. Never again would this wonderful mother and wife sing, dance, and bring joy to the lives of so many. Around him lay the bodies of Aton, Rhi'rra, Morven, Daedar...so many good people...so many innocent lives were taken.

He gently kissed Me'ra on the forehead and laid her back on the ground. Out of respect and love, he arranged her clothing to protect her decency. Behind him, the violator began to stir.

He rose slowly to his feet and grasped his spear. The man cried out in agony as he tried to crawl away on shattered limbs. Before this night, Orron would have been moved to mercy as he had been with Raulin in the forest. *Not tonight. The time for mercy has ended.* He threw his spear with such strength that it passed through the Keepers skull and buried itself a full two feet in the ground.

Exhaustion and pain finally became too great for Orron to bear, and he fell hard to the ground. He welcomed the darkness as it began to close around him. His heart and soul were filled with a strange sense of peace, not the kind that is born of happiness and joy, but the kind that comes with truly knowing one's purpose, one's destiny.

No longer did questions flood his mind. No longer did he feel helpless. He knew what his mission was. He had an identity. He now had one goal. *I am a True Keeper of the Maker's Plan. I am both Guardian and Assessor. The Age of Reckoning has come...*

PART 2
Day One of the Age of Reckoning

CHAPTER TWENTY-ONE

This city smells disgusting, Draedon thought as he strolled along the top of the southern wall. The din of travelers and Keepers streaming in and out of the South Gate grated on his nerves. Like Kor'lee, life in Farovale never really suited him. He grew up in the expansive forests of the North Woods Territory and never really adjusted to life in the cramped spaces of the various citadels he had been stationed in throughout his career. Even in the dead of winter, the smells of sewage and horse stables filled the air. *I need out of this place.*

He stopped and looked over the wall toward the expanse beyond. Farovale was located in the mouth of Havenshae Valley. Majestic bluffs rose up on either side. He had often felt that these bluffs posed a security threat. Any attacker that was a skilled enough climber to scale them could rain down destruction on the city. When he voiced these concerns to Elder Zittas, he was assured that in its many centuries of existence, Farovale had never been taken by any foe.

Unpleasant smells and defensive weaknesses were not what was really bothering Draedon this morning. He had not slept a minute the previous night. Knowing that Valtor was in charge of whatever was going on in Lillyndale made him extremely restless. It was nearing noon, and he was trying to find things to keep himself busy, hence his decision to inspect the southern defense.

What is going on between Valtor and Zittas? Since the last meeting with the two of them, he hadn't been able to shake the feeling that something very troubling was unfolding. One thing he did know was that this business with Lillyndale was not just a routine arrest. It was the start of something, but he could not quite seem to figure out what.

His thoughts were interrupted by Einar clamoring up the stairs toward him. "Sir, they have returned," he said trying to catch his breath. "Something has happened."

Draedon's heart sunk. "What is it, Einar?"

"There's…blood…everywhere. It's on their horses, weapons, tunics."

Blood. That could only mean one thing. "Where are they?"

"They just entered the North Gate and are headed to the stables."

"Stables?"

"Yes, sir. They rode on warhorses."

Warhorses for an arrest? Draedon cursed Valtor under his breath. *Bloodshed was his plan all along.*

"Thank you, Einar." He took off running toward the stables. Einar followed closely behind.

The stables were located in the southwestern portion of the city. It took Draedon and Einar almost ten minutes to reach them. When they reached the stables, they were out of breath and Einar looked as if he could pass out any moment. They arrived just as Valtor and his men rode in.

Draedon pushed his way through the throng of stable hands and Keepers. To his dismay, he saw that Einar had been accurate in his description. Blood was all over the Keepers. *Whatever happened, it was a bloodbath.*

Reaching Valtor just as he dismounted Draedon grabbed him by the shoulder and spun him around. "I demand an explanation, Captain!"

Valtor's eyes flashed with anger. "An explanation for what, sir?"

"For the blood…the warhorses," he said motioning all around him in disbelief. "This was supposed to be a simple arrest!"

"There was…a complication."

"Explain yourself, Captain!" Draedon could feel the blood rushing to his face as he shook with anger. *I knew this would happen. I knew Valtor could not be trusted!*

"The villagers revolted. We had no choice but to restore order."

"Revolted? How many were harmed?"

"None of the Keepers were harmed, sir."

It was all Draedon could do to keep from striking the insolent captain. "You know what I meant, *Captain*. How many villagers?"

"You care more about the villagers than your own Keepers?" Valtor's eyes were filled with spite, and his words were an accusation. The returning Keepers were now surrounding the two, watching the confrontation with interest. The crowd of onlookers only made Draedon angrier.

"Captain Valtor, last I checked, *I* am the Legion Commander, and I will not tolerate your insolence. I *order* you to answer the question, and keep your snide remarks to yourself."

"Yes, sir." Valtor's eyes flashed with anger, but he continued. "There were many casualties among the Heretics."

"Specifics, Captain. How many *villagers*?"

"All of them, sir. They were all killed in *self-defense*."

Draedon couldn't believe what he was hearing. Bile rose in his throat, and he had to fight back the urge to vomit. "How… why would you do this? You're telling me that unarmed villagers posed so great a threat to one hundred Keepers that they had to *all* be killed?"

"Yes, *sir*. That is what I said, *sir*." The insolence dripped off his words.

Draedon finally snapped. He grabbed Valtor by the cloak and slammed him against the stable wall. The onlookers jumped in and had to pull the two apart as they shouted at each other.

"That is *enough*, Commander Draedon!" Elder Zittas's voice rose above the chaos, silencing the Keepers. Draedon and Valtor were released. "Now, what is the meaning of this unruliness?"

Draedon pointed an accusatory finger at Valtor. "He massacred them. I *never* gave—"

"You never gave what, Commander?" Zittas said, interrupting him. "You ordered Valtor to conduct a raid of Lillyndale, *and* an unscheduled Inspection using whatever force necessary. This was their punishment for rebellion. It appears Captain Valtor carried out your orders to the letter."

Draedon was speechless. "An Inspection? Whatever force necessary? I never—"

"I have your order in writing, Commander. Would you care to read it?"

The paper they had me sign. Draedon's heart sank as he realized what had happened. He knew that he had been played.

Zittas's eyes narrowed, daring Draedon to respond. When he didn't, he cleared his throat and continued loud enough so that everyone could hear. "Your behavior toward Captain Valtor is quite honestly an embarrassment to someone of your rank; however, I am willing to overlook it this one time. You will afford these brave Keepers who have gallantly defended the Church the respect that they are due. Is that understood, Commander?"

Draedon clenched his fists tightly. He nodded slowly, anger burning in his eyes.

"I cannot hear you, Commander."

"Yes, Elder Zittas. I understand perfectly." It took all of Draedon's internal strength to keep him from striking down the pompous man in front of him.

"Very good." Zittas waved his hand. "You are dismissed."

Draedon stole a glance at Valtor who was smiling smugly at him. *Your time will come, Valtor.* He turned sharply to leave the stables.

"One more thing, Commander," Zittas said, forcing Draedon to stop and turn around. "This rebellion is your responsibility. If you cannot gain control of your territory, the Council will have no choice but to relieve you of your command."

So that's what this is about, Draedon realized. *If you can prove that I have lost control, you have the excuse you've been looking for to depose me. Something tells me that you will do whatever you can to help me lose control.*

He drew himself up and stood at attention. Now looking the part of Legion Commander he said, "Thank you, Elder Zittas, for that reminder. You can rest assured that I am very much in control."

Zittas stared at him, trying to discern the meaning of his words. After a moment, he waved Draedon away and turned to talk to Valtor. Draedon turned sharply and exited the stables. Einar joined him. They made their way through the city to Draedon's quarters in silence.

When they arrived, Draedon slammed the door behind him and sat down in his chair facing the fire. Einar settled into the chair next to him. They sat in silence for a long while.

Finally, Draedon spoke. "It's started, Einar."

"Yes, sir. It appears that it has."

"It's too soon!" Exasperated he stood to his feet so fast that his chair fell over. "We are not ready."

"We knew this was going to happen."

"I know, but what happens if we do not succeed?"

"Then we are in the Maker's hands," Einar said simply.

Draedon returned to Einar's side, righted his chair, and sat down again. "I wish I had your faith, Einar."

"I wish I had your hair, sir."

Draedon laughed in spite of himself. The light of the fireplace shone on Einar's balding head. "How do you stay so positive?"

"The way I see it, sir, this world is dark enough. I don't see the point in adding to it."

"Well said, my friend, well said. I'm afraid we are going to be in need of your good humor in the days to come…" His voice trailed as he was lost in thought.

The days to come… He had no idea what they were going to hold. As much as he wanted to believe the words he had spoken to Elder Zittas, he knew that he was very much not in control right now. *I really thought we'd have more time.*

"What do you want me to do, sir?" Einar finally said.

"Keep an eye on the battalion chiefs. We need to know who is with us."

"And Captain Valtor?"

Draedon sighed. "There's nothing we can do about him right now. We know where he stands." He shifted in his seat. "One more thing, Einar…"

"Yes, sir?"

"Put that faith of yours to good use and pray hard. It's going to take a miracle for this to work."

Chapter Twenty-Two

The sun was high in the midday sky when Orron finally awoke. Dried blood and tears caked his eyes, making it painful to open them. *What happened?* Disorientation was replaced by sorrow and anger as the horrors all around him came into focus.

Blood was everywhere. It covered his body and the ground he laid on, and the odor filled the air, overwhelming his senses. His stomach churned violently. As he slowly sat up, he saw the Me'ra's body lying next to him, and tears began to fall anew. All around him lay the remains of the villagers of Lillyndale. *So much death. So much evil.*

The winter wind sang mournfully through the trees. The sun sat in a cloudless sky that on any other day would have struck Orron as a beautiful sign of a promising day. Not this day.

He pulled himself to his feet. Darkness clouded his vision, and he became unsteady. *I'm dehydrated.*

Stumbling as he walked, he made his way to the village well. As he was about to pull up the bucket he saw streaks of blood along the edge. With horror, he realized that there was the body of a small child inside. *They will pay for this.* Fresh anger washed over him.

Turning, he made his way out of the village toward the river. Along the way he saw the bodies of so many he had called friends. When he reached the water's edge, he broke through the thin layer of ice. The water was frigid. He drank as if he had never had a drink in his life.

Once he was sated, he began trying to scrub the dried blood off his skin—a task that proved largely futile. Finally, he gave up and sat back, pulling his cloak around him. He was unsure of what to do next. Though he had not conducted a thorough search of the village, he knew that Mattox was not among the dead. When he had left him the night before, they were many hours from the village and there was no way he could have made the journey on foot anywhere near as fast as Orron had. *I need to find him.*

He sat for a while lost in thought. *What do I tell him? How can we go on without Me'ra? How will we save Ly'ra?* His thoughts were interrupted by the sound of his name being called. Looking up, he saw Mattox approaching through the fields across the river. He was running hard, and even from this distance, he could see the panic on his face. In one hand was his bow; in the other was a large stick.

Orron met him on the bridge. Unable to speak, tears filled his eyes.

"Orron…the house…it's been burned…where—" The blood on Orron's face and the look in his eyes stopped Mattox cold. "Orron, what has happened?" His voice was filled with dread.

"Me'ra…" Orron couldn't bring himself to say it. "The village was attacked by Keepers. I couldn't get here in time. They took Ly'ra."

Mattox's mouth moved, but nothing came out. He sagged against the railing of the bridge. Finally, he whispered, "Not again…"

Orron placed his hand on Mattox's shoulder. "Me'ra...they... Mattox, she's gone." Mattox's eyes filled with horror as he looked past Orron and, for the first time, noticed the bodies littering the ground.

"No, no, no..." Mattox repeated as he ran toward the village. Orron sank to his knees and covered his ears, trying to shut out the cries of agony and rage as Mattox discovered the fate of his loving and cherished wife. *How could the Maker allow this to happen?*

Even with his hands over his ears, Orron could hear and feel Mattox's screams tear through him. It was almost as though he could feel what Mattox was feeling, as if part of him was dying. His body shook with each sob.

Gradually, he began to calm himself. The fear, pain, sadness, and rage began to melt away as peace replaced it. The fire of his righteous anger was still burning brightly, but it was focused, controlled. He knew that justice was his to deal out as he saw fit. This was his task. He could not lose that anger. It had to direct him, focus him like an arrow bearing down on its target. The Age of Reckoning was coming, and he was both prophet and judge.

After a long while, he opened his eyes and lowered his hands. Everything was once again silent. He stood to his feet, and turned toward the village. Craning his head, he tried to pick up any sounds of Mattox. *It's too quiet. Something isn't right.*

He made his way quickly into the village. Me'ra was now covered lovingly head-to-toe with Mattox's cloak. Mattox was nowhere to be found.

Orron closed his eyes, and reached out his senses. He could hear Mattox's heart beating with rage. His eyes snapped open. *Cleric Osbere.*

Yanking his staff from the violator's head, Orron sprinted in the direction of the cleric's manor. *If he is still here, there's no way that the Keepers left him unguarded.*

Upon clearing the village, Orron could see Mattox rapidly approaching the cleric's house that stood on the northwest corner of the lake. Orron pushed himself faster, trying to close the gap. He saw four Keepers exit the manor to confront their approaching attackers.

Mattox reached the house while Orron was still several hundred yards away and attacked the Keepers with vicious savagery. He had discarded the bow and was wielding his makeshift club. The first Keeper that Mattox reached was brained before he could swing his mace. The other three reacted more quickly. It was all Mattox could do to keep their swords at bay with only his stick to defend himself. Still, he drove them back toward the house as screams roared from within him.

As Orron ran, he couldn't help but be amazed at the brute force Mattox was exerting on the more highly trained and skilled swordsman. He was able to meet every thrust and blow with the blinding quickness and power of his club. *Their skills are no match for his vengeance.*

One Keeper dropped his guard, and Mattox dealt him a vicious blow to the head. The other two split up and Mattox fell for the trap. He lunged for one and the other thrust his sword toward Mattox's unprotected back.

The sword never found its mark. Before the Keeper could close the final inches separating Mattox from life and death, Orron deflected the sword with his spear. The Keepers momentum turned his back to Orron. He buried his spear into the Keepers spine, killing him instantly.

Mattox let out a cry as the remaining Keeper found flesh with his sword. Orron turned to see Mattox drop his club, blood running down his right arm where the sword had cut him deeply. Before the Keeper could finish Mattox off, Orron lunged at the Keeper and tackled him to the ground. Their weapons fell several feet from where they landed.

The Keeper was well trained. He rolled hard to his right and Orron's head crashed into the side of the stone manor. Orron saw stars, and his grip relaxed enough for the Keeper to free himself and lunge for his sword. Orron pulled himself to his feet.

"By order of the Council, I have the authority to arrest you, Heretic," the Keeper said haughtily.

Calmly, Orron lowered his hands to his side. He was unarmed facing a skilled swordsman. "You can try."

They stood facing each other, waiting for the other to attack. The Keeper who lunged first. He feinted to Orron's left and tried to attack from the right. Orron waited until the last moment and spun to his left. The sword missed his chest by inches. As the Keeper's momentum carried him past, Orron landed a blow with his left fist to the Keeper's mouth. It wasn't his best shot since he was forced to use his off-hand, but it drew blood.

"You will pay for that, Maggot," the Keeper said, wiping the blood from his chin. "You will share the same fate as the rest of your friends."

Orron's eyes hardened. "No, false Keeper. It is you who has much that you will pay for."

The swordsman spun his sword around and darted at Orron. He once again dodged the blow just in time. This time, he grabbed the Keeper's sword hand. With a savage twist, he shattered the man's wrist. The sword twirled harmlessly away. Before the Keeper could react, Orron spun him around, grabbed his head from behind, and jerked it sideways. The Keeper's neck snapped like a twig, and he fell lifelessly to the ground.

Orron turned to find Mattox was no longer behind him. The front door of the manor was kicked in. He grabbed his staff and hurried up the steps and through the doorway.

The entrance to the manor was a grand foyer filled with tapestries and gilded furniture. A majestic, sweeping staircase led to the second floor. Orron could hear shouting coming from up there. Taking several steps at a time in his long stride, he hurried toward the source of the noise.

He ran down a hall passing several doors on each side before coming to the end of the hall where he burst through an open doorway. Inside, he found Mattox's massive right hand holding Cleric Osbere two feet off the ground by his neck. Unadulterated hatred filled his eyes. Curses spat from his mouth.

"Mattox, no!" Orron ran over and tried to separate them. Without even looking, Mattox batted Orron aside with surprising strength, sending him crashing to the floor.

Orron could taste blood on his lips. "Mattox, this is not the way."

Finally, Mattox turned and acknowledged Orron. "He…you saw what his kind did to my Me'ra."

The cleric's eyes were bulging as he struggled to break Mattox's iron grip. Orron walked over and placed his hand on Mattox's shoulder. "This is not the way of the Maker."

"The way of the Maker!" Mattox roared as he shook the cleric in his hands. "The way of the Maker means nothing to me!"

"I know you are in agony, Mattox. I know, because I can feel it. I am too." He looked Mattox in the eyes. "But I also know that you don't believe that. Let him go. As much as I want him to suffer for what he did, we both know that killing an unarmed man is not what Me'ra would have wanted."

The mention of her name seemed to deflate Mattox. He released his grip on the cleric's throat, who came crashing to the floor, gasping desperately for air. Mattox's shoulders sagged as he walked slowly out of the room.

"You insolent brute," the cleric said between gasps. "I will have you flogged for—" Orron cut him off with a staggering blow to the face with his fist. Blood flowed from the cleric's broken nose.

"Silence! Don't mistake my mercy for more than it is. You *will* pay for what you have done."

"How dare you—"

"Enough!" Orron said as he swung the blade of his staff around and held it inches from the cleric's face. Osbere gulped, and his eyes crossed as he stared down the length of the blade. He did not dare to speak.

"Good. You will remain in here until I see fit to deal with you."

Orron left the room and made his way out of the manor, finding Mattox sitting on the stairs looking out over the lake. He sat down next to him and said nothing. Together they stared out over the water.

Silently they sat for nearly an hour, completely lost in their own thoughts. Finally, Orron spoke softly. "I...I couldn't get here in time to save her. I..." His voice cracked, and he couldn't continue. *If only I could have been faster. If only...*

After several more minutes of silence, Mattox spoke. "You did what you could, Orron, and I thank you for...for killing those demons." Every word seemed like a struggle for Mattox to say.

Orron looked down at his hands that were scratched and covered in a mixture of his own blood and that of his enemies. *So much death. How much more will come?*

"Mattox, I got here just before...before she passed. There's something that Me'ra wanted me to tell you..." Orron hesitated. He knew this would be as hard for him to say, as it would be for Mattox to hear. "She wanted you to know that she loved you so very much."

Mattox began to cry softly.

"She wanted me to tell you that...that you can't give into your hatred."

Mattox stood up and walked a short distance away. Orron waited for him in silence.

"How can she ask that of me?" He threw his hand up and shouted at the sky. "How can you ask me not to hate them?" He looked at Orron. "You saw what those monsters did. I cannot...I will not rest until they all suffer worse than she did!"

"Vengeance and justice will be served in time. I promise you that," Orron said as he walked over and stood in front of Mattox. "But hatred will only destroy you."

"Hatred is all I have left."

"No, Mattox. You still have Ly'ra." He slammed his staff blade-first into the ground. "I made an oath to Me'ra that I *will* rescue her...no matter the cost."

"Aye," Mattox said with resignation in his voice. "Rescuing my Ly'ra is all that matters, but I will not surrender my hatred. Not now, not ever."

Orron let it go. He knew that now was not the time to push Mattox. *How can I? Why shouldn't he hate those monsters?* Even as he thought it, he knew it didn't feel right.

Mattox walked over and picked up a mace from one of the fallen Keepers. He swung it around, apparently pleased with the way that it felt in his hands. "So we go to Farovale?"

"No, right now we wait here."

"Wait here? How can we just sit here while Ly'ra—"

"Mattox, you have to trust me. They will not harm her while we are free."

"How could you possibly know that?"

"I just do. There's a lot about me that you don't understand. I don't even understand it, but you just have to trust me. Saving Ly'ra was what I was made to do. It's why I am here."

Mattox regarded him closely. "So why wait here?"

Motioning toward the manor, Orron replied, "We are going to send him to Farovale with word of what I have done here. They will send a company of Keepers—maybe more—to arrest us."

"And that's a good thing? There are only two of us." Mattox shook his head. "We can't take on a whole company by ourselves."

Orron pulled his staff out of the ground and said, "We will not be alone."

Chapter Twenty-Three

"Ouch! Watch what you're doing, girl!" snarled a weathered, old Keeper, snapping Kor'lee out of her daydream.

"Oh, I'm sorry." She forced herself to concentrate on stitching up the deep cut that he had earned on the practice field. "There, that should do it. Try to keep it dry."

"In this cursed weather?"

"I know, I know. Just try your best."

The soldier scooted off the table. When he exited the front door, a blast of cold air shot through Kor'lee, chilling her to the bone. The air stirred up the foul odors of the cramped healer's ward, which set her stomach on edge. The cold, the smells, everything about this place she hated. She longed for the clean air and freedom of the forest. *Is it the forest I really long for?*

Kor'lee blushed to herself. Since the Mid-Summer Festival, her forays into the woods had been for more than just a need for freedom. Raulin had become a constant companion on her long walks. It felt so good finally to have someone to talk to, someone who understood her misery, her discomfort with the world she was forced to live in. *Friends…that's all we are…*

In truth, she didn't really know how she felt about Raulin. She trusted him, admired him, cared about him deeply as a friend. But was there more? She didn't doubt that if situations were different, maybe. *Father would never approve.*

Just the thought of her father made her uneasy. She had heard rumors of his confrontation with Valtor when he had returned from his rather secretive mission. Something was going on, but no matter how hard she tried, she couldn't get her father to talk to her about it.

Even after her encounter in the alley with her father, things still were uneasy between them. She had grown to accept his role as the commander of these men that were guilty of so many awful atrocities, but she couldn't reconcile his proclaimed good intentions with what she saw with her eyes and heard from Raulin's stories. There was one thing that she did know. The Council was deeply evil, and someday she would be forced to make a choice. *My father or what I believe to be right.*

She shook her head and busied herself with cleaning up the area where she had stitched up the Keeper. Though she feared that this "someday" might be approaching sooner than she was ready for, she knew that she still had a job to do.

The bell above the front door chimed as someone entered. *Not another patient*, she thought to herself. It had been a very long day. Her heart sunk even lower when she saw who had entered.

"Good afternoon, fair Kor'lee," Valtor said as he came over and stood uncomfortably close to her. "You are as lovely as ever."

Keep looking at me like that, and you won't find me to be so lovely when I... She forced herself to calm down and put on her most patronizing smile. "And a pleasure it is to see you as well, Captain."

"I trust this cold hasn't been too uncomfortable for you?"

"It's been unseasonably cold, and as you can see," she motioned around the room, "they don't give us much heat to work with in here. But I've managed just fine."

Kor'lee felt very uncomfortable with the way that Valtor was staring at her. He was probing her. She was used to the lustful stares of Keepers by now, but there was something else in his eyes, something sinister.

"Good, good. I'm glad I found you in here. You've been… absent lately. What have you been up to?"

Her heart skipped a beat. *Does he know?* "Oh, you know…this and that," she said, waving her hand dismissively. "Erez has kept me quite busy around the city."

"Has he now?" he said, raising an eyebrow.

"Yes, in fact, you will have to forgive me. I have to get to the eastern ward to assist with some procedures." She motioned like she was going to leave, but Valtor was blocking the narrow aisle between the surgical tables.

"Of course, Kor'lee. I won't keep you. I can see that you are busy." He turned his body to allow her to pass. The tight aisle forced her to brush up against him uncomfortably. As she walked away he added, "I'm sure this is a hard enough time for you, what with the fallout from your father's…actions."

That stopped her in her tracks. "What are you talking about?"

"Surely you have heard about the messy business in Lillyndale." He stared at her, an evil smile twitched at the corner of his mouth.

"No, Valtor, I have not," she said impatiently. *He's enjoying this.*

He looked around conspiratorially and lowered his voice. "Well, you didn't hear it from me, but your father is quickly losing control of this territory."

"What on earth are you talking about?"

"There has been a rebellion brewing in Lillyndale for quite some time."

"A rebellion? In Lillyndale?" She laughed aloud.

"I thought the same thing myself, but your father ordered me to investigate. What I found wasn't pretty." He closed the distance between them and talked quietly, as if to prevent others from listening in. "A group of men have been providing resources for the Forest Bandits. They have been planning a full scale assault on the Keepers."

Raulin had told her no such thing. *He would have told me.* She shook her head, confident that what Valtor said was a lie. "I have a hard time believing that."

"So did your father, which is why things have gotten so out of hand. You don't have to worry, though. At your father's orders, I—shall we say—*eradicated* the threat."

She shuddered, afraid of the implications of his words. "What do you mean?"

"Your father ordered me to use *extreme* force to quell the rebellion."

Kor'lee backed away. "Wh–what do you mean by extreme force?"

Valtor sighed as if the memory pained him. "Well, I wasn't in agreement with your father on this one. He wanted to make an example of Lillyndale to discourage any further treason against the Church. At his order, I marched to Lillyndale to eliminate the threat and collect all girls eligible for the Inspection next year as punishment."

A sick feeling settled into her stomach. "What happened?"

"Not surprisingly, they resisted. Things got ugly." He shook his head, feigning disapproval at what had occurred. "It pains me to say that much blood was shed."

"And the villagers?"

"They are no more."

Kor'lee felt like she was going to be sick. "You…monster."

He bristled. "*Me?* A monster? I was simply carrying out your father's orders!"

"My father would never—"

"He most certainly did. I have his signature to prove it." He pulled a parchment out of his cloak and threw it down onto the table next to him.

With shaking hands, Kor'lee opened it. To her horror, her father's signature sat at the bottom of a document detailing the punishment that Lillyndale was to receive. She was speechless, unable to fathom the atrocities her father had authorized. Memories of the happy men, women, and children from the festival flashed through her mind. *How could he?*

After a moment, Valtor continued. "I'm sorry you had to find out this way, Kor'lee, but your father did the right thing. The threat is eliminated, and now we have the information we need to eradicate those Heretics that parade around in the forest."

Her head snapped up a little too quickly, and she knew that she was in danger of giving herself away. She didn't care. Her eyes brimmed with tears. *I have to get out of this place.* She threw the piece of paper at Valtor and ran out of the ward. As she left, she could feel Valtor's evil smile boring into her back.

Tears flowed freely as she ran haphazardly through the city, crashing into people along the way. She didn't have a plan. All she knew was that she couldn't stay there anymore.

She ran and ran, not paying attention to where she was headed. Her feet guided her as her heart broke with each innocent face of the villagers of Lillyndale that came to her mind. *How could he do this? How could he sentence so many innocent people to death?*

After running for almost an hour, she slid to a stop in front of the Great Cathedral. Her side felt like it was going to burst as she leaned against a wall panting heavily. The ornate doors seemed to beckon her, drawing her toward the opulent place of worship, a supposed place of healing. She stumbled up the stairs, through the doors, and nearly plowed into the cleric that stood just inside the entrance.

"Your head and shoes, madam."

She just looked at him with a blank stare.

"You are to cover your head and remove your shoes. This is a holy place." His voice was unkind as he looked at her as if she was not worth his time.

She did as he commanded and made her way into the sanctuary. Rows and rows of oiled, wooden benches filled the floor. At the front of the sanctuary, there ran a long altar the width of the room. It was made of wood with gold etchings of mysterious shapes and symbols. She was once told that it was intentionally made to be uncomfortable to kneel on so that those who prayed would be "uncomfortable in the sight of their Maker" or some such nonsense. Steps led up to a platform upon which stood a dais where the clerics would conduct the weekly services. High above the platform hung the symbol of the Keepers made of solid gold.

With the sun setting, the room grew darker by the minute. Faint light streamed in through ornate stained glass windows. Candles ran along the walls, casting shadows that danced eerily on the walls. The potent smell of incense filled the air.

Making her way down the long center aisle, she found a seat in a pew near the front. Sitting there in the supposed home of the Maker, she had never felt more alone. A sob escaped her throat as she buried her face in her hands. A cleric who was sitting in the front conducting his evening prayers shushed her with annoyance.

She wanted to scream at him, at the Maker, at her father, at anyone that would hear her. Anger, pain, frustration, guilt, and sadness felt like they were going to tear her apart.

Is this really what life is about? Emptiness? Suffering? Injustice?

She looked to the heavens, searching for some sign, any indication that the Maker was there, that He cared at all. *Where are You? How could You let this happen?*

Finally, when she opened her eyes she found that she was alone in the dark Sanctuary. The sun had set, and the candles were the only light in the room. A chill crept down her spine; the room seemed to swallow her in a malevolent evil. She had come here to find hope, comfort. She had come to find the Maker. After all, this was His supposed dwelling place. Instead, she found emptiness. *The Maker does not reside here.*

Wiping the tears from her eyes, she stood to her feet and gave the gilded altar one last look. She knew what she had to do. *If I do nothing, I am just as bad they are.*

She left the Cathedral and made her way toward the officers' quarters. She was relieved to find that her father was not home. Quickly, she gathered as many items as she dared. Speed and efficiency were her objectives. She packed some clothing in her knapsack. Donning pants and a wool shirt better suited for the forest, she covered herself with a warm wool cloak to hide the outfit that would have raised suspicion at this late hour. Lastly, she grabbed her bow and a quiver full of arrows.

With one last look at the room that she had called home for the last six years, she headed for the kitchen to grab some bread, some dried meat, and a flask full of water. Now that her supplies were packed, she headed for the front door. Just as she reached for the handle, her father walked in.

"Kor'lee..." he said, startled to see her standing there. He noticed the pack and quiver on her back and the bow in her hand. His eyes darkened. "Where do you think you're going at this hour?

"I am leaving, Father," she said angrily.

"Leaving? At this hour? I don't think so!" He crossed his arms, blocking the doorway.

"I *am* leaving. I can't stay here anymore!" Fresh tears began to fall.

A look of concern crossed Draedon's face. "What happened, Kor'lee?"

"It doesn't matter. I am old enough to make my own decisions."

"Kor'lee, talk to me."

Her eyes filled with anger. "I am done talking to you!"

"Why? What have I done?"

"You know what you've done!"

He raised his arms in confusion. "I have no idea what you're talking about!"

"Really?" she said, challenging him with her eyes. "What, did you think I wouldn't find out?"

"Find out about what?"

She almost couldn't bring herself to say it. "What you did... what you ordered your men to do...in Lillyndale."

Draedon sagged against the wall. His eyes filled with pain. "Kor'lee, you don't understand, I—"

"No, Father! Stop it! I cannot listen to any more of your lies!"

"Kor'lee—"

"You are a monster! Mother never would have stood by you this long, and neither will I!" Brushing past him, she ran outside and down the street toward the North Gate. She could hear her father calling out for her and trying to pursue her, but she was much faster. Weaving between buildings, she ran with all her might, trying to escape the pain her father's actions had caused.

Before long, she was able to lose him. She stopped to gather herself, drawing her hood overhead. Once she was composed, she made her way to the north gate. When she was confident that she had not been followed, she made her way to the entrance of her secret tunnel and escaped down the stairs. Once in the tunnel, she ran as fast as she could to the end where she quickly exited into the forest.

She stood for a moment unsure of what to do next. Now free of the confines of the city, the weight of her decision to flee began to settle in. Her pulse quickened as she accepted the reality of her situation. *Anyone who is not with the Church is the enemy of the Church. I am on my own now.*

Pushing her fear aside, she made her way deeper into the forest. *No,* she thought to herself. *I am not alone. I have Raulin.*

Chapter Twenty-Four

Orron wiped the sweat from his eyes as he stopped to catch his breath. The gray light of early morning lit the sky as he and Mattox prepared the graves of the fallen villagers. Despite the chill in the winter air, he still found himself sweating from the exertion of digging. At Mattox's insistence, they had prepared Me'ra's body at Daedar's Mill for burial immediately after the encounter at Cleric Osbere's manor. As was the custom of the people of Lillyndale, Me'ra would be laid to rest with Mattox's ancestors in the fields next to their sheep farm.

By the time they had finished preparing Me'ra's body night had fallen. Orron had retired to bed while Mattox kept watch over his beloved's body all night. It had been a restless night for Orron, and when he finally awoke before dawn, he found Mattox already digging the graves for his fallen comrades just outside the village. Orron found another shovel and joined him. Neither spoke as they carried out the task.

The day wore on. Time seemed to move slowly. Digging the graves was difficult work, but once they were finished, he knew that the worst of it lay ahead. Instead of digging individual holes to inter the bodies, they had decided to dig four large pits. It wasn't because they were lazy. There were too many scattered body parts to identify what bodies they came from. Their only choice was to bury the villagers together.

The sun was beginning to lower in the sky when they finally finished. Exhausted, Orron went to the river to replenish his fluids. Once he drank his fill, he sat down to rest. Mattox soon joined him.

"What are we going to do with the bodies of the Keepers?" Orron asked.

"They stay where they lay."

Orron nodded in agreement. It was considered a great insult to leave the bodies of one's enemies on the field of battle. Right now, Orron couldn't find the strength to think about digging any more graves. *After what they did to Me'ra they don't deserve any better.*

Mattox stood to his feet. "It is time to take Me'ra home."

Orron followed him back into the village where they attached a plow horse to the cart that bore Me'ra's body. She was now wrapped in a fine linen cloth that they had found in one of the villager's homes.

They slowly made their way out of the village and through the hills toward Mattox's farm. Neither spoke as they walked, both lost in their thoughts. It was hard for Orron to imagine that he had only known Me'ra for just one year. In that time, they had grown so very close. Her kindness, gentleness, encouragement, and grace had meant so much. *Now she is gone.*

Orron knew that where she had gone was a much better place. The suffering and agony of her last minutes on earth were long since replaced by the wonders of the Kingdom of the Maker. *The same place that I once called home.*

Though bits and pieces of his memory had begun to return after his encounter with Arlas, there was still much that he did not remember. Fragments of memories like shards of a broken mirror hung at the edge of his consciousness. He now knew who he was and what his mission was, but there was still much of his identity that he had yet to rediscover. It was frustrating, and the added loss of Me'ra had only furthered his sense of loneliness.

The sun was low in the early evening sky when they arrived at the farm. It took them just over fifteen minutes to dig her grave. When they finished, Mattox lifted her body off the cart and placed it gently in the ground. He knelt next to her body. Orron joined him.

They were both silent for a while. Orron was unsure of the customs of an official burial ceremony. With the villagers, they had just silently laid the bodies in the massive graves and covered them with dirt. This one was different. He felt that something should be said. Just as he was about to begin a prayer Mattox spoke up softly and mournfully.

"Most Holy Maker, I confess that I don't understand You or Your ways. First, you took my A'ra…now my Me'ra…" His voice faltered as fresh tears streamed from his eyes. "I want to hate You. I want to turn my back on You…but I…I know that's not what Me'ra would have wanted." He sighed and shook his head.

"No, Maker, You deserve more from me than that. That much Me'ra would have said. I never felt like I deserved Me'ra to begin with. Aye, maybe I didn't, but you saw fit to give me the happiest twenty-three years of my life, and for that, I am more thankful than I can express."

Mattox raised his eyes to search the heavens. The sun cast an orange glow in the clear sky as it settled onto the horizon. Orron couldn't help but notice the beauty contrasting the pain of this moment. Mattox cleared his throat and continued.

"I know that she is with You now, and I have but a few requests. Tell her that I…that I love her. Tell her that I won't give up again, not like last time. Tell her that I will see her soon." His words finished in a whisper. He kissed her linen-covered head one last time and slowly got to his feet. Grabbing a shovel full of dirt, he began to cover her body. Orron joined him, and Me'ra was committed to her final resting place.

"Goodbye, love," Mattox said as he smoothed the last shovel full of dirt over her grave. It was almost completely dark now, and with their old house burned to the ground, they had no choice but to make the trek back through the hills to the village.

When they reached the village, Orron turned to Mattox. "I have business to attend to with Osbere."

"Aye, I figured you would." To Orron's surprise he added, "I am going to sit this one out. I need to be alone. Well, that and I don't trust myself around him."

"Mattox, you should know my intentions. I plan to release him."

Mattox raised an eyebrow, but waited for Orron to explain.

"As I said yesterday, we need to draw some of the Keepers out and deal them a blow that will strike fear in their hearts. I plan to send Osbere to them with a threat that will expedite their response."

Mattox shook his head angrily. "It's bad enough that I let you stop me yesterday, but now you plan to release that man? He deserves to pay for what he has done!"

Orron looked at Mattox calmly. "I know that it is hard for you trust me, but he *will* pay for what he has done, just not right now."

Mattox fumed but did not argue. "Fine, do as you wish. I will be in the mill."

Mattox stormed off, leaving Orron alone. He sighed and headed to the Manor where he had confined Osbere. Before leaving to prepare Me'ra's body the day before, he had locked Osbere in the cellar beneath his manor. With the only exit effectively barred, it had served as a working dungeon.

Gripping his staff tightly in his right hand, he opened the cellar door. A single candle mounted on the wall provided a minuscule amount of light. Osbere was curled up in the fetal position on the floor in the far corner. He jumped when he saw Orron enter.

"P-please don't hurt me! I had nothing to—"

"Silence! Your excuses are as meaningless to me as your life." He stood towering over the shivering cleric.

"I am going to make this rather simple. You are going to tell me what happened in the village. Then I will decide your punishment."

"I told you, I had nothing to—" Orron struck the cleric in the side with his staff.

"You had *everything* to do with what happened. You and the perversion of a church that you serve." His voice echoed in the stone-walled room. "I will give you one more chance. Tell me what happened."

With a shaky voice, Osbere spoke haltingly. "The Keepers arrived around midnight while I was fast asleep. I was summoned to appear immediately in the town square. When I arrived most of the villagers had been gathered."

"Who led this attack?"

"Captain Valtor."

Orron immediately recognized the name. *The man who attacked Ly'ra at the Festival.*

"Go on."

"The Captain presented me with papers that detailed a plot against the Church—a rebellion led by the villagers of Lillyndale."

"A rebellion? Led by whom?"

"I…I don't remember the names."

Orron growled and raised his staff to strike Osbere again.

"Wait!" he cried. "I don't remember *all* of the names, but I remember the man the informant identified as the leader. His name was Mattox."

Informant? Mattox was leading no rebellion.

"Who was this informant?"

"His name was Zafilo."

That caught Orron off guard. *Zafilo? Why would he turn on his friends and family?*

"Why did Zafilo do this?"

"I don't know. Honest, I don't. Captain Valtor seemed to be the one who was driving this whole thing."

"What happened next?"

"Zafilo's father, Daedar, tried to stop him. Valtor struck him down with sword and Zafilo immediately afterward." He shuttered at the memory. "They gathered the remainder of the conspirators in the center. Captain Valtor made me read a decree from the Council and Commander Draedon stating that all girls eligible for the upcoming Inspection year were going to be taken as penance for Lillyndale's rebellion."

Orron gripped his staff tightly in his right hand. *Ly'ra.*

"A big man—Morven I think—jumped up from where they were holding the conspirators and attacked. I believe one of the girls taken was his daughter. Madness ensued." His eyes grew wide with terror, and Orron thought the cleric might be sick. "The Keepers…they…they slaughtered them all…every man, woman, and child."

"And what did you do during all of this?"

"I…I hid." Even in the dim light Orron could see Osbere trying to summon his pride. "You may see me as evil, but I do not condone wanton violence."

Orron struck him again. "You don't *condone* it? And what did you do to stop it?"

"What could I have done?" he said, rubbing his bruised ribs.

"Are you not a cleric of the supposed One True Church of the Maker? If you will not stand up for the innocent, who will?" His anger burned hotly.

"They were not innocent." Even as he said it, Orron could see the regret in his eyes. Orron raised his staff and ejected the blade. Twirling it around his head, he brought it down swiftly. The cleric screamed in pain as the blade sliced a gash across his cheek. It was not deep but blood dripped down his face.

"How dare you presume to judge the innocence of men when there is so much blood on your hands." Orron's voice was cold and harsh. "It is the Church who is lacking in innocence. This is why I have come. The Age of Reckoning has begun."

He pulled back his hood, and for the first time, the cleric saw his head and face. At the mention of the Age of Reckoning, all color drained from Osbere. The wildness in Orron's eyes spoke more threat than his words could have.

"You...you can't be..." His mouth fell open in fear.

"I am that which you fear most. I am a True Keeper and the Assessor of your guilt." The weight of his words seemed to deflate the cleric.

Orron withdrew the blade and stood up straight with both hands on his staff. His eyes burned with righteous anger. "You will share in the same fate as those whose hearts have become twisted with greed, lust, and thirst for power. The day of your reign of evil has come to an end. I have come to answer the cry of the righteous. The Maker has heard their cries and has seen your injustice. He has decided that the time for your reckoning has come."

His voice grew with each word. It was as if he were watching a scene play out from a distance. A great and powerful voice was speaking through him, and he was merely the mouth. In the darkness, his shadows seemed to grow as his presence filled the small room.

"You will go to Farovale where you will issue this warning. Burn these words in your heart for they will be your salvation or your doom." His voice rumbled like thunder, reverberating off the stone walls. Osbere shook with terror, his eyes wide open and mouth fixed in a noiseless scream.

"Repent of your sins, lay down your swords, and you will be spared. A great war like Edelyndia has never known is coming like a thunderous storm. The righteous will rise against the darkness, and the Great Light will prevail. All who stand against it will taste blood and suffering. The anger of the Maker burns like a fire that will consume all who do the work of the Fallen. Now is the time. The choice is yours. Repent and you will live. Fight, and you will die. The Age of Reckoning has begun."

Deafening silence filled the room. He was nearly as shaken as the cleric whimpering on the floor. The power that had coursed through him began to ebb. Never had he experienced anything so equally exhilarating and terrifying. It took a conscious effort to keep his hands from shaking.

Finally, he spoke again, more quietly this time. "Now, go and share that message with all who will listen in Farovale. Fail in this mission, and you will be the first to feel my wrath."

The cleric was too scared to move. Orron grabbed him by the back of his cloak, and Osbere screamed in terror. Roughly, he dragged the cleric up the stairs of the cellar in his mighty hands and threw him into the snow.

"Go! And pray that our paths do not cross soon for that will be the day of your destruction."

Without saying a word, the cleric stumbled toward the village and the road to Farovale that lay beyond. Orron knew that the cleric would finish his task. The fear in his eyes told him that the sniveling little man would not dare defy him again.

When the cleric was out of sight, Orron fell to his knees and closed his eyes. Now that he was alone, he allowed the shaking to overtake him. *What was that?* Even as he asked himself the question, he knew the answer. *The Maker.*

Deep within his soul, he heard a voice speaking to him. It rumbled with ancient power and wisdom. It was wild, untamed, and immensely good and just. The very sound of it brought tears to his eyes. For hours, he sat intently listening as the Maker spelled out what lay ahead and how to face it. Orron felt a peace flood through his spirit as he let go of his pride and fear. He knew that there was really only one way they could succeed, the Way of the Maker, and now Orron knew his plan.

Dawn began to break when he finally opened his eyes and stood to his feet. With a new resolve and purpose to his step, he made his way back to the mill. Mattox was sitting in front of the hearth when he arrived. He looked like he hadn't slept at all.

He barely turned his head when Orron sat next to him. Minutes passed as they sat in silence. Finally, he turned to look at Orron and did a double take as he noticed something different about his appearance.

"What happened, lad?"

"I encountered the Maker."

Mattox said nothing as he eyed Orron carefully. He looked back at the fire.

"Is Osbere gone?"

"Yes. He is headed to Farovale to deliver a message."

"Aye, and what message is that?"

"A war is coming. I have come to rain judgment down upon the Council," he said matter-of-factly.

Mattox studied him for a moment, taking in this bold statement.

"The Council? Lad, you *are* a mystery! How can—"

"Mattox, you need to know that this is much bigger than avenging Me'ra. We *will* rescue Ly'ra, but I will not stop until the Council is brought to justice."

Mattox remained silent. Orron could see him processing what he had just told him. Mattox didn't know what had happened to Orron in the clearing. He didn't know about Arlas or Orron's past. There's no way he could have. Still, he seemed to trust him. That meant more to Orron than he could express.

Finally Mattox spoke, "Orron, I admit that I do not always understand you." He ran his hand through his long beard. "I have spent too much of my life trying to do things my way, and all it has gotten me is…well, it hasn't gotten me far. Even if it costs me my life, I will help you rescue Ly'ra and see this through."

He offered his hand to Orron who shook it, sealing their pact. Orron knew that this was a significant oath for Mattox and a significant responsibility for Orron to bear. By offering his hand, Mattox had offered his faith and trust.

"What do we do next?" Mattox asked.

Orron gazed into the fire. "We need to prepare ourselves and fortify the village. The Keepers will come in force."

"Aye, and we will be ready." Orron was struck by Mattox's certainty and faith. His resolve was inspiring.

"Yes, Mattox. We *will* be ready. When they come, they shall taste a defeat like they have never known."

CHAPTER TWENTY-FIVE

Kor'lee stared across the rickety-looking bridge that spanned the rushing Havenshae River. Despite the freezing temperatures, the swift current of the river prevented it from freezing completely. In most cases, such as this bend, it did not freeze at all. Though she had crossed this bridge numerous times since Raulin had first showed it to her months ago, this was her first crossing alone.

She looked up at the slowly brightening sky. It looked like it would be a beautiful day. The air smelled of pine trees, and despite her trepidation over crossing the bridge, she was still able to admire the beauty around her in the early morning light. It had been a long journey through the night; all that stood between her and the final short leg of her journey was this obstacle in front of her.

The bridge was a crude structure. A long, slender, fallen tree lay across the river. Above it and a little to the side, a thick rope spanned the river, serving as a handhold. Raulin and his bandits had chosen this section as their crossing because it was well concealed by dense forest growth. Though the road to Lillyndale followed closely to the river, this particular bend was further from the road than any other stretch. It was also one of the narrowest spots, though at this moment, the distance seemed pretty daunting to Kor'lee.

Slowly and carefully, she started out across the makeshift bridge. Gripping the rope tightly in her right hand, her left arm was extended, clutching her bow to help give her balance. She inched her way along the branch, shuffling her feet, too afraid to pick them up.

Just as she reached the center, a gust of frigid wind tore across the river, sending a shiver down her spine.

Her balance wavered.

She struggled to remain upright. Her left foot slipped off the log, and her grip on the rope was all that kept her from tumbling into the water. She cried out in fear as her heart raced.

"What's taking you so long?" said a voice across the river.

She was gripping the rope for dear life, bent over at the waist. Her left leg was off the log and extended along with her left arm as she stared at the rushing water beneath her. As subtly as she could, Kor'lee glanced up to see Raulin standing across the bridge staring at her with his usual cocky smile. A freshly killed doe was draped across his shoulders. She realized that she probably looked ridiculous.

"Just enjoying the view," she replied.

"If you don't mind hurrying up, it's a bit early in the morning for me to be standing out here in the cold, especially when I know there's a perfectly good breakfast waiting for me back at the fortress."

"Well, don't let me keep you," she said with as much annoyance as she could muster. "Of course, if you knew how to build a halfway decent bridge, I'd be across by now."

"My sincerest apologies, m'lady. We are but simple men. By all means, build a better one if you know so much about bridges."

Kor'lee smiled despite the precariousness of her situation. Raulin always knew how to distract her and make her smile. *Maybe that's why I came running to you in the first place.*

Slowly, she righted herself. After taking a deep breath, she continued across the bridge. Raulin kept making a show of impatience, but she knew that he was as worried about her safety as she was. When she reached the end of the bridge, Raulin dropped the doe on the ground, and she leapt off into Raulin's arms. Safe in his embrace, she could no longer contain the rush of emotions that had plagued her throughout her nightlong journey through the woods. Tears flowed freely as she sobbed into his chest.

Raulin held her for a while in silence, stroking her hair. Finally, he spoke. "What happened, Kor'lee? Surely the bridge wasn't that upsetting."

"No...it's my father..." she said through choked sobs. "He's done something terrible. I just had to get out of that cursed city."

He held her out at arm's length so he could look in her eyes. "Well, you are safe here," he said, gesturing to the forest around him, "in *my* kingdom."

She laughed despite herself.

"Now that's a sound I'd rather hear. Let's get back to the fortress where we have some warm food waiting for us."

She nodded, and Raulin picked up the doe. They made their way down a barely visible path. Raulin filled her in on what had been happening in the woods since her last visit almost a week ago. It had been a quiet week. Winter had slowed the activity of the Keepers, which provided the Forest Bandits few opportunities to raid. Still, there were other ways they could be a thorn in the Council's side. Winter was often a time that Raulin used for recruiting new people to his cause. Most of their short journey was filled with conversation of the outlying villages that were nestled along the western edge of the Avolyndas mountain range.

The "fortress" to which Raulin was referring was little more than a collection of huts and tree houses nestled in a grove of massive, old trees that helped to provide a natural defensive perimeter. A large, swiftly moving creek cut through the northern edge of their forest bastion.

Despite its rough qualities, to Kor'lee it had become a sanctuary from her life in Farovale. Whenever she had been able to manage it, she had escaped into the woods with Raulin, enjoying long walks as they talked for hours. He was the first companion with whom she had been able to be herself in years. When her father's duties took him outside of Farovale on a few occasions, she had snuck out and stayed for a night or two among the Bandits. Raulin, always the gentleman, had set up a hut for her to give her complete privacy.

When they arrived, most of the fifty or so men were just beginning to stir. Bruschian walked over to greet them as they entered the camp.

"Greetings, fair Kor'lee," boomed the big man. Despite his imposing stature, Kor'lee found him to be a very gentle man and a fiercely loyal friend. "To what do we owe the pleasure of your company?"

Sensing her unwillingness to respond, Raulin interjected. "Why do you think? With all the savages living in that heathen city, she has been craving some real refinement—the sort only found in my fair kingdom." He winked at Kor'lee and motioned toward Bruschian with his thumb. "Present company excluded, of course."

"Hey…" Bruschian protested, feigning offense.

"Don't worry, Bruschian," Kor'lee said reassuringly. "You are my favorite brute in the whole world." She gave him a quick hug, which he returned awkwardly.

"All right, all right, break it up you two," Raulin said as he pulled Kor'lee away. "If you are done trying to woo the lady, we would much appreciate some breakfast. And if you don't mind," he said as he shoved the doe into Bruschian's arms, "please do something with this beast. I'm tired of carrying it around."

"Too heavy for you, little man?" Bruschian said with a mocking smile. "Why, this tiny thing must have been born yesterday."

"It is a fully grown doe, thank you very much," Raulin protested.

Bruschian laughed, slinging the doe over his shoulder as if it were as light as a feather. He motioned for them to follow as he walked over to the large fire pit located in the center of the camp. An elderly man was cooking venison stew. Raulin ladled a bowl for Kor'lee and himself, and they walked to the edge of camp to sit down on the gnarled roots of a towering hemlock.

After eating in silence for a while, Raulin spoke softly. "Though I am always happy to see you, Kor'lee, I sense that this visit is different from the others. What happened?"

As quickly and concisely as she could, she shared with Raulin everything that Valtor had told her. When she was done, she looked at Raulin and saw his jaw clenched in anger. Tears streaked down her face.

"I am so sorry, Raulin. I guess you were right about my father. I just didn't want to believe it. You must hate me for being his daughter." She turned away in shame.

Raulin put his arm around her and drew her close. "Kor'lee, I could never hate you. What your father did, what he stands for… that's not on you." He leaned back and looked into her eyes. "You are not your father, Kor'lee. I mean it. You are so much better than he could ever be." Then, almost awkwardly, he added, "Don't ever doubt my feelings for you."

Kor'lee remained silent. *What* are *your feelings for me?* Though it was pretty obvious that they both flirted with a romantic interest in each other, her life in Farovale complicated things to the point that she just pushed those feelings aside. *But I'm not in Farovale anymore…*

"I can't ever go back there, Raulin."

"Good," he said with a smile. "My kingdom is always sunnier when you are in it."

She shook her head. "I'm being serious, Raulin. Farovale is no longer my home, but you know my father will come after me."

"Let him try."

"Maybe I shouldn't stay here. I don't want anyone to be hurt because of me."

"Nonsense!" Raulin said. "My kingdom is a sanctuary to all who seek it. I insist. As king of this forest, you are to stay here as my loyal citizen."

"Um…your citizen?" she said as she wiped her eyes.

Raulin turned red.

"Alright, how about as my friend?"

"Just your friend?" Her heart skipped a beat and her face flushed as the words escaped her mouth before she had time to think. Her brazenness surprised her.

"Well…I…um…" Raulin was flustered by her response. Despite her own embarrassment, she couldn't help but smile. Unable to find his words, Raulin changed the subject.

"My scouts saw Valtor's company head for Lillyndale on horseback two nights ago, but we just assumed it was a routine mission. I never thought it could have been anything this serious."

At the mention of Valtor, Kor'lee was suddenly serious again. "What should we do?"

"I'm inclined to go visit Lillyndale to see if there are any survivors. I need to see this atrocity for myself."

"I'm going with you," Kor'lee declared.

"Kor'lee, I don't think that—"

She stood up defiantly. "I am not a frail little girl, Raulin."

He stood with his hands raised in surrender. "I didn't mean that. It's just that…well, I've seen the wake that a Keeper massacre can leave," he said bitterly. "It's a sight that I would never want someone dear to me to see."

"I *must* go. I have to see what my father has done."

Raulin gave in. "I understand. I'm going to talk to Bruschian. He should come with us. Why don't you go put your things in your hut? We will leave shortly."

Kor'lee made her way to her simple hut. It was a small, one room structure set between two of the massive roots of a hemlock tree. It was surprisingly well insulated from the winter weather. In the center was a small fire pit. A bed lay in the corner.

She laid her pack on the bed and pulled out her water flask, reminding herself to refill it before she left. Slinging her quiver over her back, she grabbed her bow and headed back out to meet the others.

Raulin was waiting alongside Bruschian next to the fire pit in the center of the camp. Both wore their swords and Raulin carried a bow at his side. Kor'lee joined them as Raulin was giving parting orders to one of his men. He turned to Kor'lee.

"Shall we be off?"

She nodded her head in assent.

"Alright then," Raulin said grimly. "Let's go see what evils the Keepers have wrought this time."

Chapter Twenty-Six

Orron surveyed the fruits of their labor as the sun nestled into the horizon. He had spent the last two days with Mattox turning the village into a defendable position. Though there was much work yet to be done, he was pleased with their progress.

The village was setup in a way that provided some natural defenses. The houses and other buildings were built fairly close together, so they formed a sort of corridor with houses facing each other on each side of the square. The square was located in the center of town with houses on each side. On opposite ends of the square stood the village church and town hall.

They had spent the day felling trees that would be placed as barriers between the buildings. This would force the Keepers to attack from either end. In doing so, Orron would have some control over the battlefield.

He had no idea what to expect from the Keepers when they did come. The only thing he was certain of was that they *would* come and in force. He was counting on their arrogance and overconfidence in their numbers. In any case, he knew that victory would be his.

Orron walked through the village to the square. He found Mattox sitting on the steps to the church carving sticks into sharp points.

"What's your plan with that?"

"This?" he said lifting the stick. "I figured that adding these to our barriers might encourage the Keepers to avoid them."

"Good idea," Orron said as he sat down next to him. He pulled out a knife and joined Mattox in his task.

"How many do you think they will send?" Mattox asked.

"I don't know…a company…maybe two."

Mattox whistled. "Two hundred against two?"

"We will succeed, Mattox."

"Aye, I don't doubt your resolve, lad. But two hundred…"

Orron knew that Mattox was strong of heart. It wasn't fear of death that concerned him but a fear of failing Ly'ra if they were to fall to the Keepers.

"We will succeed," Orron repeated confidently.

"When do you think they will come?"

"Well, by my best guess we still have a couple of days. Osbere said that the soldiers they left behind were supposed to capture the two of us when we returned from the hunt. They probably expected the smoke from the farm to draw us back to the village by now, if not by this morning."

Orron looked at the stick in his hand, testing the sharpness. Pleased, he moved on to another. "My guess is that they will be expecting them to bring us in tomorrow morning at the latest. Osbere should be arriving around that time. What he tells them should stir the hornet's nest. I would expect a quick retaliation."

Mattox eyed him carefully. "What did you tell Osbere?"

Orron just stared at the stick he was working on. *Should I tell him?* He wasn't sure if Mattox was ready to hear the truth about who he was. *Would he blame me for not saving A'ra, or even Me'ra or Ly'ra?* He decided now wasn't the time.

"I issued a warning...a challenge to the legitimacy of the Church. Combined with the death of the Keepers here, it is an insult they will not soon forget."

Mattox seemed to accept that. "What do we do if—*after* we defeat the Keepers here?"

Orron thought for a moment. "That plan will come when the time is right. Right now our focus is the impending battle."

Mattox tossed his stick onto his pile in frustration. "And meanwhile Ly'ra is in their hands with them doing who-knows-what to her?"

"Mattox, I know this is impossibly hard for you, but she is safe for the time being. This is just step one. We *will* rescue Ly'ra."

They both fell into silence. His heart was heavy with the suffering that he knew lay ahead. There was nothing he wanted to do more than to storm Farovale and rescue Ly'ra immediately, but that was not the Maker's plan. His strength may be greater than that of any normal human, but it was not enough. Faith was his greatest weapon right now.

He tossed another finished spike onto his rapidly growing pile. As he reached to grab another, he sensed someone approaching and stood quickly to attention. *They're right on time...just as the Maker said they would be.*

"Someone is coming," he said calmly.

Alarmed, Mattox grabbed his club. "Keepers? Already?"

"No, someone else..."

"Friend or foe?"

"That's yet to be determined." He steeled himself as he knew what was about to follow might determine the success or failure of their endeavors. Quickly, he issued instructions to Mattox and took off into the village.

Kor'lee, Raulin, and Bruschian paused at the edge of the forest. They were facing the southeastern edge of the village. The fading light cast eerie shadows. Other than the distant hum of the great waterfall, silence had settled across the village. The air was still.

"Look between the buildings," Raulin said, pointing toward the village. "There are stacks of logs and branches. Someone is preparing to mount a defense."

"Keepers?" Kor'lee asked. Her heart caught in her throat. She wasn't sure if she was ready for such a confrontation.

"I don't think so," Raulin said. "What do you think, Bruschian?"

"It's hard to tell," the big man said. He shook his head. "It doesn't look like a Keeper design...too spread out."

"True," Raulin said as he ran his hand through his long hair. "They usually prefer a tighter area to defend." He pointed at the web of branches between the closest buildings. "These defenses look to funnel people to the center, not create a true fortification."

"But what if it *is* Keepers?" Kor'lee asked.

"Good question," Raulin said. "Maybe we should go back. Though I have no love lost for the Keepers, I'm not too terribly anxious to take them head-on with just the three of us."

"It could be survivors," Bruschian offered.

"If they are survivors, we need to help them," Kor'lee added.

Raulin surveyed the village carefully. "I agree. It's going to be dark soon. I think our best bet is to wait until darkness settles in and carefully go in to check things out."

"And if there *are* Keepers there?" Bruschian asked.

"Then we retreat fast and hard. We know these woods far better than they do. In the dark, we should be safe."

It was settled. They remained there and waited for darkness to fall. Kor'lee's heart was pounding. She tried to distract herself by checking her bow and quiver for readiness. Try as she might, she couldn't keep her hands from shaking.

"Maybe you should wait here and let Bruschian and me check things out first," Raulin offered. Normally a suggestion like this would have angered her, but she knew that Raulin did not doubt her abilities. He was genuinely concerned for her safety.

"I'll be fine. Besides, if there are Keepers in there, you will need my bow to cover our escape."

"I can't argue there," he replied, giving her an encouraging smile.

With the darkness nearly complete, Raulin stood to his feet and the others joined him. "We have a full moon tonight and no cloud cover, so avoiding detection will be hard. Let's head to the nearest building. They haven't finished their defenses yet so it won't be hard to slip into the village. Let's stay close together. At the first sign of Keepers we run, agreed?"

They nodded their heads.

"Let's do this."

Raulin and Bruschian drew their swords. Kor'lee nocked an arrow and held her bow pointed down but ready. She felt her hands trembling slightly, but she breathed slowly in and out, slowing her rapidly beating heart.

They reached the building without incident. Raulin peered around the corner and gave the signal to keep going. As they rounded the corner, Kor'lee couldn't help but feel like they were too exposed. *There's too much light.*

Once they cleared the building, they found themselves in a narrow street. Kor'lee recognized it as the one where she had confronted Valtor at the summer festival.

"Where next?" Bruschian whispered.

"The square," Raulin replied.

Tiptoeing in a line, they made their way slowly and quietly toward the square. The village was very quiet. *Too quiet.*

When they reached the edge of the square, they passed a large building and entered slowly, sticking to the edge. There was no one to be found. Raulin signaled for them to follow him into the square.

"Hello there!" a loud voice said startling the three. "And who might you three be?"

Bruschian turned swiftly with his sword ready. A lone figure stepped out from behind the village church and into the courtyard.

Kor'lee couldn't see the man's face, which was covered by a hood. He appeared to be large man.

Without turning, Raulin whispered to Kor'lee and Bruschian, "He may not be dressed like a Keeper but it could be a trap." He then spoke loudly to the man who was now standing a few feet into the square on the opposite side of them. "We are three road-weary travelers. We mean you no harm."

"Yet you come from the forest brandishing your weapons? That seems mighty harmful to me."

"These are dangerous times, friend." Raulin replied.

"Friend? We shall see about that. What are your names?"

"Tell me yours first, friend, then I will tell you mine."

"I asked first, *friend*."

Raulin looked to Kor'lee and shrugged.

"Tell him," she said. "We can still run if we need to."

"These two are Bruschian and the lovely Kor'lee. As for me, my name is Raulin."

The man seemed to stiffen. "Raulin you say? Would you be the same Forest Bandit that preys on the innocent like a wolf preys on sheep?"

Raulin bristled. "I do no such thing. My men and I *protect* the innocent."

Kor'lee did not like where this was going. The man was baiting Raulin, and his pride was making him drop his guard.

As the man pulled back, his hood Raulin and Bruschian simultaneously cursed to themselves. *They know him?*

"Aye, well I beg to differ on that," the big man said angrily. He had head full of curly red hair and a bushy beard.

Raulin looked at Bruschian unsure of how to proceed. "As we said, we come as friends. We mean you no harm."

"This time…" the man replied.

"Please accept my apology for our last…um…encounter. It was an unfortunate misunderstanding."

Last encounter? What is going on here? Whatever had happened between Raulin and this man, he seemed to desire bloodshed. She reflexively raised her bow slightly.

The man glared at her. "Be careful there, little missy. You be treading on thin ice throwing your lot in with these miscreants."

Apparently, Raulin had enough. "I will kindly ask you not address the lady in such a way. If you will not let us pass in peace, you will leave us no choice but to force our way by you."

"Oh? And how do you propose to do that?" He lifted his mace and held it menacingly before them.

"We do not desire a fight, friend, but we will not shy away from one either." Raulin raised his sword, and Bruschian stepped forward, brandishing his massive sword in both hands. "Let's quit this foolish hostility. There are three of us, and but one of you."

"Wrong again," said a soft voice from behind them. Raulin stiffened and Kor'lee turned to see a blade resting against his spine. A hooded man dressed in a dark cloak held a spear, ready to deliver a fatal blow. She recognized his voice. *Orron.*

Orron's heart pounded. He knew that things were dangerously close to getting out of hand. He instantly recognized the girl to his left as the one who had saved his life at the Festival. *It is just as the Maker had said it would be.*

He leaned forward slightly and spoke calmly. "How's that shoulder healing, Raulin?"

Through clenched teeth, he responded. "It is fine, thank you very much."

"And your knee?" he said to the big man on his right.

"Fine," Bruschian grunted.

"Good, then you both remember how this could end. Let's do the civilized thing and put our weapons away."

Raulin and Bruschian hesitated then carefully moved to sheath their swords. Kor'lee lowered her bow and removed the arrow. Satisfied, Orron withdrew the blade and moved around in front of them. Mattox joined him. Orron noticed that Mattox still held his mace at the ready.

"What do you want here? Come to plunder I suspect," Mattox said with disdain.

Kor'lee spoke up. "We heard of a horrible Keeper attack and came to see for ourselves. Is it…is it true?"

"Aye," Mattox replied darkly. Orron could sense Kor'lee's countenance fall.

"As I said before, we do not mean you any harm," Raulin said. "We just came to see what happened and to see if there were any survivors."

"You are looking at them," Mattox replied shortly.

"You are all that remain?" Kor'lee asked in horror.

"Aye."

"What…what happened?" Kor'lee asked, her voice shaky.

Orron motioned for them to follow him. He led them through the square and to the narrow street that led into the village from the bridge. With his staff, he pointed to the snow covered bodies of the slain Keepers.

"The Keepers came and killed every man, woman, and child of this village—all of them innocent. Only two young girls were spared, though only so that they could be taken as selections in the Inspection. When I arrived they were…they were doing horrible things to someone I loved dearly." Sorrow filled his eyes, and Mattox looked away. "I killed them where they stood."

He looked Kor'lee in the eyes. "She was a beautiful mother and wife." He looked at Mattox who was gripping his mace so hard his knuckles turned white. "She never did anything to anyone."

Raulin looked at Mattox knowingly. He spoke softly. "She was your wife, wasn't she?"

Without looking at him, Mattox replied. "Aye, and the devils took my Ly'ra as well."

Tears streamed down Kor'lee's cheeks. Her heart broke at what she heard. Even though she had known that this is what she would find, she had not wanted to believe it. Now, standing in this empty village, she felt like she was standing in a tomb. What had once been so full of life and joy was now dark. The voices of the dead seemed to cry out for justice.

"How many were there?" Raulin asked.

"One hundred Keepers came in the middle of the night," Orron replied. "When I arrived, there were fourteen left...ten here and four guarding the cleric."

Bruschian cursed to himself. "Why would they do this?"

"They claimed to possess evidence of a rebellion." Orron looked directly at Raulin. "They claimed that the villagers were aiding your Bandits."

Raulin clenched his jaw. "That wasn't even remotely true."

"I know." Orron looked out across the field toward the river. "They create their own truth to support their desires." He turned back to the group. "It is late and quite cold. We have a fire and food. Would you care to join us?"

Kor'lee could sense that the man next to Orron was not happy about this suggestion, but he said nothing. "We would love that," Kor'lee said. There was still tension among the group, but it seemed that they were safe enough.

They made their way to a mill at the northern edge of town. Raulin and Bruschian seemed rather guarded, as did Orron's companion. In fact, the only one who seemed relaxed was Orron. He was strangely calm and collected.

When they entered the house, they found a fire burning brightly and a delicious smelling soup cooking. They had not eaten in many hours, and Kor'lee was famished. Orron served them as they sat around the fire. They ate in silence.

Orron finished first and set his bowl aside. He cleared his throat and spoke, eyeing Raulin carefully. "There is history between us that has gone unresolved long enough. Raulin, you attacked us wrongly in the forest. I only spared your life because I sensed that you were more than just a mere thief."

Raulin said nothing but held his gaze.

Orron turned to his companion. "Mattox, I know that you hold bitter feelings toward these men, but you should know that at the Summer Festival, it was Kor'lee and Raulin who came to my aid in defending Ly'ra from that foul captain."

Looking at Kor'lee, he continued. "Kor'lee, this man," he said motioning toward the man he called Mattox, "is the father of the girl you saved. It was her mother whom…whom the Keepers tormented to her very end."

Kor'lee's eyes fell to the floor. Her cheeks burned with shame. *How could my father ally himself with these monsters?*

Orron continued. "I say these things because I want you all to know that we have more in common than you may think. We all serve a greater purpose. Let us put aside our contentious past and look to a united future."

Kor'lee stole a look at Raulin. *What is he proposing?*

After a moment, Raulin finally spoke up. "I think I know where you are going with this. Let me first start off by saying that I truly and deeply regret my actions and the actions of my men." He looked at Mattox. "It is hard for me to admit when I am wrong, but I hope you accept my apology."

He offered his hand. Mattox stared at it for a moment, then he extended his own and they shook. Apparently, whatever had transpired between these four was now laid to rest.

Kor'lee knew that this was a significant moment for Raulin. She had known him for several months and had never seen him act in such humility. Her curiosity pushed her to know the full story, but she knew that now was not the time to ask.

When the apologies were accepted, Raulin continued. "As you know, we have spent many years fighting back against the Church and their Keepers. I have personally experienced the kind of tragedy that you have encountered here in Lillyndale."

He looked at Mattox, and Kor'lee could see genuine sympathy in his eyes. "I can't imagine the pain that you are feeling. I genuinely wish you my deepest condolences."

Shadows danced on the walls from the fire. In the dimly lit room, Kor'lee thought she caught the glint of a single tear falling from Mattox's eyes.

"Aye, thank you," Mattox replied.

Turning back to Orron, Raulin continued. "I am guessing that you plan to retaliate, possibly stage a rescue of Ly'ra?"

Orron nodded his head.

"What is your plan?"

"Tomorrow morning, Farovale will learn of our actions against the Keepers. I expect them to send as many as two companies to bring us in. We will kill them all."

Orron said it so matter-of-factly that Kor'lee almost believed that is was possible.

Raulin whistled. "You two against two hundred? I have seen you fight, Orron. You are one of the best I have ever seen. I'll give you that, but open battle against two companies of battle-hardened Keepers? That's madness!"

"Madness it may be, but that is what will happen. And there will be more than just Mattox and I."

"Oh? Who is joining your forces?" Raulin asked.

"You and your men are."

That brought a smile to Raulin's face. "We are? When did we sign up?"

"When you decided to come here." Orron looked solemnly at Raulin and Bruschian. "You both have seen the devastation that the Keepers have wrought. You have felt the effects first hand.

Though Lillyndale may not have supported you, other villages do. What do you think will happen to them next?"

Kor'lee realized what Orron was saying was true. Lillyndale was only the beginning. "He is right. My—" she caught herself. "The Keepers will not stop here."

Raulin looked at Bruschian, who was deep in thought. "What do you think?"

He cleared his throat and looked at Orron. "Many innocent lives have been lost because no one is brave enough to stand against them." He turned to Raulin. "I will fight with these men."

Raulin ran his hand through his hair. "I want to help you, I do, but I do not have much to offer. We have only remained free this long because we attack from the shadows. Never have we met the Keepers on the open field of battle."

"The Maker is on our side," Orron said confidently. "We will prevail."

Raulin shook his head. "That might be enough for you, but it's not for me. We only have fifty men. Even with your fighting skill, we are greatly overmatched! I feel that we are better served by warning the villages to flee."

"Aye, fleeing is what I thought was best, too," Mattox said. "The Keepers found out and slaughtered us. They will never stop."

Kor'lee's head was swirling with where this conversation was going. *Open war? Against my father?* There was no question in her mind that what Orron and Bruschian spoke was true. The Keepers had to be stopped. *But how?*

Orron looked at the staff in his hands. "I understand your concerns, Raulin. What I am proposing is madness. However, if we do nothing, if we run, how many more will die? Who will stand up to this evil if not us?"

"I agree, but facing these Keepers will be suicide!" Raulin said in exasperation.

It suddenly became clear to Kor'lee. *This atrocity happened because no one was brave enough to stand up and stop this evil. Not the Council, not the Church, and not my father.* She looked at Raulin. "It won't be suicide. We can win."

He looked at her, stunned. "Don't tell me you're buying this craziness!"

"I have lived among the Keepers all my life. They are well trained, that I will admit, but they believe in nothing. Most are only serving out their term of enlistment. We have what they lack…passion and conviction. We know what we are fighting for. We believe in it."

"Yet, every similar rebellion has been crushed," Raulin reminded her.

"I know Valtor and the leaders of the Keepers. They are arrogant. They have grown fat in their dominance." Her voice grew louder as she felt her heart swell with passion. "I think…no, I believe that we can stop them. We *must* stop them. Someone has to."

"Raulin, the time is now," Orron leaned forward and spoke softly but firmly. "If we face them here, on our terms, I know from the depths of my soul that we will defeat them. This will deal them a critical blow. The Keepers have not lost an open battle in many years."

Raulin shook his head and looked at the group incredulously. "You *really* do believe that you can win, don't you?"

"I do," said Orron with confidence.

"Well, you must have some sort of plan." Kor'lee could tell that Raulin was beginning to break.

Orron began to share his plan with the group. Raulin kept interjecting comments and questions, trying to poke holes in Orron's strategy. Kor'lee wasn't sure what to think about what she was hearing. It was so daring, so risky.

Finally, the conversation ran its course. Raulin raised his hands in surrender. "I will admit that you *do* have style. Your plan is absolutely foolish and quite frankly should never work." He had a glint in his eye. "But…I think it is *exactly* what they will never expect." He sighed. "I'm in."

Kor'lee smiled. Her heart sped with excitement. She knew the danger of what this all meant, but she felt alive. *Finally, I am doing something to stop it.* She didn't know where it would lead, but it was better than standing idly by while darkness reigned.

Orron shook Raulin's hand. "I'm glad to have you. Do you think your men will join us?"

"There will be some resistance. They will be hesitant to confront the Keepers head on."

They talked some more about what to do next. It was agreed that Kor'lee and Bruschian should return to the Bandits camp to rally them to fight. By the time they finished making their plans, it was well past midnight. They retreated to the various rooms of the house to try to catch some rest before the daunting tasks that would come with the morning.

Kor'lee had a room to herself. She stirred for hours as her mood oscillated rapidly from joy and excitement to sadness and fear. She knew that the Keepers would come in force. This battle would be fierce and deadly. She would be forced to kill, to face being killed. Deep down, she believed with all her heart that this was what was right and what was good. For too long, the Keepers had been able to do as they pleased. Someone had to stop them, and now she had the chance to matter in this coming fight.

The one thought that kept returning was that of her father. *What would he think? What happens if I have to face him in this battle? What will I do?* She tried not to think about it. *One step at a time.*

CHAPTER TWENTY-SEVEN

"There has been no sign of them, Captain," the Gate Keeper said.

"Make sure you inform me the second they arrive!" Valtor stormed off. *They should have been back by now.*

He pulled his cloak tightly around himself as he walked. A bitter chill filled the mid-morning air. He stopped to look over the wall at the forest that extended to the north. The sky was covered in ominous looking clouds. *There's a blizzard coming.*

He stood staring out at the forest for several minutes. Finally, he resigned himself to the fact that watching for his Keepers to return with the two rebels would not actually make them come any faster. He knew in his bones that something was not right.

Leaving the northern wall, Valtor ventured into the city. This time of year, the streets tended to be more deserted than in the warmer months. The only area of the city that saw continuous outdoor activity was the Keeper training grounds located in the northeastern part of Farovale. He decided to make his way there.

The sound of clashing weapons and the smell of sweat greeted him as he entered the training yard. Around the courtyard, Keepers were training with swords, lances, and bow staffs.

Archers were filling targets. Though he didn't want to, Valtor had to admire Draedon's dedication to routine and training. Even in this frigid weather, staying battle-ready was always one of the Legion Commander's top priorities. To protect the Keepers from being overly exposed to the harsh winter weather, Draedon had setup a schedule that rotated the various companies through the training area for half-day shifts. The rest of their time was spent on patrols in the valley and surrounding foothills mixed with days of rest and recuperation. Valtor was pleased to find that the company Tysion commanded was training when he arrived.

"Greetings, Marshal Tysion."

"Greetings, Captain." Tysion dismissed the Keepers. When they were alone, he asked quietly, "Any word about the others?"

"No, but I'm sure they will be here shortly," Valtor responded, trying to convince himself.

"What do you think could be keeping them?"

"Maybe the rebels were slow in returning from the hunt."

Tysion was unconvinced. "I don't know. The fire at the farm was burning very brightly. It would have lasted for many hours. They had to have seen it."

Valtor nodded his head. "They will arrive soon. How has our *other* mission been going?"

"Exactly as planned, sir."

"Good, good. And the girl?"

"She is completely unaware."

"Even better."

"Let's proceed with—" Valtor was interrupted by the gatekeeper from the northern gate.

"Sir, someone has arrived from Lillyndale and is looking for you," he said, gasping for breath.

"Someone? Only one?"

"Yes, sir. His name is Osbere, and he claims to be the Cleric of Lillyndale. He demands an urgent audience with you and Elder Zittas."

Valtor's heart sank. *Something has gone terribly wrong.* He looked at Tysion who glanced at him grimly. "Carry on, Marshal."

Valtor followed the gatekeeper out of the training yard to find Osbere waiting for him there. The cleric looked terrible. His cloak was dirty, torn, and completely disheveled. He smelled as if he hadn't bathed in weeks, and his eyes were filled with terror.

"Well, what is it, Osbere?" he asked gruffly.

"I must talk to you *and* the Elder. He must hear this." He looked around as if he were afraid of who might be watching him.

"I will decide what the Elder must hear."

"No!" he said frantically. "He told me that I must tell you *both*!"

"Who told you?"

"I...can't tell you...alone." Fear oozed from Osbere's pores, and Valtor felt a shiver run down his spine.

"Very well, follow me."

They made their way through the city. When they arrived at the Cathedral, the cleric at the door gave Osbere a stern, disapproving glare but allowed them to enter once they removed their shoes. They made their way up multiple flights of stairs. Upon reaching the Elder's door, Valtor once again heard the sounds of a struggle coming from within the room. Having learned his lesson, he knocked and waited patiently. He heard the hushed voice of Elder Zittas, and after waiting several more minutes, the door was opened by a young girl, no more than twelve or thirteen. Valtor saw signs of a nasty bruise forming on the girl's cheek.

"That will be all...whatever your name is," Elder Zittas said, dismissing the girl with the wave of his hand. She left as quickly as her feet could carry her. Valtor noticed tears streaking down her cheeks as she ran.

Clearly annoyed, Zittas impatiently said, "What do you—" His hand went to his nose as Osbere entered his room. "Who is this filthy man and how dare you bring him into my chambers, Captain Valtor?"

"I'm sorry, Your Grace. His name is Osbere. He is the Cleric of Lillyndale."

"And you couldn't have insisted that he bathe first?"

"I'm sorry, but he claims his message is urgent. The other Keepers have yet to return, sir."

Zittas understood. "Well, what is it, Cleric? What news of Lillyndale do you bring?"

Osbere looked very hesitant to speak. Fearful to make eye contact, his eyes never left the floor. "Lillyndale has fallen, Your Grace."

"Yes, I know that. It was unfortunate but necessary."

"No, Your Holiness, I mean that the Keepers that were left behind have fallen. The village is now in rebel hands."

The color drained from Valtor's face. His worst fears were realized.

"*What?!*" the Elder shouted. "How could this happen?" He turned to Valtor. "Captain, I thought you eliminated the threat."

"I…we did, Your Grace," Valtor protested. "There were only two left. I left a total of fourteen Keepers behind—some of my best I might add."

"Then tell me, Cleric, how do two worthless peasants best fourteen trained Keepers?"

Osbere clearly did not want to answer the question.

"Speak, Osbere, lest I decide to *make* you speak." Zittas was bursting with impatience.

"They…well…*he* was no ordinary peasant…"

"What do you mean? Who?" Valtor interjected.

"The one who calls himself Orron. He is not like the others."

Zittas looked confused and addressed Valtor. "I thought you said that Mattox was the leader of this rebellion?"

Valtor shrugged his shoulders. "He is!"

"No, he's not," Osbere said gravely. "This Orron is the one we should fear."

"*Fear? A peasant?* I think not!" Valtor said hotly.

"I already told you, he is no peasant!" the cleric said, his voice squeaking in terror. "He told me things…things I am too afraid to repeat." He suddenly became quiet as he looked around for invisible spies. "I am not sure that he is human."

"You have gone mad in your own fear!" Zittas rolled his eyes in disgust.

"No, I am telling you the truth! The look on his face…what he said was the truth."

"What did he say?" Valtor asked.

"He said that…well he said that he is a True Keeper of the Maker's Will."

"That's heresy and an outright lie!" Zittas practically shouted, though something about the tension in his response caught Valtor's attention.

"There's more. He said that he was the Assessor of our guilt."

"Our guilt?" Valtor said incredulously. "Does he not know that we serve the One True Church?"

Ignoring him, the cleric continued. "He gave me a message that I must deliver to you."

"Let's hear it then," Zittas said.

As if the memory pained him, the cleric winced as he began. "These are his exact words. The memory will haunt me forever." He cleared his throat and continued.

"Repent of your sins, lay down your swords, and you will be spared. A great war like Edelyndia has never known is coming like a thunderous storm. The righteous will rise against the darkness, and the Great Light will prevail. All who stand against it will taste blood and suffering. The anger of the Maker burns like a fire that will consume all who do the work of the Fallen. Now is the time. The choice is yours. Repent and you will live. Fight and you will die. The Age of Reckoning has begun."

Silence filled the room. Now Valtor was truly confused. *What on earth is he babbling on about?* On one hand, if this cleric were telling the truth, two simple men managed to best fourteen of his best trained Keepers. This was no small feat. *But a True Keeper? What does that mean?*

"He was just trying to scare you," the Elder said, but Valtor couldn't help but notice that his argument sounded weak, as if he didn't believe it himself.

"How could he have known about the Age of the Reckoning?" Osbere protested. "Only a few leaders in the Church know about that."

"What is this Age of Reckoning?" Valtor asked.

"It is a myth...a legend based on metaphorical and useless prophecies found in the Holy Writings," Zittas said a little too quickly.

He's hiding something, Valtor thought. *Whatever it is, it clearly has Osbere overcome with fear.*

"Like I said, he is lying. He's probably a cleric who deserted the Church and is trying to scare us to mask his rebellion."

"You weren't there," Osbere said, his words dripping with fear. "The way he spoke...there was tremendous power. He's no cleric. He's—"

"That will be all, Cleric. Go clean yourself up." Zittas leaned in menacingly. "If you breathe even one word of this, I will personally destroy you. Is that understood?"

Osbere nodded in submission and left as quickly as he could. Zittas drew himself up and walked over to his window overlooking the Valley. "Captain, these two rebels must be silenced immediately. We cannot have the word of their small victory inciting others to join their cause."

Valtor joined him by the window. "I agree, Your Grace, but what about Osbere's claims?"

"He's a coward and a lunatic. This Orron is a Heretic, nothing more, nothing less."

"That may be true, but he *did* best fourteen of my men."

"They were probably drunk and sloppy."

That, Valtor definitely knew to be false. These were among his best, most loyal, and disciplined men. "What are your orders?"

"Send two companies to dispatch of these men. Kill them and do so in a way that sends a message."

"And what of Draedon? After what happened in Lillyndale, he will not allow me to do this."

"I will summon him and give the order myself."

"Shall I lead the men?"

"No, send someone you trust. I need you here to keep an eye on the Commander. I do not trust him."

Chapter Twenty-Eight

Draedon stormed out of the Cathedral, nearly knocking over a cleric in the process. *Things are getting out of control!* His meeting with Elder Zittas had confirmed what he had already known. The incident at Lillyndale was just the beginning. *It's just a matter of time...*

Lost in his thoughts, Draedon wandered aimlessly through the city. Zittas had said that Valtor would send someone to "handle" the rebels. That someone was most likely going to be Tysion, Valtor's close friend and right-hand man. He was a ruthless and fierce warrior. No doubt, the rebels would be dealt with swiftly and harshly.

It's happening again. The Council was turning a violent hand to the innocent citizens of Edelyndia. *It's one thing to fight rebel soldiers on the field of battle; it's quite another to slaughter innocent men, women, and children.* What bothered Draedon most was that he knew he was powerless to stop it.

Unsure of how much time had passed, he stopped to gather his bearings. He realized his wanderings had brought him to the western edge of the city where the Citadel's prison was located. It was an undesirable part of Farovale. Buildings there were among the oldest in Farovale, and the smell of rot and decay filled the air. It was now mid-afternoon, and the sky was already turning dark.

A group of Keepers walked around a corner and was startled at the sight of their Commander. He did not visit this area very often.

"Commander Draedon, sir, have you come for an inspection of the prison?" one of them asked.

"Um, yes...yes, I have," Draedon responded, unsure of what else to say. *I guess I might as well.* He hoped the momentary distraction would ease the burden he was carrying.

"Very good, sir. I can take you there right away."

Draedon followed the Keepers through the narrow streets to where the prison was located. The building itself was a tall, imposing stone structure. Small, bar-covered windows were set high in the exterior walls.

They entered, and the prison warden greeted them.

"Greetings, Commander Draedon. It is an honor to have you here. What would you like to inspect first, sir?"

The warden was a tall, skinny man. Because his rank was considered an officer, he wore a dark cloak and was clean-shaven. His skin was very pale. Those who were responsible for the prisons in Keeper Citadels rarely saw the light of day.

Remembering that he was supposedly there on official business, Draedon asked, "What is the current occupancy of the prison?"

"Right now we only have a small number of prisoners. A few locals have defaulted on their debts. We have one man who killed another in a fight at a tavern. Three Keepers were found drunk on duty. There's the two girls who were selected in the Lillyndale Inspection—"

"What?" Draedon asked incredulously. "The two girls are *here?*"

Suddenly nervous, the warden responded, "Um, yes, sir. They were sent here by the Captain."

"And why were they not taken to the Cathedral where the selections are supposed to be held?"

"I...I don't know, sir. The Captain had them sent here with a signed order from Elder Zittas."

"Take me to them at once!" Draedon's blood boiled. It was bad enough that he was unable to stop this Inspection, but to have these young girls confined in such a vile place was incomprehensible.

The Keeper hurried into the prison and through the locked doors at the entrance to the cellblocks. Draedon had to resist the urge to cover his nose. This place smelled repulsive. The smell of human waste and men who had not showered in who-knows-how-long burned his nose.

They made their way past cells of unruly men who hurled insults at them. One man hurled something from his cell that struck the Keeper behind Draedon. He did not want to know what it was.

The corridor was long and narrow. Several similar corridors were spread throughout the prison. When they reached the end, the warden motioned to a cell and said, "The selections are in here."

Draedon looked in and saw two small girls huddled in a corner. The cell was a bare stone room. There was no furniture. One girl had red hair, the other had hair as black as midnight. The one with red hair was holding the other in her arms as she sobbed uncontrollably. There was something peaceful and calm about the redheaded girl. She stroked the other's hair as she sang softly, trying to bring her comfort. Outraged, Draedon grabbed the warden by the cloak and slammed him into the bars of the cell.

"You placed them in the same corridor as these odious men? They are just little girls! What is wrong with you?"

"I...I was just—" Draedon threw him to the ground. "Silence! Consider yourself demoted!" He leaned in, shaking with rage. "You are lucky I do not do worse. There is no excuse for this. Open this door immediately!"

"Y–yes, sir," the former warden replied as he got to his feet. He patted around his belt and turned ashen. "I…I did not grab the keys."

Draedon grabbed him and threw him down the corridor. "Well then you better get them quickly lest I decide to give you their cell as your new quarters!"

The rest of the prisoners, having heard the exchange, were now banging on the bars of their cell. Amid the assault of vile sounds and smells, Draedon's ears were drawn to the gentle voice of the little redheaded girl as she sang sweetly to the inconsolable little girl in her arms. She was so young, so pure. Seeing this girl in this wretched environment was almost too much for him to handle.

The former warden returned with the keys; with shaky hands, he opened the door to the cell. One of the other Keepers started to enter, but the daggers coming out of Draedon's eyes stopped him in his tracks. "*I* will handle this."

Draedon entered the cell slowly. The redhead stopped singing and looked at him warily. "I'm not here to hurt you," he said gently. The dark-haired girl seemed oblivious to the world. He walked over and knelt down beside the girls.

"My name is Draedon, what is your name?"

The redhead did not answer at first. She just stared at him.

"I promise that I won't hurt you. I have a daughter who looked a lot like you when she was your age." In truth, other than the red hair, she reminded him of a lot of a young Kor'lee.

She brushed her matted hair from her eyes and spoke up. Her voice was almost lyrical. "My name is Ly'ra. This is Aly'siah." She continued to stroke her friend's hair as she spoke.

"It is nice to meet you, Ly'ra. We are going to move you to a new room. Will that be all right with you?"

Ly'ra's eyes welled up with tears and her lip quivered. "I want to go home."

It felt as though someone had stabbed him through the heart. Draedon had to resist the urge to pick these girls up and fight his way out of the prison. "I'm afraid we can't do that right now, but let's get you to a nicer room. Are you hungry?"

She nodded her head emphatically. "We haven't eaten in forever."

Draedon turned and glared at the former warden who seemed to shrink from his gaze. He stood to his feet and walked over to the Keepers. He wanted nothing more than to have the girls removed from the prison altogether, but he knew that he no longer had that authority. He did the only thing he knew he could still do as Commander.

"I want you to prepare a cell for these girls in the cleanest part of the prison…as far from these men as possible. They *never* should have been placed here to begin with. I want there to be comfortable bedding and a table and chairs placed in their cell. Prepare some of the best food you can find and bring it there. I expect this to be done before we arrive. Is that understood?" The Keepers nodded and took off at a dead run.

He returned to the girls. "They are getting your new room ready for you. Are you hurt?"

"My head hurts pretty badly," Ly'ra replied. "The horrible man hit me in the head so hard that I went to sleep."

Draedon's blood boiled with rage. "May I look at it?"

She nodded and he gently examined her head. Her hair was matted with blood and she cried out when he touched the wound.

"I'm very sorry that this happened. I will get someone in here to take care of that for you right away."

He turned to one of the Keepers still standing outside the door. "Go; send for my servant, Einar. Do so quickly." Einar had extensive experience on the battlefield as a healer and taught Kor'lee everything that she knew. *Kor'lee…seeing this would have killed her.*

Turning back to Ly'ra he said, "That song you were singing was lovely. Where did you learn it?"

"My mother used to sing it for me when I was sick." At the mention of her mother, fresh tears began to stream down her cheeks. "They hurt my mother. They hurt her bad."

There was nothing that Draedon could say. His heart broke, and he had to fight back tears.

"Your friend, Aly'siah, is she hurt?"

"No, I don't think so. She's just sad. Her dad was—" Her voice was choked off by a sob as she remembered the horrible things she had seen.

"It's all right, Ly'ra. You don't have to talk about it." He placed his hand gently on her shoulder and lowered his voice so only she could hear him. "I am so sorry for what has happened to you both. I will do everything I can to help you, I promise."

A breathless Keeper returned and entered the cell. "The room is ready, sir. The food will be there shortly."

Draedon stood to his feet. "Very well. I am going to escort these young ladies to their new cell. You and the rest of the Keepers here will form a wall to shield them from the other prisoners. Is that understood?"

"Yes, sir."

He turned to Ly'ra and offered his hand. "We are going to go now. Can you walk?"

"I think so, but I don't think Aly'siah can."

"I will carry her." He bent down and gently picked her up. She barely moved. She was nearly catatonic. He held her in one arm and offered his left hand to Ly'ra. "Come now, let's get you to someplace better." She took his hand as they exited the cell and slowly made their way down the corridor.

The Keepers lined up and protected the girls from being hit from any projectiles, but they couldn't keep the other prisoners quiet. The prisoners said the most horrid things to the little girls. Draedon could feel Ly'ra shaking as she walked next to him.

Finally, they left the corridor and made their way through the winding halls of the prison. The din of the unruly prisoners faded away as they walked until they were mercifully out of reach.

Though the new cell was far from comfortable, it was clean and quiet. There was a window high in the wall that provided some natural light, and there were two beds with fresh linens. As ordered, the Keepers had placed a table and two chairs in one corner. It was far from an appropriate quarters for innocent little girls, but it was immeasurably better than where they had been kept.

He laid Aly'siah down on one of the beds, and Ly'ra sat down next to her. She placed her hand on Aly'siah's shoulder and watched over her protectively.

Draedon heard the sound of someone entering the cell and turned to find that Einar had arrived.

"I came as quickly as I could, sir. I happened to be in the area when the Keeper found me."

"Einar! Thank you for coming so quickly. Let me introduce you to a brave young lady." He turned to the girls. "Ly'ra, this is a good friend of mine, Einar. He used to be a Healer. Would it be alright with you if he looked at your head?"

She nodded.

"Ly'ra. That's such a pretty name," Einar said as he sat down next to her. He smiled at her warmly. "A pretty name to go with a very pretty girl. Now, let's have a look at that head of yours."

Draedon exited the room to find the former Warden standing at attention. "Those girls *never* should have been treated like that," Draedon said again hotly. He turned to the Keeper who had found Einar so quickly. "You, how long have you worked in the prison?"

"Three years, sir."

"Congratulations, you are the new warden."

"Thank you, sir."

"If you would like to avoid the fate of your predecessor, you had better treat these girls with the respect and dignity that they deserve. I want three meals every day with clean clothing and bedding provided daily. They are to have access to clean water where they can bathe themselves in *complete* privacy whenever they would like to. Is all this understood?"

"Yes, sir. Completely, sir."

Draedon looked the new Warden in the eyes. "I or my servant Einar will be checking with the girls regularly. If they are mistreated or abused in *any* way while they are here, you will pay dearly for it. Do I make myself clear?"

"Yes, sir. I will personally make sure that they are not harmed."

"I will hold you to that, Warden."

Einar exited the cell as the warden walked away. "I was able to close up and bandage the wound on Ly'ra's head. It wasn't too deep. Aly'siah appears to be physically unharmed."

"Physically?"

"Yes, but she has suffered a tremendous trauma. I cannot imagine what those girls had to witness in Lillyndale."

Draedon clenched his jaw. "Wait for me outside. I want to say good-bye to Ly'ra." Einar nodded, and Draedon reentered the cell. The sight of the bandage around Ly'ra's head only made him angrier. *What kind of animal could strike such an innocent girl?*

"I like Einar. He was nice."

Draedon smiled. "He is a good friend. How are you feeling?"

She shrugged her shoulders. "I want to go home."

"I'm sorry, Ly'ra. I have to go now. If you need anything, anything at all, you just ask one of the Keepers to find me, and I will come as soon as I can."

"What is going to happen to us?"

"I...I don't know." He shook his head. *What am I supposed to say?* "I will do everything I can to help you. I promise." Unable to bear looking at the fear in her eyes any longer, he left the cell and made his way out of the prison as quickly as he could.

The frigid early evening air greeted him as he exited the building. Einar was leaning against the wall waiting for him. He fell in beside Draedon as they made their way through the city toward the officers' quarters. Neither said a word until they finally entered the house. Draedon walked over to the fireplace and pounded his fist against the mantle.

"What they are doing to those girls…it's barbaric…it's…" He didn't have the words to describe what he had seen.

"Yes, sir. It is the worst kind of evil."

"This is why I have worked so hard to avoid selecting anyone. But now, I fear that even I can't stop what is coming."

They both sat down and gazed moodily into the fire. After sitting in silence for quite some time, Einar spoke up. "What are you going to do next?"

"What can I do? Zittas has all but stripped me of what little power that I had. It's only a matter of time before they find out."

"I agree. The situation is growing quite dire."

"Thanks for the optimism."

"It is not a lack of optimism, sir. It is reality. We always knew that things would get worse before they got better."

Draedon grunted in agreement. "Well, it's not all bad. Apparently, two rebels bested fourteen of Valtor's best men in Lillyndale."

"Really? *Fourteen?*" That sparked a slight smile from Einar.

"Apparently so. Zittas ordered Valtor to send someone that he trusted to lead two companies to take care of the situation."

"He will send Tysion."

"That was my guess."

"Fourteen…hmm. Those were some powerful rebels. Where would they have learned to fight like that?"

"It couldn't have been just simple Forest Bandits. I've seen what they can do. They're creative, but they're not that good."

"Were they the rebels that Valtor went there to capture in the first place?"

"I think so."

"Well, with what they did to the villagers, revenge can be a pretty powerful motivator."

"Very true." Draedon fell silent for a while.

"Einar, we both know that they are cutting me out. I'm afraid they may be on to me."

"I fear you are correct."

"It's too early! We haven't had enough time to get everything ready."

"We always knew this might happen. We will just have to accelerate things."

Draedon just shook his head. *Accelerate things? How can you accelerate something that doesn't even exist yet?* "This means anyone who is loyal to me is now in danger, including you."

"I've been in worse danger in my time, sir. No need to worry about me."

"That may be true, but there are others. We need to warn them."

"Shall I go then?"

"I fear that it is time. Start with Cleric Torker in Covenglade. They will probably head there first when it starts."

"And the others?"

"The word will spread soon enough." Draedon stood and walked over to the window. The winter wind howled in the night. "A storm is coming, Einar. A darkness is settling on Edelyndia. I just hope we can live long enough to see the morning."

Chapter Twenty-Nine

Orron shivered as he pulled his cloak tightly around him. The sun was beginning to crest the horizon, providing the earliest light of dawn. He sat atop the roof of a house at the edge of Lillyndale facing the river. Raulin, Mattox, and Orron had been trading watches for the last couple of days as they awaited the force of Keepers that Orron knew was coming. Something told him that this was the day.

He looked over his shoulder at the village. *It's not perfect, but it will do.* They had spent the two days since Kor'lee and Bruschian had left finishing the defensive preparations. They had managed to effectively create two bottleneck entrances to the village at the eastern and western edges. With Raulin's help, Mattox and Orron had been able to exceed their initial design. The narrow spaces between every house had been filled in with dense tangles of sharpened branches and vines. Anyone wishing to pass through that way would have to endure numerous cuts and worse. To Orron's satisfaction, their labor would help them control the battlefield, an incredibly important tool when facing a much larger force.

His eyes settled on the snow-covered form of one of the fallen Keepers. The freezing temperatures had prevented the bodies from beginning the decomposition process, but it was only a matter of time. Despite the insult that Mattox wanted to issue, he knew that they would have to burn them sooner or later. *There will be many more to add to the pile soon.*

It was hard to believe that it was just seven days ago when he had awakened to a new, darker world, one without Me'ra in it. Just over a year ago, he had come to this world and into the lives of Mattox, Ly'ra, and Me'ra. Now, Me'ra was dead, and Ly'ra was in the hands of the enemy. He sighed in frustration and shook his head. Deep down, he knew that this was just the beginning.

Something inside him stirred, and he became instantaneously alert. He stood to his feet and peered into the fading darkness. Though he could not see into the woods beyond the river, his instincts told him what would soon be coming through.

Jumping down from the rooftop, he ran through the village to the Mill. Bursting through the door, he found Mattox and Raulin dead asleep in front of the fireplace.

"Wake up!"

Mattox jumped to his feet and hit his head on the mantle. He cursed and rubbed the quickly forming lump. "What is it, boy?"

"The Keepers will be here shortly."

Raulin grabbed his sword and strapped it to his side. "Then the fight is on us."

"Aye, let them come!" Mattox said with a spark in his eyes that Orron had not seen in many days. "I have waited long enough for my vengeance."

Orron gripped his staff in both hands and looked Mattox in the eyes. "This is about more than just vengeance, Mattox. Stick to the plan."

"Aye, but vengeance will be mine, one way or the other."

The three men looked at each other solemnly. *Can just three of us really do this?* Orron pushed his doubt aside. *With the Maker on our side, we cannot be outnumbered.*

From the cover of the forest, Kor'lee and Bruschian watched Orron, Mattox, and Raulin spring to action.

"It must be time," Bruschian said.

The thought made Kor'lee's heart flutter. "Do you think we are ready?"

"As best as we can be."

Kor'lee couldn't help but be worried. She looked back at the Bandits that had made camp among the trees.

"There's just so few of us."

Many of the so-called "Forest Bandits" were little more than boys and old men. They were the outcasts, the marginalized leftovers whose lives and homes had been ruined by the Church. They were not battle-hardened warriors. Far from it. They were angry, homeless men and boys with the will to fight, but Kor'lee doubted whether they had the skill to accomplish much.

Though they had been waging a successful campaign of raids and skirmishes against the Keepers for the last couple of years, it had more to do with Raulin's cunning ways than their actual skill. She had never seen them in action. Raulin never allowed her to come along on one of their raids. Seeing them now, poorly dressed and even more poorly equipped, she began to have her doubts about Orron's plan.

Sensing her misgivings, Bruschian said, "We will succeed. Don't you worry, Miss Kor'lee. My father always used to say that it's not the size of the dog in the fight that matters, but the size of the fight in the dog." He looked at her knowingly. "These men have experienced great pain and injustice at the hands of the Keepers. They will fight hard and true."

Convincing the rest of the Bandits to come along had been no small feat. It took a full day of debating to get them to agree. Raids were one thing, but open battle against a superior force was quite another. Had it not been for Bruschian's bravery and confidence, they might not have agreed to join them.

Turning her attention back to the village, she saw Raulin make a few last second adjustments to the barrels he had placed at key points around the southeastern edge of the village. He then said something to Mattox that she couldn't hear and took off running toward the forest.

When he arrived, Kor'lee noticed an excitement in his eyes.

With a smile he said, "How is everyone on this fine morning?"

"Not as well as you apparently," Bruschian said grumpily. "I like how you got to sleep in the mill while we had to sleep outside in the forest."

"Hey," Raulin protested, "we had last minute details to go over."

"Is everything ready?" Kor'lee asked.

"It looks that way," Raulin said as he turned back toward the village. "Now let's see if this crazy plan actually works."

Tysion stood at the edge of the forest with two scouts beside him. From their cover, they surveyed the village. In the early morning light, they could make out no movement. The rush of the river covered up any noises.

"Maybe they fled for the mountains," one of the scouts offered.

Tysion shook his head. "Look at the gaps between the buildings. They have been fortified."

"Ah, I didn't see that."

"They are ready for a fight," Tysion replied. He stretched his back and placed his hand on the familiar grip of his sword. "And a fight we will give them."

"How do you want us to proceed?"

That was the tricky part. They really only had one choice. Even in the dead of winter, the river was wide and too dangerous to cross. "We make for the bridge. It's our only crossing in these parts."

The bridge itself was not very wide. It would limit how many Keepers could cross at a time. Tysion didn't like it. Judging by the care that the rebels had taken to fortify the village, he knew that they were prepared. They could have a trap planned for the bridge. *Well, there's only two of them. Even if there is a trap planned, we have the superior force.*

"Prepare the men for the assault. We will proceed with caution. Who knows what trickery they may have planned."

"Yes, sir."

Tysion had a full two companies at his command. It seemed like overkill for two rebels, but Captain Valtor wanted a show of force. To be able to best fourteen Keepers that he had trained personally, he knew that these rebels could fight. *But two will never stand a chance against two hundred, no matter how incredible they may be.*

Tysion kept the two companies separated. One would cross first with the other standing in reserve. Normally, Tysion would lead the first company into battle, but he was under strict orders to command from the rear. Captain Valtor was angry enough that the rebels had already accomplished what they had. He did not want to give them the satisfaction of taking down a company marshal during the initial assault.

"The men are ready and awaiting your order, sir."

"Good. Let's proceed then."

Tysion stepped out from the forest and onto a small knoll. From where he stood, he had a decent view of the village. As the first company broke the forest, he saw movement in the village. He raised his hand to halt his men. Slowly, a lone figure made his way out of town toward the bridge. He wore a dark cloak with his head covered and carried only a staff. *Maybe he intends to give himself up without a fight.*

The man walked to the bridge, and when he reached the center, he stopped. He stood with the butt of his staff on the bridge as if in defiance. Tysion's second-in-command turned and gave him an inquisitive look. "What should we do, sir?"

Tysion wasn't sure. Something didn't feel right.

He cleared his throat and spoke loudly, "I am Marshal Tysion, and I carry orders from the Church to arrest all Heretics. I also have the authority to kill on sight if I deem it necessary. Drop your weapon and your life will be spared. Attempt to resist and it will not."

The man did not budge. Turning to his second-in-command, Tysion said, "I guess surrender was too much to hope for. Send twenty men to detain him."

The orders were issued, and twenty Keepers made their way to the bridge. Just as they were about to set foot on it, the man spoke. His voice boomed across the field.

"I am Orron, True Keeper of the Maker's Will. I am the Assessor of your guilt and the vessel of the Maker's vengeance. Confess your sins, repent of your ways, and you will be spared."

The weight of his words chilled Tysion to the core. There was tremendous power in his voice. Trying to hide his unease, he motioned for the twenty Keepers to proceed. Slowly, they approached the man.

What happened next was so fast that Tysion barely had time to process what he was seeing. With swords drawn, the Keepers neared the man on the bridge. When they were mere steps from him, he was somehow transformed from completely still to a flash of blinding speed. Tysion watched helplessly as he tore the Keepers apart. In a matter of seconds, he killed all twenty men, many before they even had a chance to swing their swords. It was the most amazing and terrifying display of fighting power that he had ever seen in his lengthy military career.

It was over before it really began. With the dead bodies of the fallen Keepers littering the bridge, the man called Orron returned to his former position. From where he stood, Tysion could see a long, deadly blade protruding from the end of his staff, dripping with blood.

The man spoke again. "I am Orron, True Keeper of the Maker's Will. I am the Assessor of your guilt and the bringer of the Maker's vengeance. Confess your sins, repent of your ways, and you will be spared."

This time, the words filled Tysion with fear. This man, whoever or whatever he really was, deeply disturbed him. In all his years of battle, he had never been this unnerved.

"Sir, what we should we do now?"

Tysion shook his head to break the spell. "I…um…I mean attack. Send the remainder of the first company to dispatch of him."

The selected Keepers glanced at each other nervously as they approached. *Surely, eighty will overwhelm him,* Tysion thought to himself. *No one can survive those kinds of numbers.*

As the Keepers approached, Orron's limbs trembled, not from fear but from the power coursing through his body. He had only felt power like this when he was standing in his clearing. All feelings of fear, doubt, and insecurity were gone. The mantra coursed through him. Holy anger flowed through veins. *This is who I am. This is what I am meant to do. Injustice, hypocrisy, and evil have had their day. The Age of Reckoning has come, and justice will be served.*

The Keepers let out a war cry and closed the distance at a dead run. As they neared the bridge, they were forced to narrow their ranks. Orron smiled. *Just what I wanted.*

One Keeper was apparently faster than the rest and reached him first. It doesn't always pay to be the fastest. He didn't even have time to swing his sword. Orron's spear darted faster than lighting, impaling him through the throat and back out so fast that it took the Keeper a few seconds to realize that he was dying before he crashed to the ground in a heap.

Then the wave arrived. It was pure chaos.

Orron twirled and slashed with his spear with methodical intensity. The length of his spear gave him a distinct advantage over the swordsman. He also stood several inches taller than his foes giving him a clear line of sight.

They were well trained. He was better.

They needed the training. He didn't. He existed for this very purpose. It was his destiny.

It felt as though time had slowed to a near stop. Every swing of the sword seemed to move in slow motion. He had no difficulty parrying every blow. Spinning in a fluid motion, he and his staff felt as one. Blow after blow, he fell Keeper after Keeper. They pressed on, and he struck them down.

As more and more Keepers fell, their blood splashed on the bridge making the footing slick. He knew that he couldn't stay where he was much longer. Twenty more Keepers had already fallen. They were getting smarter. Attacking in small groups, trying to surround him. It was all he could do to keep them in front of him.

Between blows, he caught sight of the one hundred or so Keepers that remained in reserve. He saw their commander. Though he only got a glimpse, he was pretty sure he saw fear in his eyes. *The plan...I have to stick to the plan.*

With a savage burst of strength, he threw his spear through the chest of one Keeper. It flew so hard it impaled a man behind him as well.

He charged forward into the mass of bodies. Using his right elbow, he pummeled a Keeper's temple so hard that he felt the man's skull crack with the impact. He grabbed the fallen Keeper's sword cut his way through three more men.

The fury of his attack drove the Keepers far enough back to where he could turn and give the signal. Mattox appeared on a rooftop at the edge of the village. With smooth precision, he fired arrow after arrow sending a wave of burning arrows down on the bridge. Orron grabbed his spear from the bodies of the two Keepers and fled the bridge as Mattox covered his retreat.

It struck Orron how fluid Mattox was with the bow. He was calm and concentrated. He was no longer the bumbling hunter. Now, he was something more…a father and a husband fighting for the life they had taken from him.

Tysion flinched as burning arrows rained down on the bridge. What was worse was that the bridge was catching fire. If they wanted to enter the village and kill the rebels, they had to do it now.

With a roar he yelled, "Attack! Now! Attack!"

The remaining Keepers ran for the bridge. Tysion saw Orron clamor up the side building from where the archer was firing. The man paused long enough to hand Orron a bow. Now there were two archers.

Arrows continued to assault them as they crossed. Piles of men tried to press through the growing flames. *They must have put something on the bridge in advance so that it would catch quickly.*

Tysion clenched his teeth and joined the rush of men heading to the bridge. Keepers were dying all around him. Those who had fallen wounded during the first fight on the bridge now lay screaming in flames. The stench of burning flesh was overwhelming. Finally, he managed to cross the bridge.

"Sir, your cloak!" one of his Keepers yelled as he left the bridge.

He looked down and saw that the bottom was engulfed in flames. As quickly as he could he tore it off, singeing his hands in the process. Roaring in rage, he glared at the archers in the village. Suddenly they stopped firing and disappeared from the rooftops.

The Keepers gathered in the field outside the village, standing ready for whatever attacks might come. Tysion looked around. About one hundred Keepers were left. *Two men killed one hundred of my men.* He was seething with rage.

Turning to his second-in-command, he said, "We still have vastly superior numbers. We know that they probably have traps set for us in that cursed village."

"What would you have us do, sir?"

He thought for a long moment. The hailstorm of arrows had stopped as abruptly as it began. The rebels were no longer visible. His mind raced with the possibilities of what lay ahead in the village. He imagined what trickery they could be facing.

What really bothered him was the ferocity with which Orron had fought. He had never seen anything like it. *Who is he?*

"Let's divide our force in two. You will take fifty Keepers and attack the village from the front. Try to divert their attention, and we will flank them with the rest. Give me about twenty minutes to get in position then start your attack."

The Keeper nodded and began carrying out his orders. They quickly divided and Tysion set out around the southern edge of the village. They gave the village as wide a berth as they could sticking close to the tree line in an attempt to disguise their numbers. It took nearly the full twenty minutes to get his men in position around the rear of the village. He made sure his men moved cautiously.

Just as the last of his men moved into position, he heard the second-in-command give the order to attack from somewhere at the front of the village. His muscles tensed as he prepared to signal the charge.

From where he stood, the rear of the village did not appear to be guarded. Instead of drawing his sword, he pulled off his bow and nocked an arrow. Though he was not technically an archer, he possessed considerable skill with the bow. *With the way this Orron fights, I would be better off striking from a distance.*

He ordered his men to attack. They rushed past him, and he approached quickly and quietly from the rear.

―――

The Keepers passed within mere feet of where Kor'lee lay holding her breath. As they moved toward the edge of the village, she raised to a crouch. Suddenly, a massive explosion originating from somewhere at the front of the village shook the ground.

Raulin looked at her and nodded his head. "If you would please, m'lady…"

Kor'lee stuck the end of her arrow into the simmering coals and it lit immediately. She turned to the village and nocked her arrow. Taking a deep breath, she tried to calm her nerves. Though she had spent many hours practicing in the archery range, she had never fired an arrow in battle. *You can do this, Kor'lee.*

As the last of the Keepers entered the village, she took aim at the barrels lining the southern entrance. She breathed out slowly and sent the arrow toward its target. A deafening explosion rocked the ground signaling that she had hit her mark.

"It is time," Raulin said as he drew his sword. Turning to the Bandits coming up behind them, he said, "Men, the battle is on us. The time for vengeance is ours. For our families! For Edelyndia! Attack!"

With a roar, the Bandits poured out of the forest. Kor'lee followed Bruschian at the rear of the charge.

When she reached the village, Kor'lee grabbed Bruschian, and he boosted her onto one of the roofs. She was an archer, so she was of little use on the ground. Her hands shook from a mixture of excitement and fear. Calming herself, she slowed her breathing and nocked an arrow.

Taking aim, she fired her first arrow. It missed its intended target by at least four feet, burying itself harmlessly into the side of a building. She cursed herself silently. Shaking it off, she took aim again and fired. This time it hit a Keeper in the neck, and he fell to the ground. The amount of blood shocked her. She took a deep breath and brought up another arrow. Another Keeper fell.

She alternated between targeting Keepers and the barrels of black powder that Raulin had strategically placed throughout the village. The Bandits knew where they were and how to avoid their blasts.

Taking a momentary pause, she scanned the battle happening beneath her. The Keepers still outnumbered the Bandits, but the regular intervals of explosions were having a chaotic effect; however, their attention was being drawn to the center of the village. The fight seemed to be heading that way.

The houses were close enough for her to travel through the village by jumping from rooftop to rooftop. She moved slowly, stopping frequently to fire arrows. The smoke from the explosions made visibility an issue for her, but it also provided cover. Few Keepers had any idea where the arrows were coming from.

When she reached the village square, she was not prepared for what she saw. Dozens and dozens of bodies littered the ground as Orron and Mattox fought back to back. Orron fought with blinding speed. Mattox was screaming in complete rage as he bashed Keepers' heads in. From where she stood, she could tell that the battle was quickly moving in favor of the rebels. The Keepers were being cut down left and right as they were caught between Orron, Mattox, and Raulin's Bandit reinforcements. The trap that they had planned in the front of the village had worked even better than they had expected. A mighty fire burned brightly. No one could have survived. *Raulin sure knows his explosives.*

She knelt down to create a steady firing position and began loosing her remaining arrows on the Keepers below. Since she was the only skilled archer with the Bandits, they had loaded her up with all the arrows that she could carry. The battle was going well all things considered, but Orron and Mattox were still badly outnumbered. They needed help soon or they would be overwhelmed.

With a cry, Raulin and the Bandits finally reached the square and began fighting their way to the center. Kor'lee smiled with relief. She watched Raulin's progress, shooting Keepers out if his way. She knew she should be focusing on more than just him, but she couldn't help herself. She knew that he would do the same for her.

Out of the corner of her eye, Kor'lee saw Orron's head dip. She turned to see him falling to the ground with pain in his eyes. Blood spurted from a gash in his left calf. A Keeper stood over him ready to deal him a deadly blow. The Keeper's head disappeared as it literally exploded from the impact of Mattox's mace. Raulin reached the center in time to deflect another Keeper away as Orron pulled himself to his feet and rejoined the attack. He was wounded, but he still fought fiercely.

Across the square, Kor'lee saw someone climb up on the roof of a house. *Tysion.*

With alarm, she saw that he had a bow in his hands. He took aim at Orron, Mattox, and Raulin in the middle of the square. She couldn't tell whom he was targeting, but she knew that they were completely defenseless. He was at least seventy yards away. She had never hit a target from that distance.

With her right hand, she reached into her quiver and felt only one arrow left. *One shot.*

Her hands began to tremble.

Inhaling slowly, Tysion took aim. Orron was dancing around quickly, but he was confident that he could eliminate him. Even if this battle was turning into a failure, he knew that Orron was a threat that had to be eliminated. *I did not see the Bandits coming.* He cursed himself for being so shortsighted.

With Orron in his sights, he prepared to fire. Just as he began to release the arrow, he felt an intense burning sensation in his right shoulder. His arrow was sent in a lazy arch over the village and into the fields beyond as he crashed to the roof. *I've been shot!* he realized as he looked at the arrow protruding from his shoulder. Looking across the square, he spotted the distant archer who looked just as surprised as he was that the arrow found its mark. *Kor'lee!*

Shock was quickly overcome by outrage. She was out of arrows. Ignoring the pain, he tried to pull an arrow out of his quiver. *No good.* His right arm was all but useless. He was beaten. There was nothing he could do. *Beaten by a worthless woman…*

The battle was all but over. His men were routed.

He bellowed with rage and threw himself off the roof to the field below. He landed awkwardly and pain shot through his left ankle. Unsure of what to do, he lay on the ground for a moment trying to gather his strength. The remaining Keepers would either be captured or killed. *I failed.* As much as he hated to retreat, he knew that Captain Valtor needed to hear about Orron. *And Kor'lee,* Tysion thought to himself angrily. *Draedon will pay for this.*

Gingerly, he picked himself up and fled for the forest as fast as his damaged ankle would allow.

Chapter Thirty

Orron thrust his spear through a Keeper, lost his balance, and stumbled to the ground. He looked up expecting another attacker but there was no one. The battle was over. The few remaining Keepers were fleeing the village.

He rolled over onto his back and gasped for air. The battle had not lasted as long as he thought it would, but he was completely spent. Bodies lay everywhere, some dead, others dying. He closed his eyes and nearly passed out. His head was pounding.

"It's kind of an odd place to take a nap don't you think?"

Orron opened one eye to see a grinning Raulin offering him his hand. He just shook his head and smiled as Raulin pulled him up. He tried to put weight on his left leg and winced in pain.

"That's pretty deep," Raulin said. "You better get that looked at."

"I'll be fine." Orron tore a piece of his shirt of and wrapped it around the damaged flesh. It was bad, but he knew it would heal quickly.

Raulin wiped the blood off his sword. "I have to tell you, Orron, I much prefer fighting *with* rather than against you."

"The feeling is mutual, my friend. You are pretty formidable with the sword."

Mattox walked over. Blood flowed down his arm.

"You're hurt," Orron said with concern in his voice.

"Oh, it's just the wound from a week ago. It's opened again."

"Will you be alright?"

"I'll survive."

"You're not too bad with club of yours either," Raulin said to Mattox.

Mattox only nodded, too tired to speak. The three men stood silently trying to catch their breath. Kor'lee leapt down from the roof and ran over to the group.

"Are you guys all right?"

"I'm afraid you're not rid of us yet," Raulin said. "That was some pretty impressive shooting. Not bad for a girl," he added with a wink.

Kor'lee punched him in the shoulder eliciting a groan. "Hey, watch it. I've been fighting for my life while you danced around on rooftops!"

"*Danced on rooftops!*" Kor'lee said, feigning anger. "I saved your life at least five times."

"Never! I had things perfectly under control!"

"The lady speaks the truth," said Bruschian as he approached the group. He had a nasty cut on the side of his face and walked with a slight limp.

"Bruschian, how nice of you to join us! It looks like you got a little uglier in this little battle," Raulin said, obviously happy to see his old friend alive.

"Oh my!" Kor'lee said when she saw his face. "Let me have a look at that."

"It's just a scratch. Many of our men who have been dealt worse. You should tend to them first."

With a nod, Kor'lee slung her bow across her back and went in search of the injured.

"Well, lad, I wasn't sure if I should believe you, but you were right. The Keepers didn't stand a chance. What now?" Mattox asked as she walked away.

"We regroup and plan our next move."

"Regroup?" Raulin said. "We should pursue the retreating Keepers!"

"No," Orron said, shaking his head. "There's no point in wasting our energies to track the few that are left through the forest. Besides, we want them carrying a message back to Farovale of what happened here."

"But if we let them go, we will have to fight them all over again," Raulin protested.

"The boy is right," Mattox said. "There's no point in chasing them through the night. We will have plenty more to fight later anyway. Let them tell the others what a mighty force we have here."

Raulin relented. Orron looked at the group gravely. "We have dealt the Keepers a serious blow to their pride, but little more. We defeated two hundred today, but there are thousands more where they came from. They will not underestimate us again."

"What do you want us to do next?" Bruschian asked.

The mantle of responsibility hit Orron suddenly as he studied the faces looking at him expectantly. *I have become their leader,* he realized. Even battle trained and proven men like Raulin and Bruschian did not question his authority. *That's a heavy responsibility to bear.*

"Right now let's tend to the wounded on both sides."

"As far as I'm concerned, the wounded Keepers can die where they lay," Mattox said as he spat on the ground.

"Mattox, they are men like us." Orron said gently, but firmly. "Many had little to no choice but to join the Keepers. We *will* tend to their wounds."

Turning to Raulin, he said, "We need to place some scouts on the road and around the perimeter. I don't believe that they will try a counter attack, but we should be prepared just in case."

"I'll take care of it. A few of my men served as Healers before coming to the Bandits. I will have them help Kor'lee." He left with Bruschian to get things organized.

When they were alone, Orron turned to Mattox. "I know that mercy is hard for you. It is for me too. Nevertheless, we are not savages. We are not like them, thus we *must* be better."

"Being 'better' doesn't bring my Me'ra back," he replied angrily.

"Neither does lowering yourself to their level." That seemed to hit home. Mattox was slow to reply.

"As always, I know you're right, lad," he said with a grunt. "It doesn't mean I have to like it."

"You're a good man, Mattox. I'm glad to call you my friend."

"With the way you swing that staff of yours, I sure as heck don't want to be called your enemy!"

The sun was setting when Orron, Raulin, Bruschian, Mattox, and Kor'lee gathered in front of the fireplace at the Mill. They were all exhausted beyond comprehension. Miraculously, not a single Bandit was killed during the battle, though several were wounded. Only two were wounded seriously. An elderly man lost a hand while a young boy lost an eye. By all accounts, it was a resounding victory, but one that Orron was reluctant to celebrate. *Many more will die before this is over.*

No one wanted to speak, but plans had to be made. Finally, Raulin spoke up. "We all know that this was little more than a skirmish for the Keepers. We acquitted ourselves well today, but this is just the start of a long road."

"Aye," Mattox said. "But it is a sting they will not soon forget."

"True," Raulin conceded, "but it may be a sting that stirs the beast, so to speak."

Everyone sat quietly under the enormity of that truth. Though Orron knew that they were doing the Will of the Maker, their task was overwhelming. The Church obviously had not considered this small rebellion much to be feared otherwise they would have sent more Keepers.

Raulin continued, "Until today, they thought this little rebellion was just the two of you. Now they know that the Forest Bandits have joined in."

"They know I'm with you as well," Kor'lee added. Everyone turned to look at her. "I shot Tysion, their commander, just as he was about to send an arrow at one of you. He recognized me before he fled."

"They may try to use your father against you," Raulin said gravely.

"It won't work," she said with a steely edge to her voice.

Orron finally stirred. "You are all right to feel the enormity of our task. It is heavy. There is no doubt about that. We have the one thing on our side that they do not."

"Aye, and what is that?" Mattox asked.

"The Maker. He is on our side. That is all that matters."

"Fairy tales and mythology may be enough for you, Orron, but we need more than that to win this war," Raulin said, shaking his head.

Orron was about to argue the point, but thought better of it. Now was not the time for that conversation. "What do you think we need to do next, Raulin?"

"We need more men," he replied.

"*And* women," Kor'lee corrected him.

"Yes, and women that can fight like you. My point is, we need more…well…*more* of everything. I have full confidence in my men, but they are not trained warriors. They lack the weapons that we will need to take on a brigade, let alone legions of Keepers."

"I agree," Orron said. "We need more to join our cause; that is certain."

"What about the other villages in the foothills?" Mattox asked. "Surely there are men there who would fight."

"But to get to them, we would need to go through Farovale to leave the valley. There's a full legion of Keepers stationed there. I'm not sure we'd make it," Kor'lee said.

"Aye, you have a point there," Mattox conceded.

"No," Bruschian interjected. "There is another way."

"Through the mountains at this time of year?" Mattox asked incredulously. "That's suicide."

"No, it's not," Raulin said, suddenly energized. "I don't know why I didn't think of it!"

"Think of what?" Kor'lee asked.

"There's a pass that few people know about. We have used it to get supplies from the western villages. You have to scale the side of the western bluffs, but it is at a spot where the passage is not too difficult. I've never taken the pass this time of year, but it should be possible."

Then it clicked. From deep within the recesses of his spirit, Orron felt the Maker speaking to him. The others continued to discuss the best way to head through the pass, but Orron's attention was drawn elsewhere. From within, the Maker again began to speak His Will. He smiled.

"What are you smiling about?" Mattox asked when he noticed the look on Orron's face.

"I have a plan. We don't have enough time to gather as many people as we may like, but if we can gather from a couple of outlying villages it just might work," Orron said.

Raulin rolled his eyes. "Please tell me it's not as crazy as the last one."

"Oh, it might be crazier. Do you have any of that black powder left?"

Raulin smiled. "Sure do! I can tell you that I like this plan already!"

"How hard would it be to get men up on each of the bluffs around Farovale?"

"They are practically impossible to climb, especially to the east."

"Practically, but not actually impossible?"

Raulin eyed him suspiciously. "I guess it's not impossible. Why?"

Orron knelt on the ground and began to draw on the dusty floor with his finger. "Here's what we are going to do…"

Chapter Thirty-One

Draedon looked up at the sky. The clouds looked foreboding. For over a week, it looked as though a blizzard would strike at any moment, but only small amounts of snow had fallen. Still, it was unseasonably cold, which added to the gloom.

"I would like to see the state of the northern defenses, Commander. I hope they are better than the others that I have seen," Elder Zittas said with his standard air of annoyance.

Today, Draedon had the great misfortune of leading the Elder on a tour of the city's defenses. As always, Zittas was full of criticism. *You're an Elder. You haven't a clue about defensive fortifications.* To make matters worse, Captain Valtor was along for the show, very much enjoying Draedon being belittled. He suspected that this was their plan all along, to undermine his authority in front of his men.

"Yes, Elder Zittas. I am here to serve," he replied, barely attempting to hide his disdain for the man.

Evening was quickly approaching. The company of Keepers were expected to return from Lillyndale at any moment. They were about to inspect one of the archer's towers in the northeastern corner of the wall when they heard a commotion coming from the northern gate. A Keeper ran over to where they were standing.

"Commander Draedon, Elder Zittas...Marshal Tysion has returned from Lillyndale."

"Just Marshal Tysion?" Captain Valtor interjected.

Draedon glared at Valtor for speaking out of turn.

"Yes, Captain," the Keeper replied. "Only Tysion has returned, and he is wounded."

The group made their way as quickly as they could through the cramped streets toward the gate. When they arrived, they found Tysion being attended to by two Healers. An arrow was still protruding from his shoulder. When he saw Draedon approach, his face grew red with rage, and he pushed the healers away.

"*You!*" he said pointing an accusatory finger at Draedon. "You have been aiding the Heretics all along!"

That stopped Draedon in his tracks. "How dare you, Marshal Tysion! That is a baseless and reckless accusation."

"What happened, Tysion?" Valtor asked.

"We were defeated. It was a mess. The Bandits knew about our plans and came to the rebels' aid. It was *his* doing, I tell you!"

"Watch yourself," Draedon growled.

"Do you have evidence of this?" Elder Zittas asked.

Tysion pointed at the arrow in his shoulder. "*This* is my evidence!"

"What are you talking about?" Draedon demanded.

"I was shot by *your* daughter!"

A hush fell over the growing crowd that was gathering around the gate. *Kor'lee, what have you done?*

"Is...is she alright?" Draedon knew that this was probably not the time to ask, but he couldn't help himself.

"Your daughter commits treason against the Church and that's all you care about?" Tysion said angrily.

"There must be an explanation for this."

"There is! She's a Heretic!" Tysion replied hotly. "And yes, she is fine, for now. But when I get my hands on her I'll—"

"*Enough!*" Draedon shouted. Suddenly remembering his position, he drew himself up and spoke with authority "I am the Legion Commander and you will *not* address me in this manner! These are baseless accusations you are making against my daughter!"

"They are true," Valtor said smugly.

Draedon turned to him, and it took all of his strength to keep from wiping the look off his face. "And you would know this how?"

"Scouts under my orders have been observing her for quite some time. She has been sneaking out of the city for months to aid the Forest Bandits."

Draedon heart leapt into his throat. His face flushed, and blood pounded in his ears. He didn't know what to say. *He has to be lying. She wouldn't—* Then he remembered the late nights, the way she would stumble through an explanation of where she was going. His heart sank. *Kor'lee...*

"That's not all," Valtor said. "I, myself, witnessed her conspiring with Raulin, the head of the Bandits, at the Lillyndale Mid-Summer Festival."

"If you saw them at the Festival why did you not arrest Raulin?" Draedon challenged.

"I was not sure it was him until later."

"And you're just now bringing this up?"

Draedon was doing everything he could to draw attention away from Kor'lee. His only hope was to turn this into Valtor's word against his. He knew where the Elders' favor lay, but he knew there was a chance that the crowd would favor him.

"Enough!" Elder Zittas said from behind them. "I have heard enough. Captain Valtor has been keeping me informed of this investigation. There has been some damning evidence collected against you. Add this account from Marshal Tysion, and I have no choice but to remove you from your command pending a full investigation."

Draedon couldn't believe what he was hearing. He knew this day was coming, but he was still not prepared for it. "You have no right—"

"On the contrary," Zittas said coldly. "I am an Elder of the One True Church. I speak for the Maker, Himself. I have *every* right!"

"You speak for yourself," Draedon muttered to himself. He knew he was out of line, but at this point, he no longer cared.

"What was that?" Zittas challenged.

"I said you speak for yourself," Draedon said loud enough for everyone to hear. He knew he had lost. *If I'm going down, I might as well go down in style.*

His eyes flashed with defiance. "You care nothing for the Church or the people who worship there. All you care about are your own ambitions. You are unworthy to speak for the Church let alone the Maker!"

The crowd was so quiet that no one even dared to breathe. Zittas stood there with his mouth open in shock.

Draedon continued, "I have served in the Keepers for thirty-two years. I have witnessed corruption and greed that would make most men vomit. The Maker is not in your Church. He is certainly not with you!"

"That is enough, Draedon. You—"

"I will tell you when I am finished!" Draedon said angrily. "I have stood by for far too long as you and your arrogant minions have abused your power at will." He waved his arms, gesturing to the Citadel around him.

"The Keepers were supposed to be something that stood for good, for justice. Now, you think you can use them as the enforcers of your personal agendas. My daughter is the most just and noble person that I know. If standing against you to defend the innocent people of Lillyndale makes her a Heretic, then go ahead and call me one as well!"

He knew that his words would have little effect, but it felt good finally to take a public stand for what he believed in. With his left hand, he reached for the butt of his sword causing Valtor to tense and partially draw his own.

"Relax, Captain. If I wanted you dead, you would have died a long time ago. Here," he said as he handed him his sword, "I will not give you the pleasure of resisting this false arrest. I will surrender willingly."

"Arrest him!" Captain Valtor ordered. None of the Keepers moved. Draedon knew that many that were standing close by were loyal to him. Tension filled the air. *The last thing I want is bloodshed.*

"It's fine," he said the Keeper next to him. "Do as you're ordered."

"I'm sorry, sir," the man said with remorse. With reluctance, he and another Keeper grabbed him by the arm and began to escort him away.

"Wait!" Valtor said. "I will have a word with him before he goes."

He walked over and whispered into Draedon's ear. "I want you to know that I will take special pleasure in…shall we say…interrogating your lovely daughter when we catch her."

Draedon's face turned bright red with rage as the veins bulged on his neck. "You wouldn't dare touch her!"

"Oh, you can count on there being lots of touching," he said with an evil look in his eyes. That was too much for Draedon to handle. With a savage cry he yanked his arms free and grabbed Valtor by the neck. The look of sheer panic in his eyes as the air was squeezed out of his lungs was worth the sharp pain Draedon felt when he was struck in the head from behind with the butt of a sword. The last thing that he saw as he blacked out was Valtor gasping for air. He was filled with thoughts of fear and regret as he pictured Kor'lee in the wretched man's hands.

Chapter Thirty-Two

"Here," Raulin said, offering Kor'lee a bowl of something warm and unsightly. "Bruschian is a terrible cook, so it tastes awful, but the meat will help replenish your energy."

"I heard that," Bruschian said from the other side of the fire.

She gladly accepted. After taking a bite, she grimaced and forced herself to swallow. Trying to keep Bruschian from hearing, she said quietly, "You're right. He's a terrible cook."

"I heard that too!"

If her face weren't so frozen, she would have blushed. "Sorry, Bruschian. Thank you for the food."

"You're welcome, Kor'lee." He pointed his ladle at Raulin. "You are *not* welcome."

Kor'lee smiled, and even that small motion seemed to hurt. The day's journey up the side of the bluff and into the mountain pass was exhausting and painful. With all of the hiking she had done outside the walls of Farovale, she had mistakenly assumed that she would be more than ready for the difficult journey. Now, after the long day of hiking and climbing, every muscle in her body ached.

Ignoring the taste of the mushy concoction, she tore through her bowl. *It might not taste good, but the warmth sure does feel great.* The cold was every bit as bad as the difficult terrain.

They made camp in a small hollow between two boulders. Too exhausted from the hike, they decided against making an adequate shelter and opted instead for a hearty fire. Bruschian was sitting across the fire next to Mattox. Raulin was sitting rather closely to Kor'lee, something she both took note of and didn't mind one bit.

"Do I want to know what's in this?" Raulin asked.

"No, I think not," was Bruschian's curt reply.

"I figured. It's a good thing you are pretty good with a sword, or I'd have no real use for you."

Bruschian just grunted in reply. Kor'lee often wondered what drew such an unlikely paring together. Bruschian was a giant of a man, much older than Raulin. He was at least in his mid to late thirties if not older. She suspected that his incredible fitness masked his true age. He was quiet, unassuming, and humble. Though he tended to allow people to make the poor assumption that he was little more than a dumb brute, Kor'lee sensed that the opposite was true.

In complete contrast, Raulin was young, brash, and more than a little confident in his abilities. He was loud and bold, and enjoyed being the center of attention. However, like Bruschian, he had a kind heart and was a good man.

Suddenly curious, Kor'lee asked, "How did you two meet?"

Bruschian's only response was a quiet chuckle. She turned to Raulin, looking at him expectantly. Clearly wanting to avoid the question, he busied himself with picking some dirt out of his nails.

"I'm waiting," she said, pushing Raulin to respond.

He sighed. "We met several years ago in the Holy City when I was twelve or thirteen. We've been together ever since."

Kor'lee just kept staring at him, waiting for a more complete explanation. When one did not come, Bruschian cleared his throat and spoke up.

"What he meant to say is that I *rescued* him in the Holy City when he was twelve or thirteen."

"Hey, I had the situation under control," Raulin protested.

"Hardly."

"What situation?" Kor'lee asked, this time directing her question to Bruschian.

"I was walking through a corner market one day, minding my own business, when I heard this young boy crying while a woman was screaming—"

"Hey, I wasn't crying!"

"You were most certainly crying."

"I was yelling and tears were streaming down my face because she hit me in the nose."

Kor'lee couldn't help but notice that he was protesting a little too hard. "So he was crying, what happened?" she said.

"I wasn't crying," Raulin mumbled to no one in particular. Mattox just grunted in amusement and kept eating.

"Well, apparently he was trying to steal her purse. When I came onto the scene, he had his hand stuck in one of her purse strings. She had an iron grip on the other and was beating him senseless with her free hand." By this point, he was laughing which made Kor'lee laugh. Raulin did not find it quite as amusing.

"I'll never forget the look of terror on his face," Bruschian said between bursts of laughter. "You'd think the lady was a giant ogre beating him with a mighty club."

"I wasn't afraid of the *woman*. It was the *Keepers* that were running over and yelling at me that made me nervous," Raulin said defensively.

"Nervous? With the Maker as my witness, he was crying hysterically at the beating he was receiving!" Bruschian wiped a tear away from eyes. Kor'lee had never seen him laugh so hard.

It was a pleasant sound that made her feel happier than she had been in a long while.

"Anyway," he said once he was able to continue. "You are right about the Keepers. They were coming at him with swords drawn like he was some kind of Heretic trying to assassinate an Elder. I knew at that moment that I had two choices. I could abandon him to the fate of a criminal caught stealing from one of the wealthy citizens of the Holy City, which usually meant a severe beating and the loss of his right hand, or I could intervene on his behalf. He looked so pitiful, what with his ribs showing and him looking all sickly-like, so I decided to intervene. I tackled the Keepers, knocked 'em senseless, and cut the purse strings with my dagger. I threw the lady a few coins, and we made like the wind out of the Holy City. I have not been back sense."

"Neither have I," Raulin added. "It's a miserable city, anyway."

"I've never been," Kor'lee said. "What's wrong with it?"

"Everything!" Raulin said angrily. "There are starving children wandering the streets, dying every day, while the wealthy elite sit fat and lazy in front of their fires, throwing away more food in a night than I ate in a month."

"Why doesn't the Church help?" Kor'lee asked, though she knew the answer already.

"They don't exist to help people. They exist to make money and make pompous men famous."

They were all silent for a few minutes as Raulin's words hung over the group. A question popped into Kor'lee's mind. "I'm guessing that Raulin was in the Holy City to beg and survive after…well after what happened to his village. Why were you there, Bruschian?"

He shrugged. "I had just finished my final tour in the Keepers."

Kor'lee's jaw dropped. "You were a Keeper?"

Even Mattox, who had barely said a word since they left Lillyndale, looked up from his bowl at the revelation.

Bruschian sighed. "Yes. I don't talk about it much. It's not something I'm terribly proud of. People don't usually react too well to it." He was clearly referencing her and Mattox's reactions.

"I...well...it just surprised me, that's all," Kor'lee replied.

"What most people from the northern territories don't realize is that most men don't have a choice about joining the Keepers. In the southern territories, where I grew up, most families are forced to offer up their sons to pay off a crippling debt to the Church. My father died while I was young and my mom was forced to borrow money to keep our small farm. When I was old enough, I volunteered before she had to choose which one of us would go. Even though the Great War had been over for about seven years, there was still fighting going on from time to time. I was the biggest and strongest in my family, so I figured I had the best chance of surviving."

The mournful way he described his past almost brought tears to her eyes. She couldn't imagine having to join the Keepers to save her family.

"Anyway, I served the required ten years and not a day longer. When my time was done, I packed up and got out. I was going to head to the woods somewhere to get away from...well from anywhere I'd been. That's when I met Raulin."

"We spent the next several years living in the Great North Woods Territory," Raulin added. "He taught me how to use a bow and wield a sword. Eventually we ended up in Havenshae Valley where we formed the Forest Bandits."

Though Kor'lee had seen the ferocity with which Bruschian had fought in Lillyndale, she still had a hard time picturing him as a Keeper. It made her wonder how many Keepers were in fact not evil, but forced into service as he had been.

"I served under your father," Bruschian said to Kor'lee. That bit of news shocked her. Until this moment, she had never really talked about her father with him, though his identity was well known among the Bandits.

"You did?"

"Yes. I know you are having a hard time with him right now, but he was a good man and a good officer. He dealt with the peasants fairly and never committed the atrocities that most officers enjoyed doing."

She just looked down at her hands feeling ashamed. These days she was so conflicted about her feelings for her father. On one hand, she hated him for willingly serving alongside such a horrible group of men, but on the other, she knew him to be good and kind.

"I know who your father is, Kor'lee," Mattox said, finally breaking his silence.

Her heart sank. Even though she had always guessed that Orron would have told him, she still avoided mentioning her father around Mattox. It was Keepers serving under her father that had committed such atrocious acts to the woman he loved. She felt as though she was, at least in some small way, responsible for Mattox's sorrow.

She studied his face, trying to figure out how he took the news. He remained impassive, just staring into the fire.

"I know what the Keepers did to your wife…I…I'm so sorry."

He looked up and into her eyes. "Kor'lee, I know that you carry the burden of what your father and his men have done. I can see it in your eyes. But you are your own person."

That was all he said. It wasn't much, but it meant the world to Kor'lee. She had been dreading him finding out, fearing what he would think of her. He had endured so much already.

The group fell silent for a long while, each person lost in their own thoughts. Bitterly cold wind howled through the pass stealing away any heat that the fire offered.

"Well, it is late, and the night isn't getting any younger," Raulin finally said. "We have a long day ahead of us. I suggest we get some sleep. I will take first watch." Though they were high up in the mountains and safe from any Keepers, there were dangerous animals that were lurking about.

Kor'lee did not sleep well at all. She tossed and turned all through the night. Every time she closed her eyes, she saw the faces of the villagers whom she had met at the Mid-Summer Festival. She imagined her father ordering their deaths.

Morning came shortly after she finally fell asleep. Raulin gently shook her arm, dragging her awake. Though no one was eager to tackle the difficult terrain, the cold drove everyone to get moving. They broke camp quickly and continued their climb.

The second day's journey was harder than the first. When they finally decided to stop and make camp that night, they were fortunate enough to find a small cave in which they could huddle. It didn't provide much in the way of warmth, but it kept the wind at bay. Bruschian and Mattox built a small fire and the group pressed together, hoping that their collective body heat could protect against the cold. No one felt like talking, and they all spent the night in misery.

The third day of their journey was spent descending from the mountains. To Kor'lee's surprise, the descent was more exhausting than the climb. Though the terrain was less steep on this side of the pass, the grade caused her legs to burn. Every time they stopped for a quick break, her legs shook violently.

The only redeeming factor from this stage of the journey was the view. Kor'lee had seen most of Edelyndia, but nothing compared to what she saw coming out of the pass. Even though they were passing through at a relatively low altitude compared to some of the majestic peaks that were all around her, the snow-covered foothills were breathtaking.

They pressed on, pushing their pace faster than the previous two days. Raulin said that they were almost to the bottom. By mid-afternoon, the ground began to level out, and by early evening, they finally reached the road that connected the villages to the north and south. When they decided to stop for the night, they decided against making a fire. They were now in Keeper territory.

As quickly as their aching bodies would allow, they made a makeshift shelter that provided a little bit of respite from the howling winter air. Snow was beginning to fall, heralding the possible start of the winter storm that had been lurking on the horizon for over a week.

"I think that we should split up tomorrow," Raulin suggested as they ate strips of dried venison.

"It isn't safe for us to go alone," Mattox said.

"True," Raulin agreed. "There will probably be Keeper patrols throughout the countryside. Then we go out in pairs?" he offered.

"Aye, I think that wise."

"Terashale is just to the north of us. Covenglade is a ways down this road to the south," Raulin said. "I have some good contacts in Terashale that will be sympathetic to our cause. I will go there."

"I know Cleric Torker in Covenglade very well," Kor'lee offered. "He is a good man and is very close to my family. I should head there."

Raulin gave her a disapproving look. He didn't appear to like the thought of leaving her, yet another thing that Kor'lee both took note of and didn't mind one bit.

"Very well," Raulin said. "Bruschian should go with you."

Bruschian nodded in agreement.

"Aye, well then it looks like I'm with you, lad," Mattox said.

"Sounds good," Raulin said. "Then it is settled. Since Terashale is much closer to our current position, it will take you longer to return. Let's meet back here in two nights. If you are not back by then, we will come after you."

"We will be fine, Raulin," Kor'lee said.

"I don't doubt you, but we don't yet know where the loyalties of the people of Covenglade lie. They are the closest village to

Farovale and enjoy many of the luxuries that the Church has to offer."

Kor'lee knew that was far from the truth. She had seen firsthand the struggles they faced when she visited last spring, but she was too tired to disagree, so she let it go.

Questions, fears, and insecurities plagued her throughout the night. Bruschian was not overly fond of making speeches, so she knew the task would fall to her to inspire people to join their cause. *Who am I to rally people?* Now that she had the opportunity to make a difference, she was no longer sure that it was something that she could handle. *Well, either way, the task is mine. My father always said that I needed to be careful what I wished for.*

Chapter Thirty-Three

"Our scouts have just returned. The Heretics are long gone," Tysion reported to Valtor and Elder Zittas. They were gathered in the sitting room in Draedon's old quarters. A group of twenty Keepers was tearing his home apart, looking for evidence of Draedon's involvement with the rebels. Thus far, they had recovered nothing.

"All that was left was a mound of burning bodies…Keepers from the looks of it," Tysion continued. "The scouts said they could smell the burning flesh from miles away. Apparently the rebels have abandoned the town and vanished into the forest—"

"Rebels?" Zittas challenged. "They are Heretics. Do not romanticize them by giving them titles more noble than they actually are."

Tysion nodded, his face turning red from embarrassment.

Vanished? What are they up to now? Valtor wondered. "Why would they go to all the trouble of defending a town in battle just to abandon it after winning?"

"Maybe they were afraid of what our response would be," Tysion offered.

"No," Zittas said gravely. "Their victory was never about Lillyndale. It was about embarrassing the Church and the Keepers. This Orron knows exactly what he is doing."

Zittas turned and walked down the hall to the dining room. Tysion and Valtor followed.

"They are spreading word of their victory," Zittas added.

"You don't think a war will break out, do you?" Tysion asked incredulously. "Surely the peasants are not that stupid. We would crush them."

"Of course we could crush them," Zittas snapped. "But at what cost? The Council does not want another war with which to contend. It is up to us to crush this rebellion before it goes any further."

"That shouldn't be too hard with Draedon finally out of the picture," Valtor said smugly. *Finally, the position I rightly deserve is mine!* Though he was only "acting" Legion Commander, he knew that it was only a matter of time before his full promotion was made official.

Zittas moved to the wall and studied one of the paintings. It was a depiction of the Maker creating the Keepers. He was standing over the glowing form of a man, shining in brilliant white. In His right hand was a staff with many symbols on it. It appeared that He was handing it to His newly created Keeper.

Valtor smiled. He had heard the legend many times. Supposedly, the Keepers started out as some sort of otherworldly being. They then mated with the women of Edelyndia and a new breed of half-human-half-demigod soldiers were born into the world. From there, the Church was formed with these powerful beings slowly evolving into the order of clerics and Keepers that ruled today. It was all nonsense to him, but some still clung to the fantasy.

"Now that you have the reins, what is your next move?" Zittas turned to face Valtor.

"I fear that many of the battalion chiefs remain loyal to Draedon. There was much unrest over his detainment."

"Deal with them swiftly and quietly. We cannot contend with them while dealing with the rebellion."

"I will, though I feel that it is best for that to wait. If I start deposing other officers so soon after Draedon, I fear that many Keepers may desert and join the rebellion. For all his faults, Draedon managed to win the loyalty of his men."

"Captain…*Commander* Valtor is right," Tysion said. "I have worked closely with many of the men, and I believe for many their loyalties were as much with Draedon as they are with the Church."

"Yet another sign of his failures," Zittas conceded. "Very well, we can purge the ranks later. You must, however, keep a very close eye on the battalion chiefs."

"I agree," Valtor said. "I already have some of my spies working on that as we speak."

"Good, good. Now what are your plans for the Heretics?"

"Throughout the summer Inspections I noticed some troubling things. I believe that many of the clerics of this territory have been working with Draedon."

Zittas raised an eyebrow at that.

"I can't be certain that they have been working *directly* with the Heretics, but I do believe that they were aiding Draedon in circumventing the Inspections. With Draedon removed, they may choose to align themselves with the Heretics."

Zittas sat down at the head of the large table. Valtor joined him at his right. Tysion chose to remain standing. It would not have been respectful for someone of his rank to sit at a table with an Elder.

Zittas seemed lost in thought. His lips moved silently as if he were talking himself through a difficult problem. It was, in fact, a very difficult problem, Valtor realized. A rebellion among the common peasants was one thing, but if there was corruption in the Church it was quite another. Containing a rebellion with the support of a number of clerics could turn a spark into an inferno, pushing Edelyndia to the brink of war.

"This is quite troubling, Commander," Zittas finally said, "quite troubling indeed. If the rebellion spreads into the ranks of the Church…well, it could spell disaster."

"Shall I have these clerics arrested and interrogated?"

Zittas spun around. "Do you realize what you are saying? Never have the members of the Clergy been publicly detained and punished. If word spread that the Church was infected with the Heretic corruption, we could lose our control."

"What if it wasn't public?" Tysion said quietly.

"What do you mean?" Zittas asked.

"What if it looked like the Heretics were the ones who detained and…um…'questioned' the clerics?"

Valtor realized where Tysion was going. *That could work!* "Yes, yes. What if we staged it so that it looked like the Heretics were responsible? We could get the information we need *plus* the added bonus of making it appear that they were targeting 'innocent' members of the Clergy. It would be perfect!"

Zittas looked skeptical. "How would you do this?"

"It's not that difficult, actually," Tysion said. "We've done things like this before. Basically, we go in, eliminate everyone in the village, question the cleric in the process, then finish the job. We stage the town to make it look like the Heretics did it, then we send out spies to spread the word."

"That's a lot of bloodshed," Zittas said distastefully.

"But it is necessary to control this rebellion," Valtor insisted. "Like you said, if the corruption has already crept into the Church, we may end up with a full-scale war on our hands…at least in the Northern Territories."

Zittas shook his head. "None of this would have been necessary if the Council would have just listened to me and removed Draedon a long time ago." He stood up, signaling that they had reached a decision. "Very well, Commander. Make it so."

They began walking back toward the front of the house. As they walked, Valtor turned to Tysion. "Take a company of Keepers that you trust. Head to Covenglade first. I am absolutely certain that Cleric Torker was aiding Draedon. Report back to me when it is finished."

"Yes, sir." Tysion left immediately. Valtor and Zittas sat down in front of the fireplace.

"We have to get this situation under control, Commander," Zittas said with desperation creeping into his voice. "If this goes any further…" His voice trailed off as he continued to stare out the window.

"Don't worry, Your Grace. I will take care of this and get this Territory back where it should be—in line with the Church."

Zittas looked over at him solemnly. "I trust that you will. If you don't, I'm afraid the consequences will be far reaching."

There was a knock at the door and a winded Keeper entered the house.

"There…there's a man at the North Gate who insists on speaking directly with the Legion Commander."

"Have someone else deal with him, we are busy," Valtor said dismissively.

"He claims to be the leader of the Heretics from Lillyndale, sir."

Valtor shot a look at Zittas. *Their leader? Why would he come here?* "What does he look like?"

"He wears the cloak of an officer and his head is completely bald."

Jumping to his feet, Valtor ordered, "Quick, sound the alarm! If he is here, we can be sure that more are close at hand. They may be planning to attack." He turned to Zittas. "I think it is best that you move to the Cathedral, Elder Zittas. It is well fortified." Zittas nodded in agreement.

Valtor rushed out of the house with the Keeper close on his heels. Alarm bells began to ring. The city seemed to spring to life. Keepers, well trained and prepared, flowed out of buildings to their various defensive positions and assignments.

When he arrived, Valtor bounded up the stairs to the top of the wall. There, standing in the middle of the road a few hundred yards from the front gate stood a cloaked man. Even from this distance, Valtor recognized the imposing figure as the man who attacked him in Lillyndale. A chill ran down his spine. *Orron.*

Chapter Thirty-Four

Standing in the middle of the road outside of Farovale, Orron looked at the bluffs to his right and left. *They are exactly as Raulin described them.* Pleased, Orron began to brace himself for what he knew would come next. The alarm bells had been sounding for about thirty minutes when Valtor appeared atop the wall. He would never forget the man who had laid a hand on Ly'ra in anger. *You and I have much to discuss.*

He breathed slowly. Now was not the time for vengeful thoughts. That would have to wait.

The snow began to fall more heavily as the day had progressed. Now in mid-afternoon Orron could sense that they were in the early stages of what would be a heavy blizzard. *The storm has come at last.*

Since Valtor had arrived, he had been issuing orders to the Keepers behind the walls. Orron was content to wait patiently. He knew that he had a long ordeal ahead of him.

Finally, Valtor appeared to have everything set. He placed both hands on the wall and studied Orron. After a moment, he yelled to him.

"You there. Heretic. Lay down your arms, and your life will be spared."

Orron laughed aloud, making a show of his disdain for Valtor. "I requested audience with the Commander of this Legion, not his lapdog. Where is Commander Draedon?"

The insult hit home. Even from where he stood, Orron could see Valtor's face turn red.

"*Former* Commander Draedon was arrested on charges of conspiring with Heretics such as yourself. I am acting-commander and *will* receive your respect."

Arrested as a Heretic? That caught Orron off-guard. According to Kor'lee, Draedon was part of the problem, not aiding a rebellion. He shook it off and responded, "I do not and will never respect any man who picks fights with little girls."

Valtor's eyes narrowed. His snake-like voice grew in pitch as he responded angrily. "That is *enough*, rebel whelp. Lay down your arms and surrender *immediately*. This is your final warning."

With a signal of his hand, archers appeared, spread across the wall flanking Valtor. They aimed their drawn longbows at Orron. Slowly, Orron extended his hands out.

"I have come alone and unarmed to offer you a trade—my life for the freedom of the two young girls you illegally and immorally claimed in the travesty you call the Inspection."

Orron's words carried bite. Valtor appeared not to receive them well. He issued another order, and the gates opened. A full company of Keepers filed out and warily surrounded Orron.

"I take it your answer is no?" he yelled to Valtor.

"You are a Heretic! The Church does not negotiate with scum like you. I am placing you under arrest for treason against the Holy Church."

"By 'you' I assume you mean your men. Are you too afraid to confront me directly?" Orron challenged.

Valtor shook with indignation. "Detain him immediately!"

The Keepers closed quickly on Orron and threw him to the ground. Though he did not offer any resistance, they beat him mercilessly with their fists and feet as they bound his hands roughly behind him. Throughout the beating, Orron did not make a sound.

One blow from a Keeper's boot caught him in the ribs just below his right armpit. He felt the sickening crunch of bones breaking, and it took all of his self-control to keep from crying out. In fact, he knew it took more than his own strength. Over and over, the mantra played through his mind as he endured the severe beating.

As they dragged him to his feet, another Keeper struck him on the left side of his temple with the butt of his sword. Orron sagged and nearly blacked out. Still, he remained silent.

Finally, the beating ceased as he stood on shaky legs. A Keeper shoved him from behind, and he was barely able to keep his balance as they herded him through the gate and into Farovale. Once inside he was confronted face-to-face by the sneering Valtor.

"I don't know what trickery you used to defeat my men in Lillyndale. You don't look like much to me."

"This is your last warning, Valtor," Orron said weakly as he coughed up blood. "Release the girls or I will rain destruction down on this city like you have never seen."

Valtor smiled, thinking he had won.

"That is enough, Heretic. It is *you* who will feel the wrath of the Church." Turning to the Keeper standing next to him, he ordered, "Bring him with me. Elder Zittas wants to interrogate him personally in his quarters."

Orron was half-dragged, half-pushed through Farovale toward the soaring tower that he assumed was the Cathedral. His ribs cried out in protest to every movement, but he refused to give Valtor the satisfaction of hearing him cry out in pain.

When they arrived at the doors to the Cathedral, a cleric demanded that they remove their boots before entering. A Keeper had to remove Orron's for him. He did so roughly, twisting his ankle in the process. As they made their way through the elaborate and ornate hall to the stairs, Orron was sickened by the overabundance of wealth proudly on display. *This building is about making great these arrogant men, not the Maker for Whom it supposedly stands.*

The journey up the stairs was a painful one. Orron fell twice. When they arrived at their apparent destination, Valtor knocked, and they were summoned to enter. They entered a large room covered in lavish decorations and furniture.

A large, plump man was sitting proudly on a throne-like chair by the fireplace. He motioned for the Keepers to leave. When they were alone, he said, "Why don't you two join me next to the fire. It is dreadfully cold outside."

He had an air of regal piety that seemed a little too forced to Orron. Valtor shoved him into a chair across from pompous man and took the chair next to him.

Once they were situated, the man continued. "I am Elder Zittas, and who might you be?"

Orron said nothing. Zittas seemed unfazed. It appeared that this was little more than a game to him.

"I can see that having your hands bound is causing you some discomfort, but I'm afraid that is absolutely necessary…what with all the blood on your hands from the Keepers you murdered in Lillyndale," Zittas said with a feigned apologetic look on his face. Orron remained silent, as did Valtor. It was apparent that Zittas was going to handle the interrogation.

"Are you Orron?"

Zittas waited patiently as Orron considered his options. He was tempted to refuse to speak, but he ultimately decided against it. *My words will fall on deaf ears, but I must speak the message I have been given.*

He cleared his voice and said, "I am."

"Then you are the leader of the rebels?"

"I am."

"Then do you deny killing the Keepers at Lillyndale?"

"I do not."

Zittas smiled, apparently pleased at how this was going. "Tell me, why have you come here? You had to know that your crimes are punishable only by death?"

"I came to offer my life as a trade for the innocent girls you wrongfully seized."

Zittas clenched his jaw, but remained calm. Orron could see malice boiling just beneath the surface. "I'm afraid that you are mistaken. We had every right to claim those girls in the Inspection."

"You have long since overstepped your rights. Since you have refused my offer, then I have come to issue you one final warning."

Zittas smiled. "Oh? And you think that you are in a position to issue warnings?"

"I am. That is why I am here."

"No, you are here because you were arrested and brought in front of me as a prisoner."

"That was by choice. I surrendered myself willingly."

"And why would you do that?"

"I already told you."

Zittas appeared to be flustered. Orron allowed himself a hint of a smile. He was in pain, but that didn't stop him from enjoying the opportunity to confound the simple-minded Elder.

Zittas closed his eyes and rubbed his temples. With irritation evident in his voice, he said, "I thought you were here to offer yourself as a trade."

"I knew that you would have grown too arrogant and overconfident to accept my offer—hence the need for a final warning."

Zittas bristled at the insult. His eyes snapped open and he leaned forward in his seat. "You would be wise to be more cautious with your words, Heretic."

Orron ignored his warning and looked him carefully in the eyes. "It is you who should adopt some caution. The Maker has had enough of the corruption He sees in His Church. I have been sent to weed it out."

Zittas slammed his hand down on the arm of his chair. "How dare you threaten me!" All pretense of piety was dropped. "Do not presume to speak for the Maker in my presence. *I* am an Elder of the One True Church of the Maker. I, *alone*, speak for the Maker!"

"You speak only for yourself," Orron said boldly. Zittas jumped from his chair and struck Orron in the mouth. Orron barely flinched. A small smile played at the corners of his mouth as he saw Zittas shake his hand in pain from the blow he inflicted.

"How dare you! You speak nothing but heresy!" Zittas was shaking with anger.

"I serve One who is greater than you."

"How dare you, you worthless—"

"I'm not finished!" Orron's voice resonated with an authority that silenced Zittas. "This Church of yours no longer bears any resemblance to the Words of the Maker. He is love. You are drunk with power. He cares for the weak, the marginalized. You prey on them to further your ambitions. He has given you numerous opportunities to turn yourself around, and you have ignored His voice. I have come to bring justice and judgment."

Orron's voice grew with each word he spoke. Zittas just stared at him, mouth agape. His eyes simmered with hatred. Valtor just watched the scene unfold, apparently unsure of what to do.

From deep within his spirit, Orron could feel the Maker speaking. These were not his words, but the words of the Maker.

"Your pride and lust for power has blinded you. You can no longer see right from wrong. You abuse the innocent while rewarding the wicked. A Great Deceiver has turned you from the true Maker, and now you have declared yourself His enemy."

Orron slowly rose to his feet. The light seemed to vanish almost entirely in the room as the fire in his eyes bore into Zittas. "Your heart is wicked, Elder-of-nothing. Your buildings are so full of glamour and riches that you have failed to see that the Maker is no longer in them. Your church is nothing more than an institution of hollow words and empty promises. I have been sent from the Throne Room of the Maker to serve as the Assessor of your guilt. You may lay claim to earthly power, but I am a True Keeper of the Maker's Will."

Orron looked first at Zittas who was literally shaking with rage then at Valtor who seemed frozen in place. With quiet and deadly calm, he finished by saying, "Your Age of Reckoning has come."

"*Enough!*" Zittas screamed. "Commander, take this filth out of my sight. I have had enough of his heresies."

Orron gritted his teeth and looked up at the visibly shaken Zittas. "You have received your final warning."

That finally pushed Zittas over the edge. He grabbed a candlestick off the fireplace mantle and struck Orron in the head with all his might. Orron fell into darkness.

Chapter Thirty-Five

Raulin watched as the people of Terashale were busy making their final preparations. As he expected, many were more than willing to join their cause. *There are plenty who will jump at the chance to fight back,* he thought with satisfaction.

They had arrived around mid-morning, and the villagers quickly gathered in the town church, which often served as a meeting hall. The villagers of Terashale had long been strong supporters of the Forest Bandits. Whenever he could arrange it, Raulin would journey through the pass to spread word of the Bandits successes.

It had been simple really. All he had to do was share what he had seen at Lillyndale. Mattox had even added a few details of what had happened to his family, though Raulin could not imagine how difficult that must have been for him. When they had finished, the villagers were enraged and ready to charge into battle that very moment. Raulin had to work hard to convince them that they needed more than anger. Some supplies would be nice as well.

One of the reasons Terashale supported the Bandits so strongly was because of the influence their cleric wielded. Cleric

Serado was unique. He was physically imposing. Standing at just over six feet tall, he was thick with muscle, and his skin was as dark as night. Before taking up the vows of the clergy, he had served as an enlisted man in the Keepers during the uprising. Unlike many of the clerics Raulin had met, Serado was jovial and kind. His personality and appearance marked him as different, but what truly made him unique among the clergy was that he never truly left his violent past.

Now, Raulin sat with Serado, watching the villagers who were going with them gather up their meager possessions. He turned the Cleric.

"So, are you going with us?"

Serado ran his hand over his bald head. Apparently, his hair never returned after his years in the Keepers. "That is a very good question."

"We could really use you, Serado." Raulin meant it. Though he had never seen him fight, his feats in the uprising were the stuff of legends.

"But do you need me as a man of the cloth or as a warrior?"

"Does there have to be a distinction?"

Serado smiled. "Some would say yes."

"Others would say no."

"I presume those 'others' would include you?"

"Do I need to answer that?"

Serado shook his head. "No, I know where you stand." He paused and looked at Raulin carefully. "What happens when you win this battle?"

"I guess the rebellion will spread."

"It will have to. The Church will not surrender a Territory without a fight. They will retaliate."

"We will be ready," Raulin said confidently.

"Will you?" The question was asked honestly, not as a challenged. Serado gestured to the villagers readying for departure. "Tell me, Raulin. What do you see?"

Raulin thought about it. "I see people who are ready to stand up for what they believe in."

"Yes, that is true, but do you see warriors?"

Some of the villagers looked like they would be able to handle themselves in battle. Most, however, had never held a sword, let alone fought to the death.

"They will fight well. What they lack in training they make up for in conviction."

Serado nodded. "I have seen well-trained men fight without conviction. I have seen poorly trained fight with it. My experiences have taught me that it is better to have both."

"I can't argue with you there." Raulin wondered what he was trying to say. "You still haven't answered my question."

"True. That is because I do not know the answer." He sighed. "I took a vow of non-violence, but I have come to learn that the Church I swore that vow too never truly existed, at least not in my time. So, fighting does not bother me."

"Then what is your hesitation?"

Serado looked at him carefully. "Many will die in what is to come, and I'm not just talking about this battle. What you intend to do will start a war, perhaps one even deadlier than the Great War. I know the tactics of this Church. They will not just punish the rebels. They will lash out at those who do not fight as well. They will aim to undermine you by spreading fear in all those who might support you."

Raulin sat silently. He did not want to think about that, but he knew it was true. Stories of atrocities like those committed in Lillyndale were far too common a tale in these dark times. With a shudder, the dark memories from his childhood tugged at his mind. *I know all too well what this Church is capable of.*

Serado continued. "My hesitation comes from trying to determine if I am best used fighting alongside you or remaining behind to defend those who do not fight."

"Either way you choose," Raulin said as he clapped him on the shoulder, "your support is greatly appreciated."

Mattox approached them with Orron's staff in his hand. Orron had made him promise to care for it while he went off on his foolish mission. Raulin had tremendous respect for Orron, but he found him quite odd.

"When will they be ready?" Mattox asked gruffly.

"It shouldn't be much longer." Mattox was understandably impatient. Even though they weren't supposed to meet up with Kor'lee at the crossroads until the next night, Mattox had talked him into arriving early just in case the others did as well. Raulin doubted they would.

"How many are joining us?" Mattox asked.

"About one hundred and fifty," Serado said.

Mattox sighed in frustration. "That's not nearly enough!" Raulin glanced at Serado who appeared to take no offense.

"Maybe Kor'lee will have more success," Raulin offered, but he didn't really believe it. One hundred and fifty was actually pretty good considering the state of things in the villages around Edelyndia. Times were very hard, and it was going to be difficult finding able-bodied men in the dead of winter. Terashale was already on the tipping point. He knew that Covenglade was going to be a tougher sell.

Raulin looked up at the snow falling from the sky and frowned. *The weather is going to be a problem.* Crossing the mountain pass had been difficult enough without a blizzard to contend with. He knew that in places the snow would be at least waist deep. This worried him tremendously, until he remembered a trick that Bruschian had taught him many years prior. He nodded to Mattox and headed into the village.

Terashale was small, almost as small as Lillyndale, though it was very different in many ways. Unlike the wide open expanses of Lillyndale, it was tucked into the thick forests of the northwestern Avolyndas Mountain Range. Huts rarely larger than two rooms were strewn among the trees with one road cutting through the center. The heavy tree growth provided protection from the biting, often cruel northern winds. The smoke pouring from the many chimneys combined with the tree tops to create the impression of complete enclosure in the cold winter months.

Their remote location far from the Keeper Citadel provided them some relief from frequent visits and abuse, but they still had experienced their share of misery at the hands of the Church. Now that they had committed themselves fully to the rebellion everyone was on edge. Men, women, and even many children carried some sort of weapon.

He stopped at the small house of a family he knew well. The door was open as they were busy readying for departure. He knocked on the door frame before entering.

"Raulin, come in. Get yourself out of that cold," a hearty woman said, ushering him inside.

"I am sorry to bother you, Bel'ara, but I have a favor to ask."

Bel'ara and her husband Gamir had long been supporters of the Forest Bandits. Gamir had even lived and fought with them for a while a couple of years back before a seasonal illness forced him to return to Terashale. They were both about ten years older than Raulin and had never been able to have children. Though they never had to personally endure the Inspection as parents, it did not lessen their hatred for the Church.

"Anything you need, Raulin. Gamir will be back shortly."

"Actually you are the person I need to talk to. Could I perhaps have some of that cord that you weave so skillfully?" Bel'ara was a weaver, but more importantly her particular gift was making cord so strong and light that it could be used for just about anything.

"Of course! How much do you need?"

"Well," Raulin replied a little embarrassed about what he was asking. Her cord was very valuable. "How much do you have?"

She motioned him over to a large chest in the corner of the room and opened it. Inside were rolls and rolls of cord.

"Can I... um... have all of it?"

Her eyes opened wide. "I would guess that this must be pretty important."

"Yes, ma'am, it is. It just might be the key to us making it through the pass safely in time for our attack."

She smiled and nodded. "Then you are lucky that I had just finished my early winter batch before you arrived. Take it. Take it all!"

Raulin thanked her profusely. He knew this was a tremendous sacrifice for her to make. This was their only livelihood. He made a mental note to make sure that if they survived the coming battle he needed to give her family extra provisions next year.

"I won't take it all right now. I only need one roll for an experiment that I need to run."

"Well that sounds mysterious," she said with a sly grin. "Very well, you know where to find it."

She handed him one roll and closed the lid. As Raulin started to walk toward the door she stopped him.

"Now, Raulin. You need to know that I am not letting Gamir go on this crusade without me."

Raulin started to protest. He had never planned on bringing women along. *Well other than Kor'lee, of course.*

She stopped him with the stern look on her face. "Now listen here, young man. This war that you are trying to stir up will affect more than just the menfolk. We women have suffered just as bad as you have, and this war will only make it worse. There's no telling what will happen to us if you fail. You are going to need every able bodied person if you want to win this."

Raulin looked at the steely determination in her eyes as her words sunk in. He remembered what Serado had told him. *This is not just about the Forest Bandits anymore*, he realized. If they were somehow successful, what they were about to do would change the course of history for all of Edelyndia. The thought scared him.

"You are right, Bel'ara. I would be honored if you would join us."

She smiled brightly. "Good! I didn't want to have to resort to my backup plan if you said no."

"What was that?"

Bel'ara winked. "You don't want to know. Now, off with you and your little experiment."

Raulin let out a small laugh and left with his roll of cord in hand. He headed out into the surrounding forest to gather the supplies he would need. After constructing the implement he hoped would give them an edge in crossing the mountain pass, he headed back through the village to the spot where he had left Mattox waiting impatiently for the villagers to be ready to depart.

"Where have you been?" Mattox asked gruffly.

"Making these," Raulin said as he tossed his creations on the ground.

"What are those supposed to be?" Mattox studied the two objects made of scavenged sticks and the cord Bel'ara had given him.

"Snow shoes," Raulin said proudly. "Attach these to your feet and you can walk on top of the snow instead of sinking into it." Mattox tried them on and was surprised at the results. Raulin thought he even noticed the faintest hint of a smile playing at the corners of his mouth.

"Not bad," Mattox replied. "It just might work."

Together, they went through the village and showed those joining the mission how to fashion sticks and cord together to make snowshoes of their own. A little over two hours later, the last of the departing villagers said their goodbyes and the party prepared to set out on the road south. Serado found Raulin at the head of the group. Raulin noticed that he was not carrying a pack.

"I am guessing this means you are staying." Raulin said.

"Yes. I feel it is best."

Raulin offered him his hand. Serado ignored it and pulled him into a mighty embrace. "I will be praying continuously to the Maker for your success. The fate of Edelyndia is now in His hands. Goodbye, my friend. May your sword be swift and true."

Serado turned to face the gathered villagers. He lifted his arms, closed his eyes, and spoke with a booming voice.

"Most Holy Maker, I beseech You to protect and guide these brave men and women who are going and those who are staying behind. May Your face shine continuously upon us. Guard our hearts from evil. Give us the strength we will need for the dark days before us. We are Yours from the moment of our creation to the moment of our death. Do with us as You will."

Silence descended upon the village. Raulin nodded at Serado. Mattox joined him and together they led the way out of the village and into the uncertainty that lay ahead.

Later that night Raulin and Mattox sat in front of the fire where they camped for the nigh. They had made good time on their uneventful journey to the crossroads. Now, Raulin sat quietly, contemplating the events of the day while wrestling with what still lay ahead. The snow was falling quite hard, but he felt very good about their chances of making it through the pass now that they all had snowshoes. Many people were even able to make a second set for anyone who would be joining them from Covenglade. *Not a bad day's work.*

"I do believe we will make it through the pass in time after all," Raulin said confidently.

"Aye, we may indeed."

Raulin looked at Mattox with a mock accusatory stare. "Is that actually optimism that I hear?"

"Perhaps. Maybe just a little."

"Coming from you, that's pretty big news!"

Mattox suddenly became serious. "I should have known better than to doubt the Maker."

Before he could catch himself, Raulin blurted out, "I'd say you of all people should have every right to doubt Him."

As soon as he said it, he wished he could have taken it back. The pained expression that came over Mattox's face cut deeply.

"I...I'm sorry, that was—"

"No, it's fine, lad. I know you didn't mean anything by it."

Awkward silence fell between them. Finally, it was Mattox who spoke first. "I do not doubt Him, though. You should know that." His voice was quiet.

Raulin shifted uncomfortably. "You don't have to—"

"You need to hear this, boy." The stern tone to his voice demanded Raulin's attention.

"What I've been through...what my family has been through..." His voice faltered slightly. "Well, we've been through the worst kind of darkness."

He stared at the ground, trying to gather his thoughts. Raulin felt tremendously uncomfortable, which was usually the time when he would say something sarcastic or find a reason to leave. This time, however, he actually wanted to know where Mattox was going with this.

Raulin realized that they had a lot in common. Both had experienced tremendous loss at the hands of the Keepers. The difference was that he used his bitterness as the motivation to fight. Mattox turned to faith.

Mattox went on. "I was like you once. When my oldest was taken, I was bitter, angry, and full of hatred. It burned within me. You know what? I liked it!" He looked Raulin solemnly in the eye. "But I realized before it was too late that the very fire that I thought was driving me on was actually burning up anything good that was left in me. It was Me'ra—"

His voice cracked at the mention of her name. Raulin could feel long-buried emotions rising to the surface deep inside the recesses of his heart that he did not wish to confront.

"It was Me'ra who saved me," Mattox said almost reverently, oblivious to the growing tension in Raulin. "She was strong enough to tell me what I fool I was, and she was loving enough to help me come back from the dark places I had gone to. It was her unshakable faith in the Maker that showed me that He is real and still in control."

"How can you say that?" Raulin interjected angrily. He couldn't understand why this made him so upset, but somehow what Mattox was saying was bothering him greatly. "How can you say that He is in control when He lets these terrible things happen? Where was He when Lillyndale was attacked?"

Raulin's voice rose as he began to lose control of himself. He knew he was about to cross a line, but he couldn't stop himself now.

"Where was He when your wife was killed and your daughter taken?" He was nearly shouting now. "Where was He when my parents were slaughtered?"

It felt like a blow to the head as all the emotions and memories of that horrible night from his youth came flooding back. Long repressed feelings, questions, doubts, and pain returned as unwanted guests.

Mattox leaned back and looked up at the dark night sky. The stars were hidden beneath the thick cloud cover. Though the wind was still howling, the snowfall had lightened for the moment.

"How do you know that stars exist?" Mattox asked.

Raulin was startled by the sudden change in the direction of the conversation. "What?"

"You heard the question. Answer it."

Raulin thought about it for a moment. "Because I've seen them a thousand times."

"But what about now? Prove to me right now that they exist." Mattox looked at him patiently.

Raulin struggled to find an answer. "I can't," he said with a sigh.

"Why not?"

"Because I cannot see them."

"So you're saying that seeing is believing, but just because you can't see, doesn't mean your original belief was wrong?"

Now Raulin was just confused.

Mattox breathed out slowly and settled back on the ground next to the fire. He continued to stare up at the sky.

"You listen close, boy. I am going to teach you something that my Me'ra once taught me. I know the Maker is real right now in the bad times, because I know He was real in the good times. Everything that has been good in my life—Me'ra's smile, Ly'ra's laugh, the way A'ra could sing—all these things were proof of the Maker's love. I knew it then; I could feel it."

Mattox was quiet for a moment. When he spoke again, his voice was barely above a whisper.

"I would be lying if I said I could feel the Maker and His goodness right now. No, now all I feel is cold, lonely, angry, and full of hatred. But just because His goodness seems to be hidden behind a dark cloud, it doesn't mean it isn't there. I just have to wait for the storm to pass."

He fell silent. Raulin didn't know what to say or think. Though outwardly he claimed to deny the Maker's existence, he knew deep down that it was all an act. He very much believed He existed, and Raulin hated Him for it. If he acknowledged the Maker's existence, he would have to acknowledge the fact that He stood by and did nothing while his parents were killed for no reason.

A small part of him wished he had Mattox's faith. He knew that living with all of his pent-up anger and hatred was not healthy, but it was all he knew. In a way, seeing a man who had every reason to hate the Maker even more than he did but instead chose to place his trust in Him, only served to dig into his unhealed wounds.

Frustrated, Raulin rolled over and covered himself with his blanket, laying as close to the fire as he dared. He knew he would not find the answer he needed that night. Part of him wondered if he would ever find what he was searching for. *How can I when I don't even know what it is that I'm supposed to be looking for.*

CHAPTER THIRTY-SIX

The snow was beginning to fall more steadily as Kor'lee and Bruschian approached Covenglade. Night would soon be falling. The journey from the crossroads to Covenglade had gone much slower than Kor'lee had anticipated. She had hoped to arrive around noon, but Bruschian had wisely insisted on traveling farther from the road in hopes of avoiding confrontation with any Keepers. It proved a good idea as they had passed at least three Keeper scouting parties.

When they arrived, the town was quiet. Everyone seemed to be indoors. There was something unnerving about the feel of the town. Even with a storm approaching, everything was unnaturally quiet, almost abandoned. If it were not for the light in some of the windows, she would have thought that perhaps the town was deserted.

"Let's go to the cleric's manor," Kor'lee said, not realizing that she was whispering. "I think we should start there."

Bruschian nodded in agreement, appearing to be as uneasy as she was. They headed to the manor, which was located on the northeastern edge of the village, facing the square. Unlike in

Lillyndale, the cleric lived in a simple house, no bigger than any of his neighbors' houses.

When they arrived at the cleric's door, Kor'lee glanced nervously over her shoulder. She couldn't shake the feeling that something was wrong. She gave the door three sharp raps. From inside came the sound of shuffling feet and muffled voices. After a moment, she heard a voice on the other side of the door.

"Who goes there?"

"I am an old friend of Cleric Torker. Is he here? I very much wish to speak with him." She tried to sound as innocent and harmless as possible.

"What is your name?"

Unsure of whether or not she should give it, she looked over at Bruschian for help. He just shrugged his shoulders and gripped the hilt of his sword hanging at his side.

Well, they will find out sooner or later. "My name is Kor'lee."

"Kor'lee?" a voice she recognized said. After the sound of many locks being undone, the door swung open to reveal Cleric Torker's smiling face. A man she didn't recognize stood next to him.

"Kor'lee!" Torker said joyfully. "It *is* you!"

Before she could react, the little cleric wrapped her in a joyous embrace. "It is been far too long since I have seen you. With all that has happened, well, I have been worried about your safety."

Apparently, he knows that I've run away from my father. She returned the hug awkwardly. "It is good to see you as well, Cleric Torker."

"Please, please, call me Torker," he said as he held her at arm's length. His eyes were filled with such kindness. For the first time in weeks, Kor'lee felt herself relaxing. "You know I am not one who is fond of titles."

Torker just gazed at her happily as if he were lost in thought. "We have been praying that you would make it here, and now... here you are!"

She looked at him curiously. *What is he talking about?* Before she could inquire further, he turned to take in the big man standing next to her. "Heavens, me. Please forgive my rudeness. My name is Torker. Who might you be?"

"My name is Bruschian, sir. I am a friend of Kor'lee."

"Well, any friend of Kor'lee is welcome in my home." Then with a wink, he added, "Though everyone is welcome in my home, so I guess that doesn't make you all that special!"

That even elicited a grin from Bruschian who rarely smiled.

Kor'lee found it odd that the man next to Torker did not introduce himself. He just eyed them suspiciously.

"Come, come, let's get you two inside. A mighty storm is brewing!"

They were swept inside by the jovial, little man. He ushered them through his humble home to a small sitting room in the back of the house that appeared to serve as his study. In the back corner stood a small desk covered in stacks of paper and scrolls. A ring of chairs was arrayed in front of a fireplace. A group of men sat in them.

They stood as Kor'lee entered. To her complete shock, one of the men was her father's servant.

"Einar!" Without thinking about it, she ran over and gave him a huge hug. Not a man who was accustomed to showing affection publicly, Einar blushed.

"It is good to see you, Kor'lee," he mumbled self-consciously.

"What are you doing here," she asked breathlessly. "Why are you not with my father? What happened in Farovale? Is my father angry with me?"

"Slow down, Kor'lee. One question at a time please!"

Suddenly remembering that they had an audience, Kor'lee blushed and stepped back. "Sorry, I…I just didn't expect to see you here."

She looked over at Bruschian who looked lost. "Bruschian, this is Einar. He is...or was..." she looked back to Einar for confirmation.

"*Is*," he said with a nod.

"He *is* my father's servant and close friend."

"It's nice to meet you," Bruschian said.

"Likewise."

"So, Kor'lee," Torker interjected. "What brings you here in this weather?"

Remembering her mission, Kor'lee stepped back next to Bruschian. She took a deep breath, bracing herself for what she had to say and do. Pushing aside her insecurity, she began.

"Torker, Einar, you know whom my father is. For those of you who may not, he is Draedon, the Legion Commander of the Great Avolyndas Territory. Though I love my father deeply, I believe with all my heart that he is serving the wrong side."

She looked around the room at the men that were staring at her silently. Einar shifted uncomfortably in his seat.

Taking a deep breath, she continued. "I have left Farovale and have since seen tremendous injustice at the hands of the Keepers. Men. Women. Children. All have been killed indiscriminately at the hands of the Church." She paused and looked at Bruschian who stood impassively next to her.

"I have joined a group of rebels who have decided that it is their duty to fight back. I have come to ask for your support and for anyone who is willing to stand up against tyranny to join us."

Torker glanced over at Einar who returned his knowing look. Torker looked at Kor'lee and said, "So you have been to Lillyndale?"

"Yes, and I fought the Keepers there."

"You fought the Keepers and lived?" one of the men asked incredulously.

"I did as well," Bruschian said. "A full two companies of Keepers came. We turned them back." He said it rather matter-of-factly, as though it was of little difficulty.

Amazement and horror stood in apparent conflict on some of the faces of those present.

"Is it true what happened in Lillyndale?" Torker asked.

"Do you mean the slaughter of all of its citizens?" Kor'lee asked with disgust. "Yes. They were butchered as if they were little more than animals. I have seen the graves. I have heard the report from the only known survivors. Murder, kidnap, rape. These are the tools that the so-called-church used in this massacre."

Kor'lee looked over at Torker who appeared to be deeply troubled. "I'm sorry, Cleric, but this is what I have seen and heard."

He looked at her with tears in his eyes. "I do not doubt you, child. I have seen corruption and evil fill the Church that I once loved. Now, I hardly recognize it."

"Will you join us?"

He shook his head. "I have taken a vow to never lift a finger in anger against another man. But this is not a question for me." He looked at the rest of the men in the room. "We knew this day was coming. We have spent many nights in front of this fire debating what we would do when it did. It appears that we must all decide for ourselves."

The gathered men looked at each other uneasily. All knew that regardless of what they decided to do, life would never be the same. *You are either for the Church or against it.*

"If we did join you, do you have a plan?" one of the men asked.

Kor'lee looked to Bruschian. He nodded for her to continue.

For the next few minutes, she laid out the plan that Orron had come up with. When she finished, she looked at the faces of the men expectantly. It was apparent that hearing the plan had done little to alleviate their concerns.

She knew what Orron had proposed was bordering on madness. They all did, but she had seen a small force of bandits defeat two full companies of Keepers. She had also witnessed what these men could not possibly believe unless they saw it for themselves. She had seen Orron fight.

"We should gather the village for a meeting," one of the men finally suggested.

"When?" another asked.

"I hate to come across as pushy," Kor'lee interjected, "but I'm afraid that time is working against us. This plan that I have shared…we believe it will drive the Keepers out of the valley, but for this plan to work, we must act quickly."

Torker looked gravely at the group. "We must meet tonight. Let's gather in the church in one hour."

They agreed, and everyone got up to make the necessary preparations. As everyone was leaving, Einar pulled Kor'lee aside.

"I know that we do not have time right now, but after the meeting there is something I want to tell you."

Something in his eyes caught Kor'lee's attention. She wanted to press him for more information, but Torker called him over, and she was left standing alone with Bruschian.

"That went pretty well," he said.

"Yes, but I think that the next meeting will be harder."

"I agree. Convincing men to join forces against the Keepers is no small task."

One hour later, Kor'lee and Bruschian gathered with most of the remainder of the village inside the simple church. It was very unlike the opulent Cathedral in Farovale. The pews were made of wood, smoothed by age. There were no precious metals or jewels that she could see. Instead of stained glass windows, there was simple, clear glass. The altar was large, and the pulpit was small. Every time that Kor'lee visited Covenglade, she enjoyed the services ran by Torker. She had never seen him speak from the pulpit. Once, he had privately told her that he did not like feeling elevated above those he served. He considered himself no better than anyone else was.

Bruschian leaned over to her and said softly, "Torker is declaring his support by housing this meeting here."

"How so?"

"He is hosting a meeting about fighting the Church inside a church. If he were against it, he would never hold such a 'Heretical' meeting in a 'sacred' space."

Once again, Kor'lee was impressed with Bruschian's insight and understanding. "Remind me never to underestimate your brilliance, Bruschian."

He just chuckled softly in response.

When it appeared that everyone who was coming had arrived, Cleric Torker walked slowly and solemnly to the pulpit.

"Friends, family, and guests, tonight we have gathered to discuss matters of grave importance. Before we start, I want you to know that by simply sitting in this room you will be committing high treason against the Church, a crime punishable by death. If you wish to leave, I encourage you to leave now, and no one will think poorly of you for doing so." He paused and scanned the room. Not a single person budged.

"Very well, let us begin. Many, if not all of you know why we are here. The Church whose name adorns this meeting place—the Church that I am sworn to serve and uphold—has committed a great number of atrocities. Many we have seen and others we have only heard tales of." Motioning toward Kor'lee and Bruschian sitting in the back, he said, "With us tonight is the daughter of the Legion Commander of the Avolyndas Territory."

Many heads turned to look at her. She wanted nothing more than to melt into the floor. Bruschian didn't flinch. He just continued to gaze at Torker, confidence oozing off him, which gave her strength.

"Kor'lee, if you would, please come up here and share with everyone what you told me just a short time ago."

Taking a deep breath, Kor'lee stood up and walked slowly to the front of the room. She could feel every eye on her as she stood next to Torker. He gave her a reassuring smile.

Turning to face the crowd, she surveyed their faces. There were men, women, and children of all ages present. Most looked hungry, tired, and scared. *Am I doing the right thing by bringing this on them?*

"I...well...I'm not very good at this sort of thing," she admitted. "My reason for coming here is simple. My friend and I have joined a group of people much like you who have endured incredible hardship at the hands of the Council. They have decided they have no choice but to take up arms and fight back. I have come to ask you to join us."

A murmur swept through the crowd as people digested what she was suggesting. Her hands were trembling violently. She gripped the sides of the pulpit in attempt to hide the evidence of her nervousness.

She looked up at Bruschian and tried to feed off his confidence. As she was about to begin again, she shot Einar a quick glance. He was smiling at her. *What is he smiling about?* She shook it off and continued.

"I know that this is a lot to ask, and I am not going to pretend to understand what some of you would have to sacrifice and risk to join us. But I feel you have the right to know what the Council has done and will continue to do until someone stands up and stops them. Deep in Havenshae Valley there is a village called Lillyndale."

She paused, remembering the mounds of graves. "I say *is*, but what I should say is *was*. The village is no more. Every man, woman, and child was slaughtered at the order of the Council," A single tear fell down her cheek, "at the order of...of my father."

She looked down, ashamed of what her father had done, hating him for allowing such a thing to happen. "I have seen the graves. I have talked to the only two survivors. Murder. Rape. These are the actions that the Council has allowed and even promoted. An entire village of innocent people is no more because...because there was no one who would stand up for them."

Anger, shame, regret, and righteous indignation began to light a fire in her soul. Suddenly, her insecurity began to wash away as the importance of her mission drove her on. She gazed around the room at the people hanging on her every word.

"Someone has to speak for these people, because they will never speak again. They are victims in a long line of innocents victims. We have a plan. Can I promise victory? No. What I *can* promise you is that if we do nothing, evil *will* win."

She thought about saying more but instead let the weight of her words hang over the room. Torker patted her on the shoulder and smiled proudly at her.

"You did well," he whispered to her. "Why don't you and your friend wait at my house? The endless debating is about to begin."

Kor'lee nodded and walked down the aisle and motioned for Bruschian to follow her outside. They walked in silence to the house. When they were inside, they sat down in front of the fire in the sitting room.

"How did I do?" she asked.

"Very well. You had me convinced to join you."

"You joined years ago."

"True."

Kor'lee laughed weakly, and they settled in for the long wait.

True to his word, it was several hours before Torker returned from the meeting. Einar followed him into the sitting room.

"Well, I think you did very well, Kor'lee," Torker said. She could tell he had bad news.

"But..."

"But most of the villagers were too afraid to commit themselves and risk their families for such an uncertain outcome." Torker looked almost as disappointed as she was. "They did, however, agree to provide whatever supplies they could spare."

"*Supplies?*" Kor'lee said in exasperation. "These people are worse off than we are! They can't spare anything, nor could we take it if they offered."

Torker nodded sadly. "I know the time will come when they will have to fight to survive, but I just don't think they are ready for that yet."

They sat in silence. Kor'lee felt like she had failed the cause. Her mind raced with all the things she could have, should have said. Ultimately, though, she couldn't blame them for not joining. *A year ago, I'm not sure I would have joined.*

After a while, Torker stood up. "I'm afraid this old man still needs his rest. The Council insists on forcing me to live in this silly, oversized house. I have several extra rooms upstairs with fresh linens. Please help yourselves."

"I think I am going to turn in as well," Bruschian said as he stood and followed Torker out of the room, leaving Einar and Kor'lee in front of the fire.

When they were alone, Einar said, "You reminded me of him tonight."

"Who?"

"Your father. You have his passion, his fire."

At the mention of her father, Kor'lee grimaced. Angrily, she said, "My father is a terrible man."

He looked at her carefully with a sad look in his eyes. "Kor'lee, there is much you do not know about him."

"I know," she said bitterly. "And what I am learning makes me hate him even more."

"Your father loves you deeply, Kor'lee."

"That's not enough! How can he do nothing? How can he sign orders like that! How..." Tears flowed as her voice trailed off.

Einar reached over and put his hand on her shoulder. "What I am about to tell you I swore to your father that I would never tell. He never wanted you to know because his greatest desire was to keep you safe."

Kor'lee looked at him in confusion.

"Kor'lee, your father is a Heretic. Actually, he has been leading the Heretics for many years."

Chapter Thirty-Seven

Draedon was startled awake by the sound of his cell door crashing open. Four Keepers with their swords drawn entered the cell. Two kept a close eye on him while two more entered, dragging a man between them.

He recognized one of the Keepers who was assigned to watch him. Though he couldn't quite place his name, he knew him to be one of the newer recruits. He was pretty sure the man served under a company marshal who was probably still loyal to him.

"Who is that man?" Draedon asked.

"I'm sorry, sir, but I am not at liberty to say."

"Son, do you know who I am?"

"Yes, sir, but I have orders not to speak with you." The young Keeper refused to make eye contact. The other, older Keeper glared at the young man, but said nothing.

Draedon looked over to where they were chaining the man to the wall. He was badly beaten. It was clear that he had been brutally whipped for some unknown punishment.

"He looks to be in need of medical attention. He should see a healer at once."

The Keepers ignored him.

"This is *not* how the Keepers treated prisoners under my watch."

"Well, you're not Commander anymore, now are you?" the older Keeper said with a sneer on his face.

Once they were finished, the Keepers filed out of the cell, leaving Draedon alone with the man who was now chained to the wall, suspended by his hands from rings bolted into the stone. He hung there, his breaths coming in ragged bursts.

The man appeared to be young, maybe Kor'lee's age. He was bald and wore a long black cloak, much like the one that Draedon wore. It was torn and covered in blood. *If he doesn't get help soon, he may not survive.*

Draedon's right foot was chained to the floor, but there was just enough slack in the chain for him to reach the young man. He grabbed the small bowl of water that they had given him earlier during his "dinner" and started to try to clean some of the wounds through the slits in his cloak. The man did not stir.

I wonder what he did to earn such a beating. His head was devoid of hair like a Keeper officer, but he didn't recognize him. With the bloodied state of his face, he wasn't sure that he could have recognized him anyway. Since there was nothing more that he could do for the young man, he laid down and fell back to sleep.

His cell did not have any windows, so when he awoke to the sound of his breakfast being slid through the slit of the door, he had no idea what time it was. What they gave him barely constituted the word "meal." All they fed him was a few scraps of moldy bread and a small bowl of dirty water.

The only light in the room streamed through the bars of his door from the torches in the corridor outside his cell. He was in a section of the prison that was completely isolated from any other prisoners.

Remembering his new cellmate, he walked over to him to examine his condition. He gasped in surprise as he realized that the wounds had already begun to heal in remarkable fashion. Not only had the bleeding stopped, but also new skin was beginning to form over the gaps. *What the…*

He jumped at the sound of the young man groaning. It echoed in the small stone cell.

"Son, can you hear me?" he asked softly.

"W–water…" the young man managed to get out.

Quickly, Draedon retrieved his bowl and held it to the young man's lips. He drank too quickly and coughed much of it back up.

"Careful, son. You've been badly hurt."

"Thank you," he replied hoarsely. His eyes were caked with dried blood making opening them a difficult task. Draedon tore off part of his shirt, dipped it in the water, and gently rubbed away some of the blood.

"What did you do to earn such a beating?"

"I killed almost two hundred Keepers in Lillyndale," he said so simply that Draedon would have laughed were it not for the seriousness in his voice. Then he added, "Well, that, and I insulted the one called Zittas."

That did draw a laugh from Draedon. "Good for you. I hope you laid into him well enough for the both of us."

The young man regarded him closely, almost as if he recognized him. "My name is Orron."

"As in the Orron that was leading the rebels in Lillyndale?" he asked already knowing the answer.

"That's right. And you must be Draedon."

"Wait…how did you—"

"Kor'lee looks just like you."

The mention of his daughter's name caused Draedon's heart to skip a beat. "You know my daughter?"

The young man shifted uncomfortably and started coughing violently. Hanging from the chains was causing the shackles to dig sharply into his wrists. The coughing only made the situation worse.

Draedon looked around the room for something to help. He drug his cot over. It was just tall enough for Orron to sit on and therefore relieve the stress on his wrists.

Once he was more comfortable, Orron said, "Yes, I know your daughter. She came to Lillyndale with Raulin."

So it's true. Deep down, he always knew that it was. A large part of him was proud of her. *She's braver than I'll ever be.*

"Is she all right?"

"She is. She's a strong woman with a good heart."

Draedon let out a breath he did not realize he had been holding. He had been worried sick about her. It was good to know that she had survived the battle at Lillyndale. He hadn't known what had happened to her after she had wounded Tysion.

"Kor'lee said that you were the Legion Commander. Why are you in here?"

"It's complicated," Draedon replied.

"We don't seem to have anything better to do."

Draedon eyed Orron warily. "Look, I don't mean to be rude, but I barely know you. All I know is that you claim to know my daughter, and that you have killed a great deal of men."

"Have I killed any more than you have on the field of battle?"

He had him there. "Good point."

"You can trust me. Your daughter does."

Draedon looked the young man in the eyes. He prided himself on being a pretty good judge of character. It took him less than two minutes to realize that Valtor was not someone to be trusted. *Or liked for that matter.* There was something different about this boy, something in his eyes.

He decided to trust him. *What do I have to lose? It's not as if things can get a whole lot worse for me in here.*

"Well, it's a long story," Draedon warned.

He launched into his life's history, starting with when he joined the Keepers at age eighteen during the Great War. For what seemed like hours, he told him of his career in the Keepers, of his unexpected promotion to Legion Commander, and his activities with the Heretics. Orron interjected a few clarifying questions here and there but remained mostly quiet.

They broke momentarily for lunch. They only brought food for Draedon. Though Orron protested, Draedon insisted on sharing his measly portion with him. Draedon told the story of Kor'lee's birth. He laughed and cried as he recounted story after story of her childhood. Even all these years later, it was still painful to recount her mother's death. Finally, he told Orron of his painful last encounter with Kor'lee and ended his story with his arrest.

He wasn't sure why he opened up so completely to a stranger. Never had he been so open with anyone about his failures and weaknesses. It was oddly soothing, as if it was a sort of confession. Though Orron did little speaking, he did not appear to judge Draedon for his mistakes or failures.

The only way to mark the passage of time was the regular intervals in which they brought food. After dinner was served, Draedon finally went silent.

"Your daughter doesn't know of your involvement with the Heretics, does she?" Orron asked.

"No."

"Why haven't you told her?"

"I...I really don't know. I guess I was trying to protect her."

"From what?"

"I don't know. I think I was afraid that if she knew that I was aiding the underground rebellion, she would push me to do more."

"So you were actually protecting yourself," he said. Though he did not say it maliciously, the truth in his observation cut him to the core.

He sighed. "Yes, I guess you are right. I always knew that I should have done more. I could have done more."

"When I saw you at the Lillyndale Inspection, I have to admit that I wanted to hate you for what you were doing. Now that I know what was *really* going on, I realize that you saved a lot of innocent people."

"But I didn't do enough," he said bitterly. Though he wasn't sure he wanted to hear the answer, he asked, "Did you lose anyone at the massacre in Lillyndale?"

Orron was quiet for a while. Draedon could almost feel the pain in his voice when he finally spoke.

"Yes. There was a woman…her name was Me'ra. She was like a mother to me. When I arrived, I was too late. There was a group of Keepers standing around while one of them…" his voice trailed off as a lone tear streaked down his cheek. The anger and anguish in his eyes spoke more than his words could have.

"I killed them all for what they did," he said quietly.

Draedon looked down, unable to bear seeing the pain in the young man's eyes. "I'm so sorry. If I had done more, this never would have happened."

"You're right…you could have done more, but you didn't."

Draedon looked up expecting to see judgment, maybe even hatred in Orron's face, but instead saw pity.

"You have made mistakes. We all have. The real question is what will you do next?"

"What *can* I do?" Draedon motioned at the cell around him in frustration. "I'm stuck in here. My authority has been stripped from me."

"You and I will not be here long. I have a job to finish, and so do you."

The seriousness in Orron's face gave Draedon pause. *What is he talking about? There is something very strange about this boy.*

Looking at Orron's wounds, he noticed that they had continued to heal at an unnatural pace. Other than the swelling around his left eye and the bruises on his chest and back, his wounds had nearly healed. Scars were already forming where the whip had torn his flesh. Only the fresh wounds from the shackles on his wrists continued to bleed.

"Who are you?" he asked, suddenly suspicious.

"I already told you."

"No, you told me your name. I told you my life story, and you have told me little-to-nothing about yourself."

He stood up and pointed his finger warily at Orron's scars.

"When they brought you in here last night, you were bleeding so badly I wasn't sure if you would survive the night. Now…well, your wounds have healed faster than I have ever seen."

Orron shook his head. "If I tell you who I am, you won't believe me. Sometimes I have a hard time believing it myself."

"Try me."

He sighed and painfully adjusted his body. The shackles cut deeply, causing fresh blood to drip down his arms once again.

"Like I said, you probably won't believe me, but since you have been so candid about your past, I guess I owe you as much. Unfortunately, there isn't a lot to tell, because, well…there's not much that I remember. As you may have guessed by my lack of hair, I am a Keeper."

"From where?" Draedon asked. "I have been here for several years and have never seen you in Farovale."

"I'm not from…here," Orron said with a hint of a smile.

"What Territory are you from?"

"None of the ones you know."

"Wait…what?" Now Draedon was completely confused. He certainly knew all of the territories of Edelyndia, and all that existed beyond its borders was leagues and leagues of water that stretched as far as the eye could see. Aside from legends and fairy tales, there was no evidence of any other territories existing that he had ever heard of.

"I'm not from Edelyndia. Or anywhere on this world." He winced as he said it. Draedon's mouth just hung open as he stared at him.

"Are you trying to tell me that you're not...not human?"

"I warned you that you wouldn't believe me."

How can I? Though it did explain his unnatural healing, it was too much for him to comprehend.

"Look, you seem like a good man. You're honest—brutally so. My daughter trusts you, and I guess I trusted you enough to tell you my involvement with the Heretics. But *not human?* That's too much," Draedon said incredulously.

"I don't blame you for not believing me. Like I said, I had a hard time believing it too."

Draedon just stared at him in disbelief. "If you're not human, what are you?"

"I am a Keeper—what a Keeper was originally intended to be, a race of beings that the Maker created to protect and carry out His Will, not the perverse thing that the Council created."

Draedon's mind raced with questions as he struggled even to hear what Orron was saying. "I'm sorry, but I am having an incredibly hard time believing you."

"It's okay. If the roles were reversed, I'm sure I would too." He motioned with his head. "Come here and lift my shirt."

Draedon lifted an eyebrow. "Um...what?"

Orron smiled. "Trust me. Lift my shirt."

Draedon stood up and hesitated. "If this gets weird, I'm taking my cot back."

"You mean weirder than it already is?"

"Good point."

Awkwardly, he lifted Orron's shirt. Amidst the dried blood, he could make out the symbol of the Keepers tattooed on his flesh. Marking the skin in this fashion was strictly forbidden by the Church. There was no way anyone could have done this to him legally.

"Where did you get this?"

"Not anywhere in Edelyndia. I can promise you that. Touch it."

Draedon just stared at him.

"I'm serious; touch the mark."

After a moment, Draedon reached his hand out slowly and touched the blackened skin. It was hard and raised slightly. Then, he jerked his hand back in surprise. *Did it just...*

"Feel it?" Orron asked with a smile.

"I...um...I'm not sure."

"What did you feel?"

He didn't know how to describe it. "It felt like I was shocked by some source of energy."

Draedon lowered the shirt and stepped back. He didn't know what he had just experienced, but he felt disquieted.

"Something happened to me recently in the forest," Orron tried to explain. "I can't really describe it, but when I touched the mark after it happened, I reacted much in the same way."

This kid seems so honest and unassuming, but he can't be telling the truth, could he? "If you're this 'True Keeper,' then why are you here?"

"Here, as in this cell?"

"Well yes, but more than that. Why are you here, as in here, here?" He motioned around him.

"You mean in Edelyndia?"

Draedon nodded.

"Again, there is a lot I don't remember. I can tell you it started with a little girl named Ly'ra whom I came here to protect."

Ly'ra. "The little redheaded girl?"

Orron perked up. "You've seen here?"

"Yes, she's here in this prison."

"Is she all right?"

"Yes, when I found that they were keeping her here, I tried to have her moved, but Elder Zittas wouldn't allow it. I made sure she had a private cell with the other little girl...Aly'siah I believe her name was. Last time I visited was yesterday morning. They appeared to be about as well as you would expect little girls to be, locked up in a filthy prison like this."

Orron sighed in relief. "Thank you for watching out for her."

"It was the least I could do. If it were possible, I would have gotten her out of here. So you came here...for her?"

"A little over a year ago she was trapped in a rock slide. I... well, I need you to understand that there are some details that I cannot share with you right now, but I woke up in a clearing. I rescued Ly'ra, and I have been staying with her family ever since. Well, until the night of the massacre," he said, sadness creeping back into his voice.

Draedon took note of the fact that Orron was being somewhat secretive. *What details can't you tell me? You've already told me you're not human!* He let it go. Then, a question occurred to him.

"Wait, so is that how you were able to kill all of those Keepers?"

"Yes, I guess so."

"Are you telling me you have some kind of magical powers?"

That made Orron laugh which sent him into another coughing fit. Draedon looked at him with concern. "I think Valtor broke a couple of ribs that are apparently slower to heal," Orron explained.

"Healing broken ribs falls outside of your powers?" Draedon said sarcastically.

"I never said I had magical powers. I can just...I'm a deadly fighter. Let's leave it at that."

"Now that I can believe. If you faced two companies of Keepers alone and survived, you must be some kind of fighter."

"I wasn't alone. The Forest Bandits were there too."

"Still...they've never been more than an annoyance until you came along."

"Like I said, I never expected you to believe me."

Draedon was silent for a few minutes as he studied Orron. "I don't know who or what you are, but I've known a lot of good men in my life. I've also known even more evil ones. You strike me as someone who falls into the 'good' category, and that's enough for me."

"Thanks."

"Don't mention it."

Though it was impossible to tell the time, Draedon could tell by how tired he felt that it had to be late. He walked over and laid down on the floor where his cot had been.

"You can have this back," Orron offered.

"And let you hang there by your wrists? I don't care if you're not human; you were in a lot of pain. Besides, anyone that's served in the Keepers as long as I have has had to spend more nights laying on the ground than they care to admit."

Draedon laid quietly with his eyes shut. Though he was tired, his mind raced with the revelation that Orron had shared with him. *He can't be telling the truth,* he tried to convince himself.

Draedon had never been a devout follower of the Maker. He rarely gave Him much thought, but he always believed that He existed. He was just always more concerned with the people with whom he actually interacted, namely Kor'lee. He didn't know what to think about what Orron had said, but he had already made up his mind that he would trust him. Though he didn't know how much longer either of them would be alive in here, it was good to have someone to talk to.

Without opening his eyes, he asked, "Are you still awake?"

"Yes," Orron answered.

"Can I give you a piece of advice?"

"Sure."

"If we ever get out of here, I'd keep that bit about not being human to yourself. People will think you're crazy."

Orron laughed, sending him into another fit of coughs.

Chapter Thirty-Eight

"Kor'lee!" Raulin shouted as he awoke from his dream with a start. His heart raced as he tried to find his bearings. *That dream was so real.* He shook his head trying to erase the image of Kor'lee being stabbed through the heart by Tysion. Snow was falling hard as the blizzard was starting to gather strength. He sat up and found that Mattox was also awake.

"Couldn't sleep, lad?" Mattox asked.

"No, I had the most awful dream."

"Oh? So did I," he said absently. "What was yours about?"

"It was terrible. Keepers rode into Covenglade and started killing all the villagers." Raulin shuttered and shut his eyes, trying to get the image out of his head. "I woke up just as Kor'lee was dying." He heard a clatter and looked up to see an ashen Mattox who had dropped his cup.

"What is it?" Raulin asked, suddenly alarmed.

"Who was killing Kor'lee?"

"Why does it—"

"Just answer the question, boy," Mattox said, growing more anxious.

"What's gotten into you? It was just a dream." He had to think for a moment. "I think it was Tysion."

Mattox shot to his feet. "We have to go."

Raulin stood up as well as dread crept into his bones. The look in Mattox's eyes chilled him. "What is it, Mattox?"

"That was no dream," he said solemnly. "It was a vision."

"You're acting crazy, Mattox. You know I don't believe—"

"Raulin, I had the same exact dream down to every last detail. I'd say that is no coincidence."

Raulin's heart jumped into his throat. "Gather the men, we leave at once!"

It had been tremendously difficulty for Kor'lee to fall asleep. What Einar had confided in her was almost too much for her to believe. *My father...a Heretic?*

Einar told her that it all started with the introduction of the Inspections. Before then, he had been fiercely loyal to the Keepers, devoting most of his life to hunting the Heretics. Once he witnessed his first Inspection, everything had changed. He could no longer reconcile his loyalty to the ideals of the Keepers with the injustice he saw them committing. It wasn't until he was named the Legion Commander of this Territory that he officially, though quite secretively, joined the underground rebellion that was forming. The plan was to continue building support among the officers in the Keepers who felt the same way as her father. Unfortunately, the events in Lillyndale had accelerated things before they were ready.

Lillyndale. She finally knew the truth—that it was all Valtor's doing. That, she did not have a hard time believing. In fact, she was tremendously ashamed that she had believed that snake's words.

She had tossed and turned for a couple of hours. Her mind raced as she tried to understand the emotions that she was feeling. Finally, too tired to cry or think anymore, she gave in to her exhaustion and fell asleep.

Suddenly, she was dragged roughly from her sleep by someone shaking her. Her heart felt as if it were going to burst out of fear. Were it not for Cleric Torker placing his hand over her mouth, she would have screamed loud enough to wake the entire village.

"Kor'lee…Kor'lee…it's me, Torker," he said as softly as he could. She could sense the urgency in his voice. Forcing herself to calm down she slowed her breathing and tried to wake herself up.

"What is it? What's wrong?" she said after he removed his hand.

"Quickly, you need to come with me. You need to hide." He moved toward the door, motioning for her to follow.

She stood up and tried to wipe the sleep from her eyes. "What's happened?"

"There's no time!" he said as he came over and grabbed her by the arm. "Bruschian will explain. We must hurry!"

Kor'lee struggled to keep up as he raced through the house. She could hear screaming coming from outside. Torker led her through a maze of rooms to what she assumed was his bedroom. Bruschian and Einar were waiting for her there.

Before she could ask what was going on, Torker said to Bruschian, "Quickly, we must move the bed. The space is under there."

With Bruschian and Einar's help, the large, heavy-looking bed moved easily revealing the shape of a trap door underneath. Torker opened the hatch and motioned for them to get in.

"This is where we keep most of the girls during the Inspection. Stay in here and remain quiet. I will come and get you when it is safe."

Without asking any more questions, Kor'lee grabbed Bruschian's hand, and he lowered her gently to the floor of the hidden chamber. He and Einar followed behind, and Torker closed the trap door above them. Overhead, they heard the scraping of the bed moving back into place.

"How did he do that by himself?" she wondered aloud.

"Maybe he's stronger than he looks," Einar offered.

Pale moonlight streamed through cracks in the wall, just beneath the ceiling.

"It appears to be some kind of cellar," she remarked.

She hurried over the wall and peered through the cracks. Once her eyes focused, she was able to see that the wall faced the courtyard in front of the house. She could see the feet of the villagers scrambling into place as they were herded into a rough circle. Though her view was limited to just their feet, Kor'lee instantly recognized the voice of the leader of the men doing the herding.

"It's Tysion," she said as her heart sank.

"I figured as much," Einar replied. "The cleric came and woke me up just before you. As he led me to his room, he told me that Keepers rode in to the village in the middle of the night. They are gathering up the entire village. It doesn't look good."

The sounds of chaos continued for the next hour as the Keepers ran about the village dragging the men, women, and children out into the snow-covered square. Through the crack, Kor'lee could see that the snow was falling quite heavily now. The wind whipped around, causing her to shiver. *I wish I would have had time to grab my cloak.*

What she saw next made her complaint seem incredibly petty. A pair of legs suddenly made a break from the circle. Judging by their size, she guessed it was a small child. She heard a mother scream followed by the unmistakable twang of a loosed arrow. The child crashed to the ground not far from where Kor'lee stood watching, an arrow protruding from his back. Mercifully, the child appeared to die quickly.

Kor'lee jumped back from the wall and buried her face in Bruschian's chest to stifle her sobs. *Who could do such a horrible thing?*

The Keepers apparently got things under control quickly as deadly silence fell over the crowd. Kor'lee pulled herself away from Bruschian's arms and returned to the crack. The dead child was still on the ground and she had to force herself not to look at him. She had a pretty clear view of the center of the square.

"We are here because we have irrefutable proof that your village has been aiding the Heretics," Tysion said. "Does anyone dare deny it?"

No one said a word.

"Good, perhaps this will go easier than it did in Lillyndale."

From where she stood, she could hear the collective gasp of many of the villagers.

"Where is Cleric Torker?" Tysion asked.

No one responded.

"We can do this the easy way," Tysion said menacingly, "or we can do it the *fun* way. Personally, I prefer the—"

"I'm right here, sir."

Kor'lee's heart sank as she recognized the voice of the sweet, old cleric.

"There is no need for further bloodshed."

"*I* will decide that," Tysion barked as he strode out of Kor'lee's view, toward where she assumed Torker was standing.

She heard Torker gasp as Tysion struck him. Dragging noises followed as Tysion re-entered her view, dragging Torker by the hair. Tears flooded her eyes as she saw the intense pain on his face.

"Torker," she whispered quietly to herself. Bruschian was now standing beside her, looking through another crack. He ground his teeth together in anger.

"We have to help him," she said.

"We cannot. He wouldn't want it," Bruschian replied, though she could tell it pained him to say it. She returned her attention to the horror unfolding outside.

Tysion drew his sword and yanked Torker's head back. "Where are the Heretics?"

"I don't know what you are talking about," Torker said weakly. Tysion took his sword and cut a deep gash in Torker's face. The gentle old man did not make a sound.

"I'll ask you again. Where are the Heretics?"

"I...I don't know what you are talking about." With Torker on his knees, Kor'lee had a clear view of his face. Despite the horror of the situation, she admired his nobility and courage.

Tysion pushed him to the ground and said something to a Keeper standing close by that she couldn't quite make out. The Keeper came over, grabbed Torker's left hand, and held it out on snow-covered dirt.

"I am a generous man," Tysion said patronizingly. "I am going to give you ten chances to answer my question before I start cutting things off that really hurt. Where are the Heretics?"

"My answer will not change, no matter what you do to me."

With a flick of his wrist, Tysion cut off one of the cleric's fingers. Kor'lee gagged.

"This little pinkie went to market," Tysion said with a mocking, singsong voice. "Where will the rest go? I can do this all night, old man. Where are the Heretics?"

Through the pain in his voice, Torker said calmly, "I will pray to the Maker for your soul, young man."

That apparently angered Tysion because he cut off two fingers this time. Torker cried out in agony, and Kor'lee had to turn away.

"Shall we continue? Where are the Heretics?"

"I...I have already forgiven you," Torker said through ragged breaths.

With a savage cry, Tysion cut Torker's entire left hand off. Someone in the crowd screamed. Kor'lee couldn't hold it any longer and vomited on the floor. Tears flowed from her eyes, and it took all of her strength to quiet her sobs. Bruschian grabbed her from behind and hugged her tight, trying to absorb her sorrow.

"We have to do something, Bruschian. We have to!" she said between sobs.

"There is nothing we can do," he said trying to comfort her.

Through the wall, she heard bones snap and Torker cry out in agony. *This can't be happening.*

Suddenly, it dawned on her. *This is how her father must have felt all those years.*

She pulled herself away from Bruschian and faced him.

"My father stood by and let things like this happen. I cannot, I *will not* do the same. We have to go out there."

"You will just share in his fate."

"That is something I am willing to face," she said boldly, though inside her heart quaked with fear.

"Going out there is suicide," Einar said.

"Besides, the bed is above the door," Bruschian added.

"We have to think of something," she said. "Would you do it for me or for Raulin?"

Bruschian looked at her and nodded sharply.

"I will do as you ask."

"This is crazy," Einar muttered but made no effort to stop them.

The ceiling was low, but Kor'lee could still stand upright. With Bruschian's mighty frame, he had to hunch over. He bent over underneath the trap door. No longer worried about remaining quiet, he clenched his jaw and with a mighty push began to lift his shoulders. He roared as he surged upward and the bed crashed onto its side against the wall.

They had to have heard that, she thought to herself, but knew that it no longer mattered. Bruschian half-lifted, half-threw her out of the cellar and into the room. She raced through the house, burst through the front door, and yelled, "*Stop!*"

Chapter Thirty-Nine

Though the snow was falling heavily, the road to Covenglade was mostly sheltered under heavy tree growth. Raulin's side felt as if it were going to burst. After running for what seemed like hours without stopping, he knew that his body couldn't take much more. He slid to a stop and bent over, gasping for breath as the edges of his vision clouded. Somewhere behind him, he could hear the sounds of the more able-bodied men who had been chosen for the mad run to Covenglade. They numbered just over fifty strong.

Mattox reached him and fell to the ground next to him. Running for hours in the frigid air made Raulin's lungs burn.

"How much farther?" Mattox said between gasps.

"I don't know," Raulin replied. "I don't think it's far."

The trailing men soon caught up with them, each as exhausted as he was.

"We need to slow our pace," Mattox said.

"They are in danger—"

"Yes, and we will be in no position to help them if we arrive like this."

Raulin wanted to argue, but he knew Mattox was right. He looked down at his hands and legs that were shaking violently.

"I guess you're right. I could barely hold a sword right now, let alone fight."

"Kor'lee and Bruschian are strong fighters. Plus we don't know if that vision was what was happening now are what is to come."

"We don't even know if it is real!" Raulin said in exasperation.

"Oh, it was real, of that I am certain."

"How can you be?"

Mattox looked at him solemnly. "When you have been alive as long as I have, you learn to recognize the Hand of the Maker at work."

Raulin just shook his head. *There's no point in starting that debate again.*

He stood up and shook the cobwebs from his head. "We need to continue."

"Aye, but make sure to set a more reasonable pace this time."

Raulin nodded, unsure of whether or not he could. *We have to get to Covenglade before...*

He didn't want to finish the thought.

Tysion was standing behind Torker with his sword held to the front of his throat. Torker's left arm hung limply at his side, broken in more than one place. Blood flowed from the stump where his hand used to be. Tysion looked up and saw Kor'lee standing in the doorway. Shock flooded his face, and it was quickly replaced with anger. With a sneer, he shoved the old man to the ground.

"So, whore of a traitor, you have been hiding here the whole time."

"I am giving myself up. Let the cleric go."

She could sense Bruschian creeping through the house behind her. Hoping that he would see and understand her signal, she held a clenched fist in the small of her back, urging him to stay where he was.

Tysion pointed his sword at her. "You and I have business together, Kor'lee. I will make you pay for what you did."

"You mean that little scratch I gave you?" she said tauntingly. "Some powerful warrior you are, being wounded by such a dainty girl as I."

Even in the darkness of night, she could see his face growing red with rage.

"When I am done with you, you will be begging for death," he said.

Kor'lee just returned Tysion's stare. Though her heart raced, she realized that she was no longer afraid. This was what she was meant to do.

She turned her head, but instead of talking to Tysion, she began to address the gathered crowd of villagers.

"Don't you see? This is what I came to warn you about. This is the evil that is a plague on Edelyndia. This," she said as she motioned to the body of the dead child, "this is what happens when we stand by and do nothing."

"Silence!" Tysion yelled, but she ignored him.

"Who will speak for the voice of this fallen child if not you? Who will stand up to this injustice for the fallen, the weak, and the helpless if not you?"

Her voice rose to a fevered pitch and the Keepers just stared at her as if caught in her spell.

"Someone kill her!" Tysion screamed in rage.

A nearby Keeper snapped out of his reverie and drew his sword. As he approached to strike her down, Bruschian stepped from the doorway and grabbed his head from behind. With a quick twist, he snapped the Keeper's neck. The rest of the Keepers drew their swords. Tysion looked furtively around, expecting other Rebels to jump out at any moment.

Kor'lee continued, "For too long, the citizens of this land have stood by while those who claim to speak for the Maker have done whatever they please. Evil reigns because the righteous remain silent. *No more!*" She was shouting now.

She pointed an accusing finger at Tysion. "His strength is found in your fear. If you hide and remain silent, he wins. He *cannot* win. How is it that the innocent suffer while the wicked prevail? Are we not more than cowards?"

"Silence, I said," Tysion yelled futilely.

"No, I will not remain silent anymore." Kor'lee drew herself up regally and held her head high. "I am no longer afraid of you. Take my life if you want. I will gladly forfeit it if it means taking away the hold you have had on me."

She scanned the crowd. The fire of her conviction burned brightly in her eyes. "Would you rather die free from the tyranny of evil men like this and those on the Council, or would you rather live under the cruelty of their unholy reign? Men and women of Covenglade, stand up and fight. If not for truth and justice, for your very survival!"

No one moved. Tysion's face lit with a sinister smile.

"See, Kor'lee? They are nothing but cowards. Your pathetic rebellion will be crushed just like all the others have been." He raised his sword and took a menacing step toward her. "You have failed, just like your father."

A look of concern crept into Kor'lee's face.

"What? Do you not know?" Tysion asked tauntingly.

"Know what?"

"Your father is due to be executed any day now as the worthless traitor that he is. I'm sorry to say that you will not live long enough to see it."

Father! Anger welled up within her. "Then I will die alone fighting for what I believe in my heart to be right!"

"You are not alone," said Einar who strode boldly out of the house brandishing a sword. He handed Kor'lee her bow and quiver. With Einar on one side and Bruschian on the other, Kor'lee pulled the quiver over her head and stood proudly.

"We do not fear you, Tysion. Do your worst."

Just as the mightiest of fires is started with the smallest of sparks, the sight of the trio of rebels bravely standing up to the one hundred Keepers finally stirred the citizens of Covenglade to action.

Tysion lifted his sword and began to rush toward Kor'lee, but he never reached her. A roar broke out through the crowd. Men and women alike threw themselves at the Keepers. Though unarmed, they made up for it with sheer numbers. Quickly the Keeper force was overwhelmed. The fighting was so compact in the small square that the Keepers had difficulty swinging their swords.

Unlike Lillyndale, Covenglade possessed hundreds of able-bodied men and women. They were not as easily slaughtered. Bruschian and Einar threw themselves into the fray, swinging their swords with ferocity. Kor'lee remained where she was, firing her arrows, careful to avoid hitting the citizens of Covenglade, which was no easy task in the chaotic throng of bodies.

In minutes, she was down to her final arrow. Nocking it, she scanned the square for the best place to send it.

Through her peripheral vision, she saw a Keeper lunge at her from her left. She ducked just in time as he missed her head by mere inches with the swing of his sword. Still, she was too slow to avoid it completely. The hilt of his sword caught her in the temple knocking her to the ground. Her vision flashed as she nearly passed out.

With lightning-like reflexes, she rolled to the side as his sword came crashing down in the wooden porch. As the Keeper struggled to dislodge his sword from the porch, she frantically looked around for a weapon, any weapon. Just as the Keeper freed his sword, she spotted her final arrow lying at her feet.

The Keeper hefted the sword above his head. With a savage kick, she landed a blow to his groin that doubled him over. In one motion, she grabbed her arrow and shoved it into the Keeper's exposed neck. He fell to the ground, choking on his own blood.

Shaking, she stood to her feet. Her arrows were gone. Looking down, she saw the dead Keeper's sword. She picked it up and ran into the crowd.

The fire of her conviction still continued to drive her. Each swing of her sword was propelled by her will to avenge all the innocent victims who had suffered at the hands of the Keepers. She parried and thrust with a skill that she had forgotten she had. *My father taught me well.*

Having just stabbed a Keeper through the heart, she had a momentary gap in the fighting to survey the chaos around her. The battle was not going well for the villagers. They fought bravely, but the battle-trained and well-armed Keepers were regaining the upper hand, though at a heavy cost. It appeared that many of the Keepers had fallen and their numbers were a fraction of what they once were.

The villagers fared worse. The ground was littered with scores of dead bodies. Her eyes fell on a large Keeper who had just beheaded an unarmed woman. *Tysion.*

With a savage cry, Kor'lee took off running through the mass of bodies in his direction. She was so focused on Tysion that she almost didn't see the Keeper who stepped in her path. He would have landed a critical blow were it not for the mighty sword of Bruschian that cut him in half.

She continued on, reaching Tysion just as he cut down another villager.

"*Tysion!*" she yelled angrily.

He whirled around to face her, his face twisting into a wicked grin.

She pointed her sword at him. "You will pay for what you've done."

"We will see about that!" he said as he lunged for her. Kor'lee had seen Tysion in training and thought she was aware of the skill in which he fought. She had woefully underestimated him.

He attacked her with a savage flurry of blows. It was all she could do to keep her footing and deflect his attacks. His eyes were filled with utter hatred and savagery.

She continued to back up until she reached the side of a house. She had nowhere to go. Finally, one of his blows got past her defenses and cut a deep gash in her right hand sending her sword flying to the ground.

Tysion punched her in the face with his free hand, knocking her head against the stone wall. Stars clouded her vision as he grabbed her by the throat.

"Look at your failure!" he said as he forced her head to turn toward the square. Many of the brave villagers were being cut down by the two's and three's. The battle appeared hopeless.

"I had orders to kill them all quickly. Now, because of what you've done, I will personally torture the survivors."

With all her remaining strength, she turned her head to face him. "Then you only prove that my cause is just."

He dropped his sword to the ground and punched her once again. She could feel herself starting to lose consciousness. He shook her, trying to keep her awake.

"Oh, no you don't," he said. "I want you to be awake for what I am going to do to you next! You are mine now."

Perhaps the head injury gave her false bravado, but she felt no fear. She spit the blood that was pooling in her mouth into Tysion's face.

"You can take my body, but you will never own me. Today I became free."

Overcome with rage, Tysion roared and with both of his massive hands around her neck, he lifted her off the ground.

Kor'lee's lungs screamed for air as her vision began to fade. Still, she felt no fear. *This is it*, she thought to herself. *I am ready.*

The sounds around her began to fade into the distance. From somewhere that felt far away, she heard a familiar voice calling her name. It was a man, but she couldn't place it.

Suddenly, she felt the pressure on her neck vanish and her feet were once again on the ground. She gasped for breath, and her senses slowly began to return to her. The first thing she noticed when her vision came back was Tysion staring in disbelief at the bleeding stumps where his hands used to be.

She felt as though she was drugged. Slowly, she turned her head and saw what appeared to be Raulin standing next to them with blood dripping from his sword. *Is this real?*

Tysion fell to his knees and in a fluid motion Raulin separated his head from his shoulders, and Tysion's lifeless body fell to the ground with a thud.

Chapter Forty

With the arrival of the villagers from Terashale, the battle quickly turned against the Keepers. They were armed with rudimentary weapons such as clubs, pitchforks, and axes and attacked the Keepers with ferocity. Raulin had arrived just ahead of the rest, leaving Mattox to lead the charge.

The battle was soon over. Without Tysion to organize a response, the remaining Keepers folded. Most fled the village with angry villagers hot on their heels. Mattox and Bruschian managed to stop the pursuit before too much time was wasted chasing Keepers in the dark. They were far more skilled and more villagers would be killed than Keepers would in the pointless excursion.

Raulin tore a piece of cloth off his cloak and wrapped it around Kor'lee's wounded hand.

"I told you, I'm fine," she said hoarsely. Her throat felt as if it had been crushed.

"You will be once the bleeding stops. How is your throat?" he said as he gently examined the quickly forming bruises with his fingers.

"I will be fine. We need to check on the rest of the villagers."

Concern filled his eyes, but he relented. He helped her to her feet, and they made their way through the square. *So many dead,* Kor'lee thought to herself. On the western side of the square, Bruschian and a few villagers were guarding several Keepers who were lying face down in the snow with their hands behind their heads.

"Raulin, what are you doing here?" Bruschian asked with a confused look on his face.

"Well, it's nice to see you too," Raulin said drily.

"He's right," Kor'lee said to Raulin. "Weren't you supposed to wait for us until tomorrow night? How'd you know we needed help?"

"We had a vision that you were in trouble," Mattox said as he joined them.

"A vision?" Kor'lee cocked her head in surprise.

"Well…it was more like a dream," Raulin replied. He shifted awkwardly on his feet.

"I thought you didn't believe in that stuff," Bruschian said.

"I…well…let's discuss this later." It was clear that Raulin did not want to talk about it, not now, not ever.

"Kor'lee, come quick!" She turned to see Einar kneeling in the center of the square holding a bloodied body. *Torker!* In all the chaos, she had nearly forgotten about him. She ran over and knelt down beside him.

Tears filled her eyes as she saw his ruined body. Besides the torture that had been inflicted upon him, he had been trampled in the battle. His breath was coming in short, ragged bursts.

"Torker," she said as she tried to wipe the blood from his face. "Can you hear me?"

Without opening his eyes, he tried to talk, but he was overcome with coughing. Blood flew from his mouth with each burst.

"Don't try to talk," she said, trying to stop herself from crying. The beaten and bloodied old man lying on the ground had been a dear friend. Tonight he had sacrificed his life willingly to save the villagers. *To save me...*

"Kor'lee," he managed to say weakly. "You must promise me that you will forgive your father. He is a good man."

She could hold back the tears no longer. "I...I will try. I *will* try."

"That's a good girl. He...loves you...very much. He's done...so...much to save...so many." His words came in short bursts between coughing fits. With her experience as a healer, Kor'lee knew that blood and fluids were filling his lungs.

"Shh. You need to save your strength."

"My time...has come." He opened one eye and fixed it on her face. "Kor'lee...what you fight for...it is what is right. But...you must remember—" A fresh set of coughs wracked his body, and he was silent when they ceased. For a moment, she thought that he had passed.

With a faint, weak voice, he continued, "The Church...there is good in it. Do not lose faith...do not...give up on it."

Even through the sadness of watching her dying friend struggle, her anger toward the Church burned brightly. *How can he say the Church is good?*

"I have seen what the Church has done," she said bitterly. "Look what they have done to you. It is pure evil."

"No!" he said as strongly as he could muster. He lifted his head up so he could look at her.

"There are evil men...that is true. But the True Church still lives. It is not found in buildings or Councils, but in the righteous." He laid his head back down. "It is alive...in you."

His breathing became even more ragged as he slowly slid toward death's door. "Kor'lee?" he said faintly.

"Yes, Torker. I'm still here." She held the kind old man's face gently in her hands.

"Never stop...fighting. You are meant for great things. I've always seen that...in...you."

"I won't," she said as her tears fell from her face and formed small puddles. With a slight gasp, Torker breathed in his last breath and exhaled.

Einar gently placed his hand over Torker's eyes and closed them. He softly laid his head on the ground and pulled the hood of Torker's robes over his face.

"I'm sorry, Kor'lee" Einar said. "I know how much he meant to you and your father."

Kor'lee just shook her head, not wanting to believe that he was gone. Raulin slid to his knees next to her and wrapped her in his arms as she let the tears fall.

After several minutes, she pulled herself back and wiped her eyes.

"I'm so sorry for your loss, Kor'lee," Raulin said with genuine empathy in his voice.

"He was a great man." She took a deep breath and tried to pull herself together. "And the last thing he would have wanted was for me to sit here crying while people need my help."

She stood to her feet and looked around the square. The snow was stained red. Bodies lay in heaps everywhere. It was hard to tell who was a Keeper and who was a villager.

Kor'lee's head was pounding. The cut on her hand was deep and would probably need further attention. It burned, but she ignored it. She had a job to do.

"How many villagers died?" she asked.

"It's hard to tell. Over a hundred for sure. Maybe more," Einar answered.

"Let's tend to the wounded."

"We need to hurry." Raulin looked at the blizzard that was picking up steam. "If this plan of Orron's is going to work, we need to be back in Havenshae Valley as quickly as possible."

"The blizzard will slow us down." Concern was evident in Kor'lee's voice.

"Aye, that it will," Mattox said as he approached them with Bruschian.

"Can we even risk trying to make it through the pass in this weather?" Bruschian asked.

"I don't see that we have a choice," Einar replied. "Your father will be executed within the week, and I'm assuming that Orron will be as well."

"We need Orron if this is going to succeed," Kor'lee admitted.

"Then we leave tonight…with as many villagers that can survive the long journey," Raulin said decisively.

Kor'lee glanced one more time around the square. She knew that many villagers would have to be left behind. Any who were wounded would not survive the pass in this blizzard. She shook her head.

"Anyone who is left behind will die from the weather."

"Or the Keepers will return and exact revenge," Bruschian added grimly. "That is what they do."

Raulin ran his hand through his hair. "We can leave a handful of able-bodied men to protect them, but that is all. It's the best we can do. We have to leave as soon as possible."

For the second time tonight, Kor'lee caught a glimpse of the kind of decisions her father was forced to make on a regular basis. *Sometimes there are only bad options and worse options.*

"You're right, Raulin," she said reluctantly. "Let's do what we can. Completing our mission in Farovale is the best way to help these villagers in the long run."

Once again, Einar smiled and nodded approvingly. Even Bruschian seemed impressed with her assessment.

"Aye, it's settled—back to that blasted pass. Let's pray that the Maker favors us by making the journey go smoothly," Mattox offered.

"You can pray," Raulin said drily. "I'll place my trust in my snowshoes."

Chapter Forty-One

Orron stood in the center of a large, round room with Draedon by his side. They were surrounded by a circular table at which sat the ten battalion chiefs, Valtor, and Zittas. Draedon and Orron were both dressed in simple gray shirts and pants that they had been issued for this apparent trial. Their hands and feet were wrapped in chains and attached to rings in the floor.

Since he hadn't shaved in days, Draedon's beard was growing thick and scraggly. Orron's face, of course, was still as smooth as ever. Though they hadn't eaten well, they were in relatively good health. All things considered, it could have been worse. *Still staying on plan,* Orron thought with satisfaction.

Valtor stood to his feet and addressed Orron and Draedon.

"You stand before this Keeper Tribunal as prisoners accused of high treason against the One True Church of the Maker. Today, the battalion chiefs will hear the charges levied against you and will see the evidence that has been gathered. They will make their recommendation for your punishment, and I, as acting-Legion Commander, will decide your fate."

He picked up a scroll that was sitting on the table in front of him.

"Orron, you are charged with the murder of over one hundred Keepers and for inciting the murder of many more. You are also charged with heresy for spreading grievous lies and slander against the Church. Contained within this scroll is evidence of your actions as witnessed by numerous reliable sources."

He handed the scroll to the battalion chief on his right who read it and passed it on. Valtor picked up another. "Draedon, you are charged with sedition, insurrection, and failure to conduct your office in a way befitting of an officer of the Keepers. You are also charged with aiding and abetting the Heretics, both directly and through indirect means. Within this scroll are multiple eyewitness accounts of your actions and the actions of your daughter."

He handed the second scroll off as he had the first.

"Have you anything to say for your crimes?"

Orron spoke first as he and Draedon had agreed.

"I will say again what I have already told you. I do not answer to you or any other human authority. I answer only to the One who has sent me."

Zittas turned red with anger, but said nothing.

"That statement alone confirms that you are guilty of heresy," Valtor said. "Do you wish to deny your charges?"

Orron did not respond.

"Very well. And you, Draedon?" Valtor said turning to him. "Do you wish to speak?"

Draedon cleared his throat and examined the faces of the battalion chiefs. "I served with most of you for many years. I have fought alongside you. Have you ever seen me act in a way that was not in the best interests of my men?"

No one responded. Valtor appeared to be unsure of what to say.

"Are you denying the charges?" he asked.

"I will let my record speak for itself," Draedon said.

Valtor stared at him for a moment, trying to size him up. Finally, he turned and addressed the battalion chiefs.

"As acting-Legion Commander I have heard nothing that proves the innocence of these men. The evidence against them is overwhelming. I hereby find them guilty of the charges rendered. We will take a brief recess while you decide your recommendation."

The battalion chiefs stood up and left the room, followed by Valtor and Zittas. Four guards stood by each of the three exits from the room.

"Well, that went well," Draedon said sarcastically.

"Did you expect anything else?"

"No, not really. You do realize that they will probably execute us, don't you?" It was more of a statement than a question. Draedon looked calm, as if he had accepted his fate long ago.

"They will try, but they won't succeed," Orron said with confidence.

Draedon looked at him and studied his face for a moment. "Either you're crazy or you know something that I don't."

"Maybe it's a little bit of both."

Draedon just shook his head. "I'd say it's probably more of the first."

The only thing that worried Orron was the weather. When they brought him and Draedon from the prison to where this supposed trial was taking place, the blizzard was stronger than he had expected. *It is going to slow Raulin and the others.*

"Are you ever going to tell me your plan?" Draedon finally asked.

"You're going to have to trust me on that one," he replied. "Besides, you might not believe me if I told you."

"You say that a lot."

"Does it help?"

"Not one bit," he replied.

Orron liked Draedon. He seemed like a good man. They had spent the last four days crammed together in their tiny cell, and with Orron chained to the wall, the only way to pass the time was by talking. Though he never seemed to buy Orron's story fully, he felt that Draedon trusted him. Still, he did not feel it best to share his plan with him in case their captors were to torture them for more information.

Minutes passed slowly as they stood uncomfortably in the middle of the room.

"Do you think they are going to bring us some lunch?" Draedon asked, finally breaking the silence. "Maybe we will get some more of that fantastic bread."

Before Orron could answer, the doors opened, and the battalion chiefs filed back in followed by Valtor and Zittas. Once everyone was seated, Valtor stood.

"Have you reached a decision as to what your recommendation will be?"

The officer sitting to his right said, "Yes, Commander we have."

"Very good. What is your recommendation for Orron?"

"We recommend death by hanging."

Zittas smiled wickedly from ear-to-ear. Orron had fully expected this so it did not remotely phase him. He just kept staring intently straight ahead.

"Very well," Valtor said, "I will take that under advisement. What is your recommendation for Draedon?"

The battalion chief shifted uncomfortably in his seat. "For comm—um—for Draedon we recommend that he be stripped of his rank, flogged, and banished to the far reaches of the Great Desert Territory."

"That's all?" Valtor asked incredulously.

"That is our recommendation based on his exemplary career in the Keepers."

Orron quite enjoyed the look of shock and anger on Valtor's face. From what Draedon had told him about these proceedings, he knew that Valtor had the power to overrule the recommendation. Draedon also had told him that the loyalties of the battalion chiefs were very unclear at the moment. *Perhaps this will buy us some time,* he thought hopefully.

One of the doors burst open, and a Keeper walked swiftly over to Valtor and whispered something in his ear. From where Orron stood, he could not hear what their terse conversation was about. The Keeper stepped back, and Valtor stood straight and smiled haughtily at Draedon. *So much for that idea.*

"Gentlemen, some grave news has just been brought to my attention. A company of our Keepers was just attacked by a group of Heretics led by Draedon's daughter. His personal servant was involved as well. Many were killed in the brutal attack."

A murmur broke out among the battalion chiefs. Valtor held up his hands and waited patiently for them to quiet themselves.

"In light of this new information, I believe that I have no choice but to execute both prisoners as a very public display of what happens when you rebel against the authority of the Church."

He smiled and looked at his prisoners. "I hereby sentence you both to death by public execution. Your punishment will be carried out tomorrow at noon."

Chapter Forty-Two

Valtor donned his cloak and strapped on his sword in ceremonial fashion. *Today is a big day,* he thought to himself almost joyfully. *With Draedon and the leader of this insignificant rebellion dead, Zittas will have no choice but to officially promote me to Legion Commander.*

The news he received yesterday about Tysion's death was troubling and unfortunate. Though he wouldn't have called Tysion a friend, he was certainly a useful ally. His help would be missed, but the most disturbing part was that the situation in Covenglade meant that the rebellion was growing stronger. *No matter,* he thought as he straightened his cloak and prepared to leave his quarters. *Today's execution will send the desired message. No one stands against the Church and survives.*

He glanced around the room. The house that he was assigned was small, minuscule compared to the grand manor that Draedon once occupied. It lacked the refinement and luxury. *That will soon be mine as well.*

Valtor did not consider himself to be a particularly greedy man. The lust for possessions or wealth did not drive him. He was sincerely passionate about his cause. The Heretics were a blight on Edelyndia, and he possessed the strength to do whatever was necessary to eradicate them. *Though I certainly don't mind the fame, power, and fortune that will be given to me when I am finished,* he thought with a smile.

Leaving his small quarters, he was assaulted by the blizzard outside. Mounds and mounds of snow stood all over the city. The Keepers had been working day and night this past week trying to keep the roofs from caving in under the pressure. So far, they had managed to prevent too much damage. *Yet another success since I have taken over...*

He made his way through the city to where the executions were to take place. When he arrived, he was pleased to see that the preparations were nearly complete. Four Keepers were continuously sweeping the raised platform and execution device to keep the snow off it.

As acting-Legion Commander, he was given the authority to choose the methods of execution. He had wanted to make a statement with both of them, but Elder Zittas had warned that those loyal to Draedon would not react well to seeing him tortured. For Draedon, he reluctantly settled on a simple beheading. *Now Orron,* he thought to himself wickedly, *you are another story.*

Something about Orron really bothered him. It was more than just the way the insolent Heretic treated him at the Lillyndale Inspection. He couldn't figure it out, but he simply hated the man.

A chill ran down his spine, but Valtor refused to attribute it to that memory. Valtor had more leeway with how he could kill him seeing as Orron was the leader of the rebellion. *He will find no sympathy in the crowd today.*

Valtor climbed onto the platform and inspected the machine that would be used to kill Orron. It was one of his favorites. Orron's feet would be strapped into restraints at the base about shoulder width apart. His arms would be extended and fastened into wrist restraints. Slowly, the executioner would turn the machines wheel, pulling his arms up and outward. It was pure, excruciating torture. Often, bones would snap. Valtor had even witnessed one man's arm being pulled clean off.

Most often, the subject died from the extreme trauma to his body. *Orron is strong. He may take a while.* If the subject did not die from the torture, they were often beheaded or worse. *I will be very patient,* he thought with a smile.

Pleased with the state of the preparations, he turned to walk off the platform. He was greeted by Orcai, the battalion chief who had spoken for the other officers during the trial. Valtor took note of the fact that Orcai desired lenience for Draedon. He was taking note of many things these days.

"I see you are using torture. Is that necessary?" Orcai asked.

"As Legion Commander, I have the duty of selecting the means of execution. I deem it necessary."

"*Acting*-Legion Commander, sir," the battalion chief said assertively.

"Yes, Orcai, that is correct, but that is a temporary situation."

Valtor knew that Orcai would be trouble. He was a large, dark-skinned man from somewhere in the Great Desert Territory. Valtor's spies had reported that though Orcai was loyal to the Keepers, he was also extremely loyal to Draedon.

"That may be true, sir, but I would like to officially lodge a complaint."

Valtor seethed with anger. *I will not let you ruin my day!*

Every Keeper had a right to lodge an official complaint with his superior officer. In this case, Valtor was Orcai's, so he had to listen to what the battalion chief had to say.

"Go on."

"I have spoken with many of the other officers, and we feel that your decision to override the battalion chief's recommendation in regards to Commander Draedon's punishment was both reckless and unwarranted."

Valtor bristled. "That's *former* Commander."

"Yes, sir. My mistake," he said as he eyed Valtor carefully. Valtor wasn't so sure that it was a mistake.

"I have heard your complaint. Will that be all?"

Orcai just stared at him. Valtor could tell he wanted to say more, but he remained silent.

"Am I going to have a problem with you, Chief Orcai?"

He clenched his teeth and responded, "No, sir."

"Good. Now start gathering your men. The executions take place in under an hour."

As Orcai walked away, Valtor made another mental note to place him on the top of the list of officers to replace once this rebellion was taken care of. *I'm sure I can manage to trump up some charges,* he thought with a smile.

Valtor had one more thing to take care of before the execution. He wanted this to be especially painful for Orron. The way he was treated in Lillyndale still had to be answered for.

He made his way to the prison. When he arrived, a Keeper was outside waiting for him.

"Did you do as I asked?"

"Yes, sir."

"Are you sure you grabbed the right one?"

"Yes, sir. The other one has already been sent to the Holy City. You wanted me to keep Ly'ra, right?"

"Perfect."

Orron's heart raced as he was shoved onto the platform where Valtor, Zittas and the four hooded executioners were waiting for them. A large crowd of Keepers had been gathered in the square. His mind raced with all the things that had to go right for this to work. *Breathe. Connect. Focus.* The Mantra of the Wise flowed through his mind, but he had difficulty concentrating.

Two of the Keepers on the platform drew swords. One held it to his throat while the other sliced his garments. He then sheathed his sword and roughly ripped off Orron's tattered cloak, stripping him to the waist. A murmur broke out among the gathered Keepers at the sight of the mark on his chest. Despite the cold, it tingled and felt hot. Valtor stared for a moment at the mark then looked away. Orron could not tell what Valtor was thinking, but it seemed that he was working pretty hard to appear unfazed by what he had seen.

The frigid wind felt like knives being thrust into his exposed skin. *At least my wounds have fully healed.*

He looked over at Draedon who looked completely calm, almost bored. *How does he do this? He has no idea what my plan is. Either he trusts me completely or he has simply accepted his fate without qualm.* Orron admired him greatly.

Elder Zittas stepped forward to offer up a prayer for the souls of Orron and Draedon. Orron just ignored him. His words made him sick.

When he was finished, Valtor gave the executioners a nod. Two grabbed Draedon by the shoulders, while the other two grabbed Orron and moved him over to some sort of machine. *A torture device, I presume.*

He looked over his shoulder and saw Draedon being forced to his knees and his arms strapped to a short pole. The executioners pushed his head roughly down onto the pole and strapped it down. *Beheading,* Orron realized.

The crowd was dead silent as Orron was turned around and told to step back onto the contraption. His feet were strapped into the base of the machine, and his arms were spread while they attached his wrists to iron shackles. He looked to his left and saw that they had strapped Draedon's head down so that he was facing Orron. *They want him to watch.*

Valtor stepped to the front of the platform and turned to face Orron and Draedon. A sinister smile spread across his face. *Something is wrong,* Orron thought with a sinking feeling in his stomach.

"If either of you wish to beg for forgiveness and seek the mercy of the Church, you may do so now."

Orron looked him in the eye and realized that he actually pitied the man. *He has no idea how deceived he really is.*

"Valtor," Orron said loudly. Valtor smiled as he looked at him. He obviously was expecting Orron to beg for his life.

"You still have a chance to do the right thing, Valtor. Repent to the Maker, and He *will* spare you."

The smile vanished from Valtor's face. He turned to the crowd and gave a signal. To Orron's right the crowd parted and a Keeper dragged a girl to the platform. His heart jumped into his throat as he realized who it was. "*Ly'ra!*"

The executioner standing to his right punched him in the stomach, causing him to gasp for air.

Valtor grabbed Ly'ra by the hair, and she cried out as he pulled her onto the stage. She kicked and screamed with all her might, but to no avail as he savagely slapped her across the face.

Orron strained against the device, but it wouldn't budge.

"Let her go, Valtor! She has nothing do with this!"

"Doesn't she?" he replied with a sneer as he pulled her in front of the machine.

Anger clouded Orron's face as he saw the terror in her eyes. It had been seventeen days since she had been captured. He had felt every minute. Her eyes were sunken, and she was sickly skinny. They had treated her very poorly during her captivity.

Valtor leaned forward and spoke softly so that only Orron could hear his words.

"I wanted you to see her one last time." The look in his eyes was pure evil. "I also wanted you to know that her friend has already been sent to the Holy City, but I decided I was not done with this one yet."

Orron wanted to destroy him for the way he looked at her. The mantra was long gone from his mind.

"She…suits me. I have decided to keep her as my…servant. We are going to have many fun nights together."

With a roar, Orron lunged against his restraints and head-butted Valtor in the face. He could feel the sickening crunch of his nose breaking. Valtor cried out as the executioners pummeled Orron in the head and torso with multiple blows. All Orron could hear and feel was Ly'ra screaming for him.

Valtor shoved Ly'ra into the arms of the Keeper who had brought her and turned back to Orron with hatred in his eyes.

"You will die even slower for that." Blood flowed down his face from his broken nose.

"No, Valtor, it is you who will pay for this. Not just now, but for eternity." Orron's anger flowed so hotly, he felt as though it were burning him. He grasped desperately in his mind for the mantra, but it brought him little relief.

Ignoring Orron, Valtor turned to the executioner and gave him the signal. Orron could hear the turning of the wheel, and his arms began to extend until they could go no further. Then the pain began.

It started first as an ache and quickly moved to the worst pain that he had ever felt.

Breathe. Connect. Focus. Breathe. Connect. Focus.

He tried desperately to lose himself in the mantra, but the pain overwhelmed his senses. He could hear the sound of his ligaments stretching. His arms felt as if they could be ripped from his body at any moment.

The machine lifted him from the platform as his arms were pulled up and out. Soon the pain in his arms was matched by the pain in his legs. When he could contain himself no more, he finally released a savage cry.

He felt his faith beginning to slip as agony fought for control over his mind. *Maybe I was wrong.* His only thoughts were of Ly'ra and what would happen to her if he died. *I cannot fail her…*

CHAPTER FORTY-THREE

Draedon could barely stomach what he was seeing. He wanted to shut his eyes, but he felt he owed it to Orron to watch. *Someone who cares about him has to witness this.*

The barbaric device had Orron stretched further than Draedon thought possible. Draedon had been forced to watch this before, though he had never allowed such evil forms of torture under his command. *Come on, Orron! Just give in. The longer you fight it, the more horrible it gets.*

He heard the sickening pop of one of Orron's shoulders coming out of socket and Orron screamed in pain. Still, he somehow managed to stay conscious. *You're too strong for your own good, boy.*

"Just kill him, Valtor! You've made your point!" Draedon yelled angrily. He knew Valtor wouldn't listen, but he couldn't handle just watching and doing nothing.

"You're an animal!" he yelled. "This is not what Keepers do! We are better than this!" No one seemed to listen or care. He thought he saw his old friend, Orcai, turn away in disgust, but he couldn't be sure.

Then it started. Out of the corner of his eye, Draedon thought he saw the air shimmer like the edge of fire. Before he could wonder about it, the air was filled with a clamor of terrifying noises. Thunderous explosions sounded from somewhere above him. The ground shook with each concussion. Flames rained down from above. It was as if the very sky was on fire.

One of the falling balls of fire struck the platform not far from Draedon's head. It took him a moment to realize what he was looking at. *It's an arrow!*

He craned his neck as far as the restraints would allow. Through the haze of the snowy sky he thought he could see where the sounds and fire were coming from. *The bluffs…*

All of a sudden he realized what was going on. *Orron, you did have a plan!*

⌒⌒

"That's our signal," Kor'lee said excitedly as the first explosions and arrows rained down onto Farovale from the bluffs on each side. From where they were hidden in her secret passage, the sounds were muffled, but they were unmistakable.

"Aye, let's pray this actually works!" Mattox said.

The blizzard had slowed their journey through the pass, delaying the time the plan was supposed to launch. Their spies in the city had confirmed that the executions were taking place at any moment. *I hope we can get there in time to stop it.*

She started to climb the stairs to the trap door, but Bruschian grabbed her arm to stop her.

"I will go first," he said.

They could hear the cries coming from the city above. The Keepers were apparently scrambling to defend themselves from the hailstorm of fire and rocks coming from above them.

Bruschian opened the door slowly and made his way out. Satisfied, he motioned for the rest to follow. When they were all clear of the tunnel, Einar pointed toward the center of the city.

"The executions will be held a short ways to the south of the Cathedral where they always are."

Just as they were about to sprint down the main road a group of six Keepers spotted them.

"You there, stop!"

They were easy to identify as rebels. All but Kor'lee had swords drawn, which was illegal for anyone other than a Keeper.

Bruschian and Raulin jumped in front of the rest of the group as the Keepers rushed toward them to attack. The Keepers were overmatched and it ended quickly. Though Kor'lee had seen Raulin fight from her position on the roof in Lillyndale, it was even more impressive standing just a few feet away. The grace and ease with which he used his sword was a fearsome sight to behold.

"Come on," he said when they were done, "Let's go."

The group took off running through the city. The streets were pure madness. Most of the Keepers they passed ignored them completely in the chaos that the bombardment from the bluffs created. Occasionally, a few Keepers would take notice and the group would have to stop to take care of them. Even when they were able to make it whole blocks without being confronted, the confusion in the cramped streets made progress difficult.

Kor'lee's heart beat ferociously. The journey was going brutally slow. *We have to get there faster!*

Draedon looked over at Orron. In the chaos, the executioner had abandoned his post. Still, Orron was stretched far beyond the normal capabilities of the human body. *How is he still conscious?*

Orron then did something that made Draedon do a double take. *Is he smiling?*

His eyes appeared to be almost on fire. Although at first Draedon couldn't hear what he was saying, he could see Orron's mouth moving, forming words. Slowly, his voice began to grow louder. Draedon strained to make out what he was saying.

"Breathe. Connect. Focus. Breathe. Connect. Focus."

What on earth are you talking about? At first, Draedon thought he had snapped, but the look in his eyes told him otherwise.

"Breathe. Connect. Focus. Breathe. Connect. Focus. *Breathe! Connect! Focus!*" His voice rose powerfully above the chaos around him.

Then Draedon noticed the mark on Orron's chest. *Is it...?*

He closed his eyes and reopened them, assuming he had to be seeing things. *No, it is!* His eyes were not betraying him. The mark on his chest was glowing. The mark itself was still black as night, but the edges were fiery red. It appeared to be burning its way out of his skin.

Valtor spun around and his mouth fell open. Draedon squinted to try to see what he was looking at. He pulled against his head restraints but to no avail.

Draedon heard what Orron was doing before he saw it. The massive machine began to groan as the two arms that held the chains attached to Orron's wrist began to bend. *I can't believe what I'm seeing!* Draedon thought in wonder. *He's actually tearing the machine apart!*

Having seen the machine up close before, Draedon knew that it was made of the hardest, strongest wood in all of Edelyndia and was reinforced by iron. The arms were designed to handle the tremendous pull that required them to be nearly unbreakable. No human could do what he was seeing. It dawned on him. *No human...*

With a power and strength that Draedon had never witnessed in his long career, Orron pulled the arms of the machine inward to their breaking point. For a moment, it appeared that he could pull them no further. With a primeval scream, Orron threw his head toward the heavens and cried out.

"Maker...help...me..." With one last surge, Orron pulled on the chains with all his might. Draedon flinched as a tremendous boom sounded, and the arms of the machine snapped in two, sending Orron crashing to the platform.

Valtor stood transfixed as Orron did the impossible. *How...* He shook his head, half-expecting the vision in front of him to disappear.

"*Kill him!*" he yelled to several Keepers standing nearby. They jumped onto the platform and rushed to Orron. With inhuman strength, Orron grabbed one of the massive arms of the machine lying on the platform next to him and lifted it above his head, wielding it like a weapon.

Valtor quaked with fear as he watched Orron destroy the eight attacking Keepers with two powerful swings of his makeshift weapon. Enraged, Valtor drew his sword. He knew better than to try to attack Orron, lest he be torn apart as easily as the others had been.

Valtor yelled for more Keepers to attack. Twenty Keepers jumped onto the platform and tried futilely to subdue the indomitable Heretic. With Orron occupied, Valtor turned his attention to Draedon.

Dragging Ly'ra by the hair with his left hand, he made his way over to where Draedon was strapped down.

"You have lost, Valtor. Give yourself up, and he might spare you," Draedon said.

Valtor shook with rage. "*Never!* I am still Legion Commander! I am still in charge!"

"You were never commander of anything," Draedon said sharply, "and you know it."

Looking around, Valtor could see the mayhem and knew that the city was in danger of being lost. Judging by the sounds coming from outside the city, the Heretics had somehow managed to amass a mighty army. *How? How could they have done it in so such a short a time?*

"It's over," Draedon repeated. "The city *will* fall. It's only a matter of time."

Valtor feared that he was right.

"I can still kill you," he said.

He lifted his sword high above his head. Just as he was about to bring it down, he felt a burning fire in his hand. He looked up as his sword came crashing to the ground and saw an arrow piercing his wrist.

Incredulous, he whirled around to see who shot him. At the edge of the square, he saw his attacker smiling victoriously at him. *Kor'lee.*

⸺

Orron swung his weapon one more time, crushing the skull of the last Keeper on the platform. His arms burned from the tremendous ordeal he had been through. At the sound of Valtor crying out in pain, he spun around to see his hand in the air, pierced by an arrow. He followed his gaze to see Kor'lee, Mattox, Raulin, Bruschian, and a man he didn't recognize pouring into the square.

Valtor still has Ly'ra, he realized. Before he could get to her, a swarm of Keepers flooded the square and rushed the platform. With his hands still bound to the broken arms of the machine, Orron had no choice but to wield one again.

His arms felt like they had no strength left in them, so he forced himself to allow the mantra to give him power that was not his own. He lifted the massive piece of wood and metal and with a cry, attacked any Keeper that came within his range. To make matters worse, his feet were still attached to the platform, so he had little-to-no room to fight.

As the fighting wore on, his strength began to fail him. After knocking one of the Keepers over, he faltered and fell to his knees, dropping the beam of wood to the ground. A Keeper jumped onto his back and Orron grabbed him by the shoulders and threw him over his head and off the platform.

Another Keeper lunged at him, but he was cut down by a massive hand-and-a-half sword. Bruschian cut down two more Keepers, finally clearing the platform.

"It's good to see your head's still attached," the big man said with a grin. Mattox leapt onto the platform and ran over to Orron. Together, Bruschian and Mattox used the tools that the executioner left behind to free Orron's hands and feet.

Once free, Mattox helped Orron to his feet. He scanned the square for any sign of Valtor and Ly'ra. *Where is she?*

"What is it, Orron?" Mattox asked when he saw the panic on Orron's face.

"Ly'ra," he said as he gasped for air. "Valtor…has her."

"I know where he's going," Draedon said.

Orron turned to see the man he didn't recognize freeing Draedon from the post. Before Orron could inquire further, Raulin and Kor'lee joined them on the platform after finishing the last of the Keepers in the square.

Kor'lee threw herself into her father's arms. "Father, I'm so sorry," she said as tears streamed down her face.

Draedon held her close. "I am the one who should be sorry, Kor'lee. I love you so much."

"I hate to interrupt," Orron said, placing his hand on Draedon's shoulder, "but we *have* to rescue Ly'ra. You said you knew where Valtor was going?"

"Yes, sorry. He is headed for the Cathedral. That's the last place for him to hide."

Mattox handed Orron his staff that he had been carrying since Lillyndale. With deadly calm in his voice, Mattox said, "Then that is where this ends."

Chapter Forty-Four

This can't be happening! Valtor thought to himself as he crashed through the streets of Lillyndale with Ly'ra in tow. *Our plan was flawless!*

He and Zittas had been working on this for so long. First, they had to get the Council to assign him as Draedon's captain. That meant blackmailing the former captain into retiring early. Then, they had to get Tysion and several of his loyal Keepers assigned to Farovale without drawing suspicion. That required many bribes.

Their greatest successes came as a result of blind luck. One of his Keepers had spotted Kor'lee sneaking out of the Citadel during the summer not long after he had seen her with Raulin in Lillyndale. The connection was obvious. The tricky part had been to get that idiot boy in Lillyndale to turn on his friends and family, but Valtor had succeeded at that. *It should have worked!*

He stopped in front of the Cathedral and looked at its massive spires. *It's all that cursed Orron's fault,* he realized. *If it weren't for him, this never would have happened.*

The barrage of fiery arrows continued to rain down on the city. Valtor realized that by insisting that the roofs remained clear of snow he had actually turned Farovale into a giant tinder box. Fires were growing everywhere.

"Commander Valtor!" a voice shouted behind him. He turned to see Orcai running toward him. Valtor grimaced. *Not him...*

"Commander Valtor, what are your orders?"

Valtor froze. For the first time in as long as he could remember, he had no idea what to do.

"We are under attack! We need your orders, sir!" Orcai made no effort to conceal the disdain on his face, and Valtor hated him for it.

"I am going into the Cathedral," Valtor said, unable to hide the panic in his voice.

"I can see that, sir, but what do you want *us* to do?"

"Defend...um...set up a defensive perimeter."

The battalion chief looked at him incredulously.

"A defensive perimeter *where*, sir?"

"I...um...around the Cathedral!" Valtor knew that he sounded like a fool, but he no longer cared. Survival was all that mattered to him now.

"But sir, we have to—"

"You have your orders!"

Shaking his head, Orcai turned and ran back to where his men were waiting for him.

Remembering what he had come to do, Valtor grabbed Ly'ra by the hair and ran up the stairs to the doors of the Cathedral. The usual cleric greeted him at the door, but before he could say anything, Valtor grabbed him by the cloak and threw him down the stairs.

Not bothering to take off his boots, Valtor burst through the doors and into the grand hall where he was greeted by chaos. Clerics were running everywhere. The Council Guards, an elite class of Keepers chosen for the honor of protecting the Elders, were scrambling, trying to organize themselves.

Valtor spotted Zittas in front of the massive oak doors to the Sanctuary. He rushed over to him, dragging Ly'ra behind.

"What is going on, Commander?" Zittas said, the fear dripping off his voice.

"I...I don't know." Valtor didn't have an answer.

"We are under attack!" Zittas practically shouted.

Valtor hated him for feeling as though he needed to state the obvious. "Yes, Your Grace. It appears the Heretics have amassed an army."

"How could you let this happen?" Zittas screamed, pointing an accusing finger at Valtor's chest. "What kind of commander doesn't know his enemy has built an army?"

Valtor bristled. *No one talks to me like this, not even you!* He wanted with all his might to lash out at him. Whether it was witnessing the idiocy that guided Zittas's actions or the way he was being talked to, Valtor did not know, but it was as if the fog of fear that had muddled his thoughts evaporated. He was able to think clearly again.

He straightened up and replied, "We do not have time for this right now, Your Excellency. Right now, we have to ready our defenses. They will be coming for us."

Valtor was surprised by the amount of fear he saw in Zittas's eyes as it sunk in. "You mean, *he* will be coming…"

"Yes, Orron is free."

"The Sanctuary," Zittas said, spinning toward the oak doors. "We will barricade ourselves in there."

"But sir, there are better—"

"No! We must go to the Sanctuary. He can't touch us in there."

Judging by the crazed look in his eyes, Valtor did not feel like trusting Zittas's judgment, but before he could respond, Zittas grabbed the closest guard and began shouting instructions about fortifying the doors.

Amid the bedlam, Valtor heard an eerily calm voice behind him say, "He's coming for you."

He had nearly forgotten the girl he had been dragging through the streets. Looking down with disgust, he started to speak, but his words were lost when he saw the look in her eyes. Fear like he had never known began to fill his gut.

"He's coming for *you*," she said again. Each word felt like a brand searing his soul. "He is coming for you all, and there is no where you can hide where he won't find you."

Draedon led Mattox, Einar, Orron, Raulin, Bruschian, and Kor'lee through the city toward the Cathedral. He slid to a halt and ducked behind a building just before he entered the courtyard in front of the Cathedral, motioning to everybody to do the same. A full brigade of Keepers was trying to form a perimeter around the Cathedral. *With the city under attack, why would Valtor waste a brigade to defend one building?* He shook his head as he realized the answer. *Valtor only cares about himself.*

Orron peered around the corner.

"Is there another way into the Cathedral?" he asked.

Draedon shook his head. "I'm afraid not."

Orron paused to catch his breath. He gripped his staff tightly and stepped away from the wall.

"I will clear a path," Orron said as he turned to Mattox. "Get Ly'ra out alive. That's all that matters."

"Wait," Draedon grabbed Orron's shoulder. "I may have another way."

Orron looked at him doubtfully.

"Hey," Draedon said with a half-hearted smile. "I've trusted you this far, and I'm pretty sure you're crazy. It's your turn to do the trusting."

For a moment, Orron wrestled with it internally. Finally, he nodded.

"We'll do this your way."

"Father, what are you doing?" Kor'lee asked.

Draedon turned to see fear in her eyes. "I have to talk to them, Kor'lee. These are good men. They deserve a chance to do what is right."

"Don't do this alone. You could be killed!"

Draedon placed a hand on her face. "Kor'lee, I've stood to the side long enough. I have to do this. It is my responsibility to bear, no matter the consequences."

He gave her a quick hug and stepped out into the street. With his hand on the hilt of his sword, he strode confidently into the middle of the courtyard.

Battalion Chief Orcai noticed him first. He drew his sword and pointed it at Draedon.

"Commander Draedon I have orders to defend this Cathedral from all rebels," he paused. "That includes *you*."

All eyes fell on Draedon as he drew his sword slowly.

"I do not wish to fight you, sir," Orcai said.

"Then don't," Draedon said simply. Once his sword was free of its sheath he threw it to the ground in front of him. "You have been my sword brother for many years."

He looked around the Keepers who were gathered in the courtyard. With a loud voice he said, "Many of you have been my sword brothers as well. We have fought and bled together in difficult times and in good times. It has been an honor serving as your leader, but I can no longer, in good conscience, continue to serve this corrupt and evil Church."

His words hung in the air as the Keepers looked unsure of how to react.

Draedon continued. "When I joined, I thought that being a Keeper meant protecting the innocent, but it is a lie. The only thing we protect is the corrupt and power-hungry politicians that run this Church. It is not the Will of the Maker that we enforce but the will of madmen."

He looked at Orcai. "You know that what I am saying is true."

"Even if it is," Orcai said. "It doesn't change the fact that I have sworn an oath."

"An oath to do what, exactly?"

"I swore to uphold and defend the Church."

"The Church," Draedon said with disdain. "But is *this* evil thing worth defending? Tell me brothers," he said as he raised his arms. "Did you swear oaths to murder innocent men? Women? Children? Did you swear oaths to unquestionably follow any order, no matter how evil it may be?"

Many Keepers could not hold his gaze. His words cut like knives.

"You all know what happened in Lillyndale. That was not the first and it certainly will not be the last." Passion filled his spirit as his voice rose. "Yes, you all took an oath and following your orders may seem like the right thing to do, but what about *good*? Does being *right* mean having to sacrifice being *good*?"

Draedon walked over toward the edge of the courtyard so he could have a clear view of the bluffs. "Up there is an army of people that the Church calls 'Heretics,' but I see them as righteous people standing up for all that is good in this world."

He paused and scanned the faces of the Keepers staring back at him. Most were young boys, no older than Kor'lee was. "When I look at you, I see the faces of good, strong men. You know that what I speak is truth. I urge you…no I implore you. Do what is *good* and join me in my quest to end the tyranny and oppression of this hollow impression of a church."

When he finished, no one moved. He couldn't tell if his words had any effect at all.

Suddenly, Orcai stirred and walked toward Draedon with his sword drawn until he was standing in front of him. For a long moment, he didn't say a word.

Finally, he snapped to attention and turned to his battalion. "This battalion is officially under the command of Legion

Commander Draedon. If anyone has a problem with that I would suggest that you leave now."

A cheer broke out among the Keepers. Not one left.

Orcai turned back to Draedon and said, "What are your orders, sir?"

At first, Draedon didn't know what to say. He realized that he hadn't expected his speech to work. "I…um…well, what is the status of the rest of the Legion?"

"Most of the battalion chiefs will join you, sir."

"And the others?"

"We may have a fight on our hands. A battalion of Keepers loyal to Valtor are amassing on the west side of the Cathedral, preparing to launch a counter-offensive."

"Very well, send Keepers out to all the chiefs who you believe will be on our side. Send them word that I am back in charge. Have the rest of your men ready themselves for whatever Valtor may have left up his sleeve."

"Very good, sir." Orcai turned and hurried away to carry out his orders.

Kor'lee and the rest of the group joined Draedon in the courtyard.

"Nice speech, sir," Einar said drily as he looked over at Kor'lee, "but I've heard better." Kor'lee blushed.

"Thanks," Draedon said, making a mental note to ask later what that little exchange between Kor'lee and Einar was all about. "We should be clear to take the Cathedral."

"What can we expect inside?" Orron asked.

Draedon called Orcai back over.

"Yes, sir?"

"What is the situation inside the Cathedral?"

"I personally saw the Elder enter a short while ago. Valtor entered just before you arrived."

"What about a little girl? Did he have a girl with him?" Orron asked.

Orcai frowned. "I'm afraid so."

"Are there Keepers inside?" Draedon asked.

"No, but the Elder's personal guards are inside with him. They will remain loyal to him."

Draedon grimaced. "The Council Guards are a highly trained, fierce group of warriors," he explained. "Thank you, Orcai."

After he left, Draedon turned to the group. "Shall we finish this?"

Chapter Forty-Five

Kor'lee nocked an arrow as Orron and her father led their group up the steps to the massive doors of the Cathedral. Her heart was pounding so hard, she half-wondered if anyone else could hear it. Orron motioned for Bruschian to open the doors. As he was about to grab the handle, the door flew open, and a terrified cleric ran through it. When he saw the group of armed rebels, he let out a rather feminine, high-pitched scream and took off running down the stairs. Before he reached the bottom, he tripped and sprawled on the ground. His robes flew up, and much to Kor'lee's horror, he was wearing little more than an ill-fitting loincloth beneath.

She grimaced, screwed her eyes shut, and turned away. When she opened them, she saw Raulin smiling broadly. He let out a small laugh.

Kor'lee smacked him on the shoulder. "Really, Raulin?"

"Hey, it was funny!"

She turned her head so that Raulin could not see her smile in spite of herself. She was terrified of what lay ahead, but it felt good knowing that Raulin was beside her.

Orron was the first to enter the Cathedral, and the rest followed quickly behind. When Kor'lee entered, she was expecting to see a room full of heavily armed guards, but instead the grand hall was completely empty. The door closed behind them, and Kor'lee shuddered. It felt like they were standing in a tomb.

Raulin cleared his throat. "Well, that was easy. What now?"

"There are hundreds if not thousands of rooms in this place," Draedon said, frustration evident in his voice. "We don't have time to search them all."

Draedon, Raulin, Bruschian, and Einar began arguing about the best way to proceed. What was clear is that they had precious little time to find Ly'ra. Mattox said nothing, but his veins began to bulge on his neck. Kor'lee could not imagine the amount of anguish he must have been feeling.

She turned and noticed that Orron had strayed from the group. He moved to the center of the room and knelt down. His lips began to move, but Kor'lee could not hear what he was saying. Finally he spoke.

"Quiet!" He did not move, but his voice echoing through the massive foyer was enough to silence the group. "I need it quiet in here."

No one said a word.

After what felt like an eternity, he stood to his feet and pointed at the doors to the Sanctuary. "They are in there."

"How could he possibly know that?" Raulin asked no one in particular.

"He's not a human," Draedon said so simply and confidently that Kor'lee almost believed him. Raulin blinked but said nothing.

Orron walked to the doors, and after seeing that they opened inward, he gave them a mighty push. To no one's surprise, the doors didn't give in the slightest. He turned back to the group. "How do we get in?"

Draedon spoke up. "I've made it a point to spend as little time as possible in this place. Have you any idea if there's another way in, Kor'lee?"

"I've probably spent even less time than you in here," she responded. She hated that Sanctuary. It felt wrong, almost evil. Other than the mandatory weekly services that everyone was required to go to, she avoided it at all costs.

"There has to be another way," Einar said. "There obviously is a way for the clerics to come in and out during the weekly liturgy, but it will take us forever to stumble upon it. Besides, I'm sure they have heavily fortified every entrance."

"Then we go through these doors," Orron said.

He walked over to the far wall where golden statues made in the likeness of the Elders stood. With shocking strength, He ripped one from the ground in one pull. Kor'lee gasped in surprise.

"Trust me, you haven't seen anything yet," Draedon said next to her without turning his head. *Not human, huh?* she wondered in amazement.

With a grunt, Orron hoisted the statue to the side and began pounding the door with it. With each blow, Kor'lee could hear the wood groaning.

Thud. Thud. Thud. The rest of the group just watched in awe and wonder a safe distance away. Each blow sent splinters of wood flying.

With a mighty crash, the door finally gave way and splintered. Shards of wood flew into the Sanctuary as Orron threw the statue to the side. He grabbed his staff and rushed through with the rest of the group right behind him.

As Kor'lee leapt through the shattered doorframe, she heard the all-too-familiar sound of arrows being loosed. Before she could find the source, she heard Orron cry out in pain. She turned to see him crash to his knees, pierced by three arrows. One struck his right leg, one found his right shoulder, while the deadliest struck him in the chest. She had watched enough Keepers die on a Healer's table to know that this one was most likely a mortal wound.

Valtor and the two Council Guards that flanked him nocked another arrow. He was quite pleased at the results of his last shot. He stood at the front of the Sanctuary in front of the altar with Elder Zittas to his right. Zittas held Ly'ra in front of him with a knife to her neck as though she were a shield.

As the rest of the Bandits came rushing in behind Orron, Valtor gave the signal and fifty Council Guards with bows drawn jumped out from their hiding places along the wall. The Heretics were trapped. Valtor allowed himself a small smile. *Well, that was easy.*

"Drop your weapons!" he ordered. The Heretics did not move. "We have you surrounded. All I have to do is give the order." Still, they didn't move. *Foolishness masquerading as bravery,* he thought smugly.

"I will not hesitate to slit her throat," Zittas said threateningly, his voice still a little too high-pitched with fear.

Valtor could see the huge, bearded man beside Draedon trembling with rage. *I'm guessing that's the father.* The family resemblance to Ly'ra was uncanny.

"And how does that fit in with your theology?" Draedon asked accusingly.

"Do not presume to lecture me, Heretic," Zittas spat back. "I am the voice of the Maker!"

Draedon just shook his head in disgust.

"Surrender or this girl dies," Zittas said even louder as the fear began to melt from his voice. The situation appeared to be in their control.

Orron could barely hear the others talking as he struggled to remain conscious. His breath came in ragged bursts. His right arm and leg felt as though they were on fire, but the arrow in his chest caused him the most pain. He knew that it had most likely barely nicked his heart, but his lungs were already filling with blood. Each breath caused unimaginable agony.

This is it. I have failed. He wanted to feel angry...angry at himself for failing, angry at the Maker for letting this happen, angry at Zittas, Valtor, and the entire Church for all the evil they had done, but all he could feel was fear. *What will happen to Ly'ra now? Who will avenge Me'ra?*

With difficulty, he raised his head and surveyed the room. They were completely surrounded. If the rest of the group did not surrender soon, they would suffer the same fate as himself.

The edges of his vision began to grow dim. Blood poured from his wounds, forming pools on the marble floor. He knew he probably did not have long before death overtook him. With hopelessness tearing apart his soul, he looked up at Ly'ra, barely able to face the one he had failed so miserably.

What he saw on her face took his breath away. In her eyes, he saw no fear despite the blade held to her neck. There was not even a hint of the hopelessness that overwhelmed him. Instead, he saw a faith in her eyes that defied reason. In her eyes, he saw the kind of faith that moves mountains.

Suddenly, he felt a stirring in his soul. *She believes in me.*

He closed his eyes and shook his head as he realized his foolishness. *No, she believes in the Maker. He is greater. He is stronger.*

He allowed that tendril of hope to take a foothold in his spirit. As the fluid in his lungs made speaking impossible, he clenched his eyes closed and allowed the mantra to be more than just spoken words. They became the iron will of faith, not in himself or his power but in the greatness of his Maker.

Something is not right, Valtor realized. Zittas was saying something to the group of bandits, but Valtor could not hear him. His attention was focused solely on the bloodied, wounded Orron kneeling on the ground. From where he stood, he could tell that he was having tremendous difficulty breathing, but something was happening in him. His eyes were closed, but even from where he stood, Valtor could almost feel the power that seemed to be emanating from where he knelt.

The arrow that pierced Orron's chest was lodged in the symbol of the Keepers. The glowing that he had noticed on the execution platform was growing. Even though he knew he had to be imagining it, he felt as though he could almost feel heat resonating from it.

The ground began to tremble ever so slightly. The air began to fill with the smell of charged lightning. He knew he was not the only one who felt it when Zittas' voice trailed off.

Valtor tore his eyes off Orron to look at the Elder. He immediately wished he hadn't. The look of horror on his face unnerved Valtor completely. As the slight tremor began to grow into something awful and terrifying, he felt a sharp fear growing in the pit of his stomach that surpassed anything he had experienced before.

When the ground began to shake violently beneath Kor'lee, she had to grab on to Raulin's arm to keep from falling. He seemed transfixed by what was going on in front of him. Following his gaze, her eyes fell on the form of Orron. What she saw she would not have been able find the words to describe had she tried.

Though he was still on his knees with blood pouring from his wounds, he no longer looked like the Orron she had begun to know. Something was different. He was more fierce, more terrifying. His eyes were open and it seemed as though actual fire was coming from them. His mouth moved noiselessly.

She realized that it appeared as though the noise that had grown into a mighty roar was coming from him, not from his voice but from his very being. As she stared in fear and wonder, it seemed that he began to grow bigger somehow. Though his actual size did not change, his presence grew out from himself. The light in the room dimmed as flashes of light began to appear all around them.

Suddenly, she remembered the words her father had used. *Not human...*

Fear and hopelessness were now gone as a new fire burned deep within Orron. All of the righteous anger, faith, and purpose of mission that Orron had ever felt merged together into a powerful force within his soul. The pain from his wounds seemed like a distant memory. All he could feel was the tremendous energy surging through the symbol on his chest.

The roar in the room grew so loud that the ornate stained glass windows burst outward. The gilded walls of the Sanctuary began to crack as the ground shook. Though he could not see them, Orron could sense Mattox, Kor'lee, Raulin, Bruschian, and Einar fall to their knees behind him.

Orron turned his head toward the Council Guards on each side of him. Just looking at them sent them into uncontrollable panic. Incomprehensibly, they began to turn on each other, savagely killing each other with their bare hands.

He turned his gaze back to the altar and locked eyes with Valtor. Continuing to mouth the mantra, he felt the power of the Maker flowing through him like never before. With a quick motion, Valtor threw down his bow and fled through a side door out of the Sanctuary. That left Zittas alone on the stage holding the perfectly calm Ly'ra. Out of the corner of his eye, Orron could see Draedon take off in pursuit of Valtor.

The roar in the room grew to unfathomable levels, and Orron could almost feel the soundless scream coming from Zittas.

Suddenly, everything stopped.

Orron blinked. The silence was more deafening than the sounds that came before it. Looking down, he saw that the bleeding had stopped. Actually, it appeared to be frozen. He glanced around the room realizing that everyone appeared as though they were frozen as well. The colors in the world around him seemed to have dimmed to near non-existence, as a strange glow descended on the room.

Am I dead?

"No, Guardian, you are very much alive," a familiar voice echoed behind him, answering his thought.

Orron turned to see Arlas walking regally into the Sanctuary.

"How...what is happening?" Orron managed to get out. Though he seemed to be able to talk, it felt as though he was speaking under water.

Arlas raised his hands in wonder as he sat down in a pew next to Orron.

"I do not know. In all my years, I must confess that I have not seen anything quite like this."

"Like what?" Orron asked confused.

"Like this," Arlas said as he motioned around the room. "Never has the Maker chosen to focus His power in such an explicit way through one of His Keepers."

"I am doing this?"

"Well, no, you are just...shall I say...channeling this." He rubbed his chin, as he thought of a way to explain. "You, like all of the Maker's creation, are simply a vessel."

"It was never about me," Orron said as the weight of his realization settled on him. Like a veil being lifted from his eyes, Orron suddenly realized that everything he had done had been about himself.

He had needed to rescue Ly'ra.

He had needed to protect her and her family.

He had needed to avenge Me'ra and bring justice down on the Church.

It had always been about him. Looking up, he saw the frozen form of Ly'ra with the unshakable look of faith and trust in her eyes.

"When faced with the worst fear, her faith was not in me, it was in the Maker," he said with a depth of realization that lifted a hidden burden that had been weighing him down for as long as he could remember.

"Yes, Guardian," Arlas said solemnly, "and now you can finally see. You are blind no more."

With an overwhelming rush, all of the memories that had been forgotten flooded through Orron. He could remember the eons of service to the Maker as a True Keeper. Every thought, every doubt, every instance of pride became a painful reminder of just how much his existence had been about himself. Tears streamed down his cheek as he looked to the heavens.

"This cannot be about me any longer."

Arlas sat silent for moment. When he spoke, he did so with gentleness in his voice. "This cannot be about Ly'ra alone either."

Orron nodded his head reluctantly as he closed his eyes. He knew what Arlas spoke was truth. The Will of the Maker was far greater than any individual. It included His creations but was somehow more. Deep down, he knew that doing the Will of the Maker would require him to lay down his own will in its entirety.

Finally, Orron spoke. "I know what I must do."

"It is not going to be easy. Are you sure that you want to take this upon yourself?"

"What I want no longer matters. I serve the Maker completely." Though it was a simple statement, there was freedom in Orron's words that renewed his spirit.

Arlas put his hand on Orron's shoulder. "Many innocent people will die. At times, good will appear as though it is evil, and evil will masquerade as good."

Orron nodded his head. "I know."

"Good!" Arlas exclaimed as he clapped Orron on the back. "I must confess that when I first heard that the Maker had chosen you, I was filled with doubt. Now, I see His wisdom at work."

Orron looked down. Even though he had a renewed sense of purpose, it was still uncomfortable for him to be given such praise. He noticed the arrows protruding from his body that he had almost forgotten about.

"I am badly wounded," he said.

"I can see that," Arlas said with a frown.

"I am going to need some help."

He shook his head. "You know that the Maker has told me that we are not to directly intervene on your behalf…at least until it is time."

"I know, but I have something in mind that I think He will allow."

Orron laid out his plan. When he was done, Arlas smiled. "That, I think we can do."

Arlas stood to his feet and moved behind Orron. Closing his eyes, Orron prepared himself for what lay ahead.

Instantly, the roar returned and the world returned to motion.

The roar in the room seemed to reach its breaking point. Kor'lee was almost certain that if it did not stop, it would destroy everything and everyone in its presence. Suddenly, Orron began to move. With tremendous effort, he grabbed his staff and pulled himself to his feet.

He turned to the group around her and shouted above the noise, "You must all leave." No one budged. He shouted again, "You must all leave, *now!*"

Mattox looked at him in confusion, "We are not leaving! We must—"

"Mattox," Orron said with inhuman calm. "Have faith."

Kor'lee could sense the conflict going on inside Mattox. Finally, he stood to his feet and nodded at Orron. He turned to the group. Over the noise he yelled, "You heard the lad; let's go."

Raulin helped Kor'lee to her feet, and they joined the others, in following Mattox out of the Cathedral. Before she left the building, Kor'lee looked back over her shoulder. Through the doorway, she could see Orron smile and turn back toward the altar where Zittas and Ly'ra still stood.

⁓⌇⁓

Zittas screamed in hopeless rage as he saw the Heretics get up and walk out of the Sanctuary. There was no one to stop them. Then a sickening thought entered his mind as Orron turned toward him. *There's no one to stop him either.*

Blood flowed from where the arrows protruded from Orron's body. *How is he still alive? Nobody should be able to breathe let alone walk after being wounded like that!*

Still, Orron moved toward him. His steps were heavy and slow and there was pain evident on his face, but the look of wrath his eyes filled Zittas with terror.

"*Stop!*" he screamed.

Still he came.

"I will kill her! I swear I will."

His hand shook and the knife he held to her neck was covered with sweat. He attempted to dig it into her neck, but it wouldn't budge. It was as if he were holding it up against the hardest of stones. He looked up at Orron and saw him smile.

"Your time has ended, Zittas. Now you will pay for all the evil that you have wrought."

"I...I am the voice of the Maker! I have done nothing wrong!"

"*Nothing wrong?* I will tell you what you have done! You have lied, cheated, stolen, raped, murdered, and worst of all, you have harmed innocent children."

The room felt as though it filled with Orron's presence as he approached the altar slowly. Zittas could do nothing but shake in terror.

"No, Voice of the Fallen, you have done many terrible things for which you must pay." Orron stopped a few paces away from Zittas. "I, Orron, True Keeper of the Maker's Will, have assessed your guilt. The justice of the Maker shall be served. Your time has come."

Out of the overwhelming roar came the sound of a great explosion and a tremendous light filled the Sanctuary. Instinctively, Zittas shut his eyes. Nothing could have prepared him for what he saw when he opened them again.

He was no longer alone in the sanctuary with Ly'ra and Orron. The room was filled with tremendous beings. They were larger than any human he had ever seen. Their cloaks shimmered with brilliant light. In their hands, they held great staffs. Zittas opened his mouth to scream, but no sound came out.

Then, from the back of the room, he saw something move. Though he did not want to look, he couldn't help himself. Through the crowd emerged the glowing form of a great Avolyndian elk. Something about this beast frightened Zittas to his very core.

"By the Name of the Maker I command you to let her go," Orron said with tremendous authority in his voice.

The great elk gazed deeply into Zittas's eyes, boring holes straight to his soul. Suddenly, the most horrifying pain he had every experienced exploded in his head. The knife dropped from his hands as he fell to his knees, clutching his temples in utter agony.

Orron could feel prodigious power surging in the room. Lightning began to flow throughout the Sanctuary, and Orron knew it was finding every corner of the Cathedral. The Maker's judgment was extending to this unholy mockery of a place of worship. Orron snapped his head up as he heard a tremendous boom above the altar.

High above the ground there hung a massive golden symbol, the one on his chest and staff. *The symbol of the True Keepers.*

A bolt of lightning struck one of the cables suspending it from the ceiling. *It's coming down.* He looked at Ly'ra who had just fallen to the ground in front of Zittas and realized that she was directly underneath it. Summoning all of the strength he had left in his damaged body, Orron let out a savage cry and lunged for Ly'ra.

He grabbed her roughly and they tumbled off the altar just as the giant, ostentatious decoration came crashing down.

Orron held Ly'ra tightly in his arms, checking her over to make sure she was not injured. After he was satisfied, he looked back at where they had just been. As the dust began to settle, he could see blood dripping out from under the fallen decoration.

Zittas was no more.

Then, he heard a mighty sound like thunder coming from above. He knew that the source was not from the Cathedral but from the heavens high above it. A mighty wind descended down and swirled throughout the Sanctuary. The floor began to sway as the heavy wooden pews rose off the ground and began to spin around the room.

He sheltered Ly'ra in his massive arms as a light exploded into the room. Even with his eyes shut tightly, Orron felt as though he was staring into the sun. Orron knew everything that had happened to this point had been the Maker working *through* him. What was happening now was different. With overwhelming awe, Orron realized what the Maker was doing.

With a sinking feeling in his stomach, Orron realized that the Cathedral was going to be destroyed. Despite the searing pain from the light that shone around him, he opened his eyes and looked toward the door. He could feel the blood still flowing from his wounds. *We're not going to make it.*

Chapter Forty-Six

Draedon raced through the city in pursuit of Valtor. He knew exactly where he was headed. *The coward.*

The battle waged on all around him. Explosions and fire continued to rain down from the bluffs above the city. Everywhere he turned, Keepers loyal to Draedon were engaged in hand-to-hand combat with those still loyal to the Church. It was madness.

Draedon slid to a stop in front of the stables. He took a second to compose himself. When he was ready, he drew his sword and entered to find Valtor saddling his warhorse.

"You picked an odd time to go for a leisurely ride," Draedon said drily.

Valtor spun around. Draedon could almost smell the fear on him.

"*You!*" It was almost an accusation.

"Were you expecting someone else?"

"I hate you!"

Draedon had to laugh. "After all we've been through, that's the best you can come up with?"

Something appeared to click inside Valtor, and he drew himself up, trying to compose himself. "As acting-Legion Commander, I am placing you under arrest."

That only made Draedon laugh harder. He pointed with his sword at Valtor's empty sheath. "So you—an unarmed, scared little boy—are placing *me* under arrest?" He shook his head in disgust. "And what exactly are you commander of? Your army is routed, and you're preparing to retreat like a dog with his tail between his legs."

Valtor trembled with rage. "How dare you—"

"How dare I *what?*" Draedon said harshly as he stepped threateningly toward Valtor. "How dare I speak the truth? I have kept my tongue for far too long. Why? Because I respected your rank as captain of the Keepers and the decorum I was sworn to follow as Commander." He shook his head. "You are no Keeper. I'm not even sure I am. But what I do know is that you have much to answer for."

Valtor glanced around the room as if trying to figure out how to get away. "So, what, I suppose you think you are here to arrest me?" He looked smugly back at Draedon. "What are *you* the commander of? You are nothing but a filthy Heretic...you and that worthless daughter of yours."

Draedon smiled and tightened his grip on his sword. "Oh, don't worry. I have no plans to arrest you."

"So you'd kill an unarmed man?"

With his sword, Draedon motioned to a closet in the corner of the stable. "There are swords in there. Grab one so we can end this once and for all." Valtor just stared at him for a moment then backed toward the closet and retrieved a weapon.

"Do you really think you stand a chance against me, old man?" Valtor challenged arrogantly. "There's a reason I was chosen as the youngest captain the Keepers have ever had. You do not stand a chance against my sword."

"Really?" Draedon responded with sarcasm dripping from his voice. "I thought they chose you out of pity, what with that face and all."

"I am going to really enjoy killing you."

"I am going to enjoy watching you try." Draedon readied himself.

He knew the reputation that Valtor had as a tremendous swordsman. Though his arrogance was always his undoing, if the rumors were true, then Valtor was right in claiming to be formidable. *Well, I'm not too bad myself.*

Valtor smirked as he approached Draedon. With near-blinding quickness, he brought his sword up and attacked.

Matching and even surpassing his speed, Draedon easily deflected his attack and struck him in the temple with his left elbow. Valtor staggered back and shook his head slightly.

"You fight dirty," Valtor said with contempt.

Draedon laughed. "That was dirty? After all you have done you think *that* is fighting dirty?"

Valtor shook his head one more time and launched himself at Draedon. There was no question about it; Valtor was a very skilled swordsman. Trading blows, they circled each other in the expanse of the stable. Neither could get by the other's defenses.

Finally, Valtor was able to land a blow to Draedon's sword hand. The blade cut deeply just above the wrist. Draedon cried out in pain as his sword spun away to the ground with a clatter.

Wasting no time, Valtor swung again, his eyes lighting up as he looked to land the final blow. Draedon was barely able to duck away from the blade in time, but the hilt of Valtor's sword caught him in the chin. He smashed back into the wall behind him.

Valtor lunged for him and tried to swing his sword again. It was a clumsy attempt born of over-confidence and a lack of discipline. Draedon was able to catch his sword hand with both of his, but Valtor's momentum pinned Draedon against the wall, the blade of the sword less than an inch from his throat.

The majority of Draedon's weight was resting on his left leg that was stretched out in front of him. His right leg was pinned awkwardly against the wall, and he struggled to keep his balance. If he slipped in any way Valtor would have the advantage he needed to finish him off.

Think…there must be a solution! Draedon's hand burned with pain as time seemed to stand still. Valtor's sword trembled slightly as he tried to force the blade into Draedon's neck, but it did not move. Draedon's strength was fading, but his anger gave him just enough to keep the sword frozen just a few hairs away from his skin.

I can't lose to him! It was more than pride; it was a sense that dying at the hands of this man was simply not right. Draedon knew that he was far from perfect, but he had dedicated his life to stopping men like Valtor. His mind began to fill with the memories of how Valtor had talked about Kor'lee, how he had looked at Ly'ra. This man was evil.

Valtor smiled slowly. Between gritted teeth he said, "I warned you, old man. You were never a match for me. You are nothing! I will kill you. Then I will destroy everything that matters to you." His voice rasped with rage. "I *will* take your daughter, make no mistake about that! Even if, by miraculous intervention, this pathetic uprising of yours manages to succeed, know that nothing will stop me from having my way with her."

Something snapped in Draedon's mind. All form of reason drained away, replaced with an uncontrollable, burning desire to protect his daughter.

There are times in a soldier's life when he must kill another human. Though many try to deny it, Draedon knew that nearly every kill took a toll on the soldier. No matter what reason drives a man to battle, taking a human life was never meant to be easy. After every battle to this point in his life, Draedon had walked away with at least a small feeling of regret. *There will be no regret this time.*

He planted his right foot on the wall and pushed with every ounce of strength left in his body. His upper body slammed forward like a hammer and his forehead smashed into Valtor's already crushed nose. The blade of the sword bit into Draedon's neck in the process, but he hardly noticed. The force of the blow snapped Valtor's head back. In one smooth motion, Draedon pulled sharply down on Valtor's arm with his left hand and up with his right, shattering Valtor's wrist.

With the kind of speed that can only come with training and tremendous battle rage, Draedon grabbed the sword out of Valtor's hand, turned away, and spun the sword around. His back now turned to Valtor, Draedon thrust the inverted blade behind him and felt it strike home as it passed through the skin and cartilage.

Without turning around, Draedon released the sword and heard Valtor collapse to the ground behind him. He could hear him gasping for breaths as his lungs filled with blood. Draedon closed his eyes and shuddered as the rage passed from his system like water draining from a basin. He opened his eyes and turned slowly to see Valtor lying on the ground with his own sword protruding from his chest. His eyes were filled with hatred and evil. His face spoke all the horrible things that he wanted to say but could not as he choked on his own blood.

Draedon knelt down beside him. "Not bad for an old man. Enjoy your judgment day, Captain."

Valtor's tried to respond, but could only cough up blood. After several spasms, he took his final breath.

Draedon stood and walked over to retrieve his sword. His hands were shaking from the surge of adrenaline. He wrapped his wounded wrist with part of his shirt and felt the cut on his neck. It was just a flesh wound.

Draedon looked down at the body of Valtor, shook his head, and allowed himself a small smile. He found it a little unsettling that he could feel so much satisfaction after killing someone.

Then it hit him. This was the first time in his long military career when he knew he was completely on the side of justice. After years of staying silent and coming up with excuses to numb the guilt and shame, he finally knew what it felt like actually to do what was right *and* what was good. *I could get used to this.*

His thoughts were interrupted by a tremendous rumble that filled the air followed by a deafening explosion that shook the ground. Draedon felt hot air strike his face, pulling him forward then throwing him violently off his feet against the wall of the stable.

He nearly blacked out as his head struck the wall, but he fought to remain conscious. Slowly, he rolled on to his hands and knees and shook his head trying to make the spinning world around him stop. Gingerly he pushed himself to his feet and made his way outside the stable as quickly as he could. He looked toward the Cathedral. It was surrounded by a thick layer of smoke and dust.

Just then, a gust of wind blew, clearing the haze ever so slightly. Draedon couldn't believe what he saw. Amid the smoke and flames stood the collapsed shell of the building that once towered over Farovale, the very symbol of the Church as he had always known it.

The Cathedral was gone.

Draedon's heart skipped a beat as he realized that it was where he had last seen Kor'lee. He took off half-stumbling, half-running toward the wreckage that he knew lay in front of him. With considerable effort, he forced himself not to imagine the worst.

Dust, dirt, snow, and ash all merged to create a seemingly impenetrable barrier, making breathing nearly impossible. He lifted his arms over his face in a futile attempt to shield himself from the murky air.

The closer he got to the remains of the Cathedral, the more catastrophic the damage appeared. Massive pieces of debris had rained down on the surrounding buildings. Jagged pieces of stone and wood still fell from the sky as he ran.

"*Kor'lee!*" He cried her name over and over as loudly as he could manage in the stifling air, but with his ears still ringing from the explosion, he wasn't sure if he would hear her if she was able to respond.

From behind, he felt a hand grab his cloak. He spun around and drew his sword, ready for a fight. It was Einar.

"Kor'lee…is she okay?" he managed to get out. The smell of charred ruble rubble was overwhelming.

"Yes…she is…this…way," Einar said between fits of coughing. Draedon finally truly looked at Einar and saw that he had a nasty gash on the side of his face. Before he could ask if he was all right, Einar grabbed him by the arm and dragged him to the far edge of the courtyard.

Raulin, Mattox, and Kor'lee were sitting on the ground, leaning against the outer wall. All were hurt in some way or another. Without hesitation, Draedon fell to his knees beside Kor'lee and scooped her into his arms.

"I…thought you were…" He couldn't bring himself to say it.

"Father, I am fine," she said though Draedon could hear the pain in her voice. He held her out at arm's length and looked her over. She had numerous cuts, but most were little more than scratches. Then he noticed her leg. A long, nasty-looking gash ran along her left leg from her knee to her ankle.

"You're hurt," he said as he tore off his cloak and began wrapping it around the wound.

"I…I'm fine," she said weakly, but Draedon had been around war long enough to know what shock looked like.

Draedon looked around and finally noticed that Orron and Ly'ra were nowhere to be found. He turned and his eyes locked with Kor'lee's. His unspoken question was answered by the tears in her eyes.

"They...they didn't make it out. They—" Her words were cut off by the tears that poured down her face.

Raulin, not in much better shape himself, limped over and crouched down next to Kor'lee. He put his hand on Kor'lee's shoulder and gave her a concerned look. Kor'lee pulled herself away from Draedon and practically fell into his arms. Draedon felt a pang of paternal jealousy as he watched Raulin stroke his precious daughter's hair in an attempt to console her.

His thoughts were interrupted by a tap on his shoulder. He stood and turned to face Orcai.

"What happened here, Chief Orcai?" Draedon said, remembering that there was battle still underway.

"The Cathedral just, well, it just exploded!" Orcai said, still dealing with the shock of what had just happened.

"How?"

"I have no idea. We were gathering ourselves outside the Cathedral as you ordered when we were attacked by a full battalion of Keepers still loyal to the Church. They had us pinned down in this courtyard when your daughter and the others came running out. They tried to help us out, but the battle was not going well. Suddenly, there was this sound..." His voice trailed off as he searched for the words to describe it. "It was like nothing I have ever experienced. I felt this...well...it was kind of like a wave of heat that knocked me to the ground. Then there was an explosion. I've never heard anything that loud before."

He looked around the courtyard, and Draedon followed his gaze. The smoke was beginning to clear in the blustery winds of the blizzard that now seemed to be lessening ever so slightly. Massive pieces of what used to be the Cathedral were strewn throughout the courtyard. Draedon could make out the forms of many dismembered bodies. He shuddered at the thought of how many were trapped underneath the pile of wreckage.

Turning back to Orcai, Draedon asked, "How many of ours were killed?"

Orcai shook his head in amazement. "I laid on the ground for what felt like an eternity, absolutely certain that I would be crushed at any moment. The sounds of debris falling and men screaming was…it was awful. Finally, I built up the courage to lift my head. When it appeared that most of the big pieces were done falling, I got to my feet and began checking on my men." He leaned in as if to share a secret. "I have to tell you, sir, I…"

"What, Orcai?"

"Sir, not a single man loyal to you was killed. It was as if the Cathedral was a weapon aimed only at our attackers. Most of the Cathedral inexplicably collapsed in on itself and the pieces that fell struck only our enemies."

Draedon looked down at Kor'lee and realized that her wounds were not from the explosion as he had at first thought but were from the battle that preceded it.

"Not a single man?" Draedon asked, hardly believing him.

"Not a single one. Sure, most of us are pretty shaken up, but I think they will be ready to fight again soon," he said as he motioned to the Keepers strewn throughout the courtyard. Many were still sitting, but Draedon could see that they were mostly unharmed.

"Thank you, Orcai. Check with the men. When they are ready, we need to gather ourselves. We have many enemies hidden throughout this city. There is still a lot of work to be done." Orcai started to walk away to carry out his orders.

"Orcai, one more thing," Draedon said.

"Yes, sir?"

"Orron…have you seen him? My daughter says he and the girl were still in the Cathedral when it collapsed."

Orcai shook his head sadly. "No, sir, I have not. He was a brave man."

Draedon felt a deep sadness at his words. He had grown quite fond of the boy. Orcai nodded and walked away.

Draedon turned and saw Mattox on his knees in shock, seemingly oblivious to what was going on around him. He couldn't imagine what the man was going through. As a father himself, Draedon knew that if anything ever happened to Kor'lee it would most likely kill him. He started to walk over to him. Though he had no idea what he would say, he felt as though he should say something. Before he reached him, Mattox shot to his feet and a look of wonder filled his face.

"Look!" he yelled as he pointed at the ruined Cathedral.

Draedon spun around and looked at where the entrance had once stood. Now, it was replaced by the crushed remains that had fallen from high above. He peered through the murky air, trying to see what Mattox was pointing at.

"Over there," Mattox said with growing excitement. "It's *him*!"

Then Draedon saw him. Out of the haze a large form climbed out of the rubble, carrying what appeared to be a little girl. *Orron!*

Even from where he stood, Draedon could see a small smile on the lips of the girl in his arms. She was completely unharmed. Amazingly, Orron appeared to be as well. The arrows that had protruded from Orron's chest, right arm, and leg when Draedon had last seen him were now gone. His clothes that had been torn from his body before his torture were replaced by unblemished clothes as dark as night. His cloak billowed majestically behind him.

Time seemed to stand still as everyone stood in awe of what they were seeing. Though Draedon knew it was Orron, it was not the Orron he had known. He was somehow something *more*. There was a light in his eyes that burned brightly through the smoke and haze. There was no question that he was larger. He had always been taller than the average man, but now he was practically a giant. His presence radiated a power that Draedon could feel from across the courtyard. Though he appeared unharmed by the explosion, he was not the same man that entered the Cathedral a short while before. *He is no human,* Draedon finally accepted with absolute conviction.

Then he spoke. His voice boomed through the silence.

"People of Edelyndia, the Age of Reckoning has come."

His words hung over the courtyard with heaviness. Somehow, Draedon knew that everyone in Farovale was hearing this right now. He couldn't explain it, but judging by the complete lack of sound coming from anywhere in the city, he knew that this being called Orron had everyone's full attention.

He continued.

"The Maker has heard the cries of the downtrodden, the oppressed, and the weary. No longer shall evil reign uncontested in this land. No longer shall wicked men masquerade as leaders of His True Church. The Maker's Church is not a building built for the glory of man, or an institution seeking power for its own nefarious ways. The True Church is found in the souls of the righteous, those who will stand for what is good and holy, those who will place the Will of the Maker above their own desires and ambitions."

Orron paused and his eyes burned so hotly that Draedon almost felt as though he needed to shield himself from their fury.

"People of Edelyndia, hear my warning. Anyone who stands against the Maker will be struck down by His just hand. He *will* prevail."

His eyes softened as a smile crept onto his lips.

"But hear me, all you who are righteous. Have faith! The time of your salvation has come! Though darkness still hangs over this land, a new light is shining. The storm has unleashed its fury, but it has not won. Goodness and mercy shall once again warm this land. Take heart in the dark times that are still to come. Our Maker is stronger and greater than all who stand against Him and against those He calls His own!"

Silence once again filled the Courtyard. Orron walked down the remains of the front steps and made his way over to Mattox.

With a joyous smile, he offered Ly'ra to the big man who was overcome with tears of joy.

"I believe this one belongs to you," Orron said with a twinkle in his eye.

Mattox scooped her into his arms, and his joy was so great that he began to spin in circles crying unashamedly. Even the battle-hardened Draedon couldn't help but tear up. He did the only thing that seemed appropriate at the moment.

Kneeling down, he put his hand on Raulin's shoulder and said, "Sorry, but you two can have all the time you want later. It's my turn."

Embarrassed, Raulin turned a bright shade of red as Draedon pulled his daughter into a mighty embrace. All the tension, the years of strife and struggle now seemed minuscule compared to feeling that he had felt when Kor'lee fled the city in anger. Now he had his daughter back, and that was all that mattered.

Chapter Forty-Seven

Draedon stood on the wall at the southern gate, staring out at the snow-covered fields that extended into the distance beyond. He was exhausted; more than that, he was completely and utterly spent.

"You look terrible."

He turned to look at Orron who was walking up the stairs next to him.

"Please, save the flattery. It might go to my head," Draedon said sarcastically.

"I just ran into Einar. He said the last of the Keepers loyal to the Council surrendered." Orron joined Draedon in gazing out across the field. "Is the city under your control now?"

"Yes, it appears so."

"How many Keepers do you have under your command?"

"Just over two thousand, give or take."

"Do you think they are enough?"

Draedon considered the question for a moment. *No, I'd rather have two hundred thousand.* "Would it matter if I said no?"

"Not really."

They fell silent for a while, the enormity of the task that lay before them weighing heavily on their minds. Two days had passed since the events in the Cathedral. Though Draedon felt a renewed sense of hope and purpose behind their mission, it did not change the fact that it seemed quite daunting.

"How many fighters did you have on the bluffs?" Draedon suddenly asked.

Orron smiled. "Three hundred."

"Three hundred?" Draedon looked at Orron incredulously. "I figured you had a smaller force, but *three hundred*?"

"Yep."

Draedon was having a hard time comprehending it. "So you're saying three hundred men captured a city boasting five thousand Keepers?"

"Well there were several women and maybe even a few children mixed in, but yes, that sounds about right."

"So the explosions in the sky that interrupted our executions… that was just more of the Forest Bandits' trickery?"

"Yes," Orron said wryly. "Raulin has barrels and barrels of that black powder. They were basically just harmless noise-makers."

Draedon shook his head. "Well, the flaming arrows weren't harmless. My men are still trying to put out the last of the fires."

"I'm sorry about that. We knew that it would add to the panic."

There was something else that Draedon was struggling to figure out. "So noisemakers and flaming arrows…that I get, but how did you do the dreams?"

Now it was Orron's turn to look confused. "What dreams?"

"You don't know about that?" Draedon asked suspiciously. Orron shook his head and looked genuinely in the dark. "Well, Orcai told me that apparently most of his men had nightmares the night before that they were being invaded by a massive Heretic army."

Orron just smiled. "No, I had nothing to do with that."

Draedon was pretty sure that Orron had an idea what happened, but he didn't bother asking. *I probably wouldn't believe him anyway!*

What Draedon really wanted to ask him was what happened in the Cathedral before it collapsed. The trickery on the bluffs was one thing, but the power that destroyed the massive building was quite another.

He just sighed. Orron would tell him when he was ready. *Orron, or whatever was in there, managed to take down a Cathedral, but it's going to take more than that to destroy the mighty army that will be bearing down on us soon.*

"We will win," Orron said confidently, seeming to read his mind.

"There are four other Legions the same size as the one here… well when we were full strength that is." Draedon shook his head. "The Legion in the Holy City is easily twice the size of all the other legions combined."

"Some will join our side."

"More will side with the Church." Draedon turned to look over the snow-covered fields. "I have been building a network of Heretics for years. There are battalion chiefs in the other legions that are already with us, maybe even a Legion Commander or two. But what we are up against…"

Draedon was not trying to be pessimistic, but it was the reality of their situation. "We are outnumbered, we have little in the way of weapons and supplies, and we don't really know what we are going to do next."

"Still, I like our odds."

"Of course you do, you're crazy!" Draedon said sarcastically.

Orron laughed. "I'm serious. We have the one thing they think they have but don't."

"Oh? And what's that."

"We have the Maker on our side."

There was nothing Draedon could say to argue with that. With all that he had seen in the last few days, he was running out of reasons not to accept that there was a Greater Power behind their cause.

He clapped him on the back. "Well, I do know one powerful weapon we have that they don't, and that just might be enough."

Orron turned and looked at him inquisitively. "And that is?"

Suddenly serious, Draedon returned his gaze. "We have you."

For years, he had been working against the leaders of the Church, but secretly he never truly believed they would succeed. Now, he could feel a change inside himself. Something was growing that made him want to shout for joy. *Hope*, he thought to himself with a smile. *We can actually win this*!

Epilogue

Deep in the recesses of the Great Desert Territory, a lone cleric hurried through the empty halls of Elder Seiner's sprawling estate. As far as he knew, he and the Elder were the only two people in the castle that night.

The corridor was dimly lit by small candles casting eerie shadows on the walls. Though he knew that he was alone, the cleric felt as though thousands of eyes were watching him from the shadows.

When he reached the elder's private room, he paused. *Should I knock? Will he be angry at me for interrupting him?*

Before he could make up his mind he heard a voice from within the room.

"You may enter."

The voice made his skin crawl. He took a deep breath and opened the door. The Elder was sitting in front of a fireplace with his back to the door. *How can he handle that heat?* The oppressive temperatures of the Great Desert were bad enough without the added heat of a roaring fire.

"You bring word of Farovale I presume," the elder said without bothering to turn around.

"Y… yes Your Grace." The cleric tried to no avail to calm his shaking hands. Every time he was in the Elder's presence he felt complete and utter terror.

"Go on…"

"The city has fallen under rebel control, just as you have foretold."

"And the man? The one who is different?"

"He has come and is one of the leaders of the rebellion."

The elder stood up slowly and turned to face the cleric. Though he tried not to, the cleric cringed.

Elder Siedar was completely devoid of hair and his skin was leathery, almost scale-like. His fingers were unnaturally long and thin. But the most unnerving feature was his eyes. They were terrifying to look at. Almost completely devoid of white, the blacks of his eyes were startlingly large and sinister.

The cleric cowered in fear as Seidar approached him.

"The prophecy is true then," Seidar said. "The time has come. My power is nearly complete. The greatest war this world has ever known has come at last."

He rubbed his hands together in delight as his face broke into a hideous smile.

"Things are going exactly as planned. Finally, all these years that I have spent on this world planning, manipulating, and toiling are about to pay off."